Lies I Told My Sister

By Louise Ells

Copyright © 2024 by Louise Ells

All rights reserved. No part of this publication may be reproduced, stored in a retrieval system, or transmitted in any form by any process—electronic, mechanical, photocopying, recording, or otherwise—without the prior written permission of the copyright owner and Latitude 46 Publishing. The scanning, uploading, and distribution of this book via the Internet or via any other means without the permission of the publisher is illegal and punishable by law. Please purchase only authorized electronic editions, and do not participate in or encourage electronic piracy of copyrighted materials. Your support of the author's rights is appreciated.

I'm Only Me When I'm With You Words and Music by Taylor Swift, Angelo and Robert Ellis Orrall Copyright © 2007 SONGS OF UNIVERSAL, INC., TAYLOR SWIFT MUSIC, UNIVERSAL - POLYGRAM INTERNATIONAL PUBLISHING, INC., GREEN WAGON MUSIC and ORRALL FIXATION MUSIC
All Rights for TAYLOR SWIFT MUSIC Administered by SONGS OF UNIVERSAL, INC.
All Rights for GREEN WAGON MUSIC Administered by UNIVERSAL - POLYGRAM INTERNATIONAL PUBLISHING, INC.
All Rights for ORRALL FIXATION MUSIC Administered by BLUEWATER MUSIC SERVICES CORP.
All Rights Reserved Used by Permission
Reprinted by Permission of Hal Leonard LLC

Library and Archives Canada Cataloguing in Publication

Title: Lies I told my sister / by Louise Ells.
Names: Ells, Louise, 1967- author.
Identifiers: Canadiana (print) 20240364627 | Canadiana (ebook) 20240364643 | ISBN 9781988989860
  (softcover) | ISBN 9781988989877 (EPUB)
Subjects: LCGFT: Novels.
Classification: LCC PS8609.L5725 L54 2024 | DDC C813/.6—dc23

Printed and bound in Canada.
Cover Artwork: John James Audubon (1785-1851)
Author Photo: David E. Landry
Interior Design: Teagan Biersteker

Published by:
Latitude 46 Publishing
info@latitude46publishing.com
Latitude46publishing.com

We would like to acknowledge funding support from the Ontario Arts Council and the Government of Ontario for their support.

Lies I Told My Sister

By Louise Ells

46

*For Douglas Cameron Gloin,
who used to know how very much I love him*

Chapter One

BIG ROCK LAKE, FEBRUARY 2014

"I don't try to hide my tears/My secrets or my deepest fears..." I was dreaming that Tansy was singing the Taylor Swift song until the ring tone finally pulled me from my sleep.

'Umm—'

'Lily?' The voice was a pale imitation of its usual self. 'Lily?'

Not Tansy, my older sister, but my younger sister, Rose. Nine months since our argument had escalated out of control. Nine months of silence, and now Rose was calling me in tears.

I glanced at the clock. 4:00 a.m.

'What's happened? Are you okay?' Clearly she was not okay. 'Is it Mum? One of the girls?'

A jagged gasp. 'It's Kent. He's . . . he's been in an accident.'

Her husband. I let go of the breath I'd been holding. 'What do you need?'

'I need you here,' she said. 'Please.' More tears. 'I'm at the hospital.'

'On my way. I'm on my way, Rose.' I hung up. I pulled boots over my bare feet and a coat over my pyjamas, grabbed the car keys and left. When I had backed out of the driveway, I called Kathleen. I started apologizing as soon as she answered.

'Go,' she said. 'Go, go. I've got this.'

Thank goodness for cell phones, Bluetooth, handsfree. Most days of my life, I took it for granted, forgetting that for the first eight years of my life I lived without a telephone. But sometimes—like now—I sent out a silent prayer of gratitude for the technology.

'One. Two. Three.' The streets were empty; still I counted to three after I'd come to a full stop at each stop sign. Peter had taught me to do that when he gave me driving lessons and in times of stress I counted out loud. 'One. Two. Three.'

Rose was perched on the edge of a plastic chair in the far corner of Emergency. When I sat next to her, she reached for my hand and gripped it so fiercely her knuckles turned white.

'I'm here, Rose,' I said. 'I'm here. Have you called Mum? Shall I call Mum?'

'Not yet,' she whispered.

I nodded. 'Okay. Who's with the girls?'

'Carla.'

Her neighbour. Good. 'Do you need . . . what do you need?'

She shook her head. Then nodded. 'Prayers. I need prayers.'

I bowed my head, and noticed she did the same. I recited the Lord's Prayer knowing Kathleen would be praying too. Would already have prayed. I tried to remember some verses from Corinthians. 'Oh Mystery, I call God, comfort us in all our pain, that we may be able to comfort those who are hurting, with the comfort you provide.' Maybe it wasn't word perfect, but Rose loosened her grip by a little.

'I always knew he could be injured,' she whispered. 'He's a police officer. But I never . . .' She sighed. 'I never imagined it would really happen.'

We never do, I thought. We never do. 'Do you want to talk? Or do you want me to talk? Or—'

'Car crash,' she said. 'It's bad. TBI.'

'TBI?'

'Traumatic brain injury,' Rose said. 'Too much bleeding. He's in surgery now to reduce the swelling.'

I often forgot my baby sister had once been a med student, on her way to becoming a doctor. 'OK, so good, he's in surgery. That's good.' He could have been lying unconscious in the car or thrown into a ditch; he could have been found dead, hours from now. 'That's good,' I said again. 'This is a good hospital. He's getting good care.' I wanted to add, he'll recover, but I didn't know. I looked around the pale blue waiting room, thinking about all the times I'd been here

before. 'This is a good hospital. Really good. You know that.'
Rose nodded. 'I was born here. I met Kent here. Our babies were born here.'
Mine was not. But Rose didn't know about that death.
'Kent and I met here,' she said again. 'Remember?'
I nodded. 'I do. I love the story of how you met. Tell me again.'

Big Rock Lake, November 1999

I'd heard their meet-cute story so many times I sometimes felt I'd been there. Three o'clock on a Thursday afternoon in early November. Rose in her fifteenth straight hour in the emergency department—because that was the lot of med students—and not leaving any time soon because three ambulances were arriving from the scene of a bad crash. The first big blizzard of the winter had caught drivers unprepared. A transport had jack-knifed across the highway and taken out a school bus, then seven more cars had crashed into that mess in a chain-reaction. Three dead, eleven badly injured, most of them children.

At three o'clock a cop brought in a homeless man. New to the force, the cop was a little pushy and, knowing of the accident and the mayhem that was about to become the emergency room, he refused to move out of her way until the student doctor saw to the patient.

'He's not gonna die on my watch,' the cop said to Rose, standing in front of her.

'He's not going to die,' Rose said, trying to step to the right of the man in uniform.

'Red, please.' The cop moved to his left. 'Willya' take a look at him? If you don't take a look now, it's gonna be after midnight. And if he's drifted off to death by then—'

'I'll take a look at him,' Rose promised. She stepped to her left.

The cop moved to his right. 'Now, Red,' he insisted. 'Please.'

'He's warm,' said Rose. 'He's been given water, he's sleeping. He probably needs sleep more than anything. And the longer we delay, the longer he can stay warm and sleeping.' She looked directly into the cop's eyes. 'Where is he supposed to go when we discharge him, huh?'

'I'll take him to the SNAP shelter.'

Rose was growing tired of the dance and could hear sirens approaching the hospital. 'Come back around ten p.m.,' she said.

The cop shook his head. 'That'll be too late.'

'Too late?'

'My staff Christmas Party starts at 7:30.'

Rose sighed. 'So get someone else to take him to SNAP. You'd better promise me there's a bed there for him.'

'That's not what I mean,' he said. 'The party starts at 7:30 and I'd like you to come with me. Please.'

'What?'

'I'm asking you to be my date for the evening.'

Rose thought exhaustion had finally taken its toll and she was imagining things. 'Your date?' She wasn't stupid. A young, good-looking cop would have no need of picking up a date on the day of his staff party. 'You can't be single.'

'I will be, Red, if you agree to come with me.'

'That makes no sense,' she'd said. 'And I don't have time for this. And who ever heard of a Christmas party this early in the season?'

'I do have a date. But I'd much rather take you.'

She shook her head to make sense of what he was saying. 'What?'

'Do you believe in love at first sight?'

'You and the homeless gentleman? Sure.'

He laughed. 'That's okay. I believe enough for both of us. I'm gonna make myself single in order to take you out this evening, and hope that by the end of the evening neither of us is single.' He grinned at her. 'Now please, go check out that guy so I can leave you in peace. But I'll be back at six-thirty to pick you up and take you home so you can shower and change.'

'I've been working since midnight.'

'Yeah? So I'm confident you'll be off by six-thirty.'

'You're nuts,' she said.

'Yeah. Maybe.'

'We don't even know each other's names.'

'Is that the most important thing about you, Red, your name? I know you're kind, and capable, and cute as all get out, and I know I want to spend the rest of this evening getting to know everything about you. Including your name.'

Rose examined the homeless man, who was, as she'd predicted, cold, hungry, and tired. The cop used the pay phone in the waiting room, presumably to call a young lady to inform her that he wouldn't be collecting her at seven o'clock as previously agreed.

'That poor woman,' Rose always said when she told the story. 'I had no idea you were about to break her heart.'

At this, Kent would roll his eyes. 'Her heart was so not broken. She'd agreed to accompany me out of a sense of duty; we were never actually in a relationship.' Then he'd kiss her forehead. 'Admit it, Red, I called it, eh. Love at first sight.'

'I was so tired I didn't know what I was agreeing to,' Rose would reply.

Or sometimes he joked that if she really felt so bad for the girl he dumped, they could name one of their children after her. 'No,' she'd laugh. 'But only so one of our sons doesn't go through life with a female name.' That was before her children were born; at the birth of their first daughter, Kent must have had the decency to retire that joke.

Big Rock Lake, February 2014

'Hannah,' I said.

Rose looked at me. 'I told you her name? Kent wouldn't tell me for a long time, and then he swore me to secrecy.'

I started to make some non-committal murmur but was interrupted by three uniformed cops who came to lay their hands on Rose's shoulder and offer words of solace. They moved to sit a respectful distance away from us on another row of the hard plastic chairs, but Rose grasped the hand of a female officer I didn't recognize.

'Wait. Please. Kendra-' Rose started rocking in her chair as she looked up at the woman. 'Can you—? Do you—?'

The police officer looked towards her colleagues, then back down at Rose. 'I'm sorry. We don't have any details. You know we're all rooting for him.' She patted Rose's shoulder again in an awkward attempt at comfort, then joined the other cops.

'They have details,' said Rose. 'They can't share them with the family. The—' her voice broke. 'The next of kin.'

'Rose. Rose. Kent is a strong man. He's healthy, and he's stubborn, and he's a fighter.'

'I can't . . . If he dies. I can't—'

I turned on the chair and looked my sister in her eyes. 'He is not going to die! He's going to be fine! Full recovery, you'll see. He's going to be okay, Rose.'

'You promise?'

'I promise,' I said. So much conviction even I almost believed myself. 'I promise. I promise.'

'Ma'am?' A big guy in buffalo plaid held out his hand. 'Mrs. Hayton. Rich

Manikowski, with the *Big Rock Beacon*. I am so sorry about your husband. Do you mind if I ask you a few questions?'

'No.' I shook my head. 'No questions.'

It was as if the journalist hadn't heard me. 'I understand it was a single vehicle accident, on the Third Concession. Was he on duty or—'

I stood. 'No! No questions. Do you not understand me? No questions!' In my peripheral vision, I saw the three police officers standing too, moving towards us.

Rich Manikowski must have noticed them as well. 'Of course, of course. Not yet. Mrs. Hayton, your husband is in my thoughts and prayers.'

He backed away from us, skirted the three cops, and approached the woman at the registration desk. I didn't imagine he'd have any luck with her, but I didn't care. I sat again, and tried to stop trembling. *Thoughts and prayers* had long been rendered meaningless.

'So fierce, Lily. You've always been so fierce,' said Rose. 'Thank you. For looking out for me. For loving me.'

'Always,' I said. 'I have loved you since before you were born, Rose. I will love you forever.' I wanted to add that I had always looked out for her the best I could. But I couldn't. I hadn't. Not always.

'Sometimes I'm not very lovable,' she said. 'Lily—Lily, I'm so sorry about—'

I cut her off. 'I know. I'm sorry too,' I said. 'None of that matters.'

We sat in silence then, until a man in a white coat asked to speak to Rose in private. 'And my sister.'

He took us to a small bare room and spoke in a low voice.

The journalist had been correct. It was a single vehicle accident on Third Concession Road East. 'They can't tell yet if his neck or spinal cord have been injured. He's got a lot of broken bones. His breastbone punctured his lungs, and his ribs were smashed. He's lost both kidneys.'

I was glad I was with Rose, glad I was there to take notes. It was a long list to process; she looked dazed. 'Both kidneys,' I said. 'What does that mean?' I didn't know that someone could survive without a kidney.

'He needs a transplant. Otherwise he'll require dialysis three times a week for life. He'll have to restrict his liquids intake, and he won't be able to pee.' His voice wasn't emotionless, but he was very matter-of-fact.

I nodded. 'OK. Thank you. Thank you for the update.'

We were shown back to the waiting room and left alone. I took a deep breath. 'OK then, we'll find him a kidney.' As if I could pop into Canadian Tire on the way home and pick one up.

'I wish—I wish—' Rose started.

Grow a backbone, not a wishbone. I heard Peter's voice, clear as if he was sitting right beside me. I bit my lip, thinking of him waking up confused and disoriented. 'What do you wish, Rose?' If there was any way to make her wish come true, I would do it.

A deep breath. Then a whisper. 'I wonder if he was wearing his seat belt? No, I don't wonder. I know he wasn't. I wish I'd listened to you. I wish *he'd* listened to you. You told him, wear a seat belt. Your brains are more use in your head than smashed all over the road, you said.'

I winced. I had said that. Nine months ago. I'd yelled it, before screaming at him to let me out of the car. 'I'm so sorry.'

'No. You were right. You were right. I'd like a do-over. I'd like to make a different choice. I wish—' She shook her head and wiped at her tears.

We sat together, hand in hand.

Time passed. Still no news. Policemen outnumbered the other people in the waiting room. I watched as people arrived, sat, waited, sometimes left. There was a young woman in a baggy sweater, her long hair hiding her face. Deliberately? I caught myself staring at her stomach and looked away. Snuck another glance. She reminded me of myself. A long time ago. I closed my eyes. If *I* could have one do-over. If *I* could make a different choice . . .

Chapter Two

Big Rock Lake, 1990

Rose didn't know that eleven weeks after Quentin left Big Rock Lake to return to New York, I'd spent the night in this hospital. The abortion clinic.

I wanted children. But one day, not now. Having children was not something Quentin and I had discussed, but I could imagine his reaction if I told him I was pregnant, and it would not be positive. I wasn't willing to risk losing him, so by myself I made the choice between him and our baby.

A meeting with a counsellor to discuss my options was a prerequisite for the surgery. I talked about being young, and unmarried, and having plans for graduate school. That was easier than admitting my real fear that my boyfriend of not quite four months would leave me.

'Have you spoken to anyone else?' The woman was middle-aged, kind, and a mother herself I guessed. 'Your parents, a close friend, your partner?'

'Bobby—my father is dead, and I—I haven't told anyone else, no.' That was an odd thing for me to have said. Suggesting that if Bobby had been alive I might have told him? Never.

'And that's fine. It's entirely your decision. Your body, your choice.' She gave me a booklet and some leaflets. She told me exactly what to expect. She organized everything, including a ride home with a volunteer driver.

I thought I handled the situation well. I was deeply grateful that I lived in a time and a place of legal terminations. I had no last moment regrets, and felt only relief, no guilt at all, after it was over. The volunteer driver was an older woman in a chunky knit sweater who pulled the car to the side of the road when I started crying and gathered me in her arms in a tight hug. She said nothing. I don't remember her face, her car—only her sweater and that hug. I spent the following two days in bed crying, but that was simply a reaction to physical pain.

As soon as my body had healed enough, I dealt with contraception. No more risks. No more unplanned pregnancies. I was an adult woman, making adult choices. The single after-effect I acknowledged was an increased sense of insecurity, which manifested as recklessness. I had chosen Quentin over a child; I had to prove to myself that had been the right choice; I had to make sure I didn't lose Quentin. When we were together, he got all my attention. When we were apart, I barely thought about anything else. My marks, unsurprisingly, plummeted. I was let go from my waitressing job for missing too many shifts. I ignored the few provisional offers I received to graduate programs, knowing I wouldn't meet the conditions. My roommates teased me at first, then grew concerned. Finally, Larissa and Sally staged an intervention and said Quentin was no longer welcome to stay—that even if I didn't care about final exams, they did.

I was angry and more than a little scared at how alone I felt. I considered moving out but knew I couldn't afford a place of my own, considered going back home but couldn't face that either. So I told Quentin I needed a month to focus on exams, promised long nightly sessions of phone sex, and spoke of him with Rose. She was fifteen, and he had completely charmed her. She was willing to listen to me talk about the tall man with the television-worthy accent, who sent me flowers and chocolates and had given me a pair of real ruby earrings. She was more than happy to look through thick wedding magazines with me, something I told no one else I was doing. We chose dresses for both of us, bouquets and decorations, planned meals and honeymoon options.

I should have thanked my friends for making me spend a month by myself—I don't suppose I was generous enough to do so. They were the reason I scraped through with enough credits to earn my final year and graduate. Quentin came to the ceremony in June; it was the first time I'd seen him in a suit and tie, and I fell instantly in love with him all over again. I thought he'd won over my mother, and possibly liked her too, but maybe they were both pretending. He took us all—Mum, Rose, and me—to the best steakhouse in the city to celebrate. The joy was a little forced, and the conversation stilted, but I didn't care, sure as soon as we were alone he was going to drop to one knee, present me with a ring, and ask me to do the honour of becoming his wife. Or maybe not alone, maybe he would propose in front of my family and the restaurant full of strangers.

That didn't happen. He did, however, ask me to move to New York with him, and of course I said yes. I admitted that I'd been half-expecting a ring. 'Not today,' he said. 'This is your day, Lily. Today is all about you. I'm not going to let the spotlight move away from your accomplishment for one single moment.' I loved that he'd thought of that; I hadn't. His proposal came six months later, on the eve of my having to leave the States because I was a foreigner and the only work I'd found was as a volunteer at the local library. But he must have looked at wedding magazines too—there were red roses, and a diamond on a gold band, and a romantic speech. Exactly what I wanted. And I loved him so much, and I believed that love was enough to sustain a marriage. I didn't hesitate to say yes, and when I called Mum and Rose I told them that it was going to be the happiest marriage ever.

Big Rock Lake, February 2014

I looked back at the teenager with long hair and a baggy sweater. Chided myself for leaping to such an extreme assumption. No reason to think she was pregnant.

'Oh. You're crying, Lily. Please don't cry or I'll start up again,' said Rose.

I blinked back the tears I hadn't even felt welling. I wasn't sure what memory was triggering this stab of sorrow. The baby I'd never told anyone about? A time when Quentin and I had been truly happy?

'So how do we find Kent a new kidney?' I asked. 'That's our first priority, right?'

'Oh—' Rose stopped biting her lip, the closest thing to a smile I'd seen so far. 'I have wanted you to like Kent forever. I hate that it took an accident for you to care, but . . . maybe—maybe you can be friends after all?'

She thought my tears were for her husband. And she'd clearly never been fooled about my true feelings for him. 'Kent is—' I tried to assure her. 'He's the man you love. He's the father of my nieces. I love him because—'

'Yeah. I know you love him. But you've never really liked him.'

I changed the subject back to kidneys. 'Does he get put on a list? What needs to happen?'

She shook her head. 'I don't know. I don't know.'

And why should she? 'OK. Well let's go and find out. Someone here will be able to tell us.' I wanted to keep Rose busy, and I wanted to make sure we were doing as much as we could.

'What... What if he doesn't come through the surgery? If he doesn't make it...' Rose closed her eyes.

'No. No. Cheerful thoughts.'

'Like what?'

I tried to think of anything cheerful. 'A million years ago we spent a weekend together in Toronto. The two of us. Do you remember?'

'Yes, of course. A concert and museums and a spa. So decadent.'

It was a memory I cherished, and I was glad my sister felt the same way. 'We're due another,' I said. 'Beyond due. Let's plan a road trip for when Kent's fully recovered.'

'Deal,' she said. 'Deal.'

Suffolk, England, 1993

'No more tears, Lil. Deal?' Quentin said.

'Deal.' I nodded. 'I'm trying to stop crying. I'm—I'm going to miss you so much.' I wiped my eyes, blew my nose, and pulled back my shoulders. 'You warned me you'd be deployed. I didn't—I didn't know how difficult it would be—'

He pulled me close. 'I know. I know. I need you to stop crying before I start crying myself. I'm going to miss you so much too.'

'Three months,' I whispered. 'I've never been apart from you for three months. Not since the day we met. I don't know how I'll manage.'

'Oh, Lily. You'll be fine. You are such a strong woman. The time will pass more quickly than we think. Now give me a smile, please, and one more kiss. I love you to the moon and back.'

'I love you to the moon and back,' I echoed. And moments later I waved to my husband as he boarded the bus and then he was gone, leaving me alone in England.

I hadn't believed him, that the three months would pass quickly. But I was wrong, and he was right. My part-time job at the library became full-time and I bought myself an OS map and set myself the goal of walking all the local paths. We wrote letters, and twice he phoned, but the connection was poor and they were both conversations punctuated by stretches of silence and then both of us speaking over each other.

I treated myself to a new dress and a haircut before he came home and waited with all the other spouses for his return to the base. When he stepped off the bus my heart filled with so much love I gasped out loud. By the time we'd run to each other I was crying. 'I missed you! I missed you! I love you so much!'

'I'm home now, you silly goose. Why are you crying?' But I noticed his eyes were as wet as mine.

The first few weeks were blissful. I resented the hours we were apart. Every night was date night, with dinner and love making. Sometime during the third week or so, however, I realized that we were going to have to readjust to married life. I had forgotten that when he was home I had to sweep the kitchen floor every day; why was he so much messier than I was? And I'd been looking forward to showing him all the new trails I'd discovered, but he had little interest in anything longer than a half hour stroll to a pub. Cooking dinner was a chore again, and there was more laundry. The first time he went to darts I found myself breathing a sigh of relief. I made myself a tuna melt and sat on the sofa with a book I'd not opened for days.

I discovered I wasn't alone. The other wives at Book Club who'd already been through this shared all their tips with me. 'And wait till you have kids,' said one of them. 'That takes it to a whole new level.' A combination of laughter and sighs. 'But it's clear you two adore each other. You'll discover how to make it work. You'll be fine.'

And for the most part, we were.

We lived in that tiny flat on that base in Lakenheath, Suffolk, England for four years. I discovered I loved my job in the library, so much so that when my boss pointed me in the direction of a scheme that would contribute to the fees involved in my earning a Master's in Library Sciences, I applied without hesitation. I didn't even wait until Quentin got home from his second deployment to discuss it with him before I accepted the offer, signed up, and started the first two courses.

I discovered I was great at getting pregnant, but no good at keeping my babies after the first six weeks. My doctor kept up a cheerful patter. I was young, I was healthy, there was no reason to think my next pregnancy wouldn't be a textbook case. I mimicked his optimism in letters home to Mum a few times, then stopped mentioning my body's failings. There were enough daily joys to write about that I could ignore my inability to carry a baby to term. Every year I invited Mum and Rose to come and visit, but every year there was a reason why their trip had to be postponed.

I discovered that I was not as good at being a military wife as I'd assumed I would be. Too quickly I grew tired of making a friend, only for her to move on, and soon I grew jealous of all the women who found it so effortless to have babies. I was surprised how easy it was for me when Quentin was deployed, and how difficult it was for both of us when he returned, and how it didn't get any less strenuous with time. When Quentin was home, we settled into a routine which involved more spare time spent alone than together. I told myself that was fine; he was building a computer and I was writing my thesis. I tried not to think about a woman who'd once told me about the penny jar; our sex life was now entangled with my attempts to have a baby. I started each morning by taking my temperature and peeing on a strip of paper, and when either test suggested I was ovulating I insisted we have sex. I was obsessive about tracking my periods. We were happy though. Happy enough. We never argued in public, like some of his friends. We rarely argued at home.

Big Rock Lake, February 2014

'Rose! Rose! We're here.' Roses's three besties arrived in a burst.
After hugs and tears, one of them scolded her. 'You should have texted us sooner.'
I glanced at my watch. Five in the morning. I felt old. Sometimes I forgot the nine-year age gap between us, but sometimes it was all too stark. It would never have occurred to me to text a friend at this time of day. Even if I was in a hospital waiting room, my husband's life hanging in the balance. I excused myself and went to the washroom. Ran cold water and patted my face, then looked into the mirror. Caught off guard, I caught a glimpse of Tansy in my reflection. My grey eyes, my long, thin face. Rose was there too; we shared the same sprinkle of freckles across our cheeks, and long, chestnut hair. I wondered how often Mum saw her first born in me, or in Rose.
My chair next to Rose was taken when I returned to the waiting room. I looked over at Rose and her friends. I wasn't needed. I knew I wasn't my sister's best friend, hadn't been since we were children, but still this sight caused me to feel a pang of loss. I pulled back my shoulders, gave myself a pep talk. No feeling sorry for myself, not now, not ever. But especially not now, not while Kent was fighting for his life. I slipped away and walked through the hospital to the far Tim Hortons and bought myself a small coffee, which I didn't really want, as an excuse to sit at one of the tables by the window and look out into the dull grey courtyard.
I looked at my watch again. 5:15. Why was I sitting here by myself, when

I wanted to be at home with my husband? What to do? Why was I at such a loss? Why hadn't I ever become friends, or friendlier at least, with my sister's friends?

Big Rock Lake, 1999

The first time I'd acknowledged the distance between us was when I was back visiting Big Rock Lake. It must have been a trip home from . . . I worked out the date. 1999. North Carolina. North Carolina was close to Ontario and I had visited Mum and Rose on a regular basis. Rose had graduated with honours and started right in at the medical school. She was living away from home by now with a group of students. The two of us had dinner out at some point during my stay.

'What?' she asked. 'What are you looking at? Oh, I know, way over the top, eh?' It was the end of November, and the restaurant was decorated with an eclectic mixture of garlands: blue and white for Hanukkah, and red and green for Christmas. 'And too early. Even so, Merry Christmas!' She passed me a card, with a lottery ticket tucked inside. 'Remember I get half if you win.'

'I remember,' I laughed.

'You're staring,' she said.

'Yeah. At my baby sister.' In the polished young woman with make-up and a sleek bun, I could still see her five-year-old self with grubby hands and scruffy hair.

She rolled her eyes. 'I'm twenty-three years old, Lily,' she said. 'I'll be a doctor in another two years. You can't call me your baby sister anymore.'

'I've missed so much of your growing up.'

'But you love it, don't you? Living all over the world?'

'I love it,' I replied, knowing that was the answer she wanted to hear. 'You'll be able to travel too, when you're a doctor.'

'Oh, you're the traveller, not me. I'm the homebody.' She leaned in closer. 'Plus, I've met a man. I think he's The One.'

She'd had a string of boyfriends through university but none that she'd kept around for long. This time both her expression and her voice were serious.

'Introduce me?' I asked. 'Please?'

'Maybe,' she said.

'Tell me everything,' I said.

'He's a policeman. Born and raised in Big Rock Lake. We both went to

Pinesview High.' She laughed. Again, I saw the little girl I'd grown up with. Along with a hint of Tansy.

'But you didn't know him then.'

'He was two years ahead of me. Our paths never crossed.' She grinned. 'He says he was one of the bad kids, and I would never have given him a second glance back then. Ummm. What else? He calls me Red.'

'Red? Why Red?'

Rose shrugged. 'No idea. But,' she giggled. 'He gave me a copy of a fairytale called *Rose Red*. For our children.'

'Children!'

'Told you he's The One. We haven't been dating two weeks but he's as much as proposed. I've as much as said yes. And,' she looked at me, 'I know you and Quentin are happy, but I really want to have children and raise a family.'

My throat closed in on itself. I hadn't known that this was what Rose assumed. That Quentin and I were child-free by choice. 'With this cop. Whose name you haven't even told me yet.' It was easier to turn the subject back to my sister, to listen to her rave about this new love interest, than start the long story about my faulty womb.

'Oh! Of course. Kent. Constable Kent Hayton.' And she told me all about their first meeting.

'I'd like to meet him, Rose,' I said. 'I really would.'

And so we all had dinner the last night before I left Big Rock Lake to return to North Carolina. Kent was charming, and funny, and clearly besotted with Rose. He brought Mum a bouquet of flowers and gave me a framed photograph he'd taken of my sister. He'd caught her unaware and she was laughing. It was a snapshot, but it perfectly captured my sister. For someone who had met her so recently, I thought, he appeared to know her well.

After the happy couple left, Mum expressed her concerns. 'They're rushing into things,' she said. 'Rose still has two years of school left. I'm worried she'll drop out.'

I opened my mouth to assuage Mum's worries but couldn't. I didn't know my sister well enough to know which pull would be stronger: her dream of being a doctor, or her dream of marriage. 'She's eager for children,' I said. I took a deep breath. 'I hope she finds it easier than I do.'

'Oh Lily. I've wondered. I'd hoped I was wrong. I'm afraid I gave you those lousy genes.'

Not so lousy as mine, I thought. You had children. It always disappointed me when a parent tried to commiserate with me. Struggling to have a child and having one was not the same as struggling to have a child and never having one. 'I haven't given up hope,' I said.

'Good,' she said. 'You're a natural mother. Really. I know there were several years after—after, you know—when I was physically present but otherwise absent. You raised Rose, in so many ways.'

This was something we'd never discussed.

'I know how devastated I am when I lose a months-old foetus,' I said. But I heard the shake in my voice. This wasn't a conversation I wanted to have right now. Mum made a pot of tea and I set up the Scrabble board. Tradition.

'Would you consider adopting?' she asked.

I would, but it was not a topic I'd raised often with Quentin. Twice, in total. Once he'd laughed, trying to pretend I'd been joking, the other time he'd turned away as if he'd not heard me. That was a coping mechanism we'd both developed: selective hearing. I avoided answering Mum's question by mixing the tiles in their bag and drawing the first one, then pouring the tea. When I got home, I thought. Maybe I'd raise the subject of adoption with Quentin when I got home.

North Carolina, 1999–2000

But when I got home it was the run up to Christmas. There had been a chance Quentin would be useful to a Canadian Operation, to help with potential problems when the calendars turned over to the new millennium, but it seemed his expertise was not required after all. So our evenings were spent at drink parties and dinner parties and day-long darts tournaments followed by a big darts club dinner, to which spouses were invited. There were tables for eight, and Quentin and I sat with three couples he clearly knew very well. There was a danger of us growing apart if we didn't start to spend more time together. There was a party for my walking group, too, the following week, but I hadn't invited him, knowing they were people he'd have nothing in common with. Now I wondered if I should take him.

I made a real effort to follow the conversation, to try to remember what the various terms meant, and ask questions that would show I was listening and cared. One of the other women appeared to take pity on me. 'Not a player?'

'No,' I said. 'You?'

She nodded. 'I'm on Quentin's team.' She held out her hand. 'Sam Thornton.'

'Oh.' I shook her hand. 'I'm sorry. His colleague. He's mentioned you, of course, I had assumed you were a male.' I felt myself blushing. 'Shoot, that's so sexist, isn't it? I'm so sorry.'

She smiled. 'No worries. Not the first time.' She held up her drink. 'Anyhow, I'm better than all the males,' she said. 'On the darts team and in the field.' She touched her glass to mine and we clinked. 'Cheers, Lily.'

'Cheers,' I echoed.

I didn't want to ask her about her job; I thought I should probably know. And I never asked women if they had children. I avoided that conversation because it forced me to admit that I had none. So I simply smiled, and took a long slow sip of my drink. Had Quentin mentioned Sam Thornton was a woman? He must have. Back when they first met. I hadn't been paying attention. Although something was nagging at my memory.

'Your friend Sam is nice,' I said that night in bed.

'Yeah,' he said.

I waited for more, but that was it.

'I'm surprised I haven't met her before,' I said.

'Oh. You know. I couldn't name many of your librarian friends.'

'Sure you could.' I wasn't sure why I was pushing. 'We should invite them over to dinner.'

'Who? Your librarians?'

'No. Sam. Sam and...Carl is it, her husband?'

'Oh god,' said Quentin. 'Did you speak to him at all?'

I hadn't.

'You'd have fallen asleep. His life revolves around bird watching and bird calls and making lists of birds he's seen and ones he hasn't seen. Drives Sam to distraction.'

'Oh.' More than few of the walkers in my group were also birdwatchers. I remembered why I hadn't invited Quentin to the walking group's Christmas party and reversed my earlier decision to take him with me. He had turned onto his side, facing away from me, and I put my hand on his shoulder, then ran it down his back. 'Hey. Shall we?'

'Sorry, Lily. I'm whacked.' He reached for his bedside light and turned it off, leaving me staring into the dark, trying to remember the last time we'd made love. We hadn't argued, I told myself. My husband was tired—I'd been tired in the past, it wasn't rejection. I too turned to my side, but it took me a long time to fall asleep.

At my walking group party there was a Secret Santa exchange, and I was given a book of long hiking trails in the United States. I spent the next several evenings reading it, cover to cover, reading out passages to Quentin about the various walks. 'Would you consider a long walk?' I asked.

'What?'

'A long walk. Coming on a long walk with me.'

'Define long.'

I open to the first one. 'The Appalachian Trail. From Mount Katahdin in Maine to Springer Mountain in Georgia. Two thousand miles.' A vague memory. 'We talked about this when we lived in Kansas, remember?'

'No, I don't. And two thousand! Lily, are you nuts? That would take... a long time.'

I looked back at the book in my hands. 'They recommend five to seven months.' I looked back up at my husband. 'You could take six months off. You've never requested a furlough. We could do it next summer.'

'Lily,' he said. 'You sound serious.'

'I am. But not next summer, actually. I think we'd both need to train. How about the summer of 2001?'

'May I think on that?'

'Of course,' I said. 'And while you're thinking about that, there's another thing I'd like you to think about. We can agree that my body is not going to be greatly cooperative when it comes to making babies, so how do you feel about adoption?'

'Holy sh—A six-month walk. An adopted baby. Lily!'

'I'm asking you to think about the possibility,' I said again. I remembered the conversation I'd had in Kansas with a couple who were in training for the Appalachian Trail, remembering how happy they'd been, how excited to be tackling the hike together. 'It's something we can discuss in the new year.'

The new year. We brought in the new millennium with a crowd of people I barely knew, me in a new black dress and Quentin looking very handsome in his uniform. When we were reminded to fill our glasses for the countdown to midnight and Y2K, I noticed mine was empty, so I ran towards the bar. In the crush I lost Quentin and returned with a still-empty glass to find him on the four of the countdown locked in a deep embrace with Sam Thornton. I tapped her on the shoulder, and she pulled away, laughing. 'Ohmigosh I'm sorry. I've lost Carl.' And she left.

So I was kissing Quentin as we reached 1 and the ball fell on the big screen, but all I could taste was Sam's Malibu Rum and all I could smell was her perfume.

We were both silent on the drive home; I was almost too tired to think about it. But when I brushed my teeth, I studied my face in the mirror. Surely I wasn't going to be one of those wives who looked the other way? I was stronger than that.

'So?' I said, turning my back to Quentin as I pulled on my pyjamas.

'So...?'

I sighed. Really? He was going to pretend nothing had happened? 'You and Sam,' I said. 'That wasn't a friendly colleague's embrace. She had her tongue halfway down your throat.'

'Remember when you used to kiss me that way, Lily?'

I shook my head. 'Don't change the subject. Don't make this about me. What's up with you and Sam?'

'Up with us? Nothing. She was drunk, and... and I guess when she started to kiss me, I responded.' He reached for me. 'Can you blame me, Hon? How long has it been since you... since we,' he hastily corrected himself. 'I know, it's my fault too. You know how crazy busy I've been at work with all this Y2K stuff. And your schedule doesn't mesh with mine, and then you're at home when I'm playing darts and I'm at home when you're out walking...' He patted my side of the bed. 'C'mon, Lily. We can't start the new millennium with an argument. Please don't overreact.'

Was I overreacting? If a good-looking man had kissed me, how would I have responded? I couldn't be sure. I was sure that he was correct, I didn't want us to start the new year with an argument, so I said no more.

The phone woke us an hour later. 'Umm?'

It was Rose. 'Don't tell me you were asleep, Lily! It's not even two yet.'

You wait, I thought. Instead, I wished her a happy new year.

'It will be! Lily, we're engaged! We're getting married!'

'You're—Rose! Congratulations!' Fully awake now, I sat up in bed.

It was, my baby sister told me, the most romantic proposal ever. At the stroke of midnight Kent had kissed her, then fallen to his knees and held out a red velvet box and told her that he wanted to spend the rest of the millennium by her side.

'Congratulations,' I said again.

'It's the most beautiful ring,' she said.

'So, summer 2001?' I guessed.

My sister laughed. 'Oh, Lily. Not even close. February.'

'Feb—*This* February? A month from now?'

'February twenty-sixth.' She giggled. 'That's Kent's Birthday. See, so he'll never forget our wedding anniversary.'

'So soon—?'

She must have heard the 'but' in my voice. 'It's not going to be a big fancy do like yours was. I know that's what you wanted, but Kent and I just want to get married and celebrate with family and close friends.'

I felt myself stiffen. Why did I grow so defensive so quickly? What did it matter if she hadn't loved my wedding enough to want to copy even a tiny part of it? I hadn't loved it either, not the venue, not the location. And unless I looked through our photo album, I could barely remember the flowers or the menu.

'It's sounds lovely,' I said, even though she hadn't told me a thing about her plans apart from the date.

'I'll send you details,' she said. 'But make sure you keep that weekend free.'

'Of course! We wouldn't miss it for the world!' Even as I spoke, I knew that I'd be there by myself. Quentin was running an eight-week-long training session in the UK in February and March; the dates had been set for over a year.

'Rose is engaged,' I told him, when I'd listened to her and congratulated her several more times.

'And getting married in a few weeks, I gather,' he said.

'Yeah.'

'Is she pregnant?'

'Oh.' The thought hadn't occurred to me, but as soon as Quentin asked, it made perfect sense. She'd been talking about children two weeks after she and Kent had met. 'Maybe,' I said. 'I guess you'll be away.'

'Umm. Sorry.'

I leaned my head on his shoulder. 'I'm really going to miss you this time,' I said. 'I always miss you, but—'

'I know. I'm gonna miss you too, Lil.'

There were spouses who did amazing things when their other halves were deployed or away. Trained for marathons, raised money for charity, organized committees. And most of them who were my age, of course, were parenting as well as everything else. I selfishly wished that Rose had wanted a big wedding so that I could throw myself into the planning with her; but as she didn't, I did what I normally did while Quentin was away. I worked extra hours, I went on more walks, I ate a lot of one-pot pasta meals for supper, and I read in bed every night. The number one perk to working in a library was having all those books available. I read all the Appalachian Trail books we had in the stacks, then ordered some more through interlibrary loan. When I found what I discovered to be the best guidebook, I bought myself a copy, along with the necessary maps.

I took a long weekend to fly home for Rose's wedding and enjoyed seeing

Mum. I tried to quash the feeling that I barely knew my sister anymore and that she hardly noticed I was there. I wasn't needed. It was her wedding, and she was surrounded by her friends, people I didn't know. I told myself I'd have more time to visit and reconnect next time we were together, and pretended I wasn't lying to myself.

Chapter Three

BIG ROCK LAKE, FEBRUARY 2014

The hands of my watch crawled. At six o'clock I called Mum, bought three coffees, and took them back to the waiting room. Rose's friends were leaving; I was more grateful than I ought to have been. I sat next to her and passed her a coffee.

'They're good friends,' I said.

'Yeah. But I don't know why I texted them and asked them to come. I mean, I'm grateful, but...' She closed her eyes. 'I wish Dad was still alive.'

Dad. Rose was the only one who'd called him Dad. He'd always been Bobby to me. His childhood nickname had followed him into adulthood. Raised a middle-class Baptist in the American Bible Belt, he'd told people that he was a draft dodger who had escaped to Canada as part of an anti-Nam protest. It was possible; the dates almost worked. But I'd never confirmed his story, assumed it was a lie. More likely he had simply run away from the constrictions of that life. He was working as a bartender in Toronto when he met Mum, who fell in love with him—as everybody did. He was good looking, of course, she told me, but it wasn't that. He looked at you and listened to you and made you feel like there was no one else in the world.

But he would never have stepped foot into a hospital. I opened my mouth to remind Rose, then snapped my lips shut. She probably had no idea. And now wasn't the time to tell her.

Big Rock Lake, 1968–1976

Bobby. My big sister loved him. I loved him. All my friends loved him, and everyone who knew him. And our mother loved him and was content to live with him in their cocoon for many years. That was the problem.

I recall hearing Mum call Bobby 'Robert' twice. Once, when I couldn't have been more than six, she threw at him the accusation that he was well suited to this infertile land, that he was as much a failure as the commune dwellers and the farmers before him.

'This is not what we agreed on, Robert. I did not sign up for this life,' she'd said.

I remember that exact phrase, because for several years afterwards I wondered when there would be a sign-up sheet where I got to make my choice. I hoped there were lots of options—astronaut and explorer were at the top of my list—but one of the pretty girls at kindergarten told everyone that she was going to be a stewardess on an airplane and wear a pretty uniform, and that held some appeal as well. I assumed that 'mother' was not a real choice, that all girls grew up and got married and had babies, and I was pleased about that.

Bobby wasn't a complete failure—not at everything. He could make maple syrup. He could predict the start of the season to the day, knew how to tap a tree, and which ones, and then he had the patience to boil the gallons of sap needed to produce a single pint of syrup, over and over, never putting too much in the pot when the rest of us started to get bored with the whole operation. His other talent: moonshine. I'd never asked if the still was his, that is, if he'd built it, or if it had come with the land. I wondered, years later, if perhaps selling shine was one of the reasons the commune failed, disagreements between the members over the recipe, the price, the ethics. Or maybe the reason it had survived as long as it did. Certainly Bobby's recipe worked, and his charm must have been part of the reason he was able to run an under-the-counter business for so long, when everyone, police included, knew exactly what he was doing, though he gave away more than he sold. He was lucky; our county was dry in the early 1970s. When those laws were relaxed some of his business was lost. Not all of it (not everyone was comfortable writing out an order on a chit and taking it up to the small, jail-like window in the liquor store).

So, making shine. Making maple syrup. Being the person that everyone loved the most. Those were Bobby's talents. Earning a living—not so much. It was left to Mum to do that. She had been working as a reader for a publishing house when she lived in Toronto and met Bobby, and she must have been talented, because she was able to carry on doing this when they moved up north. Every two weeks a package of manuscripts was delivered, and Mum wrote all over them, then typed a letter and sent the whole pile of papers back in a padded pre-paid envelope. She had a small desk in the corner of the living room where she worked, in front of a window that provided decent natural light. I suppose this is how she spent her time when we were at school, but I didn't think much about work, money, bills being paid. It was also Mum who did all the gardening, all the preserving, all the household chores which took longer than they would have had we lived in the city rather than out in the bush. On some level I must have been aware that, had she stayed in Toronto, she would have had a different future, a future which would not have included the Old Homestead, or Bobby and their cocoon, or me.

Mum read to the two of us, often. But it was Bobby who tucked us into bed most nights. Another area in which he excelled: bedtime stories. Starting the same way, every time, with the phrase 'This time I'll tell the truth.' He made his voice serious, but we both cracked up, my sister and I, sometimes making ourselves cry with laughter, at the way he spoke to himself—the storytelling self—chastising embellishments in advance. And the stories that followed, even the one where his dog died, were funny. That one because the dog got into the raisins his mom had put aside for the Christmas cake. Three pounds of then, soaking in a full bottle of dark rum, the one exception his family made to their teetotal existence. The dog survived several hours, but then the raisins started exploding in his stomach—here Dad would start making soft belching sounds meant to replicate the raisins—and by the time the moon came out (it was a full moon, of course) he—the dog, that is—was drunk. Drunk as a lord. Drunk as a skunk. He curled up and went to sleep. It was a good death, was Dad's implication, as good a way for a dog to go as any. I don't allow myself to wonder how his own views on that subject might have changed in later years. That was the only death, the other stories involved lighter subject matter—his pop's endless, hopeless, losing battle to keep squirrels from eating the flowers in his mom's formal flower border; his best friend's trick of finding out exam questions in advance, the time he was first trumpet in the marching band for a very important parade, and his instrument was off because his friend had stuffed a sock down the horn as a joke. Then, always ending as he'd started:

'So there you have it, and that's the truth.' Again, causing Tansy and me to cling to each other and laugh. What we found so funny, I think, was how the admonishment was said with such a straight face after such a tall tale. Other mothers might have yelled up the stairs at that point, reminding Bobby that the bedtime story was designed to calm us down, not rile us up. But our mother was not the shouting-up-the-stairs kind.

I was a happy child, cheerful for the most part, I believe, good-natured, unquestioning. Tansy and I had the run of one hundred and seventy-six acres. If we wanted a tree house, Bobby would help us fashion something out of old pallets and add a rope ladder. If we needed a raft, the three of us would stuff some of the same pallets with styrofoam and Bobby would cut two branches for our poles. We explored the pond, the creek that ran through our property, the river that edged it. We made trails for summer hikes and cross-country skiing in the winter, and side-by-side sled runs so we could race each other down the hill out back on cookie sheets. My sister and I found places to camp out, watched great fields of Monarch butterflies emerge from their milkweed cocoons in the fall, and the northern lights whenever the conditions were right. If we were those children now, our mother would have homeschooled us. When I studied the stars in school, we all stayed up late to name them together. When Tansy was assigned a project about the Canadian nickel, we dismantled an old beaver lodge and Tansy took all the sticks to school to recreate it. I remember Mum sewing me an elaborate costume for a poetry recital. I can still chant all eight stanzas.

After I read a picture book in Grade One about Florence Nightingale my mind was made up; I was going to be a nurse. I started reading books with pictures on the cover of a young woman in a starched white uniform and cap. It was, said Bobby, with admiration in his voice, a vocation that I had discovered and I wondered if I would no longer be given a sign-up sheet for my choice in life because my choice had discovered me. 'But promise me, Lil, you'll never work in a hospital.'

'Bobby. You can't ask a child to make that sort of crazy promise,' Mum chided him. There was no anger in her voice, but also no room for misunderstanding. 'That hospital-phobia is your thing, don't make it hers.'

'You're right, J. You're right. Hey Lil, you work wherever you want to, hear me?' But it must have been around that time that he started muttering derogatory names for hospitals in my hearing. For one reason or another—who can say—I changed my mind about being a nurse. But no other vocation filled that gap.

There was one constant in our lives: for two weeks every August, Tansy and I were sent by bus to Niagara-on-the-Lake to visit our grandparents, Mum's own mum and dad. The novelty never wore off: a television, a telephone, a washing machine, and a dryer. Shops lining the streets, my favourite of which sold jokes. Meals in restaurants where fried chicken came in a paper-lined basket with a tiny tub of honey for dipping. The excitement of Niagara Falls. Mum saw them for ten days every Christmas, when they came to visit us, but stayed in a hotel in the city and saved the mini soaps and shampoos for Tansy and me. I'm not sure why it never occurred to me to wonder about our other set of grandparents, Bobby's mother and father.

After the accident, I was asked twice every year by well-meaning school counsellors how I was. My answer was always some variation of happy. Fine. And I was. It is remarkable that despite everything that happened in '76, my memories of my childhood on the Old Homestead are overwhelmingly happy. No doubt my memories are tainted by the rose-coloured glasses of an adult looking far back to her childhood, but I truly believe I was happy. We were all happy then.

Big Rock Lake, February 2014

'I wish you'd known Bobby before,' I said.

Rose looked at me, surprised. 'Before? Before the divorce? What do you mean? I did.'

'No, before we moved into the city,' I said. What I meant was: before the accident. What I meant was: when he was still sober some of the time.

'Oh god. No, thanks. Living off the grid like that? I would have hated it. Kent sometimes jokes about moving to the wilderness. Not me. Never.'

I didn't reply, but my inside voice was disagreeing. It was a wonderful place to have grown up. I treasured my childhood memories. I wished I had someone to share them with.

Big Rock Lake, 1968–1976

It's a subdivision in a suburb of the city now, the Old Homestead, the place where I was born—literally. Mum gave birth to me in an inflatable plastic pool (later a childhood plaything) with my father, a midwife, and a doula, in attendance. There was a cassette tape of new-age music I listened to once or twice as a teenager, not as impressed as I'd hope to be, and there was an abundance of incense, which had to be extinguished when it burned too quickly, setting fire to one of the burlap curtains, which was never replaced.

On winter afternoons when Tansy and I walked up the lane from where the school bus dropped us, it would be dark already by the time we reached the house. Mum would have turned on the lights and drawn the other curtains so the house had a gap-toothed smirk. I thought it mocked our arrival home because I could clearly see our parents—that unit of two which had existed for so long without us—getting on about their lives, our absence seemingly unnoticed. My father with a drink in his hand, my mother cutting some vegetables at the sink. Until we walked through the door, they were in a cocoon which didn't include us. I had the feeling that if one day we didn't walk through the door their cocoon would not burst.

But Tansy never saw it that way. 'Look, Lily. The house is always smiling to welcome us home,' she'd exclaim. Every day. She was the unfailingly cheerful and optimistic one, able to see the bright side of everything where I saw first the dark, the danger, the possibility of menace.

Mum never mentioned crystals when she talked about my birth, but I imagine that too as part of the scene. Tie-dye dresses and a little pot smoking along with some anti-war slogans and—long before it was fashionable—a vegan diet. Her hippie phase, she later admitted, lasted all of six months, although to her friends in southern Ontario her life living off the grid was beyond imagination.

Called the Old Homestead in reference to the original family who'd tried to farm the scrappy land, the lone evidence of their work by the time we lived there was a massive pile of rocks picked by hand from the thin, sandy soil, and (my favourite place) an orchard, the trees of which never, in my memory, bore a single apple. Between that family's son and the next owners it was left unused for years, then for some time was run as the commune and pot plantation. My parents bought all of it, one hundred seventy-six acres and three solid buildings, along with various out buildings in various stages of disrepair, the beaver pond, the creek, the escarpment running through it—for fifteen dollars an acre.

Extraordinary.

What would two thousand six hundred forty dollars buy you today, even in a remote corner of our poor northeastern county of Ontario?

Of course, even that was an amount of money that my parents didn't have back then, so there was a mortgage to be paid to the bank every month, and that was Mum's responsibility. Something an adult called Judith would do. She tried to be Judy and she tried to be Jude, but it was Judith that stuck. My father was always Bobby, but my mother was always Mum.

Big Rock Lake, February 2014

'Rose! Rose! Lily.' Mum's voice.

But it took me a moment to recognize the woman reaching for my sister, even though she was wearing Mum's green jacket and clumpy winter boots. Was it the time of the morning? The shock of the news of Kent's accident? I'd never seen her look so old. What I'd always thought of as laugh lines were etched deep in her face. Wispy grey hair framed paper skin and sunken eyes. The smile that usually lit up her face was missing, of course, and she looked bad-tempered, as she always did when worried.

This was the first time I could remember Mum looking so vulnerable. Always before I'd known that once she arrived everything would be OK. She'd had the power to magic everything better for the first eight years of my life and I'd never truly let go of the belief that she could fix anything.

'Oh.' With a start I realized what Mum might be remembering as she looked around this room. The other time she'd rushed to the emergency department of this hospital.

'I love you, Mum,' I said, hoping she could read my mind.

She looked at me, and her expression softened. 'I love you too. Both of you. More than anything else in my world. Where are the girls?' Mum's first question was the same as mine. After Rose told her, with their neighbour, Mum looked at me. 'Peter?'

'Kathleen,' I said.

Rose looked at us. 'What?' But this wasn't the time for that conversation.

'Right. Now. What do we know? Actually know? Not guesses, not rumours. Facts.'

We. It was her use of the word we. The assumption that we were all in this together, we'd deal with it as a unit. And the way she pulled an envelope and pencil from her pocket. She turned over the envelope and started making notes as Rose spoke. A list. My mother had always started with a list.

I recited what we'd been told.

But Rose wasn't listening. Maybe it was too much for her to hear it all again. 'This is where Kent and I met,' she said, launching into a retelling of that story.

Big Rock Lake, 1990

The blizzard, the accident, the young cop. I let Rose's words wash over me. Had

I told and re-told my cute-meet story when I was married to Quentin? Had I ever told it to anyone?

I was starting my final year of Art History when I met Quentin. I had come to the sad realization that I had no great interest in the courses I was taking, and my degree wasn't going to lead to any sort of job. A master's seemed one way of putting off the future, so I applied to several universities outside of Ontario, eager to travel.

My marks had wobbled during my third year, due in part to my grandparents' unexpected death, but far more to a brief but intense affair I'd had with a prof in the Psych department. It ended badly when I assumed we might go out for dinner and a movie, and he made it clear that that was not going to happen. We were not boyfriend and girlfriend, he was sorry I'd misunderstood; he was certain he'd never suggested our fling was ever destined to be more than sexual in nature. There were too many places on campus I imagined I might see him, so I avoided my classes and the library and slept with a classmate, hoping to erase the memory of my prof's mature and worldly lovemaking—the way he had worshipped my taut, unmarked stomach and smooth skin, the nicknames he'd called me. I suspected he was using those same terms of endearment for some other young woman, presumably one who was not so naive as to think there was any emotion attached to their relationship, and who had long ago figured out that the sex was just sex. Alas, for the boy in my class, he could not compare to the older man as I reimagined him, so that relationship ended too.

I barely squeaked through third year. My final year, I vowed, I'd bring my marks back up to honours level. No boyfriends, no distractions. Instead, I would concentrate on my studies, my three evenings-a-week waitressing job, and occasional evenings out with my housemates. That plan lasted through September. In early October we received our student loan on a Thursday, so on the Friday, feeling flush, we went out to dinner at a new place.

We started with a pitcher of beer and a plate of wings and perused the glossy menu. I, for one, was looking for anything that wouldn't be found at any of the other chains and was disappointed to see the usual steak, chicken, pasta. When the waitress delivered a tray of fancy cocktails we all looked up, startled, and began to explain there'd been a mistake: we'd not ordered the expensive mixed drinks. 'From them,' she'd said, winking at us and then nodding towards a table of men in military uniforms.

Sally was bold enough to walk over and thank them, pausing to flirt, while the rest of us waved our thanks. One of the men, the tallest of the group, made eye contact with me, and smiled. My best friend, Larissa poked me. 'Well we all know which one of us *he* likes!' Much giggling, and we finished our beers in order to make a toast with our cocktails, while Sally reported what she'd learned. The men, all Canadian apart from the one who fancied me, were stationed at the base. The American, Quentin, was here for three months, teaching a course in his specialty, radio and communications repair.

Before our mains were served we'd moved to a larger table, so the men could join us. The tall one squeezed in between Larissa and me. 'Hey there. Quentin Porter,' he said, with an unmistakable American accent, holding out his hand. When I held out mine, surprised that he was going to shake hands, he lifted it and brushed his lips across my skin. This gesture was noticed by everyone, and a few of his friends groaned. But it worked. I barely ate when my meal arrived and struggled to pay attention to the conversations around us. When one of the men asked about local clubs Sally and Larissa were quick with suggestions, so a few hours after we met, Quentin and I were dancing together, initially in a group for the fast songs, but for the last few slow songs we were so close I could feel his breath on the top of my left ear. At the end of the evening he insisted on buying us a cab home, even though we were not so drunk or so far away we couldn't easily have walked, and he insisted on joining us, although he'd not had a drink all evening—he never drank, he said—and could have driven his car home himself. I suppose the other men were left to their own devices. I can't recall.

My housemates were quick to get inside as soon as the cab stopped, leaving Quentin and me alone on the tiny front porch. 'I'd like to see you again,' he said, in what I now knew was a Brooklyn accent. 'Without all your chaperones.'

Perhaps I'd had more to drink than I thought because I looked at him and smiled. 'I won't sleep with you on our second date.'

He raised a single eyebrow. 'Third?'

I shook my head. 'Fifth. Maybe.'

'Ah. We'll see about that, Lily,' he said, and lowered his face to mine. I kissed him back, instinctively at first, then because he was such a good kisser. I opened my mouth and welcomed his tongue. When I felt him harden against me, I nearly caved and invited him up inside and up to my bedroom. He stood back and cupped my face in his hands. 'Lily Morris, what have you done to me?' He made it clear exactly what he meant.

I spent the next two days fluctuating between wondering what a man like Quentin (employed, handsome, sophisticated) could possibly see in a local yokel university student and reminding myself that I was not a bad catch myself (smart, pretty, young). In the end my insecurity won over my self-confidence.

I was flattered that he'd chosen me and, for the first time since the prof and I had broken up, I felt special, and in fact we did consummate our relationship on our third date, three times in a row on the single bed in my tiny room, then once again the next morning. 'Lily,' he whispered, 'you're insatiable,' and I felt a burst of joy.

'We've got six weeks,' I said. 'We'd better make the most of them.'

I immediately fell in love, and fell hard. I must have spent some nights that month by myself, and I must have done the bare minimum of schoolwork, but all I remember is working my day around Quentin's schedule. He came to the sports bar where I waitressed and walked me home after every shift, and the evenings I wasn't working I met him at the base. I thought our extraordinary sexual appetites made us special. I'd be exhausted at work, counting the minutes until midnight when I could leave, knowing I'd be asleep the moment I fell into bed. I'd tell Quentin in the car how tired I was, and he'd be sympathetic, but the moment he started to undress me, kissing my shoulder, caressing the back of my neck, all thoughts of sleep would leave me.

'You're exhausted,' he'd remind me. 'You lie back and go to sleep if you want to.' Then he'd start marvelling in a low voice at how beautiful I was, telling me what he'd been thinking about doing with me, to me, all evening.

And all thoughts of sleep, any hint of fatigue would vanish. And the next night we'd do it all again. It became an addiction, my wanting to please him, and I did things I'd never before considered, would not have thought I would ever do.

The week before he was due to leave Big Rock Lake for his base in upstate New York, I asked him, please, to clarify his intentions.

'My intentions?! You sound like my grandad.'

We were sitting in his rental car at Pointer's Park, his arm loosely draped over my shoulder. We'd stopped at the beer store and I had a little buzz on, and I knew I had minutes before he lowered the passenger seat all the way back. After which time there would be no sensible conversation. I'd never considered myself a risk taker or a particularly wild lover, but I had discovered this new side of myself. Sex in the car, where any passers-by might see us, was not the most reckless thing we'd done.

'Your intentions,' I repeated.

'My intentions. Well, here's one of them.' He described a sexual position I'd never heard of.

'Really?'

Quentin nodded. 'Not if you're not ready,' he said quickly. 'But . . . I've only got a week left on base.'

He was serious.

'You're serious,' I said.

He leaned closer to me, whispered more details about what he was imagining.

I was surprised at how instantly turned on I was. 'But it's what happens after this week that I want to talk about,' I said. 'Was this an autumnal fling for you? Do you have a girlfriend waiting for you back home?'

He pulled back. 'Lily! No! You're my Honey Bee. I thought you knew that.' He sounded genuinely shocked. Hurt.

'Well, what happens when you leave?'

'I won't be so far away. I'll come up to see you on my days off, and you can come down to visit me as well. And I have proper accommodation, a place to myself.'

We were both silent for a few moments, then he spoke again, as sincere as I'd ever heard him. 'Lily, you have to complete your degree. I couldn't live with myself if you dropped out of school so close to the end. After you've graduated in June, then we can discuss the real future. But I want to do that properly, with a glass of wine for you, in a fancy restaurant. Not in a cheap rental car when I've got a raging—.' He looked down at his lap, then looked back up at me and winked.

It was as close to a proposal as I could imagine. Romantic and funny, and everything I thought I wanted.

'And you'll need to understand that my job means I'll keep moving. Not six weeks here, six weeks there, but every two or three years. I could be posted anywhere—across the States, overseas. It won't be easy for you to make a career.'

Travel. An excuse to avoid making decisions about a career. All the boxes on my wish list were being ticked.

'And sometimes I'll be deployed. We'll be far away from each other for months at a time. It will be difficult.'

I looked at him.

'But like I said, this isn't the time or the place for this conversation.'

A car pulled up beside us, and I quickly sat up, suddenly desperate to repay his declaration, his assumption at our future, with a show of my devotion. 'So. . . is this evening a good time to, you know, d'you think?' I asked, trying to sound casual.

'Really?' Quentin appeared to be searching my expression, looking into my eyes for confirmation. 'I know I talk a good story, but are you sure this is what you want?'

'It's not something I've ever done before. But. . . with you I'd . . .' I was suddenly shy, insecure. 'I might do it all wrong,' I said.

His voice was husky. 'You're already doing it better than I could ever have dreamed,' he said. He turned the key in the ignition, then stopped, and turned to face me. 'I love you, Lily.' It was the first time he'd actually said it. And later that night he said it again, whispered over and over he loved me, how much he loved me, how much he loved me.

Big Rock Lake, February 2014

'What a precious memory,' Mum said.

I was startled. Precious? Then I remembered she was talking to Rose, talking about Rose and Kent.

'Yes, so happy,' I said. 'And you share years of happy memories. And you have so many more ahead of you. A lifetime. Watching your girls grow up, filling your home and your cottage with memories of special days and every days. You have chapters and chapters ahead of you still to write.'

'You say that with such conviction,' said Rose. 'Like it must be true.'

'Let's hope it is,' said Mum, her voice a little clipped. Was she tired and stressed, or a touch annoyed? Was she about to remind Rose, as she so often did, that I'd always been the dreamer of the three of us and the two of them the practical ones?

But I had misjudged my mother. She reached for my hand. 'Memories,' she said softly. 'You and Peter have been robbed.'

'Rose? Ma'am?' I recognized the Chief of Police from all his newspaper photos. He took off his hat and knelt by Rose. 'If there is anything—anything—you need, you ask. We're family and we're here for you.' He reassured her that Kent's salary would continue to be paid in full, and that there were additional funds available if she needed them. 'Right now, you concentrate on getting him better and taking care of your girls.'

He sounded sincere, and I gave him extra points for avoiding the tired "thoughts and prayers." He said 'family' several times. Most of Quentin's colleagues spoke of the military in the same way. Maybe if I was a different person. . . maybe if I hadn't been so scared of how easy it is to lose family, I might have embraced the military as family. And maybe things would have been different.

Chapter Four

TORONTO, 1992

Quentin was keen for a small, intimate, less expensive wedding. We agreed that marrying in a church for the sake of tradition, when neither of us had ever attended a church on a regular basis, wasn't something either of us needed, and that it made financial sense not to spend the equivalent of the down payment on a house on a single day. He pushed for New York, so it was easier for all the Americans to join us; I had always assumed I'd marry in Big Rock Lake. He would have been more than happy to be married at our local city hall, but I held out for something I considered a little more special than that, and in the end we compromised with an all-inclusive package at a hotel close to Lester B. Pearson Airport, half way between his hometown and mine.

I hated it—the bland, characterless ballroom with low ceilings and dull cream walls, the knowing that we were one of three couples being married there that weekend. I had no ties to Toronto, and this suburb wasn't even really Toronto at all. The food and music and decorations and flowers were all as they'd looked in the magazines, but I found myself longing for mason jars of wildflowers in place of the roses. I had hoped that it would be a glorious spring weekend, and we'd have photographs taken under blossom-covered trees in the hotel's front garden, but spring was late, and the parking lot was edged with the dregs of grey snow, the trees empty branches clawing at the grey, May sky.

I spent more than Quentin knew on the dress I bought for Rose, and far more than he'd ever have imagined on my own gown, and tried to keep reminding myself this was one day. It was every day after the ceremony that mattered. I scolded myself for buying into the hype, but all the same I secretly blinked away a few tears in the nondescript washroom, mid-way through the evening.

But there it was. When we boarded the plane for the short hop back to New York, it was as Mr. and Mrs. Porter, man and wife.

Married life, for the first six months, was not so different from our life as boyfriend and girlfriend had been. Quentin worked, and on the days I wasn't volunteering at the library, I tried to keep myself busy at home. I joined a group of military wives who called themselves a book club, but in fact met twice a month to drink wine and gossip, and they became my friends. There were some events on base we attended, and Quentin had a few friends who would invite us over for dinner and who we'd have over in return. Sometimes we went out to a movie, bowling, a museum. I liked our life; I was happy.

We were invited to a tenth anniversary celebration, and one of the older women, after several drinks, told me there was truth in the tale of the first-year pennies. My face must have looked blank, because she explained that if a newlywed put a penny in a jar every time she and her husband made love—here she winked at me, or had sex—the first year of their marriage, then took one out starting from their first anniversary, she would never remove all the pennies from the jar. I was determined that this should not be the case with Quentin and me, that whatever crazy hours he worked, however tired one or other of us might be, we would not let our love life slide. I had heard stories of women who planned dinner party menus while their husbands pumped away at them, oblivious. Not me. I read a different kind of magazine and made sure I surprised him from time to time with the unexpected.

Weeks before Christmas, Quentin arrived home with a box of fancy chocolates in one hand and an envelope in the other. 'Happy six-month anniversary to us,' he said. 'My new orders,' he said. 'You will not be able to guess where we're going to be living, Honey Bee.'

His good humour, as always, was infectious. 'How many guesses do I get?' I asked.

'Three,' he said.

'And if I win?'

'Your wish will be my command.'

'And if I lose?'

'My wish will be your command.'

'Ooh, I can't decide if I want to win or to lose. Is it... Texas?' He was keen to join a friend there, and it had been our first choice.

'Nope.'

Our second choice, then. The big one. 'Virginia.'

'Nope.'

'Arizona?' I decided to start with the beginning of the alphabet.

'Nope. And that's your third guess.'

'One more. Give me a clue?'

'Okay. Think of tea.'

'Boston!' I knew that much American history, although I wasn't sure if there was a base in Massachusetts.

But he shook his head, held his left hand flat, and lifted his right pinky finger, pretending to drink from a cup on a saucer. Then he put on a faux-British accent. 'No, dearie. Propah tea. With the Queen.' He pulled the sheets of paper from the envelope. 'Lakenheath, Suffolk. Wherever the heck that is.'

We looked it up in the atlas of overseas military bases, then pointed to everywhere in England we'd visit while we lived there. The seaside. Stonehenge. Windsor Castle. London, of course. 'And all that other historical stuff,' Quentin said. He opened the chocolates and passed me the map. 'To us. To England. To our new life.'

'Our new life,' I echoed. 'Hey, I guess I lost the quiz. So...?'

'Lily.' Quentin laughed. 'Have I told lately that I love you? I love you.'

And that was how we celebrated the news of our move to the United Kingdom. Expensive chocolates and sex.

We celebrated our arrival at the new base in Lakenheath the same way, in a tiny flat on the base. 'To our new life,' I said. And that became a secret mantra of mine for the following months, as I waited for our 'new' life to begin.

My days in the UK were remarkably similar to my days in the US. My new group of acquaintances comprised American military wives. The commissary on base sold American groceries; I loved going into town to buy more exotic-looking goods in different packaging but I was making more work for myself, and spending more money. There was an opening for a recreation coordinator at the health club on base, so I applied. I was shocked when I didn't even get invited for an interview and was glad I hadn't told anyone I'd submitted my resume. There were a couple of restaurants on base, but I was scared to apply for a waitressing job in case I wasn't offered one. Off base... how could I complete with the locals? I wasn't even sure if my status would allow me to work legally.

'I need a job,' I said to Quentin, after about six weeks.

'No you don't, Lily. I earn a good salary and I want to keep you. I want you to be my kept woman.'

He was joking, I knew he was, but it fell flat.

'I can't do nothing all day,' I said. I pointed out that it took me all of an hour to clean our home, an hour at most to cook supper, and that my brain was turning to mush from lack of use.

'You should get a job,' he said. 'Of course you should get a job, I'll help you find one.' But that help didn't seem to materialize, and instead I discovered a group of women who took fitness classes, often followed by lunch, and I befriended them.

One day there was a baby shower for one of our group.

'And how long have you been trying?' asked a woman sitting next to me who had introduced herself to me, but whose name I couldn't remember.

I twisted my wedding band and engagement ring, a nervous tic which had replaced nail biting. In fact Quentin and I had not come to an agreement about children. Not yet, was what he said, but I was worried he really meant not keen. After my third glass of rum punch, which so many other guests were not drinking due to various stages of pregnancy, I confided as much in this stranger.

'Oh, Treasure,' she said, clearly having forgotten my name as well. 'You don't have to wait for his formal approval. The moment that baby arrives he'll forget every one of his objections. They fall in love like a ton of bricks the first time they hold their child, isn't that right ladies?'

There was instant consent. And lots of advice. Stop using birth control. Start taking folic acid. Cut down on the alcohol. 'Stick to the missionary position and keep your legs in the air after he's...you know.' This last to much laughter, and a shrug. 'Well, it works.'

I put down my glass of rum punch. 'Okay,' I said. 'Wish me luck.'

Five days later I woke in a sweat. What had I done? Madness. This wasn't fair to Quentin. Having a child had to be a mutual decision. I told myself it had been five days, nothing had happened; I immediately went back on the Pill.

But six weeks later, after no sign of my period I bought a pregnancy kit and peed on all three sticks. Three sets of double pink lines.

I spent a day considering my options. I didn't want to terminate this pregnancy. I wanted this baby. I already loved it. So, guilty as I felt, I decided to frame it as a good news surprise. I wrapped a stick in a piece of pale blue paper with a pale pink bow and put it at Quentin's place at the dinner table.

'What's this?' he asked.

'I can't give my husband a present?' I said. 'Go on, open it.'

'Should I guess first?'

It was our tradition, after all, so I nodded, but spoke at the same time. 'Nope, nope, and nope. You'll never guess.'

Still he tried. 'A pen? A tie clip? A... ummm...'

He opened the paper, perhaps sensing my excitement. Looked at the stick he held in his hand and, it was clear, instantly understood what it was. 'Pregnant?' His voice was flat.

'Pregnant!' I said. 'Congratulations, Daddy!'

He was silent for several moments.

'I know it's unplanned, unexpected. But aren't you excited? Aren't you happy?' I asked. But I was glued to my seat. As ever, stress caused me to freeze, and there was no mistaking the stress in the air.

'We never discussed this,' he said. 'I would have thought this is something we'd discuss. A baby, Lily. This is a big decision, and you've made it all on your own.'

Instantly defensive, I stiffened. 'No birth control is one hundred percent effective. It's not a decision I made on my own,' I lied. 'And what do you mean we've never discussed this? You know how much I want us to have a child.'

'I mean, sure, in the abstract. But we didn't agree that now was a good time to start a family.'

I had to sell him on the idea but was too nervous to figure out the best way to do that, so blurted out the, 'This is perfect timing for me. I can't do nothing all day. I'm slowly losing my mind.'

'So... instead of doing some volunteer work, you decided to have a child?' It did sound selfish when he put it like that. 'It worries me that you think it's okay to bring a child into this world without asking me how I feel about it.'

'It... happened... And... But... Why did we get married if not to have children and raise a family?'

He finally stood and came to my side. 'I married you because I love you, Lily,' he said. 'I could not imagine my life without you in it. You are smart, and funny, and beautiful, and the best lover I've ever had. I married you because I want to travel the world with you and discover all life has to offer with you at my side. I want to grow old with you and one day look back at our lives and be glad that we were together every step of the way.'

'Oh—How can you be so angry at me and then say something so damn romantic?' I asked. 'How can you say you don't want a baby and still make me fall in love with you all over again?'

'Lily.' He pulled me to my feet and hugged me. 'We'll make it work, we'll figure it out. It's a shock, that's all. I was expecting us to spend the rest of our time here exploring England and Europe, just us.'

I hugged him back. 'I'm sorry.' I thought of all the wives and their advice.

'No, I'm sorry. I wasn't expecting to come home today to the news that I'm going to be a father. Hey, do you see what we've done?'

I shook my head, no.

'We had our first ever argument as a married couple. I think we survived that okay. Now I think we should go to bed and have make up sex.'

I nodded, wondering if he'd really forgotten all our previous arguments.

'Doesn't that sound like a great idea?' he persisted. He kissed me. 'Is there anything I have to know? Do I have to be extra careful?'

I shook my head. 'Love me.'

'I do love you. You're my Honey Bee.'

Three weeks later I woke in the night with a sticky sensation between my legs. In the light of the washroom I saw blood. When I sat on the toilet and wiped myself, a deep red blood clot came away on the paper in my hands. Another followed. I flushed it all away, then took a shower, sobbing into my hands. The next day I went to the doctor who confirmed that I'd miscarried. 'It happens eighty percent of the time, probably more,' he said. I assumed that was supposed to be comforting. 'You're young, you're healthy. No reason you won't have an ideal pregnancy next time around.' I drove off the base, turned up a farmer's lane in the middle of nowhere, parked the car, and sobbed.

I repeated the doctor's words to Quentin that evening, wishing he looked a little less relieved, and a lot sadder at the news that fatherhood was not imminent. 'Let's wait a while, Lily,' he said. 'Let your body fully heal, recover from the trauma, and then when we're ready...'

The next day he came home with the news that a local library was looking for a part-time assistant. I understood there was to be no interview, the job was mine, despite my lack of qualifications and minimal experience. And I understood too that his finding me a job was his way of both asking my forgiveness and asking me to wait until he was ready before we tried again for a baby. Which in any event was going to have to be postponed, as the other news he brought home was a deployment. Three months in a Middle Eastern country I'd recently started hearing about in the news but could not have pointed to on a globe.

So we celebrated our first anniversary ahead of time. On the actual day, when we were thousands of miles apart, there were cards to each other, and one from Mum, and one from Rose in her not quite adult handwriting. I hadn't told Mum about my pregnancy, given the accepted advice of waiting until the first trimester had passed, and the sad news of my miscarriage was too raw to share. So I wrote instead to both of them about the gastropub we'd been to for our early anniversary dinner, and my job, which, much to my surprise, I loved, and the coastal town I'd visited with a long pier full of old-fashioned games. I told them that my new hobby was exploring walking paths on my days off and that Quentin had joined a darts team which seemed like a surreal thing to do in the desert. I asked Rose what universities she was considering, wondered if there was one which might lure her away from Big Rock Lake, but she said she was going to be a doctor, go to medical school, and there was nothing better than reduced tuition and living at home. She missed me so much. My life sounded awesome.

Big Rock Lake, February 2014

'Lily. We've let our coffee go cold. Will you go and get some fresh ones for us, please? And orange juice and a muffin for Rose.'

Was Mum really sending me for coffee and muffins? Or did she want some time alone with Rose? It didn't matter. I was glad to have something to do, and a reason to stretch my legs. I walked back to the Tim's.

I hadn't asked Rose what muffin she wanted. I knew it wouldn't make any difference. She might not eat it, and if she did, she might not even taste it. It didn't matter. But still I studied the display as if getting the perfect muffin for Rose could somehow improve the worst day of her life, or even help Kent's recovery.

'Uh. Ma'am?'

I looked at the young man behind the counter and felt someone behind me.

'I'm sorry.' I turned to the line up behind me. 'I'm so sorry.'

'It's okay.' The tall woman behind me was wearing a white lab coat and a stethoscope around her neck. Her blonde hair was pulled back in a ponytail.

I smiled my thanks and ordered coffees and muffins—three different ones, so at least Rose would have a choice—and stood out of the way.

Indecision. One of my worst character traits. I envied the people I knew— Rose, Kathleen, Peter—who'd always seemed to be able to make decisions easily. My therapist was helping me. We'd talked about the possibility of my forgiving my younger self for the moment she'd frozen with fear instead of taking action. Why I still used indecision as a coping mechanism. And how to make good choices. *Not making a choice can be a choice. Will this still matter in five years? Five months? Given all the information you have right now, what's the best choice you can make? Is this a decision you can revisit in the future if things change?*

All good questions. Perhaps not really necessary for a muffin. They were questions I ought to have asked myself years ago, when I kept avoiding truths about my relationship with Quentin by keeping myself as busy as possible.

ENGLAND AND KANSAS, 1996–1999

After three and a half years I defended my thesis, and on a rainy June day in London I was awarded my degree. A Master's of Library and Information Studies. I was truly sorry Quentin was away, and I made sure to give my camera to lots of people to take photos to show him, but on some level I suspected that he didn't really understand what it meant to me to have earned it. Not his fault at all, but mine. It was the first thing I'd done by myself, for myself, and I hoarded the experience, never telling him how significant it felt. All the same, unfairly and illogically, I was hurt that when I got home there was a congratulatory bouquet waiting for me—not from my husband but from my mother.

When our time in England drew to a close, Quentin came home with a white envelope, a box of handcrafted chocolate truffles, and a bottle of wine for me. I had started drinking again. It hadn't helped me keep a baby, not drinking, and I'd told Quentin I was tired of the knowing looks, the winks, the smiles I got when I asked for sparkling water or a soft drink at parties. 'Everyone knows you're teetotal,' I'd said. 'They don't even notice. But they notice when I don't drink.'

'You're allowed to enjoy a drink,' he'd replied. 'No one is judging you.'

Maybe I was judging myself. We'd both grown up with alcoholic fathers; Quentin had decided not to risk repeating his father's mistakes. I liked beer and wine.

He passed me the envelope.

'Three guesses,' he said. And in his voice I heard the man I'd married. The man I loved.

'I adore this tradition,' I said. 'Italy?' That had been our first choice, so that we could explore more of Europe.

'Nope. Much closer to home.'

'Home. Somewhere in North America then.'

He laughed. 'Yes, but you have to narrow it down.'

'Umm. Give me another clue.'

'I would, Lily. But I gotta admit I know nothing about this state. I think maybe I've driven through it. Maybe...?'

'You're not selling me on wherever it is,' I laughed. 'But as long we're together it'll be fine. So... Idaho?'

'Close enough. Kansas. Fort Riley, Kansas.' We looked at a map and laughed at how little either of us knew about Kansas outside of *The Wizard of Oz*, and then we opened the Belgium truffles and toasted our new life.

In Kansas, I focused on gaining experience in different positions in the library where I worked. I also upped my long-distance walking game and hiked the Flint Hills Nature Trail with different colleagues over a series of weekends when Quentin was away. One evening we were camped near a couple in training for the Appalachian Trail. 'Let's do that,' I said to Quentin when we were both back home.

He laughed. 'Walk the Appalachian Trail? How far is it?'

'Oh, about two thousand miles,' I said.

'Two thousand miles?' He laughed. 'You cannot be serious.'

Maybe I wasn't. I laughed too. 'So I'd be on my own then, is what you're saying.'

'Pretty much, Lily. Pretty much.' He clicked on the TV. '*Law and Order* marathon starts in five minutes,' he said. 'Shall I make popcorn?'

'Sounds good. Lots of butter, please.' I snuggled on the sofa, and waited for the theme to start, and hoped there wouldn't be any dead children in any of these episodes.

He came back with popcorn and diet sodas, and we both fell asleep somewhere during the fourth episode.

The doctor I went to see said that when I stopped thinking about getting pregnant, it would probably just happen.

It didn't.

After two years in Kansas we were again given orders. Neither of us minded moving on.

'Give me a clue,' I said as Quentin put the white envelope and seashell-shaped chocolates on our coffee table.

'Mountains. Snow-capped mountains and crisp fresh air.'

'Alaska.' I knew this one. I had told Quentin that I didn't care where we went, and he was keen to join a buddy at Elmendorf, and he had the seniority to be given his first choice.

'Nope.'

'Oh. I'm so sorry, Hon. I know that's what you wanted. Can you do anything—?'

He shrugged. 'Life, you know.'

'Um. So. . . 'Wyoming?'

He shook his head, 'Nope.'

'Montana? Switzerland?'

'Nope, and nope, and you're out of guesses.'

'France? Austria? British Columbia?' I kept on going, and this made him smile.

'You are a goof.'

'I'm your goof.'

'You are. My goof and my Honey Bee.' That was a nickname he hadn't used in months. I looked at him. 'My Honey Bee,' he said again.

'I love you,' I whispered, leaning close to kiss him. Maybe I hadn't said this often enough in recent months.

'Me too.' He kissed me back. And for the first time in years, we made love because we wanted to make love with each other. I didn't even lie still for ten minutes, or raise my knees, or use any of the other tricks which I'd read about. But I did think to myself that surely this was a good start to a new life, that a baby should be born from an act of love.

So it was over an hour later when I remembered to ask him which mountainous place we were about to move to.

'North Carolina. The tar heel state.'

I laughed. 'I never would have guessed!'

Neither of us needed to look on a map, but it was tradition, so we did.

The week before we left Kansas I bought a pregnancy test in anticipation for our first week in North Carolina. The day we left Kansas my period started. So. Not this time.

Chapter Five

North Carolina, 1999–2001

In North Carolina there was a Darts League right on base for Quentin, and he joined its executive committee so was busy two nights a week and oftentimes helped out with weekend competitions. I used some of those days to go on walks, and then joined a group of hikers for regular outings. And there was a college close to the base with a job for me in their library. This time I worked in the archives which I found I liked most of all.

Quentin's seniority hadn't given him his choice of Alaska, but it did mean he was sent away to deliver two months of training. Security was so tight I wasn't even told exactly where he was.

The first few days Quentin was back were always slightly awkward, but this time it was even worse. He was jittery, unsettled, and mostly silent all through April. I served dinner in front of the television so we didn't have to pretend to make conversation. He claimed he was whacked for so many nights, I stopped reaching for him in bed. At the end of his third week home, I asked his friend, Jim, if something had happened that I should know about.

'I guess you should ask Quentin about that,' Jim said.

'I have,' I lied. 'But I know he can't share a lot of details. Did something happen? Was there a problem?'

'Oh.' Was I mistaken, or did a look of relief pass across Jim's features? 'You mean work—'

'I'm asking if something went wrong, if he's worried about repercussions,' I said.

Jim shook his head. 'No chance. He's the best at what he does. You've gotta talk to him, Lily. It's. . . it's not my call, you know.'

He was right, of course he was. But I still wanted to know what might have happened. So I asked Cheryl, the wife who always seemed to know everything that was going on, whose husband also worked with Quentin.

'Oh, Lily,' she said. 'It never gets any easier, does it? You single-handedly run the household, then they come back and everything changes again.'

'I wish I knew why things are. . . worse than usual this time,' I said. 'He was only away for eight weeks. I don't understand.'

She didn't answer me directly and instead told me about the time her husband had come home to a baby he'd never before met, and how challenging that was for all three of them. As I was leaving she gave me a tight hug, something she'd never done before. 'Take care of yourself, Lily,' she said. 'Don't lose sight of your own dreams.'

My own dreams. I cleared off the dining room table that night for dinner and put my maps by Quentin's place. 'What's this?' he asked.

'Let's do it,' I said. 'Let's hike the Appalachian Trail this summer.'

'What?'

'The Appalachian Trail. While you were away I did a lot of reading. I've planned the walk. Let's do it.'

'I—Lily, I—'

I put down my fork. 'I'm worried about us growing apart, Quentin,' I said. 'And I think this will be good for us, for our marriage. The two of us. No distractions.'

'I can't take, what, five months off work, Lily. You know I can't.'

'You can,' I said. 'I asked. You can book May through October.'

'So what. . . you think we can pack up and leave next week?'

'Yes,' I said. 'We are an awesome team, Honey. You know we—'

He shook his head. 'I can't. Sorry, Lily. I know this hike is something you're keen on, but I have to be honest, I'm not. And have you forgotten about the darts championship I'm organizing for June? And apart from anything else, Samantha wants July and August off. I'll need to be here.'

I looked across the table at the man I'd married. He didn't really want children. He didn't really want to come on a long walk with me. I had completely forgotten about his darts thing. I tried to remember what we had in common. 'Wait. What did you say?'

'I'm not keen.'

'After that.'

He shrugged.

'You said Samantha wants two months off.'

'Yeah. I mean, it's not official, but you know we all agree in advance, to make it easier.'

'Yeah. No. I mean, when did she become *Samantha*?'

'What?'

'She's been Sam since you met her. But now all of a sudden she's Samantha?'

'What are you suggesting, Lily?'

I hadn't been suggesting anything. But I saw now what I ought to have suspected for some time. I stood, leaving the table and my untouched dinner. I scooped up the maps.

'I'm going to walk the Appalachian Trail by myself. And then I'm going to move on. Somewhere else. Without you.'

Had I known that such a dramatic statement would get a dramatic reaction? That Quentin would rush to my side, assure me he loved me, didn't want me to leave. Is that what I'd hoped for?

If so, I got my wish. He swore there wasn't anything between him and Sam. That I was his Honey Bee. That he loved me.

He put on my favourite song, and held out his hand. 'Please. My wife, my love.' And for the first time in longer than I could remember, Quentin and I danced together. 'We danced on our first date,' I said.

He tilted his head. 'Really?'

I smiled. 'I guess it wasn't our first official date. It was the night we met.'

'Oh yeah! That club. . . what was it called?'

Neither of us could remember.

'That evening. You kissed my hand when we met.'

'You teased me about my accent. And told me you wouldn't sleep with me.' We both laughed. 'So long ago, hey? We were a couple of kids.'

I looked up at him. 'I think I was in love with you by the end of that evening.'

'I know I was in love with you.'

'Really?'

'I used to get so nervous, wondering what might have happened. If I hadn't been posted to Big Rock Lake. If we hadn't gone out to that place, that evening.

If you hadn't. If I'd never met you.'

He sounded so sincere, and then he lowered his face to mine and we kissed like we'd kissed when we were dating, all those years ago. Soon afterwards we went to the bedroom to make love. When we woke up the next morning, all tangled up in each other, we made love again.

'That was good,' I said, leaning into his chest.

'Ummm,' he said.

'We should do that more often.' For a few days it felt as if everything was as it should be, as it always had been, and as if it could continue to be for always.

It wasn't that simple, of course. And I hadn't been wrong. And I was a researcher, for goodness' sake, it took me no time at all to discover that Sam had been stationed at Fort Riley when we were there. So she and Quentin had known each other for longer than I'd thought. And she'd been part of the top secret overseas training session.

I did nothing with those pieces of information.

Nor did I pack the last of my things and leave for the Appalachian Trail.

We both got up and went to work in the mornings, we continued to eat dinner in front of the television. We went to events together, we laughed together from time to time. We didn't talk about Sam, or our marriage. I had always frozen when I was scared, but this was my biggest freeze yet. I looked at marital self-help books on my lunch hour, but never took them home.

So I also continued to plan my walk with care and detail, and started to think of it as being the space I'd use to figure out my future. I bought the last few things I needed for the hike, then packed and repacked my backpack. May turned into June, proper summer, and brought with it BBQs and pool parties. I caught sight of our reflection one evening as we left the house for a formal dinner and was shocked at how we looked the same as ever. A couple. A married couple. Happy enough.

Quentin saw me looking at our reflection. 'That's a pretty dress, Lily. You look really nice.'

I smiled up at him. 'Thanks.' On impulse I kissed him and sank into his chest when he kissed me back.

I was seated next to a visiting civilian. 'Awkward,' he said. 'All this small talk with people we'll most likely never see again. I'm guessing you don't really care about my job. Why don't you tell me about the next holiday you hope to go on?'

'Stop when I've gone on for too long,' I warned him, and started to talk about all the plans I'd made for the walk.

Jim was sitting across from us and heard me.

'What's that? You're going to hike the Appalachian Trail by yourself?'
I nodded, taken aback by the hesitation in his voice.
'Do you really think that's a good idea? To leave Quentin for so long?'
'No different to his leaving me for so long when he's deployed,' I said.
'But—'
'He'll be fine,' I said, wishing Jim had left the stranger and me to our conversation.

The last week of June turned into the first week of July, which meant a big parade for the July Fourth celebrations. I noticed that Sam and Carl were not at any of the events Quentin and I attended, and wondered if that was coincidence, or by design. I wondered what Carl thought of his wife's relationship with my husband.

July melted into August. I moved my backpack to the back of the closet, so it wasn't a daily reminder of my failure.

The last weekend of August there was yet another formal event. It was only the next morning I realized that once again Sam and Carl hadn't been there. My mug of coffee was suddenly too heavy for me to hold. It slipped from my hands and crashed to the floor.

'Lily! Are you okay?'
I shook my head. 'No.'
'Did you burn yourself? What—?'
'Sam's away isn't she? July and August you said.'
'Honestly, Lily? You're going to pick a fight? Now?'
'It doesn't have to be a fight. It can be a discussion. We're intelligent adults, surely we're capable of having an intelligent discussion.'
'Discussion?'
'I'm not willing to be that wife,' I said. 'You can't have it both ways. And we can't keep pretending it'll all resolve itself. One of us has to make a decision. Either you leave Sam, or I leave you.'

I stared at Quentin, hoping he'd once again deny there was anything at all between him and Sam.
'Lily—'
'I'm right, aren't I? You and Sam are having an affair?' I prayed harder for a denial.

It didn't come. 'Lily—' My husband's voice cracked. 'Please don't leave me.'

So this was how our marriage was going to end? Another woman? Yet, barely an argument. An ordinary August morning.

After I confronted Quentin, all I wanted to do was go home to Mum. She'd help me fix things. But she didn't even know my marriage was broken. Because I hadn't told her. I hadn't told anyone.

Quentin had started crying. I closed my eyes. He almost never cried and every time he did, it broke my heart. 'I need to go on my hike,' I said. 'I'll use the time to think about things, and you should do the same. It's pretty easy, Quentin. Me or her. Your wife, or your mistress.'

'Lily. Please.' I turned back to him and waited for him to say something, anything, to convince me to stay.

'Don't leave me.'

I showered, changed, and packed a few last things in my backpack, shocking myself at how truly well prepared I was. I was ready to go in less time that it took Quentin to clean the mess I'd made in the kitchen.

'That's it?' Quentin asked. 'You're going to walk out the door?'

'I need to get to Amicalola Falls State Park,' I said. 'Will you drive me?'

'Of course I will,' he said. 'That gives me seven hours to talk you out of this crazy plan.'

But neither of us said much on the drive; we listened to music, I re-read the first parts of the guidebook, and I looked at the map and calendar and the map again.

'We need to eat,' he said, when we pulled into a gas station.

'Sure,' I nodded. I left him to fill the tank, and I went into the café, ordering myself the soup and sandwich deal, and a Hungry Man's breakfast for Quentin. Crispy bacon, eggs over easy, hash browns on the grill with onions, white toast.

'See, this is exactly what I would have ordered myself,' he said, when it was delivered. 'You know me so well, Lily.'

I blew on the steaming cream of mushroom soup, but it still burnt the top of my mouth. I put down my spoon, looked at the grilled cheese, and took a sip of water.

'I need to know, Quentin.'

He knew me so well too. I didn't have to say more. He set his cutlery on the white paper placemat and nodded, once. 'I am so sorry. I—It was harmless flirtation, and then . . . somehow. . . ' He took a shaky breath. 'And it is over. I swear to you. Totally over.'

'How long was it going on?' I asked. 'Since Kansas?'

'No!' He didn't look the least bit surprised that I knew they'd known each other then. But he did look sad that I'd thought they'd been together for so long. 'Honestly, hand on my heart, Lily. It was never anything, not anything real, until we led the training session together.'

The word *real* stung. 'I see.' I wasn't entirely sure I believed him. That kiss on New Year's Eve hadn't looked like a first kiss. But that he'd been in such an odd mood since his return from the training—that fit.

'And it's all in the past. Never again,' he said.

'So you. . . broke it off?' I said. I couldn't look at him anymore, so I concentrated on stirring an ice cube from my water glass into my soup.

'She said she couldn't—I mean,' he hastily amended his story. 'We couldn't—'

I sighed. 'She and Carl have gone away to fix their marriage,' I guessed. I held my hand in front of my face. 'Actually, I don't want to know. I don't care. You should eat your food before it goes cold.'

'This is crazy,' he said, when we'd both eaten all we wanted. I hadn't touched my sandwich, so I carefully wrapped it in a clean serviette. 'It's way too late for you to start the walk. You told me you had to leave in March. It's August 26th.'

'I won't be able to do the whole thing,' I said. 'But I can do some of it.' It *was* too late to start, and I *didn't* know how far I'd get, realistically, or if I could really hike all through November. 'I cannot, possibly, spend another night in our house,' I said, keeping my voice low since the café had filled up and there were people either side of us. 'You betrayed me, Quentin. You have broken our marriage vows. And you have broken my heart.'

I stood and moved quickly to the counter to pay our bill, willing myself not to cry. While I was there I grabbed three chocolate bars and put them on the counter.

'All good?' asked the woman who took my cash.

I nodded, not trusting myself to speak.

We drove the rest of the way in silence. When we reached the trailhead with its iconic archway, where there was a single van parked, he lifted my pack out of the back of the car for me. 'Really?' he said, as I shrugged it over my shoulders and did up the belt.

I looked at him. 'What?'

'I thought you were bluffing. I didn't believe you were actually capable of turning your back on me and walking away.'

'I didn't think you were capable of fucking another woman,' I said. I heard my voice, shrill and mean. 'I wanted a faithful husband,' I said. 'And I wanted a husband who wanted to raise a family with me.'

'But you can't—You can't walk away from me, from us, from our marriage. We have to talk, at least.'

'We've had months to talk,' I said. 'I need some time alone.'

'Wait. Let me take a photo of you under the archway.' He did, and then read the notice. 'Do you know it's almost nine miles to the start of the Trail?'

'Yes,' I said.

'And you're going to start with six hundred uphill steps?'

'Six hundred and four,' I said. 'Yes.'

We were both silent for several moments. 'I'm... Good bye, Quentin.'

'I can't let you go, Lily,' he said. 'What kind of person would I be? It's not safe. You're alone... there are bears, or you could fall and break your leg... I'm scared for you.'

I was scared too. Terrified. But not by the prospect of the walk, or of being alone, or of meeting a bear. But by the realization that our marriage was ending. And not with the fireworks of a final last-ever argument, but with this surreal drawn-out whimper. I turned away before he could see the tears in my eyes.

'Lily!' He reached for me, turned me back towards him, and tried to embrace me, but the pack on my back made it an awkward half-hug. 'How do I keep in touch with you? When will I see you?'

'I left a list of addresses where you can write to me. It's on the fridge. I'll call you on my zero days, when I'm resting in a town.'

We looked at each other.

'You are actually going to do this.'

I nodded.

'But... what am I supposed to do?'

'Drive home. Think about your choices. It's me or her, Quentin.'

'I told you. It's over. I've made my choice.'

'She made it for you.'

'You don't have to do this to prove something to me. You can get back in the car and we can drive home together.'

I shook my head. 'I'm not trying to prove something to you. I'm proving something to myself.' I looked at the sky. 'I have to go now. I have to go.'

'I love you, Lily,' he said. 'I love you.'

I opened my mouth to tell him I loved him too but couldn't do it.

A group of five hikers rounded the corner and came out into the parking space, walking towards the parked van. 'Late in the day to be settin' off,' one of the men commented to another after they'd passed us. I assumed he'd intended me to hear him.

'I have to go,' I said to Quentin. As much from habit as anything I reached up to kiss him. The tears on his cheeks almost made me reconsider leaving. 'I have to go,' I said again.

'Go on your walk,' he whispered. 'But then come home. Come home to me, Lily.'

When I knew he could no longer see me I allowed myself to start crying. I walked until it was dark and couldn't see, then put on my headlamp and kept on walking until I'd reached the Black Gap Shelter and put seven miles between me and the parking lot. After I'd pitched my tent and was sitting with my cold grilled cheese and a chocolate bar I wondered how long he'd waited before he started driving home. I wondered if he might still be sitting in the car. I started to wonder what he was going to say to Sam when he saw her next but I pushed the thought from my mind. Luckily, I was mentally and physically done and fell asleep moments after I got into my sleeping bag.

Chapter Six

BIG ROCK LAKE, FEBRUARY 2014

'Ma'am? Ma'am?'

It was the server behind the Tim Hortons counter.

'Um. Your order.'

I pulled myself back to the present. The hospital. Coffee and muffins for Rose and Mum. Rose. Kent. Kent's accident.

'Sorry. Thank you.' I balanced the paper bag on the cardboard tray, and as I turned I bumped into the pony-tailed woman in a lab coat. 'Sorry.' How many times was I going to apologize today? Why was it so easy to apologize to strangers I'd never see again, yet so challenging to apologize to my sister, one of the people I loved most in the world?

After all my dithering, Rose took the muffin I passed her without even looking at it. She ate a few bites, and I guessed she had no idea what flavour it was.

'Code Blue! Code Blue!' The announcement over the PA cut through my preoccupation. There was a rush of white-coats behind the double doors.

Rose gasped. 'What's happening?'

I was about to remind her the hospital was full of patients, but noticed she was staring at the desk. And three of the staff members there were looking back at her.

'It's Kent. It's Kent, isn't it?'

'We don't know that—' I started.

But Rose was already halfway across the room. 'What's happening? What's going on?'

A young man stepped around the desk and took Rose's hand, leading her to a quieter corner. Mum and I went to her side.

'—sudden cardiac arrest... major blood loss...' I tried to focus on what he was saying.

Rose slumped against me. 'No. No.'

'We'll let you know as soon as he's been stabilized.'

Mum and I half-helped, half-carried Rose back to our chairs.

'I don't know how to do this,' Rose whispered. 'I'm so scared.'

'I know,' I said. 'I know.' I recognized that sense of terror.

Appalachian Trail, 2001

I couldn't possibly finish the Trail, of course I was aware of that. Maybe for a few days I'd imagined I could cover double the miles I'd planned, if the weather cooperated. But that was impossible. I nearly quit a dozen times that first week. All the training I'd done, or thought I'd done, had not prepared me for this relentless, endless walking, the hills, or the weight of my pack. My feet hurt, my calves hurt, my back hurt, my shoulders hurt. One day my socks got wet and I was too tired to change them; by the time I stopped to set up camp, both feet were a mess of blood and pus. The next morning I cried as I laced my boots over the popped blisters and tender skin. But I did lace them up, and then I set off, still crying.

I hadn't trained for the loneliness. I hadn't expected the long stretches of time with myself to be one of the most difficult obstacles. I found myself wishing Tansy was with me, then trying to imagine her right now. What would she be doing, would she be married, have children, where might she be living? 'I miss you,' I said, and with a start realized that was the first time I'd ever admitted it aloud. Was speaking to my sister a sign of craziness? Or a sign of healing?

My stubbornness kept me going. My refusal to admit defeat, my refusal to go back to Quentin. I needed this time to truly make the break, and to figure out what I was going to do with the rest of my life. This walk was going to be life changing, all I had to do was keep walking. So I kept walking. There were days I bribed myself with a handful of gorp every hour on the hour, days I latched on to a group of walkers to get to their finish line, days I made sure I was walking out of sight of anyone else so no one would see me cry.

The actual hiking got easier each day and at some point in the second week I started believing I'd get far enough along and could come back next Spring to finish. I had to hike the whole trail within twelve months for it to count as a 'thru hike' and that was my goal. That would mean something. The first zero day I took, I sent two postcards, one to Mum and one to Quentin. I called Mum but wasn't sure what I'd say to Quentin, wasn't sure what he'd say to me, so despite my promise, I didn't call him.

I thought a lot about the past, all the mistakes I'd made, the things I blamed Quentin for, and the things for which no one was to blame. I thought about the love affair I'd had in my third year of university. Back when I'd felt like a grown up. 'I'm sorry,' I whispered to the younger me, whose heart was crushed by the much older prof. I started spending hours a day not thinking about anything, putting one foot in front of the other. I paused, often, to stare at a view. I chatted to people I met, but never told them much. I wasn't sure if I was avoiding the real purpose of the hike, to figure out my future, or if my subconscious was working on it and one day I'd wake up with a fully formed plan.

I'd picked up my pace and was walking between twelve and fourteen miles a day now. Every night I marked off the day's route on the map with a bright yellow highlighter. It was a tiny part of the trail compared to what was left, but noting what I'd completed was motivation enough to keep going the next day.

And then, a Tuesday.

I couldn't even have sworn what day of the week it was if asked, they had already started blurring together. I was up with the sun, on the trail as quickly as possible. Until inexplicably, late morning, I was terrified. Instantly I knew I had to turn back and retrace my steps to a town I'd seen the previous afternoon, but I tried to keep going, telling myself it was an irrational fear, and I needed to walk through it. If I had met another hiker, maybe together we could have carried on, but I couldn't do it by myself. I stopped for a break, told myself I needed a cup of tea, but couldn't muster the energy to heat water, so I ate a granola bar. Kept on walking, but more and more slowly.

When I finally gave in to the terror, I turned and ran. I ran until I couldn't breathe, and then I kept going as fast as I could, retracing my morning's scant progress in a quarter of the time, speeding past my previous night's campground, rushing on until I saw the town below me and knew I was almost back to civilization.

But when did you notice the quiet, Peter asked me, years later. Really notice?

I think the truth is I didn't. I was focused on getting out, getting away from...from what? I wasn't sure. The forest was oppressive, menacing. All I noticed when I slowed to catch my breath, pull my t-shirt down my back, take a big drink of water, was that my legs and arms were covered with red welts. It wasn't poison ivy, or hornets; it wasn't a rash I'd ever seen before. I thought when I walked into a diner on the town's main street (I was forcing myself to move with the dream of a diner with french fries and an icy cold Diet Coke) people might avert their eyes, or else rush to help me. By the time I got to town, almost three hours later, my dream had changed to a bar with a platter of wings and an icy cold beer.

When I walked into the bar, I was invisible. No one noticed the hideous rash, no one watched me drop my pack by the door. Everyone was staring at the row of television screens up on the wall.

I went to the bar and waited for a bartender to acknowledge my presence. As I'd come down the mountain, I'd started feeling ridiculous and made up a story I could tell, some sentences I could say when asked. In the safety of the crowd, the bar, I started wondering if a few nights' break, a good night's sleep in a decent bed, and hot running water, might make me reconsider my decision. I tried to work out if I had the luxury of adding an extra two days to my itinerary, since I was now already going to lose one and half. I decided not to say too much to anyone in case I went back on the trail. I'd call Mum and Rose and tell them both how much fun I was having. I'd omit to mention today's weird panic attack, and focus on the views I'd seen recently, the good weather. How positive and optimistic I felt.

The guy behind the bar passed me a beer without taking his eyes from the television. There were skyscrapers and white smoke. 'What is it?' I asked, gesturing at the movie they were all watching, which was replaying the same scene, over and over.

He briefly took his gaze from the row of televisions and looked at me. 'What?' He looked at me more closely. 'Where have you been?'

'The Appalachian Trail,' I said. The beer didn't taste as good as I'd imagined it would.

'So you just walked in here? Just now?'

I put the bottle on the bar. Nodded. I must have imagined the whisper in the crowd. I didn't imagine the older woman beside me, reaching her hands over my shoulders and pulling me into a close embrace. 'Oh, Sweetie.'

I looked at her. Back at the bartender.

'Oh, Sweetie,' the woman said again. And to the bartender. 'She doesn't know.'

I turned my head back to the television screens. 'It's not a movie,' I whispered. Not a question. Whispering because no one else in the room, I realized now, was saying a word. Not a single conversation. By now my eyes had adjusted to the light, and my brain was making sense of things. It was *CNN Live*. The news. The chyron running across the bottom of the screen said, "Breaking News: Attacks Against Targets In New York And Washington. Breaking News: World Trade Center Disaster. Breaking News: Two Planes Crash Into World Trade Center Towers."

Those were the twin towers in New York City, and that was a plane, flying headlong into them.

'New York,' said the barman.

'And it's everywhere,' said the woman.

'Everywhere?' I thought of London, Milan, Vienna, Moscow. Toronto? Ottawa? Big Rock Lake? My sister and my mother. I started to shake. 'Everywhere?' I asked again.

'Washington, the Pentagon,' she said. 'We don't even know. We don't know how many people have been killed.' Later, I learned of the footage that had been shown before I arrived. People jumping to their deaths surrounded by fluttering papers, drifting more slowly to the hard earth below.

'I have to call my Mum,' I said.

She passed me her Blackberry. 'Go ahead. Call anyone you need to call.'

'I'm Canadian,' I said. 'It's long distance-'

She cut me off. 'She'll be sick with worry. Call.'

Mum was out, so I left a brief message, telling her where I was, that I was okay, that I'd call her later.

'Canadian,' the woman said. 'I would have guessed from your accent you're not from here.' It sounded like she had watched her fill of the newscast and was ready to talk.

'My father was American,' I said. Funny I didn't think to mention my American husband.

'Do you have any siblings?' she asked.

I was tempted to tell her the truth: I'm one of three. Instead, I told her the other truth. 'Yes. A younger sister.'

She passed her cell phone back to me. 'You should call her too.'

When Rose answered and I heard her voice I was suddenly unable to speak. She said hello several times, and I worried that she would hang up on what she might assume to be a prank call. Finally. 'Rose.'

A gasp. 'Lily!'

Tears filled my eyes, and I blinked furiously. 'Rose,' I said again.

'You're okay.'

'I'm okay.'

'Thank god.'

Hearing her voice was enough. I told her I'd call later, when I knew what was happening, when I'd had time to digest the news. Then I thanked the woman, whose name I never learned, and left my unfinished beer on the bar. I didn't say goodbye and maybe I was a coward to let her think I was heading for the washroom and would be back. But I knew a woman who called a stranger Sweetie, and hugged her, and passed over her cell phone, and wanted to know about her family, would also have invited that stranger home for the night. There would have been dinner at the table, or maybe in front of the television. A husband. Children who had not yet left home despite being of an age when they ought to be making their way in the world. Conversation and speculation about the attacks. Endless conversation and speculation about the attacks.

What I longed for was an anonymous hotel room, a hot bath, fresh sheets, a television that I could turn off when I chose. I felt a little guilty swinging my pack onto my back and heading back out on to the street—but not too guilty. A few blocks away I could see a Holiday Inn sign complete with an advertisement for a heated indoor pool. That sounded ideal. I could shower off the worst of the hiking dirt, then submerge myself into a warm chlorine pool to rinse away the rest of it. And underwater, I wouldn't be able to hear the news. The report repeating the same details, the film showing the plane crashing into the second tower, over and over and over again.

Later I would read that I was not alone, that many of the hikers left the trail. The fear was universal, instinctive. When the air space was shut down and the last of the planes had landed it was the absence of that background noise that caused the anxiety. We didn't know exactly what was wrong, but we knew something was wrong, and we needed to be with other people. That may explain why groups of hikers carried on, solo hikers turned back.

I suppose if I searched online, I'd find some blogs, or a community on social media, some of our number who wanted to contact others and share their stories. Back then, when there wasn't the internet in the same way there is now—I don't know. It doesn't matter. What mattered, what seemed to matter most to me, as

I walked from the bar to the hotel, was that I would not complete any more of the Appalachian Trail. I already knew that would change me. It would change my life. But there was no chance, no chance of my going back to the trail to carry on walking. It was over, clearly. I could already imagine all the people who would say, 'Oh well, there will be other walks.' The same people who would have said to me, had they known of my miscarriages, 'Oh well, there will be other babies.'

I must have been in shock. To have thought about myself in the face of the disaster. It took seconds watching the news in my hotel room to understand my walk was meaningless. So many people dead, so many more wounded. And it was clear the death toll would keep mounting. Unborn children, the rescue workers and civilians who breathed in the toxins. Later, deaths by lung disease, cancers, suicides. No one in that bar, or that town, ever asked me about the walk, and I mentioned it to very few people. No one ever saw the weird rash. I told very few people about running as fast as I could to escape an unknown terror. The two women at the Holiday Inn check-in counter were clearly traumatized, staring across the lobby at the large screen television. I had the heated indoor pool to myself. And the crisp white sheets I'd envisioned.

It wasn't until late into the evening that I thought about calling Quentin, and as soon as it registered that he hadn't been my first thought, I hated myself. How could I not have called him from the bar? This, surely, was proof that I had left him, left our marriage. This had happened in his country, his city. I imagined him sitting on our ivory sofa, watching the television, scared and shocked and saddened. Or, more likely, called into action. Communications and security would be vital now, his job more important than ever.

I called our home number and his Blackberry. He didn't answer either; I left a message on both. After I'd hung up, it registered to me that the one thing that might wipe out our final argument was an act of terrorism.

He called back after midnight. 'Lily. Did I wake you?'

'No. I can't sleep.'

'I know. Lily—' A sob.

'I'm so sorry, Quentin,' I said. I didn't want him to think I was apologizing for having left. 'So close to Brooklyn.'

'It's the worst thing. It's—I can't even begin to—We were watching *CNN*. We can't—'

'I had to turn it off,' I said. 'It's too... it's too horrible.'

'They're saying there'll be more attacks.'

'Are you safe? Where will they send you? What can you do?'

'I don't know. We—No one can—'

I'd never heard Quentin at such a loss for words. I didn't know what I could say to comfort him. I opened my mouth to ask him if he needed me there but different words came out. 'I'm going to go back to Canada, to see Mum and Rose.'

'Of course. Your family. I understand.' He made it sound as if this had always been the plan. 'I'll be here when you come home,' he said. As if I'd never left.

We spoke for another twenty minutes but said very little. Was it selfish of me to want him to ask even one question about my hike? To remember where I'd been, what I'd been doing as recently as this morning? Yes, I told myself. Deeply selfish. He could think of nothing but the attack.

'Please, will you call me again tomorrow?' he asked. I promised I would and hung up before he could hear tears in my voice. Tears for all the dead, all the widowed, all the orphaned. And a few tears for myself.

I spent three days in that town, barely leaving the Holiday Inn, and then caught a bus to a bigger city, where I was able to catch another bus, a series of buses, north to Toronto and on to Big Rock Lake. It wasn't a direct trip, and it took a long time to travel the relatively short distance. Longer because we were in a minor accident on a lonely stretch of highway at two in the morning. The accident necessitated a change of bus, and it wasn't until six in the morning that our new bus arrived, so I missed a connection. Which meant I had to spend an extra nine hours waiting in a tiny bus station in a tiny town.

I hadn't asked for a ticket to Big Rock Lake at the first station, only 'north, to Ontario.' But where else was I going to go, except to my hometown, to my mother's house? I needed to see her, and Rose, before I did anything else.

So, on a grey September day, I got off the grey bus at the grey bus station and took a cab to Mum's. She would have come to the station to meet me, but I assumed the arrival time would be too difficult to predict. In fact, the bus was three minutes ahead of schedule and many of the passengers were met by family and friends.

Mum and Rose were waiting for me with a homemade carrot cake and a pot of tea.

And there I was, home.

It was not the homecoming I'd had in mind. I was supposed to have been triumphant, accomplished, and with a solid plan for my future. But how could I complain about anything when across the States people were organizing funerals for their loved ones? How could I look at my baby sister, my best friend, and think, before anything else, 'She hasn't missed me at all'? The thought was so instant, so clear in my mind, I worried for a moment I may have spoken it out loud. 'You look so great,' I said, hugging her. 'So happy.'

'I am happy,' she said. 'Most of all happy you're home, safe and sound.' She pulled me closer. 'I missed you so much.' And immediately I felt mean for thinking she hadn't cared I was gone.

'How's Kent?'

'Working. But on his way.'

Something in her voice reminded me of her at four years old on Christmas morning, bursting to rush downstairs to discover what Santa Claus had left under the tree.

'Rose?'

She couldn't hide her grin. 'This is your day, Lily. Today is all about you.' The words sounded vaguely familiar.

'No, it's not—What are you—' And then I noticed her hand rest ever so briefly on her stomach. 'You're pregnant!'

We laughed, and hugged, and I made sure to smile, and keep smiling, and ask all the right questions, and I am confident no one could have guessed the jealousy I battled. 'Due date?' I said, and without waiting for an answer, 'Girl or boy, or will that be a surprise? Have you started thinking about names? When can we go shopping together?'

She laughed and Mum laughed and we made another pot of tea and sat 'round the kitchen table and started making lists and I really felt then, that I'd come home. 'I'll be an aunt,' I said.

'The best aunt. You'll be the very best aunt,' said Rose.

So I was able to cry then, and they looked like tears of joy, and I promised that yes, I would be the very best aunt. And I expressed amazement—true—that she was already through her first trimester, and the baby was due in early March. But it was weeks before my shoulders relaxed and I finally felt the last of that nameless fear leave my body.

Chapter Seven

Big Rock Lake, February 2014

'Rose. Rose.' Mum was holding my sister, rocking her as if she was a little child, saying her name and murmuring soothing noises.

Someone handed me a box of tissues, and I held one out to Rose.

'That's it,' Mum said. 'Blow your nose, dry your eyes. There you go. That's my girl.'

Rose took a deep breath. 'I—' her voice broke again, and then she whispered. 'I... we argued yesterday.' She shook her head. 'So stupid. The cost of Sydney's gymnastics leotard. I ordered her the official one instead of getting one from Walmart.' She lowered her voice even more. 'I didn't say I love you before he left for work, I didn't even blow him a kiss. He might die and my last words to him were said in anger. I can't stop thinking about that.'

'Because you're human,' I said. 'Oh my goodness, Rose, you didn't have to say I love you for Kent to know how very much you love him. It's in everything you do, it's in so much more than words.'

'My mind keeps returning to that stupid leotard. I'm scared that I'll cry when she wears it, that—'

'I know.' I did. 'This is overwhelming. It's easier to focus on a gymnastics uniform, and a petty disagreement, than the reality of what's happening. And that's okay. But listen to me: you have to stop beating yourself up. Let it go, please let it go.' I half-chuckled, half-sighed. 'Listen to me. As if it were that easy.'

'It reflects so badly on me. I think—I told myself I wanted her to fit in. Not be at risk of being bullied for being different. But I know half the kids will be in no-name leotards. And Sydney? She so doesn't care. I'm the snob. I'm the bully.'

'We all have regrets,' Mum said softly. 'So many regrets. But we have to live with them and move forwards.'

'Oh.' Something in Mum's tone stopped Rose's tears. 'What are your regrets?'

Mum sighed. 'So many. Big and little.' She paused. 'Not moving into town, sooner, of course.'

Of course.

She continued. 'I wonder if I should have mortgaged the house and sent your father to rehab; I didn't even think of that until it was too late.'

'Rehab?' Rose asked.

Mum carried on as if she hadn't heard Rose. 'And that damn kitchen! I have hated the layout of that kitchen since the day I looked at the house. I wish I'd had it renovated the year we moved in.'

'Oh Mum! The kitchen?!' Rose and I spoke at the same time.

'What's wrong with the kitchen?' Rose asked.

Mum groaned. 'The back door doesn't open all the way because the fridge is too close. And the broom closet is in entirely the wrong place. The pantry door opens from the wrong side. The window isn't over the sink. That oven is too narrow. And there is not one single piece of counter space large enough to roll a decent amount of cookie dough. I'd like to have knocked down the wall to the dining room and opened it all up. Put in an island.'

'Mum!' Again, my sister and I spoke as one. 'Renovate it now! Give yourself a new kitchen.'

I made a mental note to ask Kathleen for names of contractors.

'And then I'll want to change the layout of the stupid second floor. And the bathroom, and—' Mum rolled her eyes. 'If I start I'll never finish. Easier to buy a new house.'

'But—But the house isn't that bad,' said Rose. 'You must have liked *something* about it when you bought it.'

I met Mum's gaze above Rose's head. 'It wasn't the Old Homestead,' I said.

Big Rock Lake, 1976

After that spring day in '76, Rose and I never went back to the Old Homestead. When Mum collected us from the neighbours we went into the city and stayed in a room in the hotel my grandparents stayed in at Christmastime, where there were tiny bottles of shampoo and mini bars of soap. I told Bobby we had to save them all for Tansy, and, for the first time in my life, I saw him cry.

My grandparents stayed in a room next to ours, with a door that connected them. That night, when baby Rose and I were supposed to be asleep in one room, my mum and my grandparents spoke in the other.

'I can't go back,' Mum said, one night.

'You don't have to go back, my love,' said my grandmother. She was crying too.

'Not just the Old Homestead. That life. I can't live that life anymore.'

'You don't have to.' This time it was her father speaking. 'We'll buy you a house, Judith. Anywhere you like. You could come home to Niagara, or move back to Toronto. A fresh start, wherever you want.'

'A fresh start,' my grandmother echoed.

Mum chose a fresh start nine miles from the Old Homestead. A small white house on a quiet street in one of those areas of Big Rock Lake that was neither one neighbourhood nor another. Square, three bedrooms, with a blue spruce in the front yard and three maples in the back. Close enough to my school that I could get there by foot in twenty minutes; fifteen if I ran part-way.

I believe there was some resistance on my grandmother's part. They could afford to buy my mother a bigger house, more modern, in a nicer community, was my mother sure this was all she wanted? She was sure, this one was manageable, this one was convenient, this one was fine. Perhaps my grandmother's bigger disappointment was that my mother's fresh start did not include leaving Bobby.

Big Rock Lake, February 2014

'It was unfair of your parents to expect you to make a decision about buying a house right then,' I said. 'You could have rented for a year or two, then made a more informed decision.'

Mum shrugged. 'They were trying to help. Trying to do their best.'

'Um.' I wasn't ready to absolve them of all responsibility.

'They were in shock too,' Mum reminded me.
That I could believe.

BIG ROCK LAKE, 1976–1977

That August, Mum took the bus with Rose and me to Niagara-on-the-Lake. It was the first time I ever remembered her going on holiday, anywhere, and it was magical to see her hometown through her eyes. We stayed a full month, and on the way back home Mum told me she had taken a job as an editor at the university's press, that it would be Bobby who would make my school lunch and meet me after school every afternoon.

When she came home for supper after her first day on her job she announced, 'Both my girls will go to university.' I saw the look on Bobby's face at her use of the pronoun 'my.' Like a moth caught in the chimney of an oil lamp, its wings suddenly still after madly flapping, as if aware the end is near.

Children adapt—certainly I adapted. I made real friends at school now that Mum was able to organize proper playdates. I accepted birthday party invitations. I played hide and seek, and hopscotch, and skipping games with the other kids my age who lived along the street. I loved shopping in the grocery store with Mum. At home I quickly learned that playing with Rose, oohing and awing over her latest achievement, made Mum smile. This was easy for me to do because Rose was the cutest, smartest, happiest baby ever. I adored her and adored spending time with her and was proud to push her stroller along our street to show her off.

Bobby was unable to adjust to city life. The change from his days of freedom on the farm to a middle-class life in which he played no role other than house-husband must have been too difficult for him to manage. There were discussions of his finding a job, a real Monday-to-Friday nine-to-five job, but nothing ever came of them. Once I heard him sneer at something Mum said. 'A thirty-six-year-old bartender? In a city full of students who'll work for peanuts? Get real, Judith.' I missed the way he used to call Mum "J" and missed the cocoon they'd shared, that I'd once been so jealous of.

He'd pace the house, pace the back garden, pace down the street, then come inside and pace the house again. Without access to a still, he had to start buying alcohol. He tried various kinds and seemed to settle on rye and vodka. I only now understand that my mother must have loved him very much in the beginning to have stayed on the Old Homestead, and to have made that life work, and that this was now a test of Bobby's love for her, and that he had to make this life work, and that he must have known it. I do know that one evening he paced his way down the street to a dark, old-fashioned bar where he met men with whom he had at least one thing in common. What they spoke about I cannot imagine, perhaps they simply sat in silence as they drank away the hours.

Oblivious to any tension and unaffected by all the differences between *then* and *now*, was our bright, beautiful, perfect Rose. A do-over for all of us.

When Rose started at nursery school Bobby started spending more time at the bar—afternoons, then mornings too—and we saw less and less of him. He often didn't come home for supper. His drinking became more serious, and I started becoming more observant. I learned the signs, the smells, the excuses. He became mean in a way he had never been before, and the hand raising and threat of a slap less unbelievable. I started keeping a diary of my memories from my childhood at the Old Homestead, desperate to preserve the history that I now knew could so easily slip away.

But on the whole, as I say, I adapted.

And there was Peter. Peter Reynolds.

He and his parents lived next door to us in a house almost identical to ours: square, white, but with red shutters where ours were green, and a double lot so a significantly bigger garden. His mother brought us a chicken casserole the day we moved in, complete with rice, vegetables, and white bread rolls, still warm from the oven, and paper plates and plastic forks, and the next day she arrived with a bucket of cleaning supplies and scrubbed the kitchen and bathrooms while Mum and my grandparents unpacked all the boxes. She brought her son, Peter, too, who at seventeen seemed to me to be another adult. He was in Grade Twelve, one year left of high school to finish. He took me out of the way for the afternoon, to a full-length cartoon at the cinema and then to McDonald's for hamburgers and french fries. A double treat.

To repay that kindness, Mum invited them for dinner a few weeks later, when we'd started to settle in and my grandparents had gone back to Niagara. Peter noticed the unassembled bookcases, and without a word walked back home for his tool kit and put them together while his parents and my mother had a sherry. He shrugged away my mother's thanks, asking if there was anything else that needed doing.

'My bed is wobbly,' I said. 'I told Bobby but he hasn't done anything.'

'Oh, Lily Love, Daddy will fix it soon,' Mum said, blushing, perhaps flustered by her lie, or her use of 'Daddy.' She had explained to our guests that her husband was unable to join us for dinner, but I'd overheard her talking to him earlier in a thin voice. 'It's two in the afternoon and you're drunk,' she'd said. 'Go out and stay out for the evening. You are not welcome to come and embarrass me in front of our neighbours.'

'I bet your dad is super busy. Let me take a look,' said Peter, and when I snuggled into bed that night, I felt safe and secure. After supper Peter played a marathon game of Monopoly with me, then offered to come back the next day to mow the lawn.

For the rest of the year he was always around, though his visits never coincided with Bobby being at home. He always appeared to be stopping by on a whim. 'Those sugar maples are pretty in October, aren't they?' he'd say, then set to and rake all the leaves that Bobby had been ignoring. He suggested we have a big bonfire, but when I trembled with fear, he retracted the suggestion and instead left a row of neatly ties bags of leaves at the curb. Or, 'That was a heavy snow last night, wasn't it?' he'd say. 'Let me clear the worst of it for you.' An hour later the drive, sidewalk, and paths to both front and back doors would be shovelled and swept. Every so often he'd accept Mum's offer of lunch, and afterwards he'd offer to play any board game I liked, though I always chose Monopoly, because I always won.

In June he stopped by in his gown and mortarboard on his way to the high school graduation ceremony. 'We'll miss you, Peter,' said my mother.

'Not for long,' he said. 'I'm working in Algonquin Park for the summer, but I'll be back in the fall.' He had decided to go to the local university, despite offers from both the University of Toronto and Queen's. There was a full scholarship attached to the offer from our local university, and he'd chosen the concurrent Bachelor of Arts - Bachelor of Education degree. 'Two for the price of one!' he said, and it took me years to figure out his mother's cancer was the real reason he had chosen to stay in Big Rock Lake.

True to his word he was back home at the end of summer, and that fall our leaves were raked, and that winter our snow was cleared, and that continued for four more years until I turned twelve and Mum declared it was time for her grown-up teenage girl to do those jobs. Which I did, albeit begrudgingly, and never as well as Peter had. Still he'd pop by, sometimes for a meal, more often to fix a broken cupboard door, change an awkward lightbulb, or slide cedar shims under the lopsided washing machine.

The winter I was nine years old Peter taught me backgammon and chess, and when my mother told him he mustn't feel obligated he shook his head. 'If I'm going to be a teacher I'd better learn how to teach,' he said. He used the same line of reasoning when Rose was old enough to start wanting to join in what anyone else was doing, helping her with a fifteen-piece floor puzzle, over and over again. Later, after Bobby left, it was Peter who spent hours patiently coaching me in his Volkswagen so well that I passed my driving test on the first go.

I didn't think of him as any sort of father substitute; I didn't realize anyone might think I needed one. An ersatz big brother, perhaps, as I grew older and the age difference between us was not so large as it had at first appeared. I don't know how we would have managed without him helping out around the house, unclogging a drain on a Saturday afternoon in return for a toasted tuna sandwich instead of a plumber's emergency callout fee, checking the smoke alarms had working batteries twice a year, replacing the kitchen door the Sunday morning after my father arrived back at the house at two a.m. without a key and decided to break in.

BIG ROCK LAKE, FEBRUARY 2014

'And you, Lily?' Rose asked. 'Do you have any regrets?'

I hesitated. What was I willing to share? I had only ever spoken of my first pregnancy, and the termination, to my therapist, who had questioned my conviction that my first pregnancy would have been full term, resulting in a healthy birth. She'd helped me work towards revising the stories I'd told myself, and forgiving myself for ignoring evidence that contradicted my negative core beliefs.

'I regret not having been more open with you both,' I said. 'I've kept so many parts of my life hidden.' Not having had children, never having had the chance to raise a family, that was my longest running regret. I thought some more. 'My biggest regret is not marrying Peter the first time.'

'The first time?' Rose sounded genuinely confused. 'What do you mean?'

BIG ROCK LAKE, 2001

Back in Big Rock Lake after 9/11 it was amazing how quickly I slipped back into a routine, and how comfortable it felt.

'Three people, Lily,' Mum said, as she started tossing the salad. 'Set the table for three, please.'

'Oh, is Rose coming?' I got out an extra mat, more cutlery.

Mum shook her head. 'It's Thursday. Warren Reynolds always comes by for dinner.'

'Peter's dad?' I was surprised. 'You still do that?'

She nodded. 'Every week. I promised Felicia before she died that I'd feed him once a week, to make sure he got out of the house and had some conversation. I don't know that I do much by way of conversation, but I make sure he has a hot meal.'

'But—but that was years ago. She's been dead—' I paused to do the math. 'Eighteen years.'

'Umm. I guess Felicia and I both assumed he'd remarry.' She paused, salad tongs in hand. 'I hope she knew how deeply Warren loved her. He's not interested in any other woman, never has been.'

'Does Peter come?'

'Occasionally. Christmas. A few times in the summer. But no, not usually.'

Mr. Reynolds had barely changed since I'd last seen him. He was recently back from a coach tour of western Ireland and planning another trip with the same company to the Cotswolds the following spring.

I didn't remember him as a traveller. But perhaps my teenage world view had been narrow. 'You'll love the Cotswolds,' I said, describing the golden stone houses, narrow streets, and flowers that I remembered. 'And you must have some cider. And Bath, of course, is gorgeous. What was your favourite part of Ireland?'

Talk of his various holidays, and mine, took us through pre-dinner drinks and our main course. I didn't ask about Peter until we were having dessert. 'Is he well? Still teaching? Married with kids?' Though surely Mum would have mentioned a marriage if there'd been one.

Mr. Reynolds answered all my questions. His son was very well, thank you. Yes, still teaching in the same school, though there were fewer children every year. So, as well as history, he taught various other courses, one called Civics and one that was part of the new province-wide mandate to, well, he wasn't quite sure what it was for. But although Peter didn't love the subject matter, he was optimistic that it would provide job security. He had dated a few young women, off and on, and had been engaged, but that had ended. I added eleven years to my age and worked out that Peter was forty-four.

'Please say hello to him from me,' I said. 'It would be nice to catch up.'

His father must have phoned his son almost as soon as he got home, because half an hour later Peter called me. 'Lily! How lovely that you're back for a visit. Warren says you're looking very well.'

'And he tells me that you're teaching some course that will shape the minds of the younger generation.'

We both chuckled. 'It would be nice to catch up in person,' I said. 'Would you be free for drinks sometime?' I hadn't known I was going to ask him out until I did.

'That would be fun,' he said. 'How about next Tuesday evening?'

I wasn't sure how to interpret that. Was that the first evening he had free? Was there a 'young woman' his father didn't know about, with whom he'd be spending the weekend? And why did I suddenly care? I'd not seen Peter in nearly a decade, what difference would a few more days make? 'Sounds good,' I said, and we agreed to meet at a bar in a neighbourhood across the city.

On Saturday, Rose and I went shopping for the baby, then out to lunch.

'I can't believe how trendy this city's become,' I said, looking around the bistro. Apart from the accents, I could have been in a gastropub in London. 'Everything's changed so much.'

'Ooh, I'll take you to see the old farm,' Rose said. 'I wish Mum and Dad had held on to it. The people they sold it to must have made a killing. It's a housing development now, with mini-McMansions starting at three hundred thousand.'

Old Homestead, I thought. Not farm. 'No thanks,' I said. I thought of the paths to the lookout, Bobby's still, the vegetable garden, the beaver pond, our house. Would I be able to recognize anything, or had all my landmarks been cut down, filled in, paved over?

'Oh, I'm sorry.' Rose winced. 'I forget that's your childhood.'

I smiled at her. 'And I forget that it's not yours. I forget you're so much younger than me,' I admitted.

'I know, right?' she laughed. Then she smiled a real smile. 'I'm so glad you're back. Say you'll stay longer than two weeks, Lily. I mean, no need to rush back. And you handed in your notice, didn't you?'

'No need at all,' I said. 'And yes, I have no job to go back to.' Now was the perfect chance to tell her that I was considering staying for much longer, that the Appalachian Trail had been more than a solo holiday, that it had been me walking away from my marriage. I started to gather the words in my mind, but before I could, she spoke again.

'Please don't leave.'

'You sound serious.'

'I am. The whole time I was watching the coverage of 9/11 I kept thinking: Lily used to live there. If I'd lost you—'

I nodded. 'I have been wondering if people I once passed in the street were killed. Strangers to me—people whose lives I knew nothing about.'

'They're saying if we're too scared to travel ever again the terrorists have won. But I told Kent, I'm never getting on a plane, ever. Any holidays have to be within driving distance.'

'Maybe you'll change your mind.'

She shook her head. 'You should hear all the stuff Kent has to do now. For his entire career he has walked in and out of the police station. Now he has to take off his gun, walk through a security gate, sign in, sign out. He says it's a knee-jerk reaction and things will calm down, but he also says we're bringing our baby into a world that will never go back to what it was three weeks ago.'

'I think he's right,' I said. 'He's put it well.'

'I hope I'm not crazy. To bring a baby into this world.' She paused. 'I'd really like you and Kent to get to know each other. You'll love each other. Is Quint thrilled about being an uncle?' I didn't need to answer, to admit he had no idea because she barely drew breath before jumping in again. 'I'm hoping you'll get a posting closer to us and visit often. I've never forgotten how good he was with kids. Remember how he built me that tree house out back?'

I shook my head.

'Really?'

I had completely forgotten. 'If you'd asked, I'd have sworn it was Peter who built it. Seems much more his style.'

'No.' Rose was adamant. 'That fall you first met. He spent an entire weekend building it for me. He even got some other guys from the base to help, because he'd promised me it would be finished by Sunday evening.'

'Maybe, now that you mention it, a faint recollection.' I must have worked a double shift that weekend, or been cramming for an exam. I really had the shadowiest of memories of the whole thing.

'Lily! That was like, the highlight of that summer for me! And you have a "faint recollection"?' She rolled her eyes. 'I bet you were so busy sneaking around having sex with Quint that's all you thought about.'

She was the only person I knew who used a nickname for him. 'Yeah. Well.' We both laughed.

'I know you move all the time and everything, but you're planning to have kids too, aren't you? Eventually? I want my children to have cousins. The whole time we were growing up I wished we had cousins.'

'Huh. D'you know I don't think I've ever really noticed that we didn't have cousins. I mean, I had the best baby sister ever, I didn't miss our non-existent cousins.'

She jumped back to my life. 'You never told me much about your job.'

How could I explain how much I missed the library? 'Do you miss working in a hospital?' I asked.

Rose shook her head. 'Not even a tiny bit.'

'Really? Not sorry you didn't finish your degree?'

'I've never regretted leaving school. I love being Kent's wife and I can't wait to be a mother. She rolled her eyes. 'Did Mum put you up to this? She can't believe I'm perfectly happy to be a housewife, and soon a stay-at-home mum.' She sighed. 'I know she struggled, I know Dad was not always a great provider. But Kent isn't Dad. And I hated medicine. I was on the verge of dropping out anyhow, and as soon as we started dating I knew I had to make a choice.'

I bit my tongue. People the world over managed to combine med school and dating, married life, raising children. This was the first time I'd heard her say she'd been unhappy with her choice of medicine, and I wondered if it was true, or if she had told herself often enough that it had become true in retrospect. 'As long as you're happy,' I said. 'As long as, ten or twenty years from now you don't wish you were a doctor.'

'I won't,' she said, her voice slightly colder. 'Have you ever even used your Art History degree?'

She had a valid point, and I knew when to let go of a subject. 'Hey,' I made my voice light and cheerful. 'Guess who I'm having drinks with on Tuesday?'

She tilted her head. 'No idea. Maybe... Larissa? I thought she was down south somewhere.'

'Nope. Guess again.'

'One of your other roomies?'

'Peter. Peter Reynolds.'

'Really?' She sounded truly surprised, and I squashed down my immediate reaction of defensiveness. 'I didn't even know the two of you were in contact with each other.'

'We're not,' I said. 'But d'you know Mum still has his dad for dinner every week?'

'I know! Every Thursday!' said Rose. 'Apparently she made some crazy promise to Felicia on her deathbed that she'd have Warren for dinner once a week until he remarried. Canny bugger, eh? He's never remarried so he keeps getting those free meals.'

'You don't think he and Mum are...?'

Rose shook her head. 'Hah. No way. So have fun with Peter. We cross paths sometimes. You know, both of us also taking advantage of that free meal at Mum's.' She laughed. 'He's just as nice as ever. A real gentleman. Thoughtful, smart, interesting, all that. He teaches, and he gardens, and he canoes.' She patted her belly. 'I told Kent the other day, 'If you want this child to be a true-blue Canadian camper, then that's gonna be a father-son thing you two do together while this mama stays home.'

'Son! You told me you were going to keep it a surprise!'

'Oh. We don't know. Really, we have no idea. Kent would really love to have a son, so I've started calling him a boy, to try and make it so. And eating bananas and red meat too, that's supposed to work.' She held up her hand again. 'I know, I know, that's an old wives' tale. But, it can't hurt.' She grinned.

'Rose, I have missed you so much,' I said. When had my baby sister become this chatty, funny, outgoing young woman? How much more had I missed when I was away?

'Me too, Lily. Listen, I talk crap sometimes, ignore anything I said that was whacky and blame it on my hormones. That's what Kent does.'

I remembered those days, when every conversation I had came back to the sole topic I really cared about: Quentin. When had I last felt that way? I couldn't remember. I was genuinely pleased that Rose was still so infatuated. I hoped she and Kent would do better than Quentin and I had.

On Monday morning I started thinking about what to wear out the following evening and, with the excuse that I was starting to feel the cold, went to a new mall in the afternoon to browse the shops. He'd be coming from work, so he'd be wearing, what—chinos and a long-sleeved shirt? I couldn't be too dressy. Jeans, maybe, which I had, and a top that wasn't a t-shirt I'd planned to throw away at the end of the walk. I tried on a few dresses, but settled on a turquoise blouse. I paused when I passed a pair of boots. Stop being ridiculous, I told myself. It's drinks with an old childhood acquaintance. I put down the boots and drove home.

I told myself the same thing Tuesday morning as I sat in the bath and shaved my legs, and again as I got off the bus, half an hour early. For goodness' sake, I thought, I don't even know if we'll recognize each other. We may have nothing to talk about. We'd barely spoken at all since the incident with Bobby and the door. I forced myself to walk the length of the street twice so that I entered the restaurant right on the hour.

He was at a table in the corner and stood up as I walked in. Of course I recognized him, instantly. He'd hardly changed at all. Dark hair and a big smile. Blue eyes behind old fashioned glasses. A few extra pounds perhaps, but no more weight than I'd gained in the intervening years. 'Lily!' He waved, reached out his arms and I did the same, so we met in a loose hug before sitting.

'They do Spanish tapas on Tuesdays,' he said. 'I know you've led an exotic life, so wanted to offer you more than the same old, same old buffalo wings and beer. I ordered us a pitcher of sangria. I hope that's okay?'

'Sounds perfect,' I said, touched by his thoughtfulness. 'But I will correct you about exotic,' I said. 'Kansas and North Carolina hardly qualify.'

'But you lived in England for some time too, didn't you?' He filled our glasses with the dark red punch, adding a slice of orange to mine, then held his aloft. 'A toast. To the renewal of friendship.'

'To the renewal of friendship,' I echoed, as we clinked our glasses together. I took a sip—it was good, surprisingly good—and looked at the man across the table from me. 'It's great to see you, Peter.'

'Great to see you too, Lily,' he said. 'I see your mum from time to time, and very occasionally Rose, but, goodness, when you left this city you really left.'

I nodded. 'I'm not quite sure where the years have gone. I. . .' I took a steadying breath. 'I've never apologized for that day when you fixed our screen door-'

He stopped me mid-sentence. 'Nothing to apologize for, Lily,' he said. 'And so far in the past. Let's let those ghosts rest, shall we?'

A young man arrived at our table, pad and pen in hand. 'All set to order? Or would you like another minute?'

'Sorry,' I said. 'I've not even opened the menu.' I gestured across the table. 'We've not seen each other for almost a decade.'

The waiter left us and I rolled my eyes. 'A decade is half a lifetime to him. That makes me feel old.'

'You feel old? Think of me,' Peter countered. 'Well. Shall we order a selection to share? Are there any tapas you don't like? I'm not keen on sardines myself.'

When the waiter returned to take our order he brought a plate of warm pita bread and three small bowls of dip. I ripped off a corner of pita and dipped it into the hummus. It was rich with garlic, and my first thought was how much Quentin would dislike it. 'How long has it been since we sat at a table together?' I wondered aloud.

Peter smiled. 'A long time. Toasted cheese and tomato sandwiches in your mum's kitchen back when I was at university and you were a high school kid. And salted cucumber sticks. On the red and white checkered tablecloth.'

That tablecloth. I hadn't thought about it in years, but it had been a fixture of that house. 'I used to think it was so fancy, like a French café.' I laughed.

'And I loved your mum's taste in music. I thought she was so hip to listen to folk on the radio. Mine listened to classical.'

'Which now you love,' I guessed.

He nodded. 'I suppose we often turn into our parents in the end, don't we?'

I thought about that. 'I think Mum's a better person than I am. Stronger.' I didn't want to elaborate, to admit that I wouldn't have put up with Bobby for all those years.

A terracotta dish of sautéed mushrooms arrived, and a plate of grilled cheese. More garlic, and some heat. 'Delicious,' I said, ripping off another piece of pita to sop up the garlicky-mushroomy-butter.

I noticed him staring at me. 'What?' I asked.

'You haven't changed. You're just as beautiful as . . .' He blushed. 'I'm sorry. That's inappropriate.'

I felt myself blushing too.

'Ah. We'd better ask for some more bread, hadn't we?' said Peter. 'Did you drive?'

I shook my head. 'No. Took a bus.'

'Well then,' he said, and held up the sangria. 'May I?'

'Tell me everything,' I said, when the waiter had come and gone with more tapas.

He laughed. 'Not much to tell. I teach through the year, and in the summer I divide my time between escaping the city to canoe and trying to garden. I've recently bought a house.'

Exactly as Rose had said, and that made me smile. 'I'd love to have a garden,' I admitted. Quentin wasn't a fan of yard work, and although we'd had houses with yards, I'd always been reluctant to put in the necessary work to start a flower garden, knowing that in a few years I'd have to leave it behind.

'Perhaps you can give me some suggestions for what I can do with mine,' said Peter. 'It's all a bit haphazard at the moment.'

I didn't know anything about gardening, especially in this climate, and said as much, but that I'd love to come and visit. We talked about gardens, canoe routes, our parents, places I'd visited in Europe, and, of course, the Twin Towers, then circled back to gardens. It came as surprise when I swiped the last of the tomato sauce from a plate of Patatas Bravas. 'We've eaten everything?' I asked. 'I can't remember the last time I enjoyed a meal so much.' I spoke without thinking, and immediately spoke again so as not to leave space for either of us to decipher my remark. 'Delicious. Such good food.'

'Dessert?' asked our waiter, as he cleared the plates.

We both shook our heads. 'I'd love a coffee though,' said Peter, looking at me.

I nodded my head. 'Yes, coffee for me as well please.'

'Cream and sugar?'

'Double milk.'

Peter lifted the pitcher of sangria and peered inside. 'I think it's mostly fruit,' he said. But he poured the remains of the drink into my glass.

I was a little tipsy. 'What haven't we talked about?'

'Your husband.'

'Oh. Well.' I drained the last of the sangria, holding the empty glass to my mouth for longer than necessary, hoping the waiter would arrive with coffee so that I could use that as a pretext to change the subject. He didn't, so I evaded the topic by excusing myself to use the Ladies'. As I washed my hands, I stared at myself in the mirror, and asked myself what I was doing. I turned the rings on my finger, as I always did when nervous. Leave them on? Take them off? I wasn't sure. I wasn't sure about anything.

And when Peter dropped me off, I knew I wasn't sure about my feelings for him either, or his for me. Had he flirted with me, or had I imagined it? Had dinner been a one-off, or could I call him? What were the rules, these days, or were there no rules?

In the end, Peter saved me from myself; he stopped by on Friday evening. Rose and Kent were there, so he sat.

'Stay for dinner?' Mum asked him.

'Thanks, but I've come to collect Dad to take him to a talk.' He looked at me. 'I just popped in to ask you if you have plans for tomorrow.' He sounded cool, casual, like one old friend contacting another. Why had I not been able to do that in a phone call?

'No plans,' I said.

'There's an outdoor oven-making course in Blueberry Bay,' he said. 'Could I interest you?'

'Oven?'

'Oven. A box-like structure which uses heat in order to cook food,' he started.

'I know what an oven is, you goof.' I laughed. 'You sound like a teacher who tells his class there's no such thing as a stupid question.'

He chuckled. 'So this is a clay oven for a backyard,' he said. 'The course includes bread and pizza, which we then bake in our newly constructed oven. And the weather network promises a mini heat wave tomorrow.'

'Neat,' said Kent.

I wondered what Quentin would say if I suggested we go on such a course, felt disloyal, and pushed the thought aside. 'It sounds like a lot of fun.'

And it was. There were six other people, two couples and a father-son duo, and the instructor, who held these courses on his ten-acre property. We had coffee while he described the process, then went to the edge of a narrow river running through his land to collect clay. Dumping it on a bright blue tarp, we took off our shoes and socks to mix the clay and sand and water with our feet. I tried to remember when I'd last felt sand under my bare feet. A holiday to Saint Lucia four years ago, maybe? It had been a particularly good one; I remembered Quentin and I as having been truly happy. I stared hard at the pile of sand under my feet and concentrated on what the instructor was saying.

When we'd packed the sand into a pile, we sculpted it into a roundish shape, which we then carved out. It was only as the instructor started making a fire that I realized the obvious. I tried to be inconspicuous as I backed away, but Peter noticed.

'Are you okay, Lily?'

I nodded, looked away as the match was struck and the paper and kindling burst into flames, and scolded myself for letting my pyrophobia mar the day. Deep breaths, I reminded myself. Deep breaths.

After we washed our hands and feet, we gathered around a picnic table to make bread dough and pizza dough and left them to rise in the sun. The instructor took us on a tour of his property, showing us the various ovens he'd made over the years, several similar to the basic one we'd created, and a few bigger ones which were elaborately decorated with mosaics. His wife was a potter, he explained. She'd gone through a ceramic tile phase, and he used her rejects for mixed-media creations, which also explained the seascape on the washroom wall.

We put our bread in to bake and added toppings to our pizzas, then sat at the picnic table. The instructor's wife arrived with a tray of glasses and a jug of lemonade, paused at the herb garden to pluck a sprig of mint to add to it, and joined us at the table. She was bright and cheerful and had a long, thick braid down her back, and I felt a momentary stab of jealousy on Mum's behalf. I thought this was what she had had in mind when she and Bobby bought the Old Homestead. A big vegetable garden, an orchard, gatherings like this one.

There was cheese to eat with our bread, and a selection of homemade pickles and chutneys. Everything was delicious. The pizzas were the best we'd ever tasted. I couldn't tell if it was the fact that we had kneaded the dough by hand, or the fact that we were eating in a bright sunshine on a day that felt removed from the real world. 'Last slice,' Peter said to me.

When adding the toppings to ours we'd agreed to compromise: no anchovies because I didn't like them, no pineapple because he didn't like it. 'On pizza,' we had both clarified at the same time.

'Anchovies in a Caesar salad are fine,' I had explained.

'And pineapple upside down cake makes sense,' he added.

I shook my head. 'Too full. I ate too much cheese. It's all yours.'

'Nope. We have to share,' he said, taking a bite and holding up the slice for me.

'If you insist.' I took a bite.

One of the wives smiled at us. 'Newlyweds?' she guessed. She poked her husband. 'Remember when we were cute together like that?'

I must have blushed. I was glad my mouth was full, and that the instructor arrived at the table with a plate of brownies.

'So, we're cute together,' Peter said when we were driving away.

I laughed. 'I guess we are.' I thanked him again for the day. 'Are you tempted to build an oven in your backyard next spring?'

'Absolutely. I may never again be able to eat takeout pizza'

'I may never again be able to eat. I'm stuffed.'

'We still have a good couple of hours of light,' said Peter. 'Fancy a walk? There's a local hike up along the top of the canyon, then down to a cranberry bog.'

This wasn't a path I knew. I knew very little of the town, despite its proximity to my childhood home. It was a lovely hike that wound up through forest and then came out at the edge of the canyon. I kept well back and grabbed Peter when I thought he was going too close to the edge. 'Don't fall!'

'I won't,' he promised.

'It makes me nervous,' I said. 'Why aren't there fences?'

'Because you're in Canada. We trust people to be sensible.'

'Um,' I said. 'Are you laughing at me?'

'I hoped I was laughing with you,' he said. And at that, I did start to smile. Towards the end of the trail, we went down to the promised bog and paused to pick the tiny red berries that gave it its name. It was late afternoon when we reached the car, and Peter held open the door for me. 'One last coffee for the road?' he asked.

I was happy to prolong this marvellous day by another quarter of an hour. But instead of a Tim's or one of the other chains on the highway, as I'd been expecting, he drove into a part of the town I didn't know at all and pulled into a restaurant tucked on to the end of a row of expensive-looking waterfront condos.

Peter opened my door for me and I started towards the restaurant, already smelling a deep, rich roast. A child's laugh made me swivel my head. I don't know why. It was just a child, just a happy sound. It could have been any child, anywhere. In a patch of grass in front of the condo next to the café, a slim, dark-haired man was throwing a football to a similarly dark-haired boy, while a blonde woman stood by, watching and smiling. The boy jumped into the air but missed the ball. 'Again, Daddy. Again!'

'Kent!' I spoke instinctively.

At the sound of his name, the man turned towards me. Any hope I had harboured that I might be wrong evaporated. It was my brother-in-law. Throwing a ball to a boy who was calling him Daddy.

Chapter Eight

'We have to go,' I said to Peter. 'Now.'

I got into the door and did up my seat belt and looked straight ahead. As he backed away, I clenched my eyes shut.

We drove in silence until we were on the highway, heading home. 'Lily?' Peter asked quietly. 'What can I do?'

I shook my head. 'Nothing. Thank you.'

But he pulled the car into the next drive-through and ordered a hot chocolate. Then he parked the car, undid his seat belt, and turned to me. 'You're shaking.'

'I'm a little cold,' I said.

He clicked on the heat. 'You may be in shock. I think you need sugar.' He took the lip off the cup, blew on it, and passed it to me. 'Be careful, it's hot.'

'That was Kent. I didn't imagine that?' My voice raised to make it a question, in case there was any chance I'd been mistaken. I sipped the hot chocolate then put it in the cup holder between us.

'That man did look like Kent.' Peter passed the hot sweet drink back to me. 'Have another little sip.' He sat in silence while I drank.

'Was there a police cruiser in the parking lot?' My mind was replaying the scene, searching for details I may have missed.

'Yes. I think so.'

'I think so too.' *Again, Daddy. Again.* 'How old do you think he was? Five? Six? He was calling Kent "Daddy." There was a resemblance, right?'

'Someone assumed we're newlyweds,' Peter reminded me.

I looked at him. 'Because you were feeding me. And I'm wearing what is clearly an engagement ring and a wedding band.'

'Yes, appearances can be deceiving. Maybe it's not what it looked like.'

'Maybe not.' But my gut told me it was exactly what it looked like. 'What did it look like to you?'

Peter sighed. 'A family. A mother and father and their son.'

'Except the dad is my sister's husband.' I paused. 'My *pregnant* sister's husband.'

'Yes.'

'A mistress. More than a mistress. A second family.' I hadn't looked too closely at the woman, but I wished I had. Could it be the girlfriend Kent so famously dumped—claimed to have dumped—by phone the night he met Rose? Not that I knew what she looked like.

I had a sudden image of Quentin standing next to Samantha and a child standing between them. A child calling Quentin "Daddy." I opened the car door just in time to vomit on the pavement. Chunks of barely digested brownies, pizza, bread, cheese, all coated with hot chocolate. I was aware that Peter was holding my hair back from my face and making some sort of soothing sound.

'Sorry.' When I was sure my stomach was empty, I pulled myself back into the car. 'I'm sorry. I don't think I got any on your car.'

'I don't care about the car,' said Peter. 'Are you okay?'

I nodded.

'It wasn't a good idea, the hot chocolate,' he said. 'I'm sorry.'

I told him it wasn't the hot chocolate and excused myself and went inside to use the washroom where I rinsed my mouth several times and washed my face. Peter had thoughtfully moved the car when I went back out, so I didn't have to look at my sick on the ground. 'I'm so sorry,' I said again.

'You mustn't apologize. It was such a shock. I can't... I can't even imagine what you're feeling.' He offered me a piece of gum.

I took it, grateful for the burst of mint which covered the sourness in my mouth.

'I'm so sorry we stopped there.'

'There was no way you could have known that Kent would be there.' I clicked on my seat belt. 'To be honest, I'd rather not know. But now I do know.

But I'm not going to let that ruin what was otherwise a wonderful day.' I put my hand on Peter's thigh. 'Really, it was such a good day.'

'It was. Apart from those last two minutes.' Peter rested his hand on mine, then lifted it to turn the key in the ignition.

'Yes. Well.' I thought about telling him that my husband, too, had been unfaithful. Decided that I didn't want to think about that, or of Quentin, or Samantha. I didn't think there was anything left for me to vomit up, but I didn't want to take that risk. Instead, I asked Peter to remind me what ratio water to clay to sand we'd used, as if I was taking mental notes for the day when I'd build an oven in my own backyard. And then I asked him if he thought he'd use the cranberries we'd picked for sauce for Thanksgiving, and if he and his dad would have a traditional turkey dinner. Those conversations got us—me—through the drive back to Big Rock Lake.

When we neared our old neighbourhood, I looked at him. 'I don't know what I should say. If I should say anything? To Rose, I mean.'

'That's a difficult decision. Rest assured I'll say nothing to anyone.'

'Oh. I didn't mean that. I—' I wasn't sure. Maybe I had been asking him for advice. But of course, this was a decision I had to make. 'Thank you,' I said, again.

When he stopped the car and held open the door for me I thanked him for a 'mostly' fantastic day. For some reason that made us both laugh, and so I was smiling when I went inside.

In bed that night I wondered why I'd reacted so violently to the idea of Quentin having an out-of-wedlock child with Samantha. Wouldn't that make it easier in some ways, make our separation more final? I sat up, startled. When had I stopped thinking of it as final? When I'd set off on the Appalachian Trail I'd had no plans to ever return to him or to our marriage.

Rose and Kent dropped by the next day. I waited to see if he would come up with a story. If he'd make a deliberate comment to me. 'Wasn't it odd the way our paths crossed yesterday?' I thought he might say. 'I told Red that the last person I expected to see while I was on an undercover job was my sister-in-law.'

I wasn't sure how I'd react if he made such a claim. He'd not been in uniform. But undercover? I hadn't looked closely at the police cruiser, couldn't even say for sure if it was a City of Big Rock Lake PD. But the boy's voice. Laughter, and then *Daddy. Again Daddy.*

But Kent said nothing. Not even when I told them about the oven-making course, the bread, the pizza, the walk along the canyon path, the berries we'd picked.

Rose asked to see them and I told her I'd given them to Peter. 'He's going to make cranberry sauce for his Thanksgiving Dinner.'

'We'll have jellied, from a tin,' she said. 'Kent's favourite.'

He nodded. 'Sugar and red food dye number ten,' he joked. 'Nothing to do with a fruit of any description.'

Before last night, I would have laughed. Now, his tone of voice irked me. Arrogant. I caught myself staring at him from time to time during the afternoon; if he noticed, he said nothing. I suspected it wouldn't be impossible for me to find out more information. Figure out if she was the first girlfriend or not, if that boy was Kent's son. Who she was exactly, and if she was aware—she must be—that Kent was a married man. How often he visited, what sort of financial support he was giving her and the child. Based on no evidence at all I thought she might be a lawyer, making a salary sufficient to own a townhouse on that lake and raise her son. I wondered what the boy's name was.

'—earth to Lily. Hello,' Rose was saying.

With a start I looked up.

'You were a million miles away.' She laughed. 'Why so pensive?'

'Thinking about names,' I answered. 'Have you started thinking about names? For your baby,' I clarified.

Kent laughed. 'You know your sister. She must have a dozen lists by now.'

It was a safe subject, and although Rose wasn't willing to share the shortlisted names for a boy or a girl, she was happy to tell us the names she'd rejected, and why.

A thought occurred to me. 'Any chance it will be twins?' I couldn't bring myself to look directly at Kent. 'Any twins in your family?'

For the split second between my asking and his reply, I willed a positive answer. A laugh, and a casual, well, yeah, there's my identical twin brother of course, who lives pretty close to where you were yesterday, and has a six-year-old son. These things happened in fiction all the time, didn't they?

'No,' he said. 'No twins that I'm aware of. Of course I'm adopted, so I wouldn't know.'

'Oh. Adopted. I don't think I knew that.'

He shrugged. 'Not something I mention much.'

'So you could have a twin. Separated at birth.' Did he not understand why I was asking?

'Lily! Good grief what's with this twins obsession? We want one healthy child!'

So did I, Rose, so did I. But I said nothing.

Big Rock Lake, February 2014

Rose was staring at her phone. 'There are details.'

'Details?'

'About the accident. On Facebook.'

Why was she looking at social media? To help the time pass? To remind herself of recent happy family memories? 'Well. You can't believe everyth—'

But she was already pointing at the screen. 'There was a moose. That's what pushed him sideways into the rock face. It was bad luck that the airbag didn't deploy, apparently that can happen when a moose hits a car side-on. But he was lucky, too. He was thrown from the car before the car was crushed. And someone was driving the opposite direction, saw what happened, pulled Kent to safety, and called the ambulance.'

'I don't—'

'That's who posted. The other driver. A reminder, I guess. Moose are out. Moose are big animals—they'll crush a car. Life is uncertain. Go home and hug your loved ones.'

I wasn't sure what response she expected from me. It seemed irresponsible of anyone to post details online. Even a witness. It was too soon, too early to know how well—if—Kent was going to survive the accident.

Rose turned to look at me. 'So maybe. You know. Maybe it's a good thing he wasn't wearing his seat belt. He was thrown from the car. Maybe not wearing his seat belt saved him.'

What could I say. Maybe it had. I had been wrong before. So many times.

'I wish—'

I wondered what percentage of sentences spoken in emergency waiting rooms were never finished.

Mum answered Rose with the exact words I'd been about to say. 'What? What do you wish, Rose? If I can make it happen, I will.'

Big Rock Lake, 2001

The evening after I saw Kent with his secret son, Mum and I played our now ritual two games of Scrabble, and after, I took the phone to my bedroom and rang Quentin. I had carefully calculated the time change and knew he'd be playing darts. I'd written out a brief message. So I was taken aback when he answered the phone. 'Lily?'

Of course, he'd have been able to figure it was me from the call display number.

'Hi.'

'Hey. It's so good to hear your voice.'

I scrunched up the message I'd planned to leave on the machine. 'I said I'd call you... so—'

'Thank you,' he said.

'You're not at darts.'

'No. I didn't want to miss your call.' As if he'd been waiting by the phone.

I wasn't sure I believed him but had to give him points for a quick answer. 'It's warm here,' I said. 'The leaves haven't started turning at all.'

'They will. And then the snow will fly.'

Were we really reduced to talking about the weather? Couldn't I tell him about the outdoor oven I'd built yesterday, the bread dough I'd made, the walk? I knew I couldn't. If he started telling me about such an outing, I would want to know who he'd gone with, and if he mentioned a female name, even that of a childhood neighbour, I'd be suspicious. Nor could I tell him that his brother-in-law was being unfaithful to his sister-in-law; fidelity wasn't a topic I could raise anymore, maybe ever again.

'A new Ben Stiller comedy is showing,' he said. 'The trailer looks funny.'

'I don't think it's playing here yet,' I said. Based on nothing. I hadn't checked the movie listings once.

'It'll run for a while,' he said. 'I won't go see it until you get home.'

Home? Why had I phoned him? What could he possibly say to change my mind? I looked at the crumpled message. 9/11 was already too much loss, how could I heap more loss upon that? 'Home.' I took a deep breath. 'Um. Have you had your orders yet?'

'Within the next two or three weeks,' he said. 'They're late. 9/11 pushed everything back.'

That made sense.

'I've started packing.' That was usually my job. 'I'm glad the Christmas decorations are already boxed.'

'Ah.' We'd amassed them over the years. I'd miss them, the memories they represented. We had a real Christmas tree every year and had developed a ritual for the evening we decorated. After the lights and the hanging baubles, Quentin made me a glass of mulled wine while I added a strand of silver tinsel to the tip of every branch. Then we turned off all but the lights on the tree, sat, and enjoyed it. Like an old married couple, he'd joked the first year. Which is what we'd become. Almost.

'Don't know if I can decorate our tree without you, Lily,' he said with a note of real sadness in his voice. And I thought the 'our' was not deliberate. 'And the packing. You're way better at packing than me.'

Because you've never done it before. 'Maybe Samantha will help you,' I said, wincing at the spite in my voice.

'Lily. Don't—'

I shook my head. That had been a mean jab, and it wasn't like me. 'I'm sorry. I don't want us to argue,' I said. 'I'm going to go now.' I said goodbye and hung up.

I lay on my bed, thinking about the Christmas tree decorations. The delicate blown glass we'd bought in Venice, the red-breasted robins from a farm shop we stopped at on a country walk in England, the pieces of cheese from Wisconsin. Such a random collection, but each with a memory attached. I thought of the past nine years, how many memories we'd amassed that we shared. Who could I turn to now and ask, 'Remember when we... ?' about a path we followed, a meal we ate, a view we saw? It was so often just the two of us. Quentin was my mirror and keeper of my past.

He's not the guardian of all your memories, I told myself crossly. It's not true that no one else was there. I was there.

I dialled Peter's phone.

'Hey, glad you called,' he said when I said hello, as if he too had been waiting by the phone. As if every man I might possibly telephone was sitting by the phone waiting for my call. That made me smile, and I relaxed.

'I've washed our cranberries,' he said. 'Can I freeze them raw, or do I have to do something special to them?'

'Raw. Well, that's what Mum always does.'

'She'd know. And when I make the cranberry sauce do I cook them from frozen?'

'Yes.' This I knew. I owned a copy of an English Christmas cookbook with three different recipes for cranberry relish. 'Your decisions will be orange zest or grated ginger and red wine or port.'

'That's simple,' he said. 'Orange zest and port. No contest.'

'So decisive! And your stuffing, bread-based or sausage-based.'

'Both, of course. One each end.'

'Ooh, I'm impressed.'

'This old bachelor has a few tricks up his sleeve,' Peter said.

'Not so old,' I teased.

By the time we hung up we'd spoken for over an hour. Talking about

Thanksgiving Dinner had led to talk of traditions, and of our childhoods, and the ways the neighbourhood had changed and ways it had stayed the same, and how different teenagers were to when we'd been that age. And somewhere along the line Peter had invited me to come to the school's pancake breakfast-for-dinner on Wednesday. 'It's an annual event,' he'd said. 'The staff cook, the students serve, and all the money raised goes to our charity of the year. This year it's the Alzheimer's Society.'

'Can I bring Mum?' I asked.

'Of course.'

'And shall we bring your dad, as well?'

'That's a sweet thought, thanks, but he goes to the Legion on Wednesday evenings. I doubt he'd change his routine to eat a few pancakes.'

There were more than a few. Mum discovered a group of colleagues from her office there so we sat with them. I wobbled when I was passed the syrup and, much to my surprise, discovered it was real maple syrup. The smell that always took me back to Bobby and the Old Homestead.

'. . . daughter, Lily, you remember?' Mum's voice pulled me back, and I focused on the conversation. I took several deep breaths to relax and tried to have a good time. Peter grinned and waved at us from behind the giant griddle. He called me later that night to thank me for coming and reported the number of pancakes he had cooked. 'Give or take several dozen.' He admitted he'd actually lost count after the first half an hour.

'How much money was raised?' I asked.

'I'll let you know,' he said.

'Well it was lots of fun,' I said. 'But you must be running on empty.'

'I don't want to cook another pancake for a while,' he admitted.

'Tomorrow's Thursday,' I said. 'Mum and I are cooking for your dad. Why don't you join him?' I quickly added, 'If you're free, of course.'

When Rose phoned a half hour later and asked me if I wanted to go to a movie the following evening, I had to say thank you, but no.

'You sound giddy,' she said. 'What's up?'

'No giddiness here,' I lied.

I looked at myself in the mirror when I brushed my teeth. I was thirty-three years old yet felt as if I'd been transported back to my university days. I hoped I didn't sound giddy when I spoke to Peter, but I saw a certain giddiness in my reflection. It was possible, too, that it was easier for me to fill my spare time visiting with him than worrying about what Rose did or did not know about the blonde woman in Blueberry Bay, whose son called Kent "Daddy."

On Thursday we told both our parents about the oven-making course, even though Mum had heard the details from me already. 'It was a lovely property,' I said. 'It reminded me of the Old Homestead.'

'Ah. You were wearing your rose-coloured glasses,' Mum said. 'I bet they don't have to use their jelly pot to catch rain coming through the roof, and cover the inside of the windows with plastic to keep out the ants, and chop enough wood to keep the stove going all winter, or—'

'Ants? I don't remember ants,' I said, cutting her off.

She tilted her head. 'The summer you were two. I was terrified you'd eat them. You'd put anything into your mouth.'

'D'you remember the flying ants on that camping trip, Dad?' asked Peter.

'Your mother picked that campground,' Mr. Reynolds said. 'I wanted to go to Manitoulin Island.' We all chuckled at his adamance.

'I've never been to Manitoulin,' I mused. We hadn't gone on family camping trips. I wondered if those childhood trips were why Peter had worked at provincial parks through his university years.

'I think you'd enjoy it,' said Mr. Reynolds. 'It's like stepping back in time.' He described the swing bridge, the colour of Lake Huron, the small villages and their local museums. 'And the walking is first rate,' he said. He looked at his son and shook his head fondly. 'Remember all the walks we dragged you on? All you wanted to do was sit on the beach and read.'

'Come for a walk with me on Saturday?' Peter asked as we said goodbye.

'I'd love to,' I said.

On Friday, knowing Kent was working, I spent the day with Rose. I wanted to tell her that I'd left Quentin before any more time passed. But despite a long, relaxed lunch, and stroll along Main, popping into a few shops, I didn't find—or make—a good opening to raise the subject. In a secondhand bookstore in the travel section, I started to tell her, but when I saw a book of long walks in North America, with a picture of the Appalachian Trail on the front, my heart sank and I moved away. At the back of the store there was a table with a display of gardening books, and I started flipping through them.

'What have you bought?' Rose asked when we met at the till. She had an armful of picture books.

'Garden design.' I showed her.

'Since when do you garden?'

'It's exactly what Peter has been looking for,' I explained. 'Companion plants and what will thrive in this zone and how to make best use of sun and shade and space.'

'Oh.'

'He'll love it,' I said. I heard myself speak and wondered when I'd last bought a gift for Quentin with as much confidence.

I gave it to him in the car the next day when he came to collect me. 'This is perfect, Lily. Exactly the book I've been looking for.' Almost word for word what I'd told my sister. 'Thank you.'

Suddenly embarrassed, I said, 'It's secondhand.'

'Even better. If we're lucky there'll be some notes from previous readers about what really works.'

If *we're* lucky. Was that a turn of phrase? Or a slip? I gave my head a shake. I couldn't dissect a throwaway sentence and try to read too much into it. 'So when will you tell me where we're going?'

'You'll see,' he said. He looked down at my feet. 'Good. Good walking boots.'

'Bought and broken in for the Appalachian Trail.'

'Of course.' He navigated onto the highway. 'You haven't told me anything about that. How was it?'

'I didn't finish,' I reminded him. 'I only walked two weeks of it.'

'You walked, by yourself, for over two weeks. Not many people can say that.'

I chuckled. 'Half empty versus half full. Are you always this cheerful and optimistic?'

'I try to be. I am well aware some people find it annoying.' Did *some people* include his ex-fiancée? 'I think it's a good reminder to be grateful for what I have.'

I hadn't told a single person anything about the walk, neither Mum nor Rose—or anyone. 'I was finally getting into a good rhythm,' I said. 'It was a steep learning curve, having to be completely self-sufficient. The last three days I had found a routine that was working well.'

'Were you lonely?'

'A little. Maybe if I'd gone on longer, but I think I was too tired to be lonely. And I did see other walkers on the trail from time to time, most days. And it was so beautiful. Every time I thought there couldn't be a more gorgeous view, I turned a corner down the path and there was a better one.' I tried to describe some of my favourites. 'I have photos,' I said but I hadn't had them developed.

'We'll have views today,' he promised.

And he was right. It took me a long time to figure out where we were going, until we turned off the highway at Espanola. 'Manitoulin Island?'

'You said the other night that you'd never been. We'll do the Cup and Saucer Trail, which will be crazy busy, but is a must, and then we'll have a picnic lunch on the shore of Lake Huron, and for dinner we'll drive out to my favourite fish restaurant on the coast. At some point I'd love to hear all about your master's thesis.'

The day whizzed by.

'One last treat,' said Peter. 'We have a half hour until the swing bridge closes again.' He led me to a small ice cream shop.

I was looking at a map of the island on the wall. 'How did I not know what a big island this is? Over a thousand square miles. There's so much more to see. It's tempting to find a B & B and explore some more tomorrow.'

Peter said nothing, until he'd passed me my ice cream. 'I wasn't sure—' I'd never heard him falter and hesitate over his words like this. 'I did consider asking if you'd pack a bag and make a weekend of it. But—'

Neither of us said anything and his last word hung in the air between us.

'Oh, you're right. This ice cream is so good.' Was he considering separate rooms, or twin beds in a shared room? Had he even thought that far? Was it too late to change our minds? All we'd need was a toothbrush, really.

He was looking down at his watch '—next crossing, we'd better make sure we don't miss this one,' he said.

'Today was the best day. Thank you, Peter,' I said, as I got into his car. 'You know you don't have to hold the door for me every time.'

'I know. But I want to,' he said.

'Your parents were so happily married,' I said, remembering his father holding the door for his mother.

If he wondered at my line of thought, he didn't query it. 'The happiest marriage I know,' he said. 'They set the bar high.'

My eyes were heavy after the day of fresh air and exercise and an early start and good food. 'You should be married,' I said. 'You'd be a great husband.'

'Well, thank you.'

I thought of the way he'd cared for me the other day after the shock of seeing Kent and then the embarrassment of being ill. 'You'd be a great dad, too,' I added.

The swing bridge snapped into place and the traffic ahead of us began to move. He started the car and we drove away from the island. I turned my head to watch it grow smaller, then sat up straight and dug my nails into my hand so as not to fall asleep. It was a losing battle. 'I might doze for ten minutes or so,' I said. 'Sorry to be so antisocial.'

'No worries,' said Peter. 'Will the radio keep you awake?'

'Nuh-uh.' And that was the last I spoke until I felt my shoulder being gently shaken. I struggled to come to the surface of a deep sleep, floundered to locate myself.

'We're back at your mum's.' Peter was whispering from my right. 'I almost didn't want to wake you, but it'll get chilly soon.'

Back home! I sat up and blinked. 'I slept the whole drive home? I'm so sorry! Such lousy company.'

'Not at all.' He held open the door.

'Thanks again for a great day,' I said. 'G'night.' Without thinking I leaned towards him to kiss him but at the last moment realized what I was doing. 'Oh. I'm—I'm still half-asleep,' I said, lifting my hand and scooting off and inside before he could reply.

Inside the house I knocked my forehead with my hand. Why had I done that? And why, having started, hadn't I finished? If I was going to blame a near kiss on being tired and disoriented—which was the truth—then why not actually kiss him and get away with it? It would have been so easy.

I unlaced my boots and crept up to my room as quietly as possible. Mum had left a note on my bed. Quentin x 3. *"I'll wait by the phone."* I could hear his plaintive cry through Mum's handwriting.

I hadn't planned to phone him. But I also hadn't guessed Peter was going to take me on a seventeen-hour long excursion; I thought we'd go for a walk, have a picnic, and be home mid-afternoon. I looked at my watch. Too late to call Quentin now. He'd want to know why I was coming home so late, and where I'd been, and who I'd been with.

I lay in bed and thought about what I could say. 'A friend and I went for hike,' I tried. I started again, 'You remember Peter, my old neighbour?' But why would an old neighbour and I drive for hours to go on a hike? I hadn't mentioned the tapas, or the oven-making course, or the dinner with his dad. I sighed with frustration. I had no obligation to explain my whereabouts to Quentin. I owed him nothing. It might be kinder of me to break off all contact. I'd had time to start living a life without him. I should let him do the same.

I wasn't sure if it was the fact that I'd been so fast asleep in the car, or if it was the anticipation of the things Quentin might assume, or the realization that not so long ago I would have cared if Quentin was out until midnight with a female friend, but that I no longer did, but I couldn't go back to sleep.

Why would he assume anything, I asked myself. Why would he not trust you? Why would he ever imagine that you'd have an affair to get back at him?

And where had the thought come from? I wasn't having an affair with Peter. And yet. . . I had almost kissed Peter goodnight. I wanted to kiss Peter goodnight. I was sorry I hadn't kissed Peter goodnight. I closed my eyes and imagined kissing Peter. He'd be gentle, I thought. Firm, but gentle. I turned onto my side and tried to remember all Quentin's strengths, what it was I loved about him, why I was so hurt that he'd cheated on me, but I kept drifting back to the idea of Peter's lips on mine. What if we were in a bed & breakfast right now... what if he and I were naked in a double bed... what if he was trying to behave like a gentleman but—

It was late when I woke the next morning.

'Good day yesterday?' Mum asked me.

'Great day,' I said, pouring coffee and sitting down to tell her all about it.

'D'you know I've never been to Manitoulin Island,' she said when I'd covered all the highlights. 'Bobby and I often talked about going but it never happened.'

How many times had she made plans with Bobby and thought there was even a remote possibility they'd come to fruition? When was it she stopped believing anything he said? 'We should go,' I said. 'A mother-daughter holiday. Next summer. It would be great.'

'That sounds like fun,' she said.

Rose walked into the kitchen. 'What sounds like fun? And why aren't you dressed, Lily?'

'Slept in,' I said. Then, seeing that Kent was behind her, I excused myself to go and get dressed.

'A proper Thanksgiving Dinner,' Rose was saying when I went back to the kitchen. They were all sitting at the kitchen table with a fresh pot of coffee, Rose with pen in hand and list in front of her. 'I'm so excited.'

I wasn't entirely clear what was exciting to her. Planning the big meal? Hosting it in her own home? Or perhaps celebrating a holiday which had not, so far as I could remember, been celebrated at all when we were young. I had no recollection of Thanksgiving at the Old Homestead; after we moved to the city we had gone out to a buffet lunch once, a proper treat for me, Mum said, not to have to cook and wash up. But not so much a treat that it was ever repeated.

I watched Kent smiling at his wife with a mixture of love and pride, and I said a brief prayer that she'd still be this happy when she was my age. That she really hadn't enjoyed med school and would never have any regrets that she'd quit. That Kent was a twin separated at birth and had no idea about his look alike, and that the boy I'd seen was not his son.

'—roast or mashed?' Rose was asking.

'Mashed, for sure,' said Kent. 'Potatoes are a vehicle for gravy aren't they?'

'I thought you said stuffing was a vehicle for gravy,' Rose teased, poking him. Mum and I were there, and part of the group, but those two were in a bubble of their own. I tried to remember the last time I'd teased Quentin. I thought of the previous day when I'd teased Peter.

'And we'll have leftover turkey for weeks.' Rose looked up from her list to Kent. 'We should have more than four people. D'you think Jim and Carrie would like to come?'

Kent shook his head. 'They're spending the weekend with both families down south. What about Naomi and Don?'

'Naomi's vegan. We'd need a separate menu. She can't even eat the mashed potatoes because I put butter and cream in them.'

'Oh yeah.' Kent's tone made it clear what he thought of non-meat eaters, and I wondered if he knew Mum was a lapsed vegetarian, that I had eaten no meat for the first three years of my life.

'Too bad Quentin can't fly up,' said Rose.

I murmured some non-committal agreement that North Carolina was too far away to come for the weekend. Soon, soon I had to tell Mum and Rose that my marriage was over. I owed them—and myself—that honesty. And I owed Quentin a phone call, or, at least, I wanted to call him before he called back. Although the person I really wanted to speak to was the person I'd spent the previous day with.

'What about Peter and his dad?' Rose said. She looked at Kent, then Mum and I. 'Would that work?'

I didn't trust myself to speak. It was as if she'd read my mind.

'That's a lovely idea,' Mum said.

'Sure,' said Kent. 'Neither of them is veggie, eh?'

'You have Peter's number don't you? Will you ask him, Lily?' Rose was making notes about a seating plan.

I said I would, but before I could make the call, the phone rang. Quentin. I took it up to my room.

'I'm sorry you missed my calls yesterday,' he said. 'But I'm glad we're connected now. How are you, Lily?' His voice was gentle, the question concerned. As if I'd been sick.

'OK. You?'

'Empty. Lonely. Missing you like crazy,' he said. 'Have you booked a flight home?'

I am home. I'm not coming back to you. But I only thought those words. Instead I said, 'I haven't found a great deal yet.' Not technically a lie, since I hadn't even started looking.

'Yeah. The prices are whacky. And everyone's saying that you need to leave hours ahead of time to get through security.'

'I guess.' I realized with a start that I hadn't thought of the Twin Towers once yesterday. The first day since the attack that I hadn't thought of it. I wondered if I could tell Quentin this, or if it would be too soon for him to hear that life for me would carry on post-9/11. Or if my saying I'd not thought of it yesterday would lead him to question more closely where I'd been and what I'd been doing and who I'd been with. Better not to broach that subject. 'How's work?'

'Yeah, it's nuts. The guys were joking that we'd be better off coming to work nude—save dressing twice every morning.'

I smiled at the image of a line of naked guys waiting to get into the office.

'Hey. I bet that made you smile,' he said. 'I miss that—my Honey Bee smiling.'

His Honey Bee. How long had it been since he called me that?

'Always and forever you will be my Honey Bee,' he said, as if he'd read my mind. I knew he believed what he was saying, right now, in this moment. He kept talking, as if he hoped that he could find the right words, some magical combination, to draw me back. 'I know we have to finish that conversation we started.' As if we'd been discussing holiday plans, or a paint colour. 'It will be better face to face, Lily.'

'I don't know that there's much more to say,' I said. I closed my eyes. 'You vowed that you would be faithful to me, and you weren't.' I wasn't sure what hurt more, that he'd had sex with Samantha or that he'd thought he was falling in love with her. 'I'm not sure I can ever trust you again.' I took a deep breath; hours ago I'd been fantasizing about sharing a bed with Peter. I was no better than him.

'Lily—'

I shook my head. This whole conversation had the tired air of something already said. Because, of course, it had all been said before. 'I want a family and you don't.'

'You are my family. I want you.' He took a deep breath. 'If you need a child to make you happy, then let's discuss having a child.'

'Really?' My voice must have sounded a cross between surprise and disbelief. This was one hundred and eighty degrees from the last conversation we'd had about children.

'I love you, Lily,' Quentin said. 'I screwed up and I feel guilty and I hate myself. If I could go back and change things I would. I miss you, and I want you to come home and I want us to fix things between us and get back to that perfect place we had.'

It was never perfect, I thought. And we can't go back.

As if he sensed my thoughts, he said, 'Don't say anything right now, just book a ticket and come back, please. We'll go to counselling. I'll earn back your trust. Please, Lily, please come home.' His voice broke.

'I'll let you know,' I said. I wasn't sure what I was going to let him know.

'I love you, Lily,' he said before he hung up. His voice was thick. 'I love you more than anything.'

I sat on my bed for several minutes, trying to decide what I felt. Detached, impassive, emotionless. I didn't care that my husband was miles away, alone and crying. I didn't care that he was hurting. I didn't care that he was sorry, that he was suggesting marriage counselling. I didn't care. I looked down at my left hand and twisted my rings around on my finger. The gold band was intact, but the circle it represented had been broken. I wasn't sure there was any marriage counsellor on earth who could make our union whole again.

I lay back against the pillows on my bed and dialled Peter's number. This call would cheer me up.

No answer. I called his Blackberry.

It threw me when I heard his phone ringing down the line and echoing at the same time in the house. Moments later there was laughter from the kitchen.

'Lily, Peter's here!' Rose yelled up the stairs. And when I joined them, there he was, sitting at the table, looking as if he belonged, although over-dressed in suit and tie. 'Our two guests are confirmed,' Rose said to me.

'Hey, Lily,' said Peter.

'Hey, Peter,' I replied, 'You look sharp.'

'That's exactly what I said!' said Rose.

Peter blushed. 'I take Dad to church,' he said. 'Today was my day to read. Isaiah 9:10.'

'"The bricks are fallen down, but we will build with hewn stones: the sycamores are cut down, but we will change them into cedars,"' Kent quoted. 'I guess that's a good one, post-9/11.'

I looked at my brother-in-law. The surprise on my face must have been evident.

'Eight years of Bible study. You never forget,' he said, shrugging.

'True enough,' Peter agreed. He passed me the milk and a bright yellow paper bag. 'Your jam,' he said.

'Ooh, thanks. I was so tired when we got in last night.' So tired that I left the jam in your car, and so tired that I nearly kissed you. I took the jars out and lined them up on the table. 'Presents from Manitoulin Island. Wild blueberry for you, Mum, and raspberry for you, Rose. Kent, I wasn't sure what you'd like, so I went for the best seller, hawberry jelly.' I had actually bought the hawberry for myself, but it seemed churlish not to give Kent a jar too.

'That's sweet of you, Lily,' said Kent. 'Thanks.'

Maybe that wasn't Kent I'd seen playing ball with the boy. Maybe a stranger had turned at the sound of my voice—maybe he was about to say, 'No, sorry, that's not my name,' but we left too quickly. I could almost believe I'd been mistaken. *Almost.*

'Let's make some toast,' said Rose, 'so we can try them all right now.' She stood and went to the bread drawer and plugged in the toaster. This was so Rose-like, to take charge, make a plan, and then go for it.

There was something else in the bottom of the bag, and I pulled it out, surprised. A bar of fudge that I'd considered buying and then left on the shelf, worried about the calories. 'Oh.' I smiled at Peter. 'You snuck that in when I wasn't looking. Thank you.' I looked away quickly before I started thinking too closely about the thoughts I'd had the previous evening. 'It was such a great day,' I said to everyone. I looked across the kitchen at Rose. 'Have you been?'

Kent answered for her. 'When did we go, Red? The August long weekend, eh? It was lovely.'

'If we win the lottery we'll buy a cottage there,' said Rose. 'Or maybe Temagami. Or in the Haliburton Highlands.'

Kent coughed, as if embarrassed. 'We have a lot of plans for our mythical lottery win,' he said.

'Don't forget we split it if either of us wins,' I said to Rose.

'I won't forget,' she said. She held up her hand and we joined pinkie fingers. 'Sister's club forever.'

'What? What's this?' Kent asked.

'Lily and I agreed years ago,' Rose explained, 'whichever one of us buys the winning ticket, we split it two ways. But there'll be enough for a cottage for each of us.' Rose didn't sound embarrassed at all by her talk of lottery wins. 'Don't worry, I have a list for all the ways to spend our share.'

'My sister is a list-writer. Same as Mum,' I reminded Peter.

'Someone around here has to be organized,' Rose said. 'Keep you lot in line.' She placed a plate of toast in the middle of the table, along with small plates and knives and the butter dish.

'Speaking of lists,' said Peter, spreading a piece of toast with the blueberry jam, 'Do you have a baby registry anywhere?' At Kent's blank look he added, 'For gifts, so your baby gets the toys and whatnot you want it to have.'

'I thought that was for weddings,' said Kent. 'Didn't we have one of those for our wedding?'

'We did,' Rose answered. To Peter she shook her head. 'We're not asking for presents. We'd like best wishes. And,' she smiled, 'maybe you could pop by and assemble the crib.' She turned back to Kent. 'It was Peter who made my first crib for me.' She told the story while we ate toast, interrupted by Mum and I correcting or adding details.

'I don't think so, Mum,' said Rose at one point.

'You were barely three weeks old!' Mum pointed out. 'I believe I have a clearer memory of the event.'

'Um, I was there too. Do I get a say in how it really happened?' Peter asked.

We all laughed, and I relaxed into the sound.

Home, I thought to myself. This is home. Toast and jam for lunch, eaten at the kitchen table. Laughter. Childhood memories which none of us completely agree on, memories we are going to pass on to the next generation. 'I love this,' I said.

'I do too,' said Kent, misunderstanding me. 'They're all good, but the raspberry is my favourite.'

But something of what I was thinking must have come through in my voice, because Rose looked over at him. 'We should make the most of this weather. Will you fire up the BBQ and we'll have everyone over for dinner?'

'There's a plan, Red,' he said. I wondered if he really wanted Peter and me there. 'Will you all come?' Rose asked us.

'Sounds great,' I said as Mum said that she'd love to, and she'd bring a salad.

'Ask your old man too,' Kent said to Peter.

'Thanks,' said Peter. 'What can we bring, a bottle of wine?'

Rose smiled. 'That would be lovely.'

And just like that it was settled. Peter went off to tell his dad and Mum cleared the kitchen table. Rose pulled me aside. 'Is a BBQ . . . open flame . . . okay? You never talk about your fear, but—?'

I nodded, but couldn't quite meet her eyes, embarrassed at what I considered my weakness. 'Starters or dessert?' I asked. 'What shall I make?'

'Is there time for you to make a raspberry pie?' she asked.

'I have some raspberries in the freezer,' Mum said.

Rose laughed. 'I knew you would.'

I stood. 'Always time to make a pie,' I said, reaching for an apron from the hook at the top of the basement stairs.

She and Mum hugged goodbye, even though they'd be seeing each other in a few hours' time. 'I'm jealous that you two live so close,' I said as Mum and I walked Rose and Kent to their car.

'Can't you convince Quint to get a civilian job and move back?' asked Rose. 'I love having you here.'

She and Kent drove off, and I put my arm around Mum's shoulders. 'I miss you.'

'I miss you too,' she said. 'I love having you home.'

Home. There it was, that word again.

'I haven't made pastry in ages,' I admitted. Quentin didn't eat much dessert and the rare times I made quiche for a potluck I bought pastry to be sure it would be successful. 'Will you help me?'

"Course I will,' she said. And we had so much fun making the raspberry pie for supper that we made a deep-dish apple as well, and then cheese straws with the leftover scraps. We took everything to Rose and Kent's backyard, which was glorious in the late afternoon sun. I accepted the bottle of Corona Kent passed me from the ice-filled tub and helped Rose set the picnic table, then the two of us sat at one end, me with my beer and Rose with a lemonade, and ate cheese straws while we watched as Mum plucked off deadheads and Kent fussed with the barbecue.

'Should we go and help Mum?' Rose asked.

I shook my head. 'She's happy. And I'm too idle. Would you really like a summer cottage? I didn't know that.'

'A summer cott—Oh, this morning's conversation. When we win the lottery.' She laughed. 'Yeah, we would,' she said. 'A simple one, not a McMansion. Close enough that we could go for weekends without too much traffic. Somewhere on a lake, in a forest, away from all the hustle and bustle of real life. Low maintenance. A creaky front deck, a screen door that slams shut, a big old pine tree out back where we can hang a tire swing, a dock for the canoe.' As she carried on describing it, I almost forget it didn't yet exist. 'I want to make sure our children have lots of time to play outside, like we did,' said Rose. 'Not all TVs and video games. Not rush-rush from one formal activity to another.'

I smiled at my sister. 'You're going to be such a great mum.'

'It's what I want more than anything else in the world,' she said. 'To be a mother. To raise happy, healthy children.' She looked at me and narrowed her eyes. 'With cousins.' She took a long drink of lemonade. 'I wish Quint was here.'

Another chance, the opportunity to tell her that Quentin had cheated on me, and our marriage was over. 'I'm not—It's—You and Kent are so happy,' I said slowly. 'I love seeing you so happy...' I hesitated. It was on the tip of my tongue to say, *But Quentin and I aren't happy. Our relationship is broken, I want out, I've left.* But I hesitated.

'I know. I know this is still infatuation, and the honeymoon phase, and it's going to get more difficult when the baby comes along, and at some point in the future the way Kent tosses his dirty socks towards the hamper, but not in to the hamper, will cease to be cute, and my bossiness will irritate him. And he does earn a good salary, but if I don't get a job then we'll have to make sacrifices. Children are expensive. And the summer cottage fantasy is just that, a fantasy. We both know that.'

Somehow the subject had changed. I'd not been fast enough to say what I meant to, and Rose had misunderstood my unfinished sentence.

'But right now, sitting with you in the sun, and smelling the burgers, and watching Mum potter about my disaster of a garden... Sure it would be great to smell Filet mignon, but I'll take this. I love this. And next year there'll be a baby lying on a blanket in the sun, and the year after that a toddler lurching about, and five years from now maybe two kids to run after.' She looked at me, her wide blue eyes glistening. 'I know to many people it might seem like nothing special, but I know this is the good life. I love my life.'

'I'm so happy for you,' I said. 'I hope you'll always be this happy.' I looked across the patch of lawn towards Kent. How was it possible he had a son, a part of his life, that Rose knew nothing about? How could he keep such a big secret from his wife? There had to be more to the story. Or maybe, maybe it wasn't a secret between them. Maybe Rose knew all about the boy, and figured it was none of *my* business. I felt my face flush with embarrassment, and I looked away.

Chapter Nine

BIG ROCK LAKE, FEBRUARY 2014

Time in a hospital waiting room doesn't follow regular rules. I watched the hands of the clock on the pale green wall—they barely moved—yet people came and went, chairs filled and emptied and were filled again. It was impossible. Then the hands of the clock stopped moving entirely, even though one of the police officers brought us bottles of water and I drank some, then used the washroom, then sat down and drank some more. Rose dozed, her head on my shoulder, but only for a few minutes.

Quentin and I had watched a movie about the D-Day landings before our trip to the Normandy beaches. I remembered how long the movie was, and how nerve-wracking. The soldiers, waiting for the right combination of water and tides, waiting to land. And, then, for many soldiers, waiting for help that never came, and finally realizing that they were waiting to die.

I shook my head of that last thought, and stood patiently to wait to speak to the young man at the desk to ask if there was an update. There was no news, sorry. You will be told as soon as we have any news. But I was given a clipboard with paperwork to complete for Rose, and I was able to do that.

'This is a basic medical screening,' I read to her. 'Then, if it looks like your kidney will be a good match, you'll be given a full evaluation.'

'Full evaluation.' I wasn't sure if she'd heard and understood me, or was repeating a few words.

'Yes. Physical exam, chest x-ray, EKG, urine testing, blood tests including tissue typing and crossmatching—' I stopped reading when it became apparent Rose wasn't listening to a word. 'Good. We'll start here.' I filled in her name and date of birth. Name and date of birth of the intended recipient. 'Do you know your blood type? Do you know Kent's?'

'I have that in a file,' she said. She looked down at the phone. Closed the Facebook page she'd been reading. Clicked on an app. Blinked several times, then passed me the phone. 'I can't—'

Her eyes were welling with fresh tears. She couldn't see.

'Oh, Rose.' I put down the paperwork and held my baby sister in my arms. 'Oh, Rose. It's going to be okay. It's all going to be okay.' But as I said that I happened to look over her shoulder at the young man behind the desk. He was being told something by a doctor, and then they both looked in our direction. I guessed there was an update. I guessed it wasn't good news. I held Rose tighter to me. Bad news could wait.

Big Rock Lake, 2001

'Rose seems very happy,' I said to Mum as we set up the Scrabble board for a quick game the evening of the impromptu BBQ.

'I hope so.' Mum pulled a P and took back my A. She looked at me. 'Are you and Quentin as happy as Rose and Kent?'

Avoiding her gaze, I pulled seven tiles and arranged them on my rack. A blank, an H, and a bunch of regular letters. There ought to be a bingo if I could see it. I shook my head. 'No.'

Mum pulled her seven tiles.

THE. HEAD. DATED. I rearranged my tiles. 'I'm not as sure of who I am as Rose is. She knows what she wants and she asks for it. She didn't say, "yes, please bring dessert." She said, "please bring this specific dessert".' EAT. HEAT. HEATED.

'Was that the purpose of your long walk? To figure out who you are? *Find yourself*, as we would have said in the sixties.'

Why had I thought my mother wouldn't understand? I was her daughter. She'd raised me, she loved me, she knew me.

'Yes,' I said. 'And now. . . I'm still not sure where I'm going. But I don't think. . . I don't think Quentin and I are going to make it.'

'Would you like to talk about it?' she asked gently. As she asked, I knew she'd been waiting for me to tell her since I got home. She was giving me time, and space, and wouldn't pry, and she was going to love me whatever I told her or if I chose to tell her nothing.

I looked down at my rack of letters. I picked them all up and placed them on the board. 'The bank is a C,' I said. 'CHEATED.' And the tears that had been threatening began to fall.

Mum took the Monday off work, assuring me she had months' worth of days in lieu. 'We don't need to talk, we don't need to do anything at all,' she said. 'But it's been a whirlwind of you off with Rose, and you off Peter, and I'd like to have you all to myself for a day.'

We spent the morning raking leaves, first ours and then Mr. Reynolds. 'You don't have to do that,' he called out. 'Peter will come by and take care of them.'

'All those years Peter raked our leaves,' I said. 'This is the least we can do.' And even though I loved the idea of a day with Mum, and even though I knew Peter was at work—it was a Monday during the school term—I couldn't help but wonder if he might arrive at any moment to visit with his dad. I immediately felt guilty.

'There's a new bistro downtown I've been looking for an excuse to try out,' Mum said. 'That's where I'm going to treat you for lunch.'

It was in the old bank on Main Street, a lovely red brick building. I was pleased they'd not torn it down. Inside, the decor left no doubt as to the restaurant's theme. Black and white photographs of Paris landmarks (the Eiffel Tower, Moulin Rouge, and Notre-Dame), paintings of narrow streets, cafés with awnings, and a selection of framed menus covered the walls. Small tables were covered with thick white tablecloths.

'Fun,' I said, when Mum ordered us each a virgin *Kir Royale*. 'Authentic,' I added as I sipped it.

The menu looked authentic as well. *Pâté de Maison*, *Croque Monsieur*, *Duck Confit*. I had a bowl of *moules* which came with a side of crisp *frites*. After I'd eaten the mussels, I dipped crusty french bread into the bowl to sop up the creamy white wine sauce.

True to her promise, Mum didn't mention Quentin or probe for any details of his affair. We chatted—a drumming group she'd joined, her job, baby gifts for Rose, my walk. 'I would have started by saying I didn't finish, and I didn't even walk two hundred miles,' I said, 'but Peter reminded me that what I did do was an accomplishment in its own right.' I had been very careful not to say his name as often as I thought it, not to turn the conversation to him.

'He's a wise young man,' Mum said. If she was thinking anything else, she gave no indication. 'I am so proud of you. What was the best day, or your favourite stretch?'

There was a sudden influx of diners—office workers, we guessed—who all arrived, ate a salad or a sandwich, and left within half an hour.

It was over dessert—we shared a chocolate mousse, super rich but light as a cloud—and tiny cups of strong coffee that I blurted out another hurt.

'All my so-called friends knew,' I said. 'That's almost as humiliating as the affair. Knowing that I sat at a dinner and everyone there was aware Quentin was—' I paused. 'That he was with Samantha. Humiliating isn't the right word. I'm angry. Angry that he was cheating on me in full view of everyone. But no one told me.'

'Would you have liked someone to tell you?'

'Yes. No. I don't know. I was the last to know. What an idiot. They must have been laughing at me behind my back for being so stupid. I thought they were friends, but now, looking back, I was so totally alone.' I sniffed, determined not to cry.

'Or they didn't want to risk losing you as a friend,' said Mum. 'They wanted to be there for you if you needed them—after you did find out.' She took a tiny spoonful of the mousse. 'I don't know if I'd be brave enough to tell a friend her husband was having an affair.'

'I would,' I said. 'Now, for sure I would. I'd risk losing a friend in order to tell her the truth. I was so careful not to marry an alcoholic, and not to marry someone unemployed. I forgot to add other items to the list when I was choosing my husband.'

Mum shook her head. 'There is no exhaustive list,' she said. 'And people do change. They can change for the worse, but they can change for the better too.'

'Do you ever regret marrying Bobby?'

'Did I wish he was different? Yes, often. But do I regret our marriage? No. Not for a moment. Not for a single moment.' She hadn't had to consider her answer at all. She reached across the table. 'How could I?' She stroked the top of my hand. 'He gave me you and Rose, the two greatest wonders, the two most important people in my life. And before that he gave me Tansy.'

'It's difficult not to wonder what might have happened...'

'If.' Mum nodded. 'If. If we'd stayed on the Old Homestead, where I was much better able to keep his drinking under control.'

'That wasn't your job,' I said. 'He was an adult.'

She nodded. 'I know. But I made a commitment when we said our vows, and I thought I could stand by that.' She sighed. 'I forgave him and forgave him, and kept lying to myself about the depth of his addiction. How could I be honest with him when I wasn't being honest with myself? If Bobby had stopped drinking. . . or tried to make a life in the city with us. . . who knows. Although, I'm sure I could have lived with his alcoholism and I never expected him to hold down a job. But his lies . . . his constant lies. In the end, I couldn't live with his belief that truth was optional.'

I shared a few more details about Quentin's infidelity. It wasn't a single time, couldn't be excused as a 'mistake.' Quentin had slept with another woman. The same one. Many times. 'I must be partially to blame,' I concluded. 'There are always two sides to every relationship.'

Mum shook her head. 'How can blaming yourself be helpful?'

'I don't know what to do with all this anger, and hurt, and sadness. And I know I have to move forward.' It felt as if my life was passing me by, and I had nothing to show for it—no children, no career, no accomplishments. I knew I had to decide what it was, exactly, that I wanted, and then go after it. But that was the problem, I wasn't sure what it was I wanted.

'Whatever you do,' she said. 'I love you. Know that. And I see accomplishments—many.'

The weather had turned while we had lunch. Sunny when we went inside, grey clouds covered the sky and a wind whipped leaves along the sidewalk. 'Fall's here,' I said. 'What a great thing to have had dinner outside last night. I bet that'll be the last one for some time.' When overcome by emotion, talk about the weather. It worked.

We went back home for warmer jackets and then walked along the lakeside boardwalk and a short distance up the escarpment.

We were still full from lunch, so opted to open a tin of soup for supper. We played another game of Scrabble, and then watched a British murder mystery on TV. 'Thanks, Mum' I said, hugging her as we went off to bed. 'This was the day I needed.'

'Me too,' she said. 'I love you, Lily.'

I took the phone with me and lay on my bed. It would spoil the mood to phone Quentin, but I needed to tell him that I needed more time, that I wasn't going to book a plane ticket any time soon. I thought of our conversation yesterday, sighed, and pressed re-dial.

'Hi there.' It was a warm, friendly voice.

'Peter?'

'Yes. Hello, Lily.'

'How did you know—?'

'Call display,' he said. 'You called me.'

'I did,' I said. 'I called you yesterday, but you were in the kitchen.' So when I'd pressed re-dial, thinking Quentin was the last person I'd phoned—'You must think I'm a numpty.'

'Cute and quirky,' he said. 'But not a numpty. And listen, since you have called me, what are your plans for Friday evening?'

I grinned down the phone. 'No plans.'

'Great. I weaselled out of chaperoning the high school dance by claiming a prior date. Which was not the truth. So may I, please, have the honour of a date with you on Friday evening, if you're not averse to going out with a liar? It will make me feel far less guilty.'

'A date with you on Friday evening sounds lovely,' I said. I meant it.

'I mean,' his words tumbled over each other, 'of course not a *date* date. But the Friday evening of a long weekend could be busy, so I'll book somewhere to be safe,' he said. 'How does French strike you? There's a new bistro on Main.'

'Chez Laurent,' I said. 'Mum played hooky and we had lunch there today.'

'Oh. Shall we go somewhere else then?'

'No. No. I'd love to go back. The food was excellent, and there's lots on the menu I'd love to try. That sounds like a great choice. And what other exciting plans do you have for your week?'

'Hm. Boy Scouts on Tuesday, a church fellowship committee meeting on Wednesday, and Big Brothers on Thursday.'

'Boy Scouts? Big Brothers?'

I heard him chuckle. 'Yeah, I'm a pushover when it comes to volunteering for any sort of youth group. It didn't sound as if he regretted either commitment. 'But, you know, you have to give back to your community.'

I thought of the volunteer work I'd done in England, purely for selfish reasons; I'd needed something other than coffee mornings with other military wives to fill my days. 'You are such a good person, Peter.'

'Oh, I don't know about that. Dad tells me the neighbourhood elves raked all his leaves this morning.'

'Ha. And then the wind came up this afternoon, so now the rest of them will have fallen.'

'And what else did you and your mum get up to on your sneaky day off?'

'We saw a blue heron,' I said. And even though we'd spent most of the weekend together, I was surprised to note, when we said goodbye, that once again Peter and I had spoken for the best part of an hour.

The moment I hung up, the phone rang again and I answered with a smile, wondering what Peter had remembered he wanted to say. 'Yes?'

'Hello, Lily.' At the sound of Quentin's voice my heart sank, and I wished Peter and I had spoken a little longer, so the line was busy. 'How are you? How was your day?'

I considered telling him that Mum knew about his affair, but I said nothing. I thought of all the details I'd shared with Peter—the waiter in a white apron, the birds we'd seen, the murder mystery we'd watched, and how Mum had solved it long before the fictional detective had. 'Good,' I said.

There was a long silence, then we both spoke at the same time. 'Have you looked at plane tickets?' he asked, precisely as I started to say that I had not looked at plane tickets.

'I thought—'

'I need more time,' I said. 'I'm not ready to come back to you. I don't know that I ever will be.'

'I—I don't understand, Lily.'

I sighed. 'I'm not sure if what we have is worth salvaging.'

He gasped. 'That's harsh.'

'I'm trying to be honest. You know, more honesty and fewer lies from the start might have helped us avoid so much... pain.'

Our conversation did not improve, but I didn't want to argue, so I asked him to give me time, and rang off. More honesty and fewer lies. I had never told Quentin about our very first baby, the pregnancy I had decided to terminate. I cringed. Mum said that Bobby believed truth was optional. Could the same be said of me?

First thing next morning I acted on an unspoken promise to myself and went next door to rake Mr. Reynolds' lawn of all the newly fallen leaves. As I raked Mum's lawn, I remembered my adamant vow not to hide knowledge of an affair from a friend.

Rose was my best friend.

So why hadn't I told Rose that I'd seen Kent with another woman? And a boy who called him Daddy? I had found myself liking Kent on Sunday, and Rose clearly adored him. It's none of your business, said one side of me. She deserves to know, said another. I couldn't decide which voice belonged to the angle on my shoulder and which voice belonged to the devil.

You're not one hundred percent sure it was him, I told myself. If you're wrong, it's a wild accusation to make. And maybe she already knows and thinks it's none of your business.

For the first time since Quentin had admitted his affair with Samantha, I considered why none of my friends had been able to bring themselves to tell me about it. My husband was a tall American man. Easily mistaken for another tall American man. Especially if he'd been in uniform at the time. It would have been equally easy for my friends to question what they'd seen as it was for me. Or maybe they too told themselves that I might be aware of the relationship...

Or you're a coward.

Or I was a coward, not in fact willing to risk my friendship with my sister in order to tell her what I believed to be the truth.

Rose wasn't my best friend. She was my only friend.

I imagined confronting Kent. Then I thought about the risk of losing Rose, and knew I wasn't going to do anything.

I filled the rest of the week with the baby shower planning, and other little chores, and time with Rose and Mum, and every day a local walk. I also went back to the mall and, without hesitating, bought myself a lacy black bra and panties set, and a little black dress. Passing by a nail salon I stopped on a whim and had a manicure. 'Doing something special for the long weekend?' the young woman asked me as she rubbed oil into my skin.

'A date tomorrow night,' I said, blushing as I spoke.

'Ooh. Friday night date night with your hubby and you still get excited,' she said. She paused to turn my twisted engagement diamond to the front of my finger. 'How long have you been married?'

I didn't want to correct the misunderstanding; it would involve too much explanation. 'Ten years next May,' I said. The truthful answer to her question.

'Ten years. And you still—Wow. I want a marriage like yours,' she said. 'Mind you, you're doing all what the magazines say you should. Date nights and making an effort with your appearance. I guess it works, huh? Any kids?'

'Not yet.' Also the truth. 'But I'd love to have at least one.'

'Well. Maybe Friday's the night, eh?'

I gave her an extravagant tip as I left, and she winked at me. 'Good luck.'

I tried not to think about the fact that I was cheating on my husband. Emotionally, for sure.

And if you're not thinking about the possibility of sex on Friday night, asked the devil on my shoulder, *then why did you blow sixty dollars on two scraps of fabric which Peter won't see unless you undress in front of him?*

The truth was, when I was alone in bed each night, I thought of little else. The simplest, gentlest fantasies. Peter holding my hand as we walked down a street, Peter kissing my lips at the end of the day, Peter telling me he loved me as we snuggled in bed.

When Quentin phoned that night and interrupted the fairytale love story I was telling myself, I was short with him. 'I asked for time,' I said. 'You need to give me time. I'm staying here for now.'

His voice trembled. 'I'm losing you, Lily. I can feel I'm losing you. Have you found someone else?'

'Of course not,' I lied, feeling a mixture of guilt and anger. 'Why would you think I need someone else? Why wouldn't you assume that I'm happy by myself?'

'I love you, Lily. I know you. You're a sexual, sensual woman.'

'Now it's all about sex? Because you cheated on me, you think I'll do the same to you? An eye for an eye? It doesn't work that way.' I cringed at my words.

'It's always all about sex,' he said. He sounded as if he genuinely believed that.

'Well I'm not thinking about sex now,' I said. Another blatant lie as minutes previously I had been wondering if black lace had been the right choice, or if Peter was more of a white cotton panties man. If Peter preferred the missionary position or would like me on top. 'I can't think about you without thinking about you and Samantha. I wonder what she has that I don't. I wonder what she did for you than I never did. I wonder what you saw in her. I wonder how many times you've seen her this month. I wonder what else I don't know, who else you've cheated on me with—' Where had I pulled these lines from? I sounded every bit the hurt wife, the wife whose husband had been unfaithful. If this was my role, some part of me seemed to feel I ought to play it to the hilt.

'Lily... Lily.' Quentin appeared to be at a loss for words. 'Have you given up on us? Is our marriage over? Is that what you're telling me?'

'I told you it was over. I left you. What's changed?'

'I ended it with Samantha, I told you. I promise you. 9/11 was a real wake up call. If I'd lost you... I know how good we have it, Lily. I—'

I closed my eyes. 'I need time, Quentin. Do me a favour, don't call me tomorrow, or over the weekend.'

Another long silence. 'If that's what you need me to do,' he said. 'I love you, Lily. Whatever you do, whoever you're with, don't forget you have a husband back home who loves you.'

His last words left a sick taste in the back of my throat. Maybe he did know me as well as he claimed to. Maybe there was something in my voice that gave away my growing feelings for Peter. My asking Quentin not to phone had freed me from any possible worry that he'd phone tomorrow when I was out, but I was now no better behaved, was just as dishonest, as he'd been when he'd snuck behind my back with Samantha. I tried to push away that thought and get back to the happy place I'd been, but it was hopeless. Enjoy the weekend, I finally told myself. Enjoy the weekend, see where you are on Monday, and then make the big decision on Tuesday.

It was pouring rain Friday morning. Despite that I asked Mum to drop me off at the start of the escarpment walk on her way to work. 'Can I still loop all the way around Maple Lake?' I confirmed. I could, she said, but reminded me that it would take me six hours. 'That's what I was hoping,' I said. I packed a lunch and pulled on layers of clothes topped with my raincoat, and waved goodbye to her from the trailhead. The rain lessened to a relentless drizzle from a grey overcast sky, a perfect match to my mood. Had I stayed home I'd have fussed. This physical exertion was exactly what I needed.

I thought about what I'd said to Mum. That I'd risk losing a friend in order to tell her the truth if I knew that friend's husband was cheating on her. I didn't know if Kent was actually cheating on Rose. I thought he had fathered a child and was playing some role in that child's life, but I had no idea if that woman I'd seen was his mistress, or an ex. Or if I was completely wrong.

At the top of the escarpment I sheltered under a spruce, peeking out between branches at the lakes far below. There were answers, I had to allow myself the luxury of time to find them.

It was five past four when I turned into our road. Time for a half-hour power nap, then a shower before I dressed. The walk had blown away my foul mood, and I was once again looking forward to my evening. There was a florists' van parked in our driveway, the deliveryman lodging a box against the front door.

Had Peter sent me flowers?

The man looked at his clipboard, peering at what must have been rain-soaked notes. 'Lily Porter?'

'Yes,' I said. 'That's me. Thanks so much.'

There was a pile of mail on the front mat. I stepped over it so as not to drip water on it, then, once I'd put down the flowers and hung up my raincoat, I picked it up. Mostly junk mail, one bill, and at the bottom a white envelope addressed to me. Inside was a card and a long letter from Quentin. I glanced at it but didn't read it. It could wait. I poured myself a glass of water, drank it, and then opened the box. A bouquet of nine calla lilies. My favourite flowers. The card read *You asked me not to phone, but I am thinking about you every minute of every day. I love you, Lily.*

With a sigh I arranged the flowers. They were striking. If I could plan my wedding all over again, I'd carry calla lilies as my bouquet. I gently rubbed one of the creamy white petals. With another sigh I retrieved the letter and sat next to the flowers to read it. It was a combination of heartfelt apology, promises for the future, and pages of remember whens. Quentin knew me well; he shared our favourite memories in detail. Ducking into a pub to avoid the rain one evening, we played in a pub quiz and won. Ordering from a French menu we discovered we'd asked for frogs' legs and tripe. Taking a wrong turn, we ended up on the Blue Ridge Parkway and just kept driving and driving, unable to believe the beauty. As I read his words I was back in those moments with him—precious, happy moments. With a start I saw that I had left myself barely twenty minutes to shower and dress before Peter arrived.

My hair was still damp, and I'd rushed my makeup, so I wasn't as polished as I'd envisioned. I hesitated for a moment before pulling on the new underwear, and didn't look at myself in the full-length mirror until I was in the dress. 'You're pretty,' I said to the mirror. 'Now smile, and enjoy this evening.' But I was nervous when the doorbell rang, and at the last moment I looked into the living room and saw the lilies in full sight. It was too late to move them.

'Is it still raining?' I asked. 'I could have come out to the car.'

'I wanted to make sure you had an umbrella,' he said. 'Hello, by the way.'

I smiled at him. 'I'm sorry. Hello.' I touched my hair. 'I went for a walk today and I was late home and my hair's still wet and—'

He cut me off. 'And you look lovely. So lovely. Shall we?' If he was surprised not to be invited in, he gave no indication.

'I'm still fretting about the other day,' I said. 'The woman and child. I haven't said anything to Rose. I don't know if it's my place, or not. I really don't.'

Peter turned to look at me. 'Sometimes doing nothing, while you consider all angles of the decision, is a valid choice. As long as you're aware that that is the choice you're making. Sometimes it helps me to talk through a decision, the pros and cons, you know. If you ever want to do that, Lily, I'm here to listen.'

'Thank you, Peter.'

The restaurant was buzzing, all but three tables full, when we arrived. 'Goodness. I'm so glad you booked,' I said. 'What a difference, what a crowd.'

The waiter, the same one from Monday, seemed equally surprised by the number of guests. 'Live music starts soon,' he said, as if that's what we'd come for, or perhaps to apologize in advance for any delay. 'Chef's backed up a bit, but here's some bread to start you off.'

Peter thanked him and assured him that we were in no rush. 'A glass of wine?' When I nodded, he asked which one I'd prefer.

Peter's next sentence was drowned out by a trio warming up, and when they started playing it became clear that conversation would be an effort. 'Not quite the ambiance I had in mind,' Peter shouted over Blue Rodeo's 'Til I Am Myself Again."

Ten minutes later the waiter arrived with, not two glasses of wine, but a bottle. Peter shrugged at me, and poured us each a glass.

I smiled and took a sip. 'At least it's good music.' From the shake of his head I could tell Peter hadn't heard me.

I finished two glasses before the waiter reappeared to take our order and was halfway through my third by the time our bouillabaisse arrived with a garlicky rouille and hot croutons. 'Smells like it was well worth the wait,' I shouted at the waiter, who replied with a brief smile of thanks.

We devoured the seafood soup and scooped up the last of the thick sauce with chunks of baguette. 'I love that you love garlic,' I said to Peter. 'I love that you love food.'

Peter shook his head and held his hand to his ear.

When the waiter stopped by to put another basket of warm baguette on our table and tell us our mains would be up soon, Peter asked him if he could ask the band to lower their volume. 'Yeah, sorry about this. It's our first time trying this out.'

He came back a few minutes later with a second bottle of wine. 'On the house. Manager says sorry.'

Peter held his hand over his glass, but I picked up the new bottle and added a splash to mine. 'Louder music, more wine.'

I tried to remember where that quote had come from. Was it a novel I'd read, or a movie I'd watched? I wondered what Peter's favourite movie of the past year was, opened my mouth to ask him, but knew it would take several minutes of speaking very loudly to be understood. I'd ask him another time.

The steak, when it came, was perfectly cooked. Delicious. The Béarnaise sauce was rich and creamy, sharp with tarragon and lemon. Crispy *frites* and a robust salad filled the rest of the plate. I took several bites of my meal to "All Shook Up." But I'd eaten too much bread. 'I won't have room for dessert,' I said.

'Sorry?' Peter rolled his eyes, then stood and came to stand next to me. 'This is nuts. The table's so small I'm bruising my knees, but I can't hear a word you're saying over Elvis. They did not think this through.'

It was the angriest I'd heard him, and he was, by any scale, only mildly irritated. For some reason that made me laugh, and he responded by laughing too. 'If you can't beat 'em, join 'em,' I said. I stood and took his hands in mine, 'May I have the pleasure of this dance?'

There was no room between our table and our neighbours, so we wound our way closer to the band. Peter didn't drop my hand but reached instead for my waist and pulled me close, then twirled me away and pulled me back.

'You can dance!' I said, childishly pleased that my new dress swirled so beautifully around my legs. The wine had eliminated any self-consciousness I would have felt in other circumstances, dancing in too small a space, in front of strangers, in a place not designed for dancing. But with such a strong leader, all I had to do was follow. I knew people were watching us but was surprised by the round of applause at the end of the song. I grinned at Peter.

The band, seeing the reception their Elvis song got, carried on with more '60s rock and roll. By the third song several other couples had joined us on the makeshift dance floor, and the waiter and his manager hastily pulled the few empty chairs out of the way, making as much space as possible. About half a dozen songs later the band gave us all a breather, returning to Elvis and playing "Can't Help Falling in Love." Peter pulled me close to him and we moved in small circles, possibly at a slower tempo than anyone else who was dancing.

I looked up at him and sang along with the lyrics. He looked down at me as the lead singer started singing the chorus again. I lifted my face to his and kissed him. Finally, my lips on his. It was everything I'd imagined. Gentle, firm. I sank into the kiss and teased his lips open with my tongue. I was dimly aware of the song ending beneath the taste of garlic on Peter's tongue, the tiny chip in one of his back teeth, the way he was holding my head in his hands that made me feel safe, wanted, loved. I reached for his neck, wound my fingers in his hair, pulled him closer.

'Get a room!' someone heckled in the pause between songs.

Peter pulled back a fraction of an inch, his cheeks red.

I had forgotten we weren't alone but knew nothing would wipe the grin from my face.

He took my hand, leading the way back to our table. Our mains had been elegantly wrapped in a silver foil swan for us to take home, and there was a bill and two chocolate truffles on a silver tray. It was my turn to pay, but Peter had already pulled out his wallet and was holding out my coat for me. We made our way to the cash register at the front door. 'We shouldn't charge you at all,' the manager said. 'You were great. You've been dancing together for years, haven't you? Proper rock and roll moves those were.'

I smiled to thank him and smiled again as he held the door for us, too deliriously happy to form a coherent sentence.

After the heat of the restaurant and the sweat I'd built up dancing, the cold night was a shock. I assumed we'd go to the car, but Peter walked several metres away from the door of the restaurant until we were standing under an awning in the light of a streetlamp. He put the silver swan on the ground. Carefully. Precisely. As if keeping the leftovers intact, a tactile memento of this evening's meal, was of utmost importance. Slightly dizzy, I kissed him again, but withdrew when it was clear he wasn't responding the same way as he had on the dance floor. 'Peter?'

He cleared his throat. 'So. Where are we going, Lily?' he asked.

'Well...' I whispered, moving a fraction closer. 'We could go back to your house.' As chat up lines went, it was clumsy. But I was confident he knew what I was suggesting. And when he reached for my left hand, I thought that it had worked, that he was going to walk me to his car, take me home. And it felt right.

But he gently held up my left hand, positioning it between us, looking down at it. My gaze followed his, and I thought how lovely my nails looked, and wondered if he had noticed them, how pretty they were. I would tell him about the manicurist. I'd remind him that the woman at the oven-making course thought we were cute together.

'Lily.' He touched my rings. 'I have to ask you your marital status.'

'My—?' It took me a moment to shift my attention from my pretty nails.

'I have to know what's going on here before we kiss each other again, before we... before we... do anything either of us might regret.'

Too fragile, my bubble of happiness burst, falling, to the dirty sidewalk at our feet, to be washed down the drains by the grey autumn rain.

Peter was too good a person, too kind, too honest for me to lie to. 'I don't know what my marital status is,' I said. 'I... left him in late August.' My voice broke. 'But 9/11 changed things. I don't understand why, or how, but it did.' I paused. Peter waited. 'So—we're still in contact. And I haven't asked him for a divorce.'

Peter nodded. 'That sounds like the truth, and I thank you for that.' He bit his lower lip. 'That extravagant bouquet of lilies. Safe to assume they're from him?'

I didn't want to meet his eyes, but nor could I look away. Why had I put the flowers on display like that, like they meant something? I nodded.

'He's trying to win you back,' Peter said. It wasn't phrased as a question.

'He's trying,' I said softly.

I watched as a look of pain crossed his face and wished I could erase it, wished above all else that I hadn't been the cause of it. He nodded. 'I wish you all the best, Lily, I really do, whatever you decide. But I can't—I'm not going to get involved with a married woman. That's not the kind of man I am, or want to be.'

'I understand,' I said. 'I guess that's one of the many things I love about you.'

We stood for what felt like a long time under the patch of awning, until I started shivering. 'You're cold,' said Peter. 'I'll take you home.' He walked me to the car, where he opened the passenger door for me. I watched him in the rear view mirror. He paused several times and I wondered if he was re-thinking, wrestling with his conscience.

When he opened his door and got in the driver's seat, he resembled his father for a moment, and I saw him as an older, more vulnerable man. I felt a rush of guilt.

'I'm so sorry, Peter. I—I drank too much, I'm a fool. Forgive me?'

'Nothing to forgive,' said Peter. 'And don't think that I'm not tempted. I'd be a damn lucky man, and maybe I'm the fool not to spend one night with you at the risk of a broken heart.'

It was the last line. He didn't want to be hurt. I knew what that felt like, to be hurt by someone you cared for. I hadn't understood until that second that I was playing the other role this time. The role of the person who used someone, toyed with their emotions, and then walked away. Except I wasn't planning on walking away. 'I'll ask him for a divorce tonight. I'll leave him, I don't love him. I wasn't using the word love flippantly,' my words tumbled over each other, and I knew I sounded desperate. 'Please, Peter. Please give me a chance to make this up to you.' I moved towards him, but he gently held me back.

'If you leave your husband, you have to leave him on real terms, for real reasons,' he said. 'You can't leave him for me; I won't take that responsibility.'

I didn't like myself at all. 'I'm making it worse, not better. I don't know what else to say.' As if there were some magic words that could take me back to the moment an hour ago when I'd been feeling safe and wanted and loved. 'I bought beautiful new underwear,' I said sadly. 'It's so pretty.'

'I can imagine,' he said softly.

'I thought—I thought—'

'I know,' he said. 'We've known each other since the day you moved in. We've been friends for so long. It would be so easy, and so, so. . . comfortable to fall in love with each other.'

'You've been Mr. Right all along, haven't you,' I mumbled. 'Right in front of me and I never knew till it was too late. If you proposed to me—'

He cut me off. 'You'd say yes. But I'm not going to do that.'

'I'm sorry we won't go canoeing next summer,' I said. 'I was really looking forward to that.'

'Me too.' I wanted him to add, *another time maybe*, but he didn't.

'But I think it really is over between Quentin and me, so maybe I'll be back here by next summer.' In time for canoeing, and camping, and building an oven in his backyard, and, and, and—I looked over at him. 'Do you think you might—' I wasn't sure what I wanted to ask. Would he wait for me?

He knew what I was asking. 'I'm not going to make any promises,' he said. 'I'm not going to stop living my life in the hopes you get a divorce and give yourself time enough to recover and then want to explore what we might have together. But if things do go that way, then yes, of course I hope you'll look me up.' He didn't say anything about remaining friends, or keeping in touch.

'With my luck you'll be married yourself by then, with a couple of kids.'

He said nothing for several minutes. 'Maybe your marriage is broken beyond repair. Maybe it isn't. You owe it to yourself to give yourself the chance to figure that out.' He turned the key in the ignition.

The drive was silent. But I wasn't quite ready for a final goodbye. 'Will you still come to Thanksgiving Dinner at Rose's on Monday, Peter. Please?' I asked when he pulled up in front of my childhood home.

'I will still come to Thanksgiving Dinner at Rose's on Monday, Lily,' he answered. 'Yes.' But I thought he sounded tired, and I wondered if it was easier to honour a prior commitment than make excuses to Rose and to his father. I wondered if he was doing this to help me save face, so that no one guessed I'd been the cause of our falling out.

Wordlessly I unbuckled my seat belt, opened the door, and closed it behind me. I stood by the side of the driveway, and as he pulled away I held up my hand, something between a wave and an acknowledgement that he was leaving. He did a U-turn in the street and was gone. I had never felt more alone in my life, not even at the loneliest moment of my aborted walk, or the nights when Quentin had been away on deployment.

I listened to the sounds of the fall night, the rain on the tarmac, the muted traffic from the highway, somewhere in the far distance a siren. City sounds. I had a sudden longing for my childhood home, when on a night like tonight there would have been a mouse scurrying through leaves, a swooping owl, a creaking birch.

I replayed the events of the evening: the uneven start, my race to inebriation, the high of dancing, the even higher high of kissing, and then the swift, painful plummet. I thought of a triptych of Icarus I'd seen in a museum in Europe. In the first panel his face radiated joy, in the second the wax of his wings was melting and he was frantically trying to stop his descent, in the third he was still falling, but it was clear he'd accepted his fate. I was falling, for sure, but I wasn't sure I'd accepted my fate. I wondered if Peter might have a change of heart, and so I waited for half an hour, in case his car came driving back up the street. Of course, it didn't, and when my teeth started chattering I finally went inside and slowly walked upstairs, to the room where only a few hours earlier I'd dressed in anticipation of... of a very different ending to this evening.

Still shivering, I stripped off and got into bed. Maybe I'd ring Rose and tell her I was ready to go and see the housing estate that had been built on the Old Homestead. Maybe I needed to say goodbye to my childhood. I was thirty-three and I had to grow up, or whatever it was I'd not yet managed to do, fix whatever it was that was so damaged that I had propositioned an old friend. Propositioned him and more, asked him, expected him, to save me from myself.

I closed my eyes, curled into a ball, and waited for the morning, and the rest of my life.

I awarded myself an Oscar for the performance I played that weekend.

Saturday morning I suffered silently through the worst hangover I'd had in years, running a bath to cover the sounds of my vomiting in the toilet, and discreetly pouring my coffee down the kitchen sink because the mere smell of it made me retch. I forced myself to be super cheerful as I cleaned and cooked and decorated for the baby shower with Mum, claimed I was still full from the previous night's dinner to excuse my need for lunch, and knelt down on hands and knees to pretend to scrub a patch of the kitchen floor when I was overcome by a dizzy spell. By late afternoon the mild painkillers in Mum's medicine cabinet were no longer taking the edge off my headache.

Somewhere in my pack I had a bottle of Tylenol Extra Strength in case of a sprained ankle on the Appalachian Trail. I'd never fully unpacked my first aid kit, and now I dumped it upside down and shook it. I rooted through the things on the floor, pausing to pick up two boxes of tampons. Crushed, but unopened.

I remembered buying one box months before I left for the walk, when I was obsessively packing and repacking, making my pack as light as possible. The second had been on hand at home. I begrudged packing it, resentful of the extra weight, but I knew I'd need them and there was no point leaving them behind. I'd left that house in North Carolina planning to never return. So... so when had I last had my period? Not on the walk, not since I got back to Big Rock Lake.

I left the mess on my bedroom floor and went down to the calendar on Mum's bulletin board, lifted it off, turned it back to August. Sunday, August

26th I'd left North Carolina, not bleeding. I moved my finger from Sunday to Sunday, muttering to myself. September 2nd, 'walking.' September 9th, 'walking.' September 16th, 23rd, 30th, 'here.' Tomorrow was the 7th. 'Six weeks.' *Six weeks!*

I turned back to August. Then July. Trying to remember the last time I remembered having my period, for sure. In my growing confusion I couldn't recall any significant detail that would pinpoint a date of any period during the summer. When I was training for the walk—nothing. Arguing with Quentin—nothing. At work—nothing. Spending afternoons at the outdoor pool on base—nothing.

But I recorded my period obsessively, so that I knew when I was ovulating. My tiny diary would have a red dot by the days I'd bled. I went back upstairs and flipped back through August, July, June, May, April. April 23rd - 27th. The last red dot was April 27th. I closed my eyes. Quentin had been back for several weeks by then, and I'd been worried about him. Told him I wanted to do the walk together... and he'd said "Samantha" was taking two months off in the summer. We'd argued. Then had make up sex...

Again I counted weeks on the calendar.

If that was correct, if I'd conceived on that day in late April, then I was well through my first trimester and halfway through my second. I counted the weeks again. Looked through my diary more carefully, in case I'd missed a red dot.

I tidied away the mess of first aid stuff and tampons and then I sat on the bed. Held my hands over my stomach. Maybe. Maybe this time- I stopped myself from finishing that thought.

Mum yelled up the stairs, asking if I was okay.

'Fine. Just fine,' I lied.

Chapter Ten

'I'm going out for a second, Mum,' I said, pulling on my coat and lifting her car keys from their hook.

I drove to a pharmacy I didn't know on the other side of the city, bought three packs of pale pink and blue balloons and some matching streamers and two pregnancy kits, and walked to the Timmy's next door, bypassing the coffee counter for the small washroom stall. I ripped open a box, peed on the stick, and closed my eyes. When customers rattled my door, I called out some sound to indicate I was there and let them wait for the other stall to become available. After five minutes I took a deep breath and looked down. The two bright pink lines could not have been clearer.

I dropped the stick in the garbage can, gathered my coat around my shoulders, and left, whispering some word of apology to the line of women waiting for a toilet.

I wanted to be happy. I wanted to be gloriously, gloriously happy. But I wasn't going to allow myself that luxury. I wasn't even going to think of this as a baby; I wasn't going to risk falling in love—yet again—and having my heart broken—yet again.

My headache was gone, replaced with something that I couldn't even begin to name. Get through today, I told myself. Then get through tomorrow. Then worry about the day after that.

I turned on the radio in an attempt to drown out my thoughts. '—everything you wish for,' the chirpy announcer was saying. She sounded about sixteen. I turned off the radio. Get through today. Then get through tomorrow. Tomorrow. Rose's baby shower. I let out some harsh noise that was a combination of a cry and a laugh. Pulled myself together and went home to blow up the balloons I told my mother I'd decided we absolutely needed and then hung them around the living room with tendrils of streamers.

'Didn't those lilies arrive at the perfect time,' said Mum, surveying the room. 'Doesn't the room look lovely.'

'Lovely,' I echoed. The balloons and streamers were tacky by comparison and I considered taking them down, but didn't have the energy. 'How about a cup of tea and a game of Scrabble?' I couldn't concentrate, but it was easier than trying to hold a conversation. We played two games, Mum trouncing me both times. 'This was your night tonight, for sure,' I said. 'Rematch tomorrow after the party's over?' I said I was tired—true—and went off for an early night.

I was saved by my not having slept more than an hour Friday night after the disaster of my date with Peter. My body, beyond stressed, took control and shut itself down. I slept for nine hours solid. In the morning I showered to cover the sound of my crying, but no tears came. I paused as I soaped my stomach, then focused on washing my hair. Before I went downstairs I went back to the washroom, opened the second test. Just in case. I left it hidden behind a pile of books on my bedside table. I'd check it later. Just in case.

Because of stress, I told myself. Stress could do odd things to a body. Surely a false positive pregnancy test could simply be a result of stress. And a woman who'd left her husband, started a long solo walk, lived in the world of 9/11 and all its news coverage, fallen in love with a friend who didn't love her in the same way—surely that woman could be said to be stressed enough for her body to react in odd ways to a pregnancy test. I showed none of my usual signs of pregnancy—no morning sickness, no tender breasts. I put the stick out of my mind and went downstairs, surprised to discover, when Mum passed me a plate of toast and scrambled eggs, that I was hungry. And that the coffee was good. And that I found it easy to shut down the part of me that ought to have been thinking about the possibility that I was pregnant and waiting for the signs of a miscarriage.

When Rose arrived at two, ostensibly to collect Mum's big turkey platter, all her friends yelled surprise.

'What?! No! Oh! I should have guessed this morning,' she said. 'Kent went on and on about how I should wear a skirt instead of jeans today and I had no idea why. He wouldn't shut up about it.' She laughed. 'He'll be pleased he met his obligation.' She looked around the room. 'Carrie! You were supposed to be down south for the weekend. I can't believe—! Kent was so convincing.'

All the women laughed at Kent's deviousness, and I smiled as well as I could. It was easy to stay in the background, organizing games, piling the gifts in front of my sister, excusing myself to make another pot of tea, offering around the finger sandwiches, the scones, the tiny cupcakes iced in pastel colours. Rose was the centre of attention and all eyes were on her, as they ought to be. She was opening the presents when the doorbell rang, everyone hooting with laughter at the tiny onesie that read 'Keep Calm: My Daddy's A Policeman.' It rang again before I registered that someone was at the door and got up to answer it. I thought everyone we'd expected was here, but perhaps one of Rose's friend's plans had changed at the last moment and she was coming to celebrate.

A tall man was standing on the front porch. It took me a split second to recognize my husband.

I stepped outside and pulled the front door closed behind me. 'Quentin—?'

'I'm not so good with words, you know that.' He dropped to his knees and pulled a small red box from his pocket. 'I love you, Lily, and I always will. Will you forgive me, please?' When I didn't take the box from his hands he fumbled with the catch and opened it. Nestled on a bed of ivory was an emerald ring I'd once seen and coveted. I stared down at it. 'Remember that holiday on Saint Lucia?' Quentin asked. He knew I did. 'Those long walks along the beach. Our own private deck where we watched the sun set while we drank virgin Pina Coladas in our hot tub.'

Of course I remembered. It was one of those picture-perfect holidays, a week out of time. We spent the whole week together, leaving the resort a single day to go into town. That was when I'd seen this ring, or one very like it, and fallen in lust with it. At the time I thought it embodied all that had been so perfect about our week. The Caribbean was the same emerald colour, and everything—the sand, the pool, the palm trees, the bright flowers—seemed to sparkle in the sun. That was before Samantha, or at least, before I knew about Quentin's affair with her.

'We were so happy then,' said Quentin. He stood up, held out my left hand and looked down at it. I had a moment of déjà vu—Peter holding out my hand and looking down at it in a similar way, worry etched in his features as worry now showed on Quentin's face. It was incredible that my nails looked as pretty now as they had then. Surely a million years had passed between those two moments.

'Let's get that back. Together,' Quentin said, and slipped the emerald on to my finger, above my engagement ring and wedding band. 'Say yes,' he whispered, and leaned in to kiss me. The softest, gentlest kiss.

A door closed, there was the sound of footsteps, and a car starting. I caught a flash of silver as the car drove off and knew without needing to see any more that Peter had dropped his father off after Church, then no doubt stayed for lunch to help around the house. And had he glanced at this house when he left his own, or looked as he drove by, he'd have seen me standing on the front porch kissing my husband.

'Friend of yours?' Quentin asked.

I wondered if he'd felt me stiffen. 'Neighbour's son. Peter.'

'Lily?' Rose was at the door. 'Are you—Oh, Quint! You did come! You've made it up for Thanksgiving!' She engulfed him in a hug. 'I knew you'd come. Well get in here, both of you, it's freezing.' She grabbed his hand and pulled him into the house. 'Look, everyone, my brother-in-law's come all the way from North Carolina.'

I was glad that my mind was already compartmentalized, that I was operating on automatic, that I could shift my act of happiness at Rose's shower gifts to an act of happiness at Quentin's unexpected appearance. He excused himself for a moment to go back to the rental car and returned with a teddy bear the size of a Saint Bernard, a big bow around its neck, wrapped in an airline-approved plastic bag.

I gave him points for buying a gift, even if it was over the top and ridiculous. All of Rose's friends oohed and aahed, and I was reminded how loveable Quentin was to people who saw this side of him. How much I loved this side of him.

After her guests had left, when Kent arrived, we sat amongst the balloons and streamers and piles of gift wrap and Rose took full credit for the surprise. 'I didn't tell either of you,' she said. 'In case he couldn't get the time off work, or, you know, post-9/11 travel.' She grinned and looked at her brother-in-law. 'I knew you'd come. I knew you'd make it.' I wondered what sort of conversation she'd had with him. Had she mistaken my wanting to go for long solitary walks as a sign of sadness? Had she warned him that I was striking up a close friendship with Peter? 'Are you surprised, Lily? Are you totally surprised?'

'I am totally surprised,' I said. 'Beyond words.'

'You had no idea, did you?'

'None.' Had he known Thursday evening, even as we argued, that he'd soon be seeing me for a, what had he called it, face-to-face discussion? I didn't ask. 'I thought Mum and I were in charge of the surprise-giving today,' I said.

Get through today, I told myself. Get through tomorrow.

'—truly thankful tomorrow,' Rose was saying.

Tomorrow. How would I face Peter tomorrow, with Quentin sitting at the table? I spun my rings on my fingers, looking down when they didn't turn like they usually did.

Rose followed my gaze. 'Lily! Oh my gosh, that's gorgeous!'

Quentin beamed. 'She fell in love with it on Saint Lucia and I knew I'd taken a picture. I went through all the holiday photos to find it, so I could make sure it was identical.'

'It's stunning,' said Rose. 'Ooh, I'm jealous.'

'Oh thanks for that,' Kent said to Quentin with a mock scowl. 'How am I gonna top that, eh?'

Both men laughed.

I wanted to tell my sister: Don't be jealous! You have a husband you truly adore. You live in a house where you can raise your family and live into retirement. You're pregnant with a planned, wanted baby. You're part of this community. You live the good life. I'm jealous of you.

But then Kent said something else and, without looking at him, I heard the boy calling out to him. *Again, Daddy. Again.* I wasn't jealous of Rose, not so much. Maybe she didn't know her husband as well as she thought she did. I looked down at the sparkling green ring again, wondering if I could force it to represent that happy week in Saint Lucia, or if every time I looked at it I would instead think of Samantha.

Supper was easy to get through. All the baby shower leftovers to eat, and Rose talking a mile a minute. 'Red,' Kent said at one point. 'You gotta let the others have a chance.' But he smiled as he said it, and she wrinkled her nose at him. She appeared to be oblivious to the fact that her husband didn't address a single word to me, or I to him.

When Rose and Kent drove off, the trunk of their car full of presents, the enormous bear taking up the entire back seat, Quentin went to the washroom and Mum looked at me. 'Are you okay?' she asked.

I nodded. 'I will be.'

'I can insist he sleeps in the other room if you'd like,' she said.

I shook my head. My twin bed wasn't really big enough for two. We'd be cramped, and neither of us would sleep well. But it would be too difficult for me to explain to Quentin that my mother knew about his affair. That she was looking out for me. *Get through today. Get through tomorrow.* I hugged her. 'But thank you.'

When he reappeared in the kitchen, I reached for the Scrabble board. 'Mum and I play every night,' I said. 'Would you like to join us?'

I had expected him to say no, to turn on the TV, but he sat down and joined in with a show of spirit. For a split second I was touched. He hated boardgames; this truly was a sign he was making an effort. But one game of Scrabble wasn't enough to make up for all those hours with Samantha, all those lies he'd so easily told me.

'Big day,' Mum said at ten o'clock, as we finished the game.

'And Thanksgiving tomorrow,' I said. 'Yes, time for bed.'

I turned to Quentin as soon as I shut the bedroom door. 'It's a beautiful ring. But this doesn't mean I instantly forgive you.' What I wanted to tell him was that if he was expecting sex, that wasn't going to happen.

'I know. It's only a ring. I wanted to make a grand gesture, but I know it's the little things I do every day for the rest of our lives that will really make the difference.'

If nothing else, he'd been reading up on what he was supposed to say, and he had delivered that line well.

'There is one more thing,' he said, reaching into the pocket of his overnight bag. He held up an envelope. 'Our new orders. And plane tickets for Tuesday.' And a tiny box of my favourite chocolates. Tradition.

'Orders,' I said. Then, 'Tuesday?' So soon. I turned my back to change into pyjamas. 'Did you really come because Rose asked you?'

'I came to get you, to take you home,' he said. 'I didn't want to choose our new place without you. So Canadian Thanksgiving worked perfectly.' I hated the way he had always called it Canadian Thanksgiving; I never said 'American' Thanksgiving when I spoke of his country's holiday. 'I've booked us three days of viewings with an agent next week. Off-base, Lily.'

Another sign he was trying. In our past two locations I'd asked to live off-base, but he had argued that it made no sense for either of us. That it was easier to fit in, that the on-base lifestyle was a good one. He passed me the envelope again and I put it down on the top of the dresser, unopened.

He was trying. I could tell he was trying.

'I miss you,' he said. 'I'm lost without you. A disaster.'

He took off his watch and looked for somewhere to put it, moved the pile of books on the bedside table to make space and, at the same moment, we both saw the white plastic stick. Even from across the room the two pink lines were clear. So bright they were glowing.

He dropped his watch and grabbed the stick, turning to stare at me. 'Is this—? Does—? Are you, we—?' He strode 'round the bed in three short steps. 'Pregnant? Lily?' He held up my chin to look into my eyes, where I was sure he could see the answer, and then threw his arms around me.

'If I hadn't been there, at our last big argument, I'd believe you're happy with this news.'

'Happy? Happier than ever!'

I wasn't going to get myself get pulled in simply because he was saying what I'd waited so many years to hear. 'You didn't want a baby. You never wanted a baby.'

'That was old me,' he said. 'Stupid me, selfish me. New me knows that, more than anything, I want us to be a family of more than two.' He did look genuinely happy. I almost believed him.

'I almost believe you,' I said.

'Believe me. Please believe me. I was an idiot, an ass, and I am going to spend the rest of my life making it up to you, making you the happiest woman ever, being the best husband and dad you can imagine.' He kissed me again, then knelt and kissed my stomach. 'Welcome, Little One,' he said. 'I love you.'

I hadn't thought of the baby as more than a problem I would have to deal with at some point, another decision I'd have to make. My husband's words transformed it into a person. A person Quentin claimed he already loved. I put my hand on my stomach, and he put his on top of mine. Our baby. Our baby. This changed everything, and the choices I thought I had to make were choices I had to make with the baby's father.

Quentin stood and looked at me. 'Come to bed, Lily.'

The bed was too small for two people. When we got in, the only way to be at all comfortable was for Quentin to curl around me. Instinctively I leaned my head into the crook of his arm, like I used to when we were first married, when we use to lie in bed like this and make plans for our future. Was this meaningful, this gesture I made, or simply muscle memory?

He was asking when the baby was due, if I thought it would be a boy or a girl, when we could start thinking of names, how far along I was. For years this was what I'd longed for, now I wished I could feel even half of the enthusiasm and joy he was expressing.

'I know this is my second chance. I'm not going to fuck it up this time,' he said. 'I need you to believe me. I need to know there's hope for us. Especially now. We need to fix us for our baby's sake.'

I thought of my childhood, how Mum had essentially been a single parent. That wasn't the life I wanted, for my baby for myself. But nor did I want to raise a child in a relationship devoid of trust. Sacrifices were going to have to be made, whatever choice I made.

'Hey, don't forget to open the envelope, Lily,' Quentin said. 'You're gonna be super excited. But first, three guesses.'

The game we always played when he got notification of his new posting. I couldn't even remember what we'd discussed, or if we had discussed our options. Maybe at that point he'd thought he'd be going somewhere with Samantha. 'I don't know,' I said.

'I'll give you a clue. We won't need a snow shovel.'

'Florida? California? Spain?' I didn't care.

'Nope, nope, and nope, and you've used up all your guesses.'

He wanted me to smile, to be excited. Could he not tell that I wasn't even sure if I'd be on the plane with him on Tuesday? I sat up and reached for the envelope, but before I opened it he blurted, 'Honolulu! We're going to live in Hawaii!'

'Honolulu,' I echoed. 'Hawaii.'

How's this sound? We'll find a place on the ocean. We'll sit on our lanai and watch the sun set every evening. We'll eat fresh fish and fresh pineapple and fresh mango. We'll grow them in our backyard.'

'Is Samantha going to be in Honolulu too?'

'No.' He reached for my hands. 'No, Lily. It's over between me and Sam. I swear, it's completely over. I don't even know where she and Carl have gone. I haven't asked. I don't care.'

It would be easy enough to find out, and if I decided to go 'home' with Quentin, then I would find out. Keep your friends close, but your enemies closer and all that. 'So July and August, the make-or-break holiday she and Carl took... it worked?'

'Let's not talk about them,' Quentin whispered. 'Let's talk about us. The three of us.' He held me, and I felt his chest heave. He was crying. 'I missed you so much. I'm fucking useless without you.'

He cried so rarely.

'Please don't leave me, Lily. We're months away from our ten-year anniversary. We've made it this far. We're going to have a baby. Come to Hawaii for a fresh start with me. I promise I'll... I promise... Whatever you need me to promise,' he finally said. 'Remember how much we love each other.' His voice broke with more tears.

'Shh, shhh,' I said, starting to cry myself. 'It's going to be okay, Quentin. It's going to be okay.' And together as we held each other and cried, I believed, for the first time in months, that maybe the last ember of our love hadn't been totally extinguished, and maybe there was hope for recovery. Maybe "okay" was a stretch. But maybe it wasn't.

In the cold light of morning, after a night of broken sleep, I wondered what it was that had made me cave so easily, so quickly, and as I showered reminded myself that I didn't have to do anything I didn't want to do. I could choose not to get on the airplane the next day. I could choose to raise my baby by myself. I couldn't actually envision myself not getting on the plane, but I kept telling myself it was a choice I could make. I told Mum over breakfast that Quentin had been posted to Hawaii. I thought I could read her thoughts in her guarded comments: do you want me to be excited? Are you going to be safe? You are welcome to stay here for as long as you like. I divided up the previous day's newspaper and passed out different sections, so as to avoid conversation.

When I walked out on the front porch, pie in hand, Peter's car pulled into his dad's driveway. I put the pie into the trunk of the rental car and stood, waiting. He'd seen me, I knew, and I wondered if he was hoping I'd go back inside and leave him in peace. But just as his car door finally opened and I thought I'd have a few moments alone with him, Quentin came outside with the other two pies. 'Here you go, Lily,' he said, putting them next to the first one. 'They won't get squished, will they?' He sounded every inch the caring husband. He looked up at the sound of Peter's car door closing.

'Hi.' He strode across the short distance between them. 'Pete, isn't it?' He held out his hand.

What could Peter do but shake it? 'Hello, Quentin.'

I looked at the two men, wondered what each was thinking. I couldn't compare them; they were so different from each other. One was my husband of nearly a decade, and the father of my unborn baby. The other—What was Peter, really? A neighbour, a childhood friend, a man around whom I'd recently spun a romantic fantasy.

'Still teaching?' Quentin asked Peter. I wondered again if Rose had said something to Quentin. How else he would have remembered what Peter did?

Peter nodded. 'Still in the Army?'

Quentin nodded. 'That's right. Lily and I are off to Hawaii next.'

'Hawaii,' said Peter.

Quentin turned to wink at me. 'Can't you imagine my beautiful wife in a bikini?'

Like a dog pissing at the base of a tree, he was marking his territory in no uncertain terms.

'I'd better make sure Dad's ready,' said Peter. With a curt nod he took his father's front steps two at a time.

'Not much of a conversationalist, your Pete,' Quentin said to me. 'C'mon, let's see what else we can do to help your mom.'

I didn't think there was any point calling him on the use of "your." It was better to let it go. If he did suspect anything was amiss, I didn't want to give him any further cause to wonder. But over pre-dinner drinks and nibbles at Rose's I heard him further goading Peter while Rose, Mum, and I did the last-minute preparation in the kitchen.

'So the kids you teach go on to university, right, Pete?'

'Some of them,' said Peter.

'Is that still a useful option?' Quentin asked. To Kent and Mr. Reynolds he probably sounded as if he was making an effort to show an interest in Peter's career. 'I mean, is there a job at the end of it all for them, or a whack load of student debt?'

'Good point,' said Kent. 'How many people do you know with a degree who've never used it?'

I looked at Rose, who was also listening. 'I guess that would be the two of us,' I whispered.

'Oh, he didn't mean us,' she said quickly.

Kent was ploughing on, talking about trades and skills, that's what this country needs. 'I don't know about the States—'

I could picture Quentin nodding, as if he'd given the question serious thought. 'Same. Same. We used to be a country that manufactured the goods we sold, now we ship in all the crap that China wants to send us. Plastic garbage that we toss away when it's broken instead of repairing.' This was a conversation he liked, and had often with his colleagues, and I knew he'd hold forth for the next quarter of an hour on the problems with the motor industry and others. The difference being that this time, it was somehow all Peter's fault.

'This is a rant,' I whispered to Rose. 'The most efficient way to stop him is to serve dinner.'

But she misunderstood me. 'Aww, cute,' she said. 'Let him have his rant.'

I hid in the kitchen until the last dish was on the table, and Kent was clicking his fork against his wine glass. He asked my mother to do the honours and say grace, which she did.

'Amen,' we all echoed. I carefully unfolded my table napkin and put it on my lap.

'When do we get to make our big announcement?' Quentin whispered.

I shook my head. Not in front of Peter, I wanted to say.

'Please, Lily?' he said. 'Please?'

What did it matter? Everyone was going to know sooner or later.

'Okay. Sure.' I tried to sound less reluctant than I felt.

Quentin looked at Rose, perhaps understanding that she was his ally in all things. 'Yesterday was your day, Rose, your celebration. But do you mind if we combine your Thanksgiving feast with our good news?'

'Share, share,' said Rose. 'Please.'

'Well...' I felt people turn to look at him. I looked down at my plate, then reached for the cranberry sauce. Peter had brought it and I knew it was made with the cranberries we'd picked together.

'Our next posting has been announced.' Quentin paused, clearly for effect. 'Our baby will be born in Hawaii!'

'Baby?!' Rose screamed.

'Goodness!' said Mum at the same time.

'Congratulations,' said Mr. Reynolds.

I couldn't take my eyes from my plate. I didn't want to meet Mum's gaze. Most of all, I couldn't bear to look at Peter. Whatever he had thought of me, whatever excuses he had been willing to make on my behalf, there was no way for me to explain in any sort of coded language that when I'd propositioned him on Friday night I didn't know I was pregnant with my husband's child.

Rose had jumped up, was now behind me, throwing her arms around me and mock scolding. 'You! I told you! I told you Kent and I want cousins for our kids and you never breathed a word, not a word of this!'

Could Peter figure out it was news to me too? I wanted him—needed him—to know this was news to me too.

'We just found out yesterday evening,' I said. 'It's very unexpected—'

'The best unexpected gift ever,' said Quentin. 'We're both so very grateful.' His voice trembled with the right note of emotion. No wonder I'd been so easily fooled by his stories of late nights at the office.

'A grandma twice in a year!' Kent said to Mum. 'You must be thrilled.' I didn't hear her response.

'And wait. You said something about Hawaii?' said Rose. She looked at me. 'Is that news too?'

Quentin laughed. 'We thought it would be New England. Maybe Germany. We're going to grow a garden full of calla lilies and pineapples and mangos.'

'Hawaii is so... so... so far away,' said Rose. 'A long plane ride away.'

'We'll have a guest room. You'll have to come and visit,' said Quentin.

'Nice!' said Kent. 'How does January through March sound?'

There was laughter, though not from Rose or Peter.

It crossed my mind that I could burst into tears and no one would mind. Overcome with emotion, overcome with joy, it would be acceptable. But my eyes were dry as dust. I found my voice. 'This beautiful meal, Rose,' I said. 'Everyone, please, we mustn't let the food get cold,' I said. I spooned more cranberry sauce onto my plate.

'A toast,' said Kent, standing. 'To family, to friends, to the future.'

We raised our glasses. 'The future,' I echoed. Still I couldn't look up into Peter's face. A few feet away. A million miles. It occurred to me that, had things gone differently on Friday night, and was this day not actually happening in real life, he would have found out sooner or later. That even if we'd slept with each other—and I assumed Peter was man who would use protection—we would both have done the math and known he was not this baby's father. But then—.

I was passed the gravy and automatically poured some, watching it run down the mashed potatoes, forging a path to the plate. I couldn't think about what might have happened if things were different. Things were not different. I was going to have a baby, and I was going to raise it with its father. I was going to get on that plane on Tuesday and I was going to live in Hawaii. Not so long ago those two sentences might have been the best ever. I reached for my wine glass and remembered that alcohol was now off limits. Now that I knew I was pregnant. Peter had to realize I hadn't known I was pregnant on Friday—I would not have been drinking alcohol. I took a big drink of water. I started my mantra again in my head: get through today. Get through tomorrow.

I got through the meal. As soon as he could, Peter made his excuses. Saying he had exams and essays to mark, he left his dad to enjoy pie and coffee and asked us to drop his father back home. After thanking Rose, he waved at the room in general, and turned away from the table.

I opened my mouth to call after him, but what was I going to say? "Sorry? Stop? Stay?" I said nothing and watched him go. If he turns around—If he turns back and says my name, I won't go to Hawaii. If he—

He left the dining room, and I heard him pause at the door to put on his boots, and then I heard the door close behind him. He hadn't looked back.

I helped Rose clear the table for dessert. When I put the glass bowl of Peter's cranberry sauce on the kitchen counter she said, 'Oh, toss that. Kent won't eat it.'

But I couldn't throw it out. It represented time together spent picking berries in the late afternoon sun. It was the last physical reminder connecting me to Peter, to these past three weeks, to a potential life I'd glimpsed so briefly, in such vivid technicolour, which had now faded to the sepia photograph of an era long gone. I ate it, all, until it was gone.

'When are you due?' Rose asked me.

I counted out on my fingers. 'The end of January?' I guessed.

She hugged me. 'I love that our babies will be the same age. I just wish... Oh, you're going to be so far away.'

'I know,' I said.

'I can't believe it,' said Rose, her voice as sad as I felt. 'You only got here.'

'I know,' I said. 'I know.' A single tear.

'And now you're leaving. Tomorrow.'

'I know,' I said again. And knew that whatever I told myself about choices, I would get into the rental car the next morning for the drive to Toronto, and there I would get on to an airplane that would take Quentin and I off to our new home. Far, far away from this city, and my family, and Peter.

Chapter Eleven

BIG ROCK LAKE, FEBRUARY 2014

Were emergency room chairs supposed to be this uncomfortable? Were the fluorescent lights intended to be this harsh? I shifted my position, and blinked, but it didn't help.

'I'd like to amend my regret,' I said. 'It's more than not marrying Peter sooner, when maybe there would have been time for us to adopt. I shouldn't have gone back to Quentin.'

'*Gone back to* Quint? What are you talking about?'

Of course Rose didn't know what I was talking about. She didn't know I'd left him. 'After 9/11. No, I mean before. When I started on my walk—'

'Your walk?'

'The Appalachian Trail.'

Rose's face was blank.

'It was a turning point in my life.' I shouldn't be upset that Rose didn't appear to remember it at all. But I was.

'Oh my god, Lily. What was that? Two weeks? I'm sorry I forgot about a two-week episode in your life. But what did that have to do with Quint?'

'He'd had an affair,' I said. 'I'd left him. But the terrorist attack... it changed things. And then I discovered I was pregnant with David.'

Rose's face was no longer blank. 'He—You—You'd left him? And you never breathed a word of it? You never said anything?' We both noticed heads turning as people heard our raised voices.

I spoke softly. 'I tried—I wanted to tell you—'

She shook her head. Spoke through clenched teeth. 'BS. If you'd wanted to tell me, you would have. You would have made the time and found a way.' An eerie echo of our fight at her cottage.

'You're right.'

We were both silent. I stared hard at the bulletin board. I'd read every sign and poster a dozen times, but now, through my tears I couldn't make out any of them. The pale green sheet had details about a support group for children of alcoholics. The yellow one was...? A reminder about paying for parking before you left the building? The one with tattered edges... I had no recollection. I'd been staring at these pieces of paper for hours, but now I couldn't remember what they said.

I fought the sense of panic, closing my eyes and picturing a circle, adding the numbers one through twelve, making the final clock say ten past eleven, then ten to two. A deep breath. My memory was still functioning.

'Did you know, Mum? Did you know any of this?' Rose demanded.

'I did. But it wasn't my place to tell you.'

'No. No it wasn't. It was Lily's.' My sister spoke of me as if I wasn't there.

More silence. My therapist often reminded me that no one could read my mind, and that I had to speak up if I wanted my voice to be heard.

'You're right,' I said again. 'I'm sorry, Rose. I know that's not good enough, but I'm sorry I was too much of a coward to tell you.'

'Coward?'

'You were so happy, you and Kent. Your big house, your first pregnancy. I was jealous. I didn't...' I wasn't sure what I'd intended to say. 'Your life was perfect.'

'Oh please. We were adults. No one's life is perfect.'

'I know that. I knew that.'

'Oh my god.' She broke off, pulled her phone out of her pocket, and began staring at its dark screen.

I could feel her pulling further away from me. 'I'm sorry. I'm sorry.'

'Well.' This from Mum. 'I'm glad you two are finally sharing things.'

'So am I,' I said. 'I really wish I'd shared a lot more over the years. The shitty stuff as well as the good stuff.'

'I didn't teach you, as children, how to have the difficult conversations.'

'I'm not going to blame you, Mum. It's on me.' I'd seen enough therapists over the years, knew that communication—honest communication—was one of the things I found most difficult.

Rose put down her phone. 'Well what else haven't you told me?' she asked in a whisper.

Hawaii, 2001–2002

When we arrived in Hawaii, we went to counselling and Quentin did every assignment, answered every question, as if he was going to be given a mark at the end of the course. We were asked to be honest with each other, but I held back any mention of the time I'd spent with Peter and what I had thought it meant to me at the time. I didn't talk about my first pregnancy and termination. And nor did I tell either Quentin or the therapist about my encounter with Kent and his son. *Again, Daddy. Again.*

Sometimes I said nothing, because it was easier than struggling to express in words thoughts I could barely explain to myself. Other times I presented a version of the truth. 'I thought you were infallible,' I said. 'You've been knocked off the pedestal where I'd put you, and it's a shock.'

'I was never perfect,' Quentin said, tears welling in his eyes. He cried a lot. Maybe someone had told him that tears in the therapist's room were worth bonus points towards the final exam.

'Can you imagine how difficult it was for Quentin to live up to that impossibly high standard you'd set?'

I'd chosen a female therapist, worried a male would somehow side with Quentin, male to male. I hadn't counted on a female being charmed quite so quickly and thoroughly by my husband. But then again, I too had been instantly charmed by Quentin when we first met.

When she asked me about my relationship with my father, I gave few details.

I was honest when I spoke of my fear of Quentin cheating again. Of how difficult it was to believe him when he called me to tell me he'd be late home from work.

'Our country was attacked by terrorists in September,' the therapist said.

'I understand that,' I'd said. 'I understand my husband's job description has changed since the attack. I understand what he does. I understand we are at war.' But I felt that I was not expected to be able to fully understand, as I was not really an American.

I wasn't sure how to talk about how different the reality of Hawaii was to my expectation. It had taken less than a day with a real estate agent to comprehend that we would not be living on a beach, or even be able to afford a view of the ocean. There would not be a garden with fresh pineapple, mangos, or calla lilies. Fort Shafter was seventeen miles from Honolulu, and even I could understand that there was no advantage to living so far away. We moved into a two-bedroom townhouse on base, and soon, apart from the warmer weather, we could have been living anywhere. I felt a like a tourist who goes to Paris and eats poutine. It took half a day to drive around the entire island—I had not known it was so small. Apart from the days we tried to go exploring, when we resembled every other tourist walking along the beach or climbing the volcano or visiting Pearl Harbor and the USS Arizona, there was little to indicate where we lived.

I found a temporary job in the university library which would last until mid-January. This worked perfectly for me; I'd have two weeks off between the end of the job and our baby's due date. I took a bus to the city each morning to go to work in the air-conditioned building, and a bus back home after work. I knew it wasn't Toronto, or St. Louis, or Milwaukee. . . but it could have been.

Quentin agreed to the ultimatum I set: if he was ever again unfaithful, our marriage would end, and after three months of intensive work, the therapist declared us in full recovery. She said our marriage was probably stronger than most, that the infidelity had forced us to initiate difficult conversations that many couples avoided all together. I didn't feel recovered, but nor did I think another six sessions, or sixteen, or even sixty sessions would make any difference. Maybe all I needed was time, and our baby to keep me busy, because I had not yet made any friends. But there were moments—when Quentin and I were decorating the nursery, or sitting on the back deck with iced tea, or when he held his hand on my stomach to feel the baby kicking—that I looked at him and thought, 'Okay, we're okay. I love this man. The father of my child.' I could imagine our future. We even resumed our love life. Sort of.

My last day of work I felt sick all day. I pushed through the nausea until mid-afternoon. Something was wrong. Dreadfully wrong. I called a taxi to take me to the hospital and left a message for Quentin to meet me there.

The midwife held a Doppler machine against my belly. 'When was the last time you felt your wee one moving?'

I closed my eyes. This morning? During the night? Why couldn't I remember? 'Is. . .is everything okay?'

'I'd like you to have a scan,' the midwife said. 'Give me a moment?'

She seemed to spend longer than usual setting up the ultrasound, but as soon as Quentin arrived she was ready for us both. By then I was panicking.

He burst into the room. 'Is this it? Labour?' He stopped grinning as soon as he looked at me. 'Lily? Are you in pain?' He reached for my hand. Looked at the midwife.

After the scan she took a deep breath. 'I'm so sorry—'

I shook my head, turned away from the screen and closed my eyes, willing her not to finish the sentence.

'—I can't find a heartbeat.'

The rest of the day was a blur. Another ultrasound, another expert. I was moved to a private room, away from the maternity ward, and given some medication that knocked me out. I was woken by contractions and remember gripping Quentin's hand through the labour, praying that they were all wrong, that our baby would be fine.

The longest hours of my life. I asked for drugs, for a C-section, for more drugs. But I had to stay conscious, and I had to push.

'It's a boy,' Quentin said, his voice breaking.

I waited for my son's first cry.

It never came.

He was wrapped and passed to me.

'He looks like he's sleeping,' I whispered.

The midwife nodded. 'He's a bonny child.' As if he was alive. 'What's his name?'

Quentin spoke through tears. 'David. After Lily's grandfather. It means beloved.'

We stayed with him for the day, holding him, singing to him, telling him how much we loved him.

It wasn't until after we'd said our final goodbyes that I started to cry, and after half an hour of wracking sobs, clinging to Quentin, I was given a shot of something and knocked out again. When I awoke the next time Mum was there, sitting beside me, my hand in hers.

Big Rock Lake, February 2014

This time it was a woman who took the three of us into the side room to deliver the news.

'An update?' I asked. 'Please tell us it's good news.'

She hesitated, and Rose interpreted the silence to mean the worst possible news. 'No. No. Not... gone—I can't—'

'No!' The woman reached for Rose's hands. 'Not gone.'

Rose fell against Mum, so it was my job to listen and take notes. A stroke. And then another stroke, the second one more serious. More bleeding on the brain, and the original swelling wasn't going down as quickly as hoped. Kent was being put into a medically induced coma.

Back to the waiting room. 'What if Kent—What will I do if he—If he—'

Rose couldn't say the word, but I heard her question: What will I do if Kent dies? I knew the answer but said nothing: You'll survive. You'll have no choice.

Hawaii, 2002–2006

Quentin demanded answers, but there were none. No explanation for baby David's death. Sometimes these things happened, we were told. My body would heal, and the next time I got pregnant there was no reason I wouldn't carry the foetus to full term and deliver a healthy baby. The same speech I'd already heard from so many different doctors.

Mum stayed with us for several weeks and together we dismantled the baby's room. We packed away the crib and all the tiny clothes and toys, took down the mobile and the wall mural, replaced the animal curtains with plain white cotton.

I don't remember much of that spring. It was hot, and I kept our bedroom curtains drawn against the sun and heat. Sometimes Quentin must have come home to find the single coffee cup he'd left by the sink ten hours previously still there, with no sign that I had moved from the bed. Sometimes I forgot Quentin had also lost a baby. Sometimes I forgot that I had ever left him. Sometimes I forgot that I hadn't.

In early April, Rose gave birth to my niece, Madison Mary.

One day in late July, Quentin made me shower and dress for dinner; he had grilled fresh tuna and followed a recipe for pineapple salsa. I complimented him and meant it. He told me the university had rung to ask if I could come back to work in the library in September. Permanently, full-time. He said it was my choice, but he hoped I'd say yes. He had found a support group for parents who'd lost a child to stillbirth and signed us up. It was time, he said, that we try as best we could to resume our married life. I recognized that my days of inactivity would not be allowed to go on indefinitely, and that I had to start playing the role I once knew by heart: wife, worker, sister, daughter. So I tried to imagine what it was I'd ever done before David, and tried as best I could to give a performance that was good enough. I sent emails to Mum and Rose with as much cheerful news as I could find to include. I signed up for an evening course at the university which could, if I wanted, lead to a doctorate down the road. In the support group I wondered out loud why I had dared to imagine this pregnancy would end any differently than any of my others, then cried, because it had ended so differently. I thought I'd grieved after my miscarriages—I hadn't understood what grief was.

I managed to discharge my duties from Monday to Friday; on the weekends I again retreated to the cool darkness of the bedroom.

One Saturday when I woke from a long afternoon siesta, I heard Quentin speaking in a low voice on the phone downstairs. I slowly picked up the receiver in the bedroom and held my hand over the mouthpiece. '—not coming to terms with it,' he was saying. 'If you could, I know this is difficult, and I hate to ask you, but maybe if you could not send quite so many photos of Madison?'

'Oh shit, Quint, of course.' It was Rose. 'She keeps saying she's fine. She keeps asking me for updates. I wondered, but—'

'She doesn't want to worry you,' my husband said to my sister. 'You know how Lily is.'

What was that supposed to mean? How was I?

'Is there anything else I can do?' Rose asked. 'I mean, I'm so far away, but—?'

'Could you come and visit, d'you think? I know she misses you.'

There was a moment of hesitation. 'I miss her too. It's . . . We priced tickets, it's expensive. And a long way. I'm not sure—'

'Don't worry about the tickets,' Quentin said. 'Let me give you tickets. And you could break the trip if that would be easier. A night in Vancouver or LA?'

I wanted to hang up the phone but didn't want either of them to know that I'd been listening in, so I waited until they'd discussed further details, and both had promised to email and agreed to keep the planned trip a surprise from me until it had been finalized. As soon as they said goodbye I hung up, and when I heard Quentin coming up the stairs I turned onto my side and closed my eyes and let him think that I was still asleep.

I knew Quentin was trying. I had to act surprised and delighted that Rose and Kent and baby Madison were coming to visit. And maybe, I thought, I would be able to talk to Rose in person in a way I couldn't in an email. I had not realized that Rose and I would not have any time alone together. For a tiny person who did little more than drink and sleep, Madison seemed to take all of Rose's time and attention. I wasn't jealous of my niece; I simply hadn't anticipated how her birth would change the relationship I shared with Rose.

'She's beautiful,' I kept saying. 'She's perfect. She's lovely.' I oohed and aahed over the tiny fingernails, the pudgy belly, her bright blue eyes.

'I know. I know, right?' Rose was besotted, and Kent equally so.

'My chin, I think, but Red's nose, for sure, don't you think?'

It was a baby chin, a baby nose. I agreed, and wondered if things had been different, if I was holding David in my lap, would Quentin and I be this consumed with every detail of his looks, and bowel movements, and burps, and noises? This holiday was going to centre around Madison's schedule, and I accepted that I was now on the outside of a circle of three. Even when Quentin presented us with vouchers for an afternoon at the spa, Madison came too.

'Ah, look at you all tanned and slender,' Rose said when we stepped into the whirlpool. Madison was sitting in her car seat by the edge of the hot tub. 'I feel like a pasty beached whale by comparison.'

'Yes,' I snapped. 'Of course, I would give anything if the greatest of my worries was how to lose my baby weight.'

'Oh—Lily. Lily. I'm sorry,' Rose was instantly horrified and upset. 'I didn't— I'm devastated. I don't know what to say. I've been—' She was saved by an older woman stopping to coo over the baby, asking after her name and exact age, telling Rose how bright her daughter looked. The woman then joined us in the whirlpool, and we were able to resort to the usual twenty questions about our visit, which hotel we were at, what did we think of that tour over another, oh you live here, you lucky thing, but do you miss the seasons, how can you bear to be so far away from your sister and her baby? This was a conversation I could manage.

Another moment of tension came on the second-last afternoon when I suggested we find a babysitter and the four adults go out for dinner.

'Oh,' said Rose. 'No, thank you. We've never left Maddie alone, you see. And—we couldn't, not here, not with a stranger.' I assured her that I'd found a highly recommended babysitter, but she wouldn't be swayed. She laughed. 'We'd be those nightmare new parents anyhow, on the phone every five minutes, checking in. If you guys need a night off baby duty, the two of you can go out,' she suggested. 'Kent and I are fine on our own.'

That wasn't what I'd intended, I explained, we'd have plenty of nights for dinner out after they'd gone back to Canada. I didn't want to miss a moment of their visit. Should we go to a child-friendly place of their choosing, or would it be easier to have dinner here at home?

When the guys were on the balcony, Rose tried to further justify her reluctance to leave Madison. 'You may have forgotten, but Kent's adopted. So Maddie is actually his first biological relative. The first time he held her...' She grinned. 'It was so precious.'

I bit my tongue.

Rose gave me a long hug at the departures gate. 'I love you, Lily,' she'd said fiercely. I was surprised to see tears in her eyes. 'I am so so sorry about your baby.'

'David,' I said. 'His name is David.'

'David,' she repeated. 'I—I should have asked you... if you wanted to talk about him, about...'

His death. His stillbirth. She couldn't even say the words. And maybe if our roles were reversed and I was the sister holding a live, healthy baby in my arms, maybe I'd be struggling to say those words.

'But I'm so glad you're okay, I mean, as okay as possible.' She hugged me again. Told me again that she loved me.

I wanted to tell her that I wasn't okay, but I wasn't sure what she could do with that piece of information for fifteen hours on a plane.

'I love you too,' I said, returning her hug. 'Thank you for flying, I know that was stressful for you.' Then I kissed Madison. 'I love you too. Don't forget your old aunt. Come back and visit often.'

'We will,' Rose promised. 'This has been so great.' She hugged Quentin and whispered something I couldn't hear.

When we were walking through the parking lot, I reached for Quentin's hand. 'Thank you. That was lovely. Although it was a long two weeks in some ways, wasn't it?'

'It will be nice to have our place to ourselves again. But it's always good to see your family. You enjoyed all that time with Rose, didn't you?' He sounded anxious.

Be truthful, I told myself. He's your husband. If you can't tell him the truth, then who can you tell? Tell him that you feel you didn't have any real, quality time with Rose, that you feel more alone now than you felt before she came, that it was too difficult to see her baby. Her living, healthy baby.

But my words weren't the right ones to properly explain what I was feeling. I sounded churlish and ungrateful in my own mind, like I wanted to argue, as I had so often in the past. I wasn't supposed to know this entire trip had been his treat—a generous treat. I had seen the price of the tickets. 'It was fantastic,' I lied. I squeezed his hand. 'And I loved watching you with Maddie. I always knew you'd be a good dad.' The closest thing to acknowledging our loss I'd said outside the safety of the support group.

'I hoped it would help, you seeing your sister,' he said, embracing me in a hug. 'But if I'd known it would work this well, I'd have asked her out long ago.' He chuckled. His tone grew more serious. 'But, truly Lily. I'm so thankful you're better.'

I'm not better. I will never be better. But it was easier, safer, not to say those words out loud. To pretend that I was 'better.' 'You've been so patient,' I said. That was true. 'I know it hasn't been easy for you.'

We got in the car, and I had a momentary flash of Peter holding open the passenger side door for me. I shook the memory from my head.

'Lily? What's up?' Concern in his voice.

'Nothing. Kicking myself for forgetting to say a proper goodbye to Kent,' I said. When had it become so easy to lie?

'Send him an email,' said Quentin. 'Tell him you think Madison definitely inherited his ear lobes.' We smiled at each other. Quentin started the car, and we drove towards our home, our life, our future.

Their holiday was an annual vacation for four more years. But the year Maddie's new sister, Aidan, was two, and air sick all the way from Toronto to LA and then LA to Honolulu, Maddie cut her foot on a clam shell on the first afternoon, which turned out to be the single sunny day of the twelve-day visit. With the beach a wash, literally, and Maddie not even able to swim in a pool, and Aidan teething and fussy. All the other tourists also seeking indoor entertainment for their children, and our two-bedroom townhouse no longer really big enough for everyone, especially with most of the day spent inside, the twelve days dragged. Kent and Quentin grew quieter and more polite to each other as the time went by.

Maddie chose this holiday to learn that having a baby sister meant she would never again have both her parents focused solely on her, and she tried to rectify the imbalance with ever more outrageous behaviour. She refused to eat whatever she was offered the first time, even if it had been her absolute favourite the previous meal. She insisted on changing her outfit at least three times each day, and once worn, declared everything dirty and wouldn't touch it until it had been laundered. I wanted to joke that she was late for the terrible twos, or ask if it wasn't supposed to be the youngest who was the spoiled child, but didn't want to risk having my comments met with hostility or be taken as aggressive. Occasionally I wanted to point out that she was not starving and would eat when she was hungry, and allowing her to call the shots at this age was dangerous. But I was very aware that I was an aunt, not a parent, and I did not have the right to offer advice.

I understood we were beyond the time of flared tempers when Madison managed to break our brand new television screen and Quentin merely laughed it off. 'Never mind, it's only money, right? We'll earn some more.' I had not mentioned to Rose that Quentin's new title at work brought with it more work and longer hours, not a raise in pay. Or that I was now working part-time due to the time my research required. Or the price of my degree. Nor had I told Rose about our new obstetrician and the monthly fertility treatments and how much they were costing us, financially, physically, emotionally.

I noticed she had taken down the photograph of David hanging in the spare room, and when I asked her about it she said it would be too difficult to explain a ghost cousin to the girls.

Big Rock Lake, February 2014

'You took down our photograph of David,' I said now.

Neither Rose nor Mum had a clue what I was talking about. Of course not. They'd been worrying about Kent, not reliving my past.

'When you came to visit us in Hawaii the last time, Rose. You said you didn't want to explain a ghost cousin to Maddie and Aidan.'

'I don't remember.'

'No. No reason you should. It was a fraught time.'

'Fraught? We loved our holidays with you. I was so jealous—you lived in Hawaii! But a picture of David—he was dead, Lily. You hung a picture of a dead baby on the wall of the guest room.'

My baby. They were the only pictures I had of my baby. 'He looks like he's sleeping,' I whispered. 'He looks like an angel, watching over his cousins from heaven.' I opened my wallet to the tiny black and white photo I carried with me. 'An angel cousin, not a ghost cousin. I wanted his portrait to inspire love and comfort, not fear.'

Rose looked at the photo, then at me. 'I wish you'd said something. I wish you'd explained that to me. Of course I could have done that for you.'

'For me, yes. But also for your girls. For Quentin.'

'Lily... I can't read your mind. I never could. I didn't know. But I am truly sorry—that must have seemed callous and it must have hurt.'

'I guess... I guess I always wanted you to be able to read my mind. So I didn't have to say the difficult things out loud.'

Hawaii, 2006–2007

That last holiday I raised the topic of pregnancy once. Rose, happy now to leave her two children with a babysitter she'd never met before, was the one who suggested an adults-only dinner, though our husbands declined the invitation and sent us out alone. Rose ordered us each the cocktail of the day; clearly she hadn't noticed that I'd not had a sip of alcohol since she'd arrived. As the last five attempts at artificial insemination hadn't worked, one drink might not make any difference to the success or failure rate of this current round of medications and shots. But it wasn't a risk I was willing to take.

'Cheers,' she said, clinking her glass to mine when the multi-coloured drink arrived bedecked with tropical fruit and a pink flamingo stir stick. 'My god, I'm shattered. Everyone says two kids is easier than one, but that's a crock.' She laughed. 'Not that I'd change a thing, of course, and they're growing up so quickly, but it will be nice when Aidan is sleeping through the night.' There had been a lot of crying, and in fact I suspected no one had slept through any night.

'I'm sorry we had to cram you all into one room,' I said.

'Maybe we'll rent a time-share next year,' Rose said.

'Maybe we'll have won the lottery and have a four-bedroom house on the beach,' I said. I picked up the rum punch, then put it down without a sip and drank my water instead. 'We're having fertility treatments,' I said.

'Oh.'

'It's my body, not cooperating.'

'I didn't... know...'

'David was our miracle.' I had convinced myself that my first pregnancy would also have resulted in a healthy baby, had I only been brave enough at the time.

Rose was silent for a long time. She finished her drink, and I passed her mine. I opened my mouth to tell her that I was aching for a child, and my anguish was unbearable. There were days I wished I'd been the one to die. 'It's a shame the weather has been so lousy,' I said.

'I know.' Relief in her voice. A painless subject. 'Ugh. I bet it's sunny the minute our plane lifts off.' She smiled. 'Maybe you could come back to Canada next time. It really would be easier for us not to have to travel all this way. You know, with the girls.'

What I knew was that Quentin was still paying for their plane tickets and everyone was happy to pretend that he wasn't. I bit back a comment about looking a gift horse in the mouth. 'We were back home for Christmas last year,' I reminded her. Despite repeated invitations, Mum had not come back to Hawaii since her emergency visit when David was born.

'And that was great. You should come in the summer too,' she said. 'The weather never disappoints in Ontario, you know that. Guaranteed sunshine.'

I looked at her; she appeared to be serious. 'I think it rains in the summer in Ontario too,' I said, waiting for her to smile. She didn't.

'Oh, look, let's not talk about the weather. This is the first time in ages it's been just us. Let me tell you all about Maddie's dance recital. It was the cutest thing. Here, I have a video of it on my camera.' I was glad the screen was so small that I couldn't tell which child was my niece.

I took them to the airport myself on the day they left, and we said goodbye long before their plane was due to depart. I left them to wander through the shops rather than seeing them through security. I stopped for blood work on the way home, was not surprised that the results were not what had been hoped for, and took a detour to walk along a short stretch of beach, once again packed with tourists, as the sun (exactly as predicted) had come out. When I heard a plane above me, I shaded my eyes and looked up. It might have been the one Rose was on, it might not have been, but all the same I waved.

I anticipated that in six months or so I would receive an email from my sister saying that they had decided to give us a break this year, they'd booked an all-inclusive in Florida, or one of the cheaper Caribbean islands, that it was such a great deal, and so much closer, and a colleague of Kent's had a condo nearby and kids the same age as the girls... It was so vivid a picture that I almost sent her the suggestion when I got home. But instead, I wrote to Mum:

> *I miss the seasons. Almost five years have passed and the only way I really know that is because my newborn baby niece is now a four-year-old hellion. I'm sorry not to have made any friends other than fellow ex-pats, all of whom leave eventually. I am neither fish nor fowl—not a local who really belongs here nor a tourist who has two weeks to do nothing. The child-free wives of Quentin's colleagues are all newlyweds in their twenties or women whose children have grown and left home—I struggle to*

> make conversation with either group. Quentin loves this life, and has asked to stay on, despite the stress of his new job. He hopes to work here through to retirement and then get the same or similar job as a civilian; if he never leaves, he'll be happy. I have tried to see his attraction to this place, but have failed. I'd rather be back on the mainland, close enough to you to visit for a weekend, play a game of Scrabble, sit at the kitchen table for a cup of tea. I want to reminisce about the Old Homestead with you, and tell you that I don't think I can keep trying for a baby this way and having my heart broken month after month. Those magical weeks when I lived with you in Big Rock Lake after 9/11 feel like a dream that might have happened to someone else. I miss you so much, Mum.

I looked at the words and felt tears welling in my eyes. It wasn't fair to offload all my sadness onto my mother. I deleted the email, word by word, and started again:

> It was lovely to see Rose—aren't the girls growing up quickly?!—shame that the rainy season started early, resulting in lousy weather, but it was super to have so much time for us all to chat and catch up.
> It's Thursday evening your time, so you must be about to sit down for dinner with Mr. Reynolds.

I cc'd Rose, so she knew what version of events I'd told Mum. In this, at least, we were in full agreement. Keep Mum happy.

Mum's reply came moments later:

> I love it when we're on the computer at the same time! You feel so much closer. Sad news, I'm afraid—Warren had a stroke, a bad one, and the house has been put up for sale. I fear the Thursday Night Dinners have come to an end. I feel I did well by Felicia, but have not truly fulfilled my side of the deal.

That took me a moment to digest, to remember that Mr. Reynolds was Warren to everyone except me.

> So sad! What's the prognosis? And how's poor Peter coping? And, Mum, you have **more** than met your side of the deal! How many dinners d'you reckon you've cooked Mr. Reynolds over the years?

I sat in front of the computer, waiting until I heard the ping of an incoming message.

> Warren survived the stroke—he was lucky it happened on a Sunday and Peter was with him. He is recovering slowly, still in the hospital but a longer-term solution will have to be found. I gather no one thinks he'll be able to cope on his own—hence the 'For Sale' sign next door. Guess how much they're asking? (Do you remember what your grandparents paid for this house in 1976?) I saw Peter and his partner the other day when I was visiting Warren—he looks tired, as one would expect. I suppose I look tired too.

We all look tired, I thought. We all are tired. Rose is tired because she's raising two children, one of whom appears to run the household. Aidan is tired because she's teething, and Maddie because her sister's screaming keeps her awake at night. I'm tired because I'm almost forty and I've lost all hope in IVF and I don't have a single close friend. Quentin is tired because he's working extra-long hours and his wife is unhappy.

Of Peter's partner, I asked Mum for no details.

'I'm so sorry about the television,' I said to Quentin when he got home. I'd made an effort with dinner, grilling mahi-mahi, and making proper side dishes. I poured myself a small glass of chilled white wine.

He shrugged. 'No use crying over spilled milk. But I think we'll have to rethink the arrangements before their next visit.'

'I agree,' I said quickly. 'This house isn't big enough for a family of four plus us. I think, perhaps, this should be their last visit. For now.'

'You'd be okay with that?' Quentin asked.

'It was exhausting. Their whole visit was exhausting,' I said. 'I'm exhausted. Aren't you exhausted?'

He smiled. 'I am exhausted. But she's your sister—'

'And I love her, I do. And I love those girls, even though one of them is spoiled rotten and the other does nothing but cry. But...' I raised my glass and clinked it to his. 'To us,' I said simply.

'To us,' he echoed. He looked pointedly at the glass. 'Are you sure it's alright to have a drink? That won't mess up... anything?'

'I think—I think we need to consider taking a break from the IVF,' I said. 'A break. For a few months. I mean, I'm not making an executive decision, we'll discuss it, of course, but—'

He was shaking his head. 'No discussion needed. I agree. I so very much agree, B.' I thought again of how tired we all were; Quentin was so tired he'd started shortening my nickname from Honey Bee to B. He clinked his glass against mine again. 'I hope you really enjoy it, that wine. You must have missed it.'

'Do you know what I miss?' I had planned this speech, which wasn't entirely true, so I didn't give him a chance to guess, but said what I thought he might want, or perhaps even need, to hear. 'I miss making love with each other without first checking my body temperature or stabbing myself in the thigh. I miss cuddling in the morning when perhaps we don't want to have sex. I miss holding your hand when we walk along the beach without feeling the gesture has to be foreplay. I miss evenings, like this one, when we can admit we're shattered and want to fall into bed and go to sleep.' It was what I'd intended to say to sway him if he was reluctant to stop the IVF, but I wanted him to hear it all the same. Sex was the glue that had held us together—and had nearly split us apart—and I wanted him to know that it was still important to me. Even though I wasn't at all sure it was.

He kissed me, and said dinner smelled lovely and I understood that to mean thank you, he had heard me, and yes, he too was looking forward to resuming our love life, though not that very night, tired as we both were. Or that week, as it turned out, or very often at all in fact.

A month later he was told that he was being deployed and I said the timing worked well because I was finishing the last course I needed for my doctorate; all that was left was to write my dissertation. He couldn't quite mask his surprise but I forgave his not having remembered that a PhD was the ultimate goal with all these courses I'd been taking. It wasn't something I spoke about at home. In the past he might have made a joke about higher education, or Jack of all trades, master of none, but he simply said he was glad I'd be so busy while he was overseas, and asked me to recommend a novel or two he might enjoy while he was away.

'Seriously?'

'Seriously. Reading has been your constant love. I figure there must be something to it.'

Early in the new year I had a letter from the clinic asking us what were our plans for the rest of our fertilized eggs, and a bill for their storage, and could I please contact them to confirm if they should be stored or destroyed. I knew this was not a decision I should make without consulting the owner of the sperm, the would-be father of those potential babies, so that evening I spoke to Quentin about it. But I was clear that my mind was made up: I didn't want to get pregnant again. I didn't think I could survive nine months of anticipation, knowing that at the end of it all I might lose another baby. We. We might lose another baby.

The next day I contacted the clinic and told them we had no plans for further inseminations, that we both felt the treatment had run its course, that as I was approaching forty years of age we had no need for storage, thank you. We were given an appointment to further discuss this decision with one of their members of staff, but I didn't go. And then I spent money I'd been saving in our baby account on a television to replace the one Madison had broken and took a day off working on my dissertation and hiked up to a waterfall not noted on any tourist map. I stripped off my clothes and slipped into the pool at the base of the falls and said goodbye to all the children I'd not been able to bear and scattered some wildflower seeds in memory of David.

When Quentin got home and had settled back as much as could be hoped, I asked him if he'd teach me how to throw a dart.

'Seriously?'

'Seriously. You love darts. I figure there must be something to it.'

We discovered I wasn't completely hopeless, and we started playing together several times a week.

In May I was conferred with my doctoral degree, a PhD in Library and Information Studies. I had intended to invite Mum to come to the commencement ceremony, and I think she would have made the trip, but in late March we had had a shock and in early April I had found an unopened condom in a pair of Quentin's jeans when I was doing the wash. I'd said nothing to him. I was almost grateful to the woman, whoever she was, for relieving me of the pressure to have sex with him more often than I did, which was so infrequently we sometimes went for weeks with barely any physical contact at all. Since his return from this recent deployment, nothing. I decided, this time, I would wait and see rather than confront. I knew I was avoiding the truth; we had agreed during the long-ago sessions of marital counselling that I had the right to issue an ultimatum, and I had. If he had another extra marital affair, if he was unfaithful, either sexually or emotionally, then our marriage would end. I had been warned that I had to be sure I would live up to my end of the bargain, told that if I chose to stay in the marriage when I knew he was being unfaithful then no ultimatum I ever issued again could be taken seriously. Of course those sessions of therapy were so far in the past that I imagined the ultimatum might no longer be valid. Well beyond the statute of limitations.

All the same, I waited out the summer. And the fall. And when in mid-October Quentin said maybe it was time we discuss holiday plans, I said maybe it was time to discuss plans for the longer term.

When I asked who she was, he looked almost relieved that it was out in the open. 'Beatrix Johnson.'

A colleague. I vaguely remembered her name having been mentioned. I thought she'd been in Iraq. 'Beatrix.'

'Bea,' said my husband.

'Bea,' I echoed. 'I see.' Some time ago I'd thought he was so tired he'd shortened 'Honey Bee' to B, but he was so tired he was calling his wife by his mistress's nickname. Confirmation that this relationship had been going on for well over a year.

'Maybe if we hadn't lost David. Or if you loved this island life the way I do. Or if my deployments had been easier on both of us.'

'Maybe,' I said. 'Maybe if I was better at making friends. Or if we'd started sharing our hobbies sooner.' I thought of all the other things we hadn't done, or things we could have done differently.

This time there were no arguments, no begging for forgiveness, no promises of counselling and never doing it again, no pleas for me to reconsider leaving. I was shocked at how little our day-to-day life changed; he was out of the house, working or otherwise, the same hours as he'd always been. I went to work at the library then came home and cooked dinner, and like any other couple we passed evening hours watching television or reading. We continued to play darts. He took great pride in introducing me as 'His wife, the Doctor.'

One night, after we had turned out the lights, he turned to me. 'I do love you, Lily.'

'I know,' I said. 'I know.'

'You'll always be my Honey Bee.'

He started to cry, and I held him and comforted as best I could. I understood that he would never have been the one to leave, that he would have been content to carry on as we had been ad infinitum. I wondered why Beatrix Johnson was not demanding more action on his part—perhaps she was married herself and a part-time lover suited her—but I wasn't curious enough to bother finding out. I thought how sad it was that we were breaking up just when we had truly learned how to live together, and said as much. 'You've become my best friend. I'll miss our companionship so much.'

'That breaks my heart,' he said. 'You've always been my best friend.'

There was no intention on my part to make any grand statement to mark my departure. I remembered with amazement the last time, planning my long walk which would, I had believed at the time, change everything. I didn't have the energy now to even consider the amount of planning involved in such a scheme, let alone actually walking. I wandered around the condo, picking up a vase, staring at a picture on the wall, holding an ornament in my hand. All the memories I'd once thought so important to preserve were now going to fade. I thought about packing but was in no great rush because I liked my job and my colleagues, and I wasn't unhappy. Although I'd decided to leave, I wasn't without regrets, and I had nowhere specific to go. I spent some weeks composing an email to Mum and Rose telling them that Quentin and I had filed for divorce and I would be back in Canada in late November.

Chapter Twelve

Big Rock Lake, February 2014

'Hey, Rose.' It was a police officer. Kendra. She was holding up a phone. 'Some of us... if it's okay with you... we've set up a GoFundMe page for Kent. For you and the girls.'

Rose looked confused, then nodded. 'That's—Thank you.'

I peered at the tiny screen. 'Two thousand three hundred dollars.'

'Yeah,' Kendra seemed embarrassed. 'It's only been up a couple of hours and, you know, a lot of people aren't aware yet. The number will climb. It's going to make a difference.'

'No, no. That's amazing. It already has,' I said. 'So generous. Thank you.'

'I, uh. I have to go now, get my kids off to school, you know. But we won't leave you alone, Rose.'

Rose nodded, thanked the woman again. 'Kendra's taking her kids to school? Now?'

'Yes, and Carla will take your girls,' Mum assured her.

As if on cue, a text arrived for Rose from her neighbour. 'It's pyjama day,' she said. She showed Mum and me the photos Carla had sent.

'I'm right on trend,' I said, pointing at my kitty cat pyjama legs. 'First time in my life.'

Rose looked at me. 'I hadn't noticed. You didn't even get dressed. You came straight here.'

'You needed me.'

'I did. I do.'

'I haven't always been there when you needed me. I'm sorry, Rose. Not that sorry is enough.'

My sister reached for my hand. 'It's enough. It's enough.'

It must have been shift change for the police. Nine officers left the hospital, all stopping to say words of comfort to Rose, then seven more arrived, also stopping to talk to Rose.

'Like a family,' I mused out loud. 'I could have embraced the military as a family if I'd let myself.'

'Both of you,' said Mum quietly.

'Both of us?'

'You both married men in uniform, with steady jobs. The polar opposite of your father.'

In uniform. I thought that was perhaps code for men who belonged to structured organizations. Workers with a clear career path set out for them. Even Peter, as a teacher, had had some of that stability.

'But Kent's a lot like Dad too,' said Rose.

'Really?'

'He adores his children. He makes us all laugh. He tells ridiculous stories. He loves puttering around outside.

That was how Rose remembered Bobby? Not as an argumentative drunk?

'I'm glad you have such happy memories of your father,' said Mum.

I tried to think back, way back. I knew I had equally happy memories, from the time before. Of course I did. 'Memory's odd—'

Rose spoke too. 'Time's odd—'

Mum was smiling. 'You remind me of the twins sometimes. Speaking over each other, saying the same or almost the same thing.'

'You first,' I said to Rose. 'Time . . .'

She shrugged. 'I dunno. I feel like I've completely lost track of time.'

'Me too,' I said. Time in the emergency waiting room had become a meaningless blur, like those six years in Hawaii.

Big Rock Lake, 2007

My arrival in Big Rock Lake that late November held with it a remarkable sense of déjà vu. It was a grey afternoon and I took a cab from the tiny new airport through the grey weather, the grey city streets lined with small piles of dirty grey snow.

The cabbie was chatty. 'That's a nice tan. Been somewhere nice?'

'Honolulu,' I said.

'I hear that's a lovely place. Rest and relaxation, was it? Nice to escape this lousy weather.' He was being friendly; I didn't correct him.

'Um. Winter proper must be on its way,' I said resorting to a safe topic.

'We always start to hope, this time of year, don't we?' He gestured to the edge of the road with a sigh. 'A white Christmas, the snowmobile trails open in time for the holiday. That'd be nice.'

I knew how this conversation went. 'Then by mid-February we'll all start complaining that it's too cold and too dark, and wondering how long until Spring.'

He chuckled, agreed.

The city had grown and changed yet again. The Reynolds house—no longer theirs, I reminded myself—had been refinished on the outside, a modern combination of grey stone and siding, and it looked as if a professional landscaper had renovated the front garden. I wondered if it had been gutted and updated inside, as well. Our house looked as it always had. Mum's door opened before the cabbie parked and Madison and Aidan spilled on to the front porch. 'Aunt Lily! Aunt Lily!'

'That's a super welcoming committee you've got there,' said the cabbie. He carried my bags up to the door and I paid, then over-tipped him with American bills. 'Are you sure?'

'I'm sorry,' I apologized. 'I haven't got any Canadian money.'

'But this is way too much.'

I waved away his protest, pleased that someone, at least, would feel cheerful today.

Mum and Rose were at the door, there were hugs all round. In the kitchen there was a massive 'Welcome Home Dr. Aunt Lily' poster, made by Madison and Aidan, covered with photographs of the three of us. On the table, a homemade carrot cake, three mugs for tea, and a bottle of bright red juice. I examined the poster in detail, oohing and awing.

'It's time for cake now,' said Madison. 'And we have some very exciting news.' She looked at her younger sister, who nodded. Clearly they had practiced the timing and delivery of this exciting news.

'We're going to be big sisters!' There was squealing and jumping and laughter.

It took me a moment to translate their words. 'Rose!' I looked at her, saw instantly beneath the baggy sweater what I ought to have noticed first thing. It took me a second to remember the word I had to say: 'Congratulations!'

She nodded, beaming. 'Due in May. And this time you'll be here for it all,' she said. 'Not the exotic aunt flying in with presents, but here for the everyday miracles—first steps, the first words.' There was more: two heartbeats. Twins.

I had amassed years of practice at play-acting, so it was not a challenge to be Pleased Sister or Excited Aunt for the rest of the afternoon. And at dinner I even managed to be Civil Sister-in-Law.

'Twins!' I said, several times. That was enough for everyone else to leap in with calculations as to the number of diapers that would be needed, suggestions for renovating the guest room into a nursery, amazement over the luck of wishing for one more child and being given two, the chances they'd be boys.

'You once asked me if Kent was a twin,' said Rose. 'D'you remember?'

'No,' I lied. 'I thought you had three older sisters,' I said to him.

'Yeah, that's right.'

'Auntie Kimberley, Auntie Angela, and Auntie Jennifer,' recited Madison. I was delighted that the brat I remembered had grown into a lovely child. It was a single short period of her life, I reminded myself, and it had been a poor holiday for everyone. Not a great time to judge anyone's true nature.

'I wonder why you thought Kent was a twin,' said Rose.

'The two Ks maybe, Kent and Kimberly,' I said. Where had that lie come from? 'Will you give your twins matching names, do you think?'

The happiest moment of my evening came after dessert, when Madison got down from her chair and came over to mine. 'Will you cuddle me, please Aunt Lily?' she asked. 'I've missed your cuddles more than anything.' Without waiting for an answer, she sat in my lap and lay her head against my chest. My hands automatically reached to circle her. I would never be able to hug my own child. This was the next best thing.

I looked down at her dark head and fell in love with her exactly as I had when Rose had first put her into my arms. 'I remember when you were a tiny baby,' I said.

'Was I a very naughty baby?' she asked.

'No. You were the best baby ever. You never cried, you never fussed at all, even when you were teething.'

'Pah!' said Rose. 'Don't you believe everything your aunt tells you, Maddie,' she said.

'It's true,' I whispered to the girl on my lap. 'You were the best.'

'I was a very fussy baby when I was teething,' said Aidan. She sounded proud of the fact. 'We went to your house and nobody got even one wink of sleep!'

'Now that is a true statement,' said Rose and I at the same time. We both laughed.

'Ohhh, I remember that,' said Kent. 'Are we completely crazy, Red, to be starting this all over again?'

'We are,' said Rose.

'You are,' Mum said at the same time. More laughter.

'And what if the doctor has missed a heartbeat?' I said. 'What if you're having triplets?'

'Ahh. Stop it,' said Kent. 'Red, make your sister stop.' For a moment we all laughed together, and I forgot that I didn't like him. He was family. The father of my nieces, the husband of my sister, who was my best friend in the world. I was surrounded by family, and I was home.

At dinner time, still surrounded by my loved ones, I pictured Quentin sitting alone at our glass-topped table. Before I'd left, I had cooked and frozen a month's worth of dinners for him, left them neatly labelled in the freezer, then wondered, as I'd done so, if it was an odd thing to do. Had he found them, and eaten one this evening? Or had he and Bea gone out somewhere to celebrate his freedom? I held my cellphone in my hand for twenty minutes thinking about calling him, just to hear his voice. In the end I wrote a brief text. *Arrived safely. Miss you.* I added a heart symbol and pressed send before I could reconsider.

Sitting on the planes from Honolulu to LA, LA to Toronto, then the puddle jumper to Big Rock Lake, I had told myself I'd stay in my hometown until I made a plan. I had no idea what that plan might even involve.

The next day I put a piece of paper and pencil in front of me on the red and white checkered tablecloth. In May I would turn forty. Rose would give birth to her twins. Mum would retire from her job. This summer Rose and Kent would celebrate eight years of marriage; Quentin and I had not made our fifteenth anniversary. I stared at the paper for half an hour, then put it away.

'I don't even know where to start,' I told Mum. 'I'm further behind than I was twenty years ago.'

'You don't have to decide everything all at once,' she said. 'Do you remember how little I did the years after Bobby and I separated?'

I thought back to that time. Told her, honestly, that I didn't. 'You'd always done everything,' I said. 'Nothing really changed. Apart from you didn't have to chop wood, or grow our food, or deal with the million and one other things living on the Old Homestead required.'

My mother smiled at me. 'Bless you. I forget you were still so young then. You know, some days it doesn't seem so long ago. Every so often I read an article in the paper and start to think, "I should cut that one out for Bobby," before I remember he's gone.'

'Time is odd,' I agreed. 'I've just spent six years in Hawaii and I could sum it up in a few sentences.' I'd met tourists who'd spent two weeks there, but because it was the holiday of a lifetime, they could speak of the island for hours, giving a moment-by-moment breakdown of their experience.

'I'm sorry to have left my job,' I said. 'I shall miss that.'

'There's a posting for a job in the university archives if you're interested. It could tide you over,' said Mum.

They were desperate; the previous archivist had left six months earlier. I was interviewed two days after I submitted my resume, and there was a message on the phone when I arrived home from the interview, offering me the job. Three weeks after I left my job in Hawaii, I was starting a new, but nearly identical job, five thousand miles away. To tide myself over, I told myself. Until I had a real plan.

Big Rock Lake, February 2014

'Hey, Lily.' I looked up at the sound of Kathleen's voice. 'Rose.'

My friend draped a silver-grey shawl over my sister's shoulders, then knelt down and pulled her into her arms. 'We're all praying,' she said. 'For you, for Kent, for your girls. This is our hug for you, knitted with love.'

'This is so beautifully soft,' Rose said. 'And I don't . . . I don't even go to church.'

'I've brought the church to you,' whispered Kathleen. She held Rose for several minutes, then turned to hug me. 'Peter is fine,' she whispered. 'Don't you worry about a thing.'

'I didn't call work. I just remembered.'

Kathleen shook her head. 'I've got your back. Family first.'

'She's so kind,' Rose said, after Kathleen had left.

'Yes, she's wonderful.' It had taken me so long to find such a good female friend, but it had been worth the years of loneliness. 'She's been wonderful from the very first time we met.'

Big Rock Lake, 2007–2008

During my first day of work at the university I was introduced to everyone in the library, then taken to the lunch room. I was shown how the fancy coffee machine worked, presented with a cake that read "Welcome, Lily!" and a mug with daisies on it. 'Closest thing we could find to a lily in the campus shop,' said a woman. As she served the cake, she told us about the Zumba classes she'd started. '—said shake your booty but I heard booby, so what the heck.' She demonstrated her booby shake to hoots of laughter.

One thing I *had* learned as a military spouse was how to integrate myself into a new group of colleagues. 'I'm the person hiding at the back of the room who turns right when everyone else is turning left,' I said.

'Yes! And when I remember what a flipping 'grapevine is' the instructor changes it to a 'reverse grapevine'!' The booby-shaking woman grinned at me. 'I'm Kathleen. You are going to fit in with us perfectly.' Later that week she admitted they'd been worried. 'All we knew about you was that you come from Hawaii and you have a PhD in Library and Information Science.' She pointed at herself. 'Born here and never left. Grade Thirteen. Fourteen if you count my victory lap.'

'I actually come from six miles away,' I said. 'And my degree was mostly a way to avoid going stir-crazy on a small island.'

'Stop it!' She mock punched me in the upper arm. 'Never let me hear you downplaying your intelligence. I'm not even qualified for my position by today's standards. Thank goodness I've been working here so long they can't get rid of me.' Later I learned that she was only one course away from her undergraduate degree, and already accepted into an MILS programme. She laughed. 'I love having a friend who has a doctorate.' And I understood I was being given the chance to make a friend who wasn't going to move away in six months or a year. A friend who had, apparently, already decided she liked me.

There was more than enough work to keep me busy, to stop me dwelling on the past or worrying too much about the future. I told Mum I'd find an apartment, but she said she enjoyed my company, so I stayed. Outside, the snow started to fall in earnest and it was dark by four o'clock. Christmas came and went. One Thursday evening in January, I asked Mum how Mr. Reynolds was doing. 'It's odd,' said Mum. 'You wouldn't think I could lose touch with a neighbour I've known over thirty years, but after his stroke, after he left the hospital...'

I tried calling Peter, but that number was no longer in service. There wasn't a Reynolds listed in the phone book at his address, and when I rang the school where he'd taught his whole life, they said he was on an extended leave of absence. They were happy to take my number and leave a note for him, but he'd not checked for messages for some time. Would I like to leave my name? I thanked them, but said no.

Winter finally gave way to spring. We had a retirement party for Mum the weekend before the twins arrived. Two girls. Sydney and Mackenzie.

'Odd names,' Mum said to me when we were alone. 'But I daresay people thought I was odd to name my daughters after flowers.'

'I love the names you chose,' I said.

'I've always disliked Judith,' Mum said. 'I tried to be Judy or Jude, but no.'

'I remember that,' I said. 'And I remember Bobby calling you J.'

My mother's features softened, and I wondered if she was recalling a specific moment, or just the sound of Bobby using her nickname. 'Am I making this up, or did he have a beautiful voice?'

'Dreamy. Rich. Yes, he had a gorgeous voice. Persuasive.' She chuckled. 'He convinced me that if we moved to a scrap of bush, seven miles from anywhere, we'd watch sunrises and sunsets and live happily ever after. I wanted to believe him. I so wanted to believe him.'

A hint of a memory appeared and immediately vanished. My parents arguing in low voices when I was supposed to be sleeping. My mum, clearly angry, muttering that she wished she could believe him. She so wanted to believe him. And Bobby, pleading with her, teasing her. Why was I convinced that at the time I knew he was lying to her? But his words had worked; moments later the unmistakable sound of kissing.

Kathleen quickly became more than a colleague. She refused to let me stay buried in the archives all day, dragging me out for coffee, for lunchtime walks around the campus, and to occasional evening events. When she discovered it was my birthday there were streamers on my desk, and a bag of gourmet coffee, and fancy cupcakes for our coffee break. One Saturday she invited me to dinner, and when I arrived I discovered I'd been seated next to a pharmacist friend of hers, William, recently divorced. 'Ah,' he said. 'Another of Kathleen's cunning plans to keep me from wallowing in misery.' At the end of the evening he told me that I was lovely, really lovely, and clearly an interesting and intelligent woman. 'Kathleen would love me to invite you out. But it's too soon for me to think about dating. I have two children and they have to be my priority right now.' He was sorry, maybe in the future. Perhaps we could keep in touch?

Perhaps, I echoed. But neither of us gave the other our phone number.

Monday morning Kathleen apologized. 'You're both such lovely people. I hate to see you so alone, and so sad.' I assured her I wasn't sad. I joined her book club, though I politely declined her requests to join her church. I thought about signing up for a photography course, and realized that if I didn't soon formulate a plan I'd put down roots. I voiced my concern to Kathleen, momentarily forgetting she had been born and raised here, married her high school sweetheart, and raised three children. 'Roots are a good thing, Lil,' she said. She knew a little of my past. 'All that moving about, now's your chance.' The next day I found a bright yellow flowerpot on my desk with a card: *you'll have to wait and see what it becomes—hint, it's got roots*. I blinked—I had befriended Kathleen more quickly than anyone, anywhere, ever before.

That evening there was a manilla envelope waiting for me at home, postmarked Honolulu. I pulled out a decree absolute and a sheet of creamy notepaper. I looked at Quentin's handwriting through my archivist's gaze. At once as familiar and as distant as a notation in a famous hand.

> *Dear Lily,*
>
> *I have held on to this paperwork for several weeks, hoping to find the right words to include. You would be much better at knowing what to say. I am sorry that I was not the husband you deserved. I wish I could have been. I am sorry too that there isn't a child in this world who is the combination of the very best of both of us. I think of David often.*
>
> *You will find attached a cheque. Please don't try to work out how much it cost you per day to be married to me. . . please don't ever wish away those years of our life. . . what we shared will always be priceless. I owe you everything.*
>
> *I do not mean this next paragraph to be hurtful—I want you to hear the truth, and to hear it from me. My relationship with Bea did not last. I suppose an affair built on lies and deceit is bound to fail. I see that now. I am dating a woman you don't know. Her name is Sonia Moore, and if things were very different—if you met each other in different circumstances—I believe you would be friends. She drags*

me out for long hikes, she is a keen Scrabble player, she gives me books to read.

I learned from our marriage how not to be a husband and hope I will not be such a failure the next time around. I have not yet proposed to Sonia, but I am going to, and it is my hope that it's not too late for us to raise a family, if we are able to have or adopt children. This, especially, I wanted you to hear from me.

I hope you wear your emerald ring. I hope you look at it and think of me with more fondness than bitterness. Remember that black and white movie we watched in the park in Suffolk? They always had Paris. You and I, we'll always have Saint Lucia. And a million other happy memories as well.

Lily, you will always be my Honey Bee.
With love,
Quentin

I read it, then read it again. I unclipped the cheque and put it on my lap, then put the letter back on top of the decree absolute and slid them both back into the envelope and sat quietly. I thought about that outdoor film festival, sitting on a rug with pints of cider and bags of crisps, watching *Casablanca*. I thought of the view of the Caribbean we'd had from our private hot tub. I imagined a younger woman meeting Quentin for the first time and found I truly wished them both luck.

We had agreed on a no-fault divorce and a fair division of our assets. All the same, I was surprised by the amount of the cheque and wondered if guilt had induced Quentin to add on some extra. It would be enough for a down payment on a small house, and a month later I stood in a real estate office with a lawyer and took possession of a winterized cottage by the lake which sat on a quarter acre.

'Aha!' said Kathleen when I told her about my new house. 'Real roots. Now I can give you a lilac bush for your garden.'

The day I moved in I took off my shoes and walked along the tiny stretch of pale brown beach in front of my—*my*—house. I looked across the dark blue water to the opposite shore and thought of the emerald sea and white sand of Lanikai Beach, my favourite spot on the island. Had I really lived in Hawaii for six years? I knelt down and pulled a handful of weeds, then sat back and watched as the gentle waves filled in the cavity. Soon all trace of the hole was gone. If only it could be that easy to fill the holes in my life.

Big Rock Lake, February 2014

'What did Kathleen mean, Peter is fine?'

I took a deep breath. 'He's not... He's not well.'

'What—?'

'Maybe now's not the time to talk about my problems. Not while we're waiting for news about Kent.' I looked towards the desk. Why wasn't there more news? What was going on?

'Or maybe now is the time?' Rose asked. 'Seems like a good time to share all the important secrets we've been hiding from each other.'

Sometimes my baby sister was far wiser than I was. I nodded. 'It's his memory...' I still struggled to use the label. Took another deep breath. 'It's Younger Onset Dementia.' It was easier to give an example. 'He came into the study yesterday and told me he'd made me coffee. With cream and brown sugar, for a treat, he said. I thanked him and we went to the kitchen. And told him that I don't like cream or sugar in my coffee. Double milk. I like double milk.'

I'd passed him the mug he'd given me. 'Here. You enjoy this one.' I poured myself a fresh cup, noting that it was already cold—how long ago had he made it?—and added milk. I resisted the urge to immediately scrub the counter, which was covered with granules of brown sugar and grains of coffee.

Peter had looked heartbroken. 'I thought you liked cream.'

'I do. I love cream. Just not in my coffee,' I said. 'But I recognize and love the fact that you gave me cream and sugar as a treat. Thank you, Darling.' This was as strength-based and optimistic as I could be. I remembered being touched that he'd remembered, in 2001, how I drank my coffee. And again when I returned. He used to ask waitresses for milk, not cream, for me. Now, he was shaking his head and looking like a puppy who'd been scolded for bringing his master the wrong pair of slippers.

I could have let it go. Perhaps I should have let it go. Taken one sip for the sake of it, then discreetly poured the sweet coffee down the drain. But, I argued with myself, I couldn't let every little thing go. I let dozens of moments pass by every day—but surely I had to be honest too. Dementia didn't get to win every time.

'I guess I never knew how you drink your coffee,' he said.

'You knew. You know. A lot of days you know.' I hugged him. 'You know a lot of things.'

'But one day I'm going to forget them all.'

I couldn't leave those words hanging between us, but I wasn't sure what to say. He had stated a fact, and it was correct. One day he'd have no memory left. This house, my face, his past would all be unfamiliar to him.

'Not today.' I'd forced cheer and lightness into my voice. 'But not today.' It was the best I could do. 'And speaking of today, what would you like to do today?' Not a good question, I told myself, too late. Offer a few options, don't ask an open-ended question.

'We could. . . garden?' he said, uncertainly, as if worried that he'd given the incorrect answer on a test.

I'd taken a sip of my cold coffee. Could he not see the snow outside? Did he not remember the heavy coat, hat, scarf, and mitts he'd worn the previous day? 'That's a great idea, Hon. Let's plan next summer's garden. Let's get ahead of the game so we're ready to plant as soon as we can next year.'

'Yes, let's plan,' he said. 'You can write a list. You like writing lists. And I have a book.' He left the kitchen and went off, I was sure, in search of the book I'd bought for him at the second hand bookstore all those years ago.

I listed other examples for Rose. 'He's losing the ability to read. He's never sure what day it is. Sometimes he asks where his dad is.'

Rose was crying. 'But—But—In June he was—'

'I know. It's been such a steep decline. They say the earlier it hits, the faster it progresses. But he's been especially unlucky.'

'How are you—? What do you—?'

'He goes to a day programme while I'm at work. I'm super lucky; it's at the university. So he thinks we're both going to work together every day.'

'Oh, Lily.'

'Your sister is an angel,' Mum said. 'I watch her and wonder where she learned that patience. I'd never manage.'

There were tears in my eyes too. 'From Peter,' I said. 'Peter taught me.'

Big Rock Lake, 2008

House bought, job secured, I realized I had made the decision to stay in Big Rock Lake. Apparently returning to my childhood home was my plan. I spent several evenings a week with Rose and her family and issued Mum a standing invitation to dinner once a week. Ironically, our night became Thursday, which had always been Mr. Reynold's night. 'Routine for so long,' she said. 'Funny how we're such creatures of habit.' But I couldn't spend all my free time with my family. I scanned the local newspaper for events with which to fill my spare time. The first Tuesday of each month the Horticultural Society hosted a guest speaker or two; in July it was a pair of television gardeners who promised anyone could transform an unremarkable piece of land into a show stopping display of flowers, or a vegetable garden to supply food for the summer and winter both. I was undecided until the last moment, then went because I worried the two guests would be speaking to an empty room.

I scolded myself for my narrow-mindedness when I entered the packed hall and wondered if every month's talk drew this many people. I should arrive earlier next time, I told myself, taking a seat in the second-to-last-row, from where I had a limited view of the stage.

There was banter, of course, and a new book to be sold, and perhaps I'd have laughed at more of the jokes if I'd ever watched their show and understood their references. But I learned a lot and took copious notes. After the talk there was a break, with tea and squares, before an open Q&A with members of the local Society. I noticed a number of people leaving, having bought a signed copy of the book, but by then I had some real questions about the zone we lived in and what I could realistically expect to grow in my garden, and how the wind from the lake would affect the length of the growing season. I stood in the line for the coffee urn. One of the slides had shown a magnificent display of lilies, but surely that had been taken in southern Ontario, where milder winters and a longer summer made a significant difference to what plants could thrive.

'Lily?' The voice at my right shoulder startled me and for a split second I forgot my name. Remembering, I hesitated a moment longer. Would it be seen as somehow boastful to grow lilies in my garden, as if proclaiming my own name? 'Lily?' again.

I turned with a smile in place. 'Hello.' And then a real smile. 'Peter!'

'I wasn't sure it was really you,' he said.

'I've aged.' I smiled.

'No. No, not at all.'

Someone coughed discreetly. I apologized, filled my cup with coffee, added milk, and backed away.

Peter was waiting behind me, carrying two cups.

'So are you—'

'I called your old number—'

We both spoke at once, laughed nervously, waited for the other to begin. 'You first,' I said.

'Where do you live these days? Are you back visiting your mum?'

'Here,' I said. 'I live here. I've bought a house by the lake. With a patch of land.' I made an awkward gesture to the stage. 'Maybe a garden.' I took a sip of the coffee. 'And you? Do you still live here?'

He nodded. 'Never left.' He looked at my left hand, but my ring finger was curled under the cup. 'And Quentin—?'

'We're divorced,' I said. The word was so blunt. So final. 'And you? My mum mentioned—oh, gosh, your dad. I was so sorry to hear of his stroke.'

Someone jostled me, and there was an announcement from the stage that the second half was to begin. 'Shall we go for a proper coffee and catch up after the Q&A?' he asked.

'That would be nice.' I nodded at his two cups. 'Yours is getting cold.'

'Yes,' he said. 'I think the person sitting on my right has gone. Come join us?'

Us. A wife? Unlikely, as he'd made a point of asking me my marital status and inviting me out for coffee. I followed him to the front of the auditorium and watched as he passed one of the cups of tea to an elderly gentleman. 'Warren,' he shouted. 'Look who I've found. It's Lily. Judith's daughter, Lily.'

The old man slowly turned to face me and held out a hand, which I took in mine. His skin was paper thin and covered with age spots. 'Lily,' he said. 'Welcome home, child.' It was a lovely greeting, and I understood what people really mean by the phrase 'years melted away' because other than his white hair and frail air, Peter's father hadn't changed.

He was caring for his dad, Peter told me two hours later over a coffee at a new independent on Main Street which boasted an in-house coffee bean roaster. He'd moved him into his house, where they were, he said, 'rubbing along.'

I told him I'd called his school.

'They've been very good,' he said. 'I'd amassed a ridiculous amount of unused holiday time. Though to be honest, I don't know if it's truly a leave of absence or an early retirement. I'm not entirely sure I'll go back.' It was a young man's gig, he said. Teaching had changed since he started out. Interactive whiteboards in place of chalkboards. Tablets in place of books. Unspoken orders to make sure everyone in the class moved up a grade every year. 'Kids who couldn't do the work, who didn't pass their exams, used to fail.' That was no longer acceptable.

I understood that it wasn't safe to leave his father alone for long stretches of time. He'd had a number of small strokes recently and was failing at an alarming rate. His father, always sharp as a tack for years, could no longer read, though he held the newspaper in front of him every morning. His hearing had gone and as a result his balance, too. 'Deaf as a post,' said Peter. 'Apologies if I start shouting at you, it's the volume I'm used to.'

'It's so good of you,' I said.

He shrugged, but there was no unhappiness or even resignation in the gesture. 'There is no one else to care for him.'

'And by "caring" you mean—?'

'I look after him,' he said, as if that clarified everything. 'He's not able to cook for himself, or wash very well. I pay his bills and make sure his friends come to visit, and I help him bathe and monitor his medications and drive him to his various appointments and listen to him reminisce. Our caseworker says at some point he'll need to go into a home with professionals, but I hope to keep him at home.'

I thought of my mum, so fit, so healthy. 'I don't know that I could wipe my mother's bottom,' I said. Too late, I wondered if that was crass of me, no doubt he had also experienced this sort of hands-on care with his mother, when she was ill.

'Of course you could. You can do anything for the people that you love.'

He was so sincere, so matter-of-fact. For him it was non-negotiable. You looked after your loved ones, whatever that involved. You simply did whatever was required.

This was something I had not thought of before. Were I to grow ill or frail, who would care for me? I tried to imagine Quentin in that role and failed to produce a clear imagine. Perhaps with Sonia Moore? Again I found myself wishing them both luck.

The waitress came to warn us that she would be closing in fifteen minutes and offered us free refills, perhaps as a consolation, or perhaps to save throwing away freshly perked coffee. 'And more cream on its way,' she said.

'Milk, please,' said Peter. 'Lily drinks her coffee with double milk.'

He had remembered when ordering the first cup. I was touched. 'I enjoyed the presentation this evening,' I said. 'Does your dad still garden?'

'He likes to fiddle about. Between us we keep the worst of the weeds down. But the truth is I take him to all the talks, regardless of whether or not he really has any interest in the topic. I think it helps to keep him active, and out and about, you know? It would be too easy for us to sit in front of the television every night. I don't want that to happen.' He took a deep breath. 'Lily. Your mum told me about your son. I'm so very sorry. I don't have the words.'

'There are no words.'

He put his hand on top of mine, and squeezed it.

Had the coffee shop not closed, we might have stayed there longer. 'It was really lovely to see you,' I said, as we stood by my car in the parking lot. I meant it.

'Come to dinner on Friday? Warren and I would love your company. You'll have to brave my cooking, I'm afraid. And it will be insanely early—five o'clock.'

In fact, his cooking was not bad at all. Chicken Parmigiana over pasta, with salad on the side, followed by homemade apple pie. I complimented the pastry. 'We took a course, didn't we Warren? Everyone thought we were there to meet women, but I really wanted to master pastry. They taught us six different kinds, though I'll confess I use the same one for everything.'

My initial impression, that Peter's father was the same man I'd always known, had to be revised. He was charming and polite but quiet and, it was clear, struggling to follow our simple conversation about Tuesday evening's talk, the plans I had for my garden, the work that needed to be done on my house.

We washed up together while Warren sat in his easy chair with a book on his lap and fell asleep. 'A stroll?' Peter suggested. 'Have you seen the new waterfront area? They've finally finished it. The whole industrial park is now a really attractive boardwalk with flower gardens and a big playground.'

As we walked, I asked him about neighbours from the old days—people we'd known because back then neighbours knew each other—the ones I'd played with as children. Some surprises: a death in an accident at the mill, a windfall job working for a startup company, the unexpected birth of quadruplets ('too bad, a few years later and they'd have made a reality tv series of them all,' Peter joked). And the more quotidian lives: a third marriage, a move to Toronto, a grandchild.

'Have you kept in touch with everyone on the street?' I asked, smiling, to make sure he knew I was teasing.

But he answered seriously. 'I've never left Big Rock Lake, remember,' he said. 'And it really is a small place in many ways. You'd be surprised how many of the same people I see all the time. And Facebook, of course. I've re-connected with dozens of people I barely knew thirty years ago. Only social media would consider us friends, but it's an interesting way to glimpse other lives. You don't have a Facebook page.'

So, he had looked for me.

'I don't. I was never sure how much of my life I'd share if I started one. And now...' I didn't want to have one glass of wine too many one evening and start searching for the Facebook page of a young woman called Sonia Moore who lived in Honolulu. I didn't want to see photos of an engagement ring, or wedding dress, or baby bump. I wished her and Quentin well, but I didn't want to be party to their lives. I let the rest of my sentence drift away, unsure what I was going to say. 'But you searched for me. That's nice.'

'I was always sorry with the way I left things between us,' he said. 'Unfinished.' He sounded sincere. 'You didn't know. You couldn't know—weeks before you and I reconnected, my fiancée had broken off our engagement because she'd been seeing another man.'

'I was back in Big Rock Lake because I'd discovered Quentin had been having an affair,' I said. 'I'm sorry I didn't tell you that at the time. It was so raw. I was so embarrassed. I'd failed at my marriage, failed at my long walk, failed at making it clear to him that I'd truly left.'

We walked in silence for some time, but it felt as if any and all missteps and misunderstandings between us were forgiven. Stopping at a row of benches by a playground, we admired the view of the lake, and Peter described the gardens through the seasons. Teams of volunteers came out every day to help; it was something he'd hoped his dad would be able to do on his own, but that hadn't worked out. The playground was busy with shouting children and chatting parents, and there was a row of food trucks in the parking lot, selling hand cut fries, tacos, ice creams.

'I meant to serve ice cream with the pie,' said Peter. 'May I make it up to you now?' He bought two soft cones and we sat on a bench down by the water's edge.

'Rose and I are Facebook friends,' Peter said.

I was surprised she'd never mentioned that and said as much. 'Ah, she has many hundreds of friends, she's probably forgotten I'm one of them. It is an odd thing—our paths never cross, that I'm aware of, even though we live no more than a few miles apart. But I knew she had two daughters, and now the twins.'

'That is odd,' I agreed. 'And, slightly...'

'Creepy. Yes,' Peter agreed cheerfully. 'In the wrong hands that sort of information could be... could be misused.'

'Quentin is going to remarry and hopes to have children.' I hadn't told anyone. I didn't want Rose or Mum or even Kathleen to think I was regretting our divorce. 'The times I lost our babies—lost, what a stupid way to describe it—it was my body's failing, not his. So there's still hope for him.'

'I'm so sorry,' he said. 'Seeing Rose's children must be... bittersweet.'

'Very.'

'I had always hoped I'd have children.'

'When I blew out the candles on my fortieth birthday cake in May, I wished that I could let that dream go,' I admitted.

'Difficult, that one, isn't it?' he said. 'You think *one day it will be my turn* until you understand that no, that particular *one day* isn't going to come.'

It seemed an evening for honesty. 'A new friend at work introduced me to a divorcé with two children. If he'd asked me out—he didn't—I would have said yes, in the hopes of meeting his children.'

Peter nodded. 'A ready-made family, even if only part-time. I dated a woman with children for a similar reason.'

'Dated?' I clarified. 'Past tense?'

He nodded. 'Yes. When I moved Dad in with me it... it changed things.'

'Ummm.' I could understand that.

He nodded again. 'I'm so sorry you've had so much heartache, Lily.'

'Ah well. Time to move on.'

'Easier said than done sometimes,' said Peter. 'Well, we've finished our cones. Shall we walk again?'

We said goodbye at my car, and I left him to drive home and help his dad to bed, promising I'd be back for dinner again soon. Or return the invitation in my new house. I drove home the long way around, stopping at Pointer's Park, where Quentin and I had come when we were first dating. It looked much worse for wear, the café had been torn down, and there was no sign of any playground. Perhaps everyone now went to the new waterfront area. Whatever the cause, it was a sad place. A scruffy teen sat at a broken picnic table, smoking. Still, I sat in my car and remembered happier times, when I'd had my whole life ahead of me, and had at the time imagined Quentin and I as an elderly couple returning to this park to hold hands and watch the sun set.

Odd that, although I'd met Quentin here in Big Rock Lake, I could recall few other physical places with linked memories. The base, I suppose, and the house the girls and I had lived in. I tried to remember where else we'd hung out during our courtship, our special places, but drew a blank. There must have been dinners, movies, bowling, mini golf. But I couldn't pinpoint a specific location that was 'ours'—somewhere I could return to now that would spark a memory.

But the few weeks I'd spent with Peter in 2001 had come flooding back as we'd walked and spoken. The bank-as-French-bistro on Main Street of course, although it had since closed. The farm where we'd taken the oven-building course. The path above the canyon and through the forest to the cranberry bog. The tapas bar, still going strong, Kathleen assured me.

Kathleen's husband, Frank, ran a landscaping company. The next day I asked her how busy he was, if there was any hope he'd have time this summer to come and dig up my yard, lay new sod, build raised beds for flowers and vegetables, and plant an oak tree. 'Of course he'll have time,' she said. 'I can organize that much at least. But that sounds like a big job. You should get quotes from a couple of other companies too. I can't guarantee he'll give you the lowest price.'

'I don't want the lowest price,' I said. 'I want the best person to do the job.'

'And you know he's the best, how, exactly?'

'Because he's married to my friend.' I smiled. 'And I'm pretty sure she'd never settle for second best.'

'Darn right,' she said. 'And FYI, I'm not going to let you settle for second best either.'

'What a gift,' I said.

'What's that?'

'Making such a good friend at this age.'

On Saturday I was woken at seven by the sound of a truck pulling into my driveway. I pulled on a sundress and went outside. 'Morning, Lily,' said Frank. He passed me a Tim's. 'Walk me through your yard and paint me the picture of what you envision, talk to me about your budget, and I'll let you know what can be done and what's unrealistic.'

The budget was easy. I'd sold the emerald ring Quentin had given me, shocked at the amount I'd been offered.

I had invited Mum and Rose and all the kids for Sunday lunch. By the time they arrived, the transformation had already started. I gestured at the various patches of mud in the brand new grass. 'Tomatoes, green beans, zucchini there. Herbs over there, flowers there, and there, and that's where the oak will go.'

'Wow.' Kent, jiggling one of the twins on his hip, was impressed. 'You're really going for it.' He looked over at Rose, who was feeding the other twin. 'I shouldn't be surprised. You are Red's sister.'

'Roots,' I said. 'It's time.'

'What about a sugar maple?' asked Rose. 'Pretty in the fall, and you could tap it in the spring. In memory of Bobby,' she added.

Aidan tugged on my shorts. 'Who's Bobby?'

'My daddy,' I explained. 'Your Grampa. When I was a little girl, we lived in the bush and he tapped the maples and made maple syrup every spring.'

'Your daddy was Mumma's daddy too,' said Madison. She looked at her mother. 'But you didn't live in the bush.'

'No, that's right. I grew up in Granny's house in the city.'

'And Bobby was Granny's husband,' said Madison. 'And you nearly called me Bobby but with an i.'

'That's right,' said Rose. 'But shall I tell you a secret? I am very glad your name is Madison.'

'Me too,' said Madison. 'Madison Mary.'

Aidan was much more interested in the maple syrup than boys. 'Will you make maple syrup, Aunt Lily? And then will you make pancakes?'

I promised her that we'd make pancakes together one day. She was disappointed to discover that we weren't having pancakes for lunch. 'Maybe me and Maddie can come for a sleepover,' she suggested. 'And in the morning you can make pancakes.'

I looked at Rose for confirmation that would be okay.

'Sounds like a great idea,' she said. 'Will you take the twins as well? Joking. Sort of.'

'I used to have sleep overs at your house all the time,' said Madison. 'When you lived by the swimming pool in the sunshine.' She looked at me and smiled. 'I'm sorry you don't have a swimming pool anymore, but it's much nicer to see you all the time. And I think this lake is better for swimming than a pool,' she lowered her voice. 'Aidan can't swim yet. She thinks she can, but she can't really.'

I relayed the conversation to Kathleen the next day at lunch. 'The last time they visited, it rained non-stop and she cut her foot on a shell. All she remembers is sunshine and the swimming pool.'

'Bless 'em,' said Kathleen. 'Not wishing my life away, but I can't wait for grandchildren to fuss over. Now did my husband live up to your expectations?'

'And exceeded! I can't believe how much he accomplished in a single weekend.'

'Good. I gave him strict instructions of course.' She laughed.

'What a gift,' I said again. 'Making a best friend at this age.'

Chapter Thirteen

July became August.

Peter and I had developed a routine, with my visiting for supper at his house, then leaving his dad to fall asleep in the living room while we went out for a walk. 'Not very exciting, I'm afraid,' Peter apologized on the third evening I visited. 'And a bit like having a chaperone monitor our conversation.'

'I don't want anything more exciting,' I said. 'But I would like to repay your hospitality. Won't you both come to mine next Thursday? We'll have two chaperones then.'

It wasn't a great success. Peter's dad was confused by the seating arrangement at the picnic table on the deck, the view of the lake, Mum's presence. 'Should be getting home for dinner,' he said to Peter at one point. 'Dinner at the kitchen table. Always eat dinner at the kitchen table.'

'You remember Judith,' said Peter. 'She and Mom were great friends, and she had you to dinner on Thursdays for years.'

'I remember, of course I remember,' said Warren. 'Everyone always on about my memory. Of course I remember.' But it was not clear that he did. I served individual lemon mousses for dessert and Warren shook his head when I passed him the ramekin. 'What's that? I don't know what that is.'

'Lemon mousse,' I said. 'I know Felicia won your heart with a lemon meringue pie.'

He muttered something under his breath, and it wasn't until Peter passed him the teaspoon that he started eating it. With no apparent interest in the food, simply doing his duty as he'd been asked. 'My watch is broken again,' he said at one point.

'There's a good repairman I use,' Mum said. 'I'm taking him my clock this week. Would you like me to take your watch at the same time?'

Peter gently shook his head at her, mouthed 'no thank you.'

Peter said sorry as they left. 'He's not having a great day.'

'No need to apologize, goodness. Are you sure we can't have his watch fixed?'

'Thank you, no need. He's convinced his watch is broken, but in fact he's forgotten how to tell the time.'

'Oh, Peter. Oh, I'm so sorry,' said Mum. 'I didn't—I assumed—.'

'It's called vascular dementia,' said Peter. 'A side effect of the most recent strokes.'

We looked it up after they'd left. Impaired blood supply to the brain.

The next week, at Peter's house, his dad seemed no better. He asked me what the grated cheese was for, then asked me to sprinkle it on his noodles for him, as if he was unsure how much to take or where to put it. I watched him struggle with the pasta, and I quietly reached over and cut it up, as I had recently done for Aidan, and put a spoon in his hand. 'That's better,' he said.

For dessert there was blueberry pie from a box. 'Store boughten,' said Peter. 'I hope this won't lose me points.'

'No lost points,' I assured him.

His dad picked up the piece of pie on his plate with his hand and ate a bite, not noticing that half the filling had fallen on to his lap.

'Oops. Never mind,' said Peter. He started to wipe his dad's lap.

'Get away,' said the older man. 'You're not my wife.' He looked at me. 'Do you know where my wife is? She's been gone for some time now and I can't remember when she's due home.'

I put down my fork and blinked away tears.

Peter knelt at his father's side. 'Mom loves you, Dad. Your wife, Felicia, loves you.'

'I know that.' Warren was cross. 'I was asking when she's due home.' He pushed himself away from the table, but as he stood he got a foot caught in the leg of the chair and he lost his balance.

Peter grabbed for him and managed to keep him upright. 'Okay, Dad. I've got you. Maybe you should have a lie down, what do you think?'

I put away the untouched pieces of pie, did the dishes, cleaned the blueberry stain as best I could from the kitchen chair, wiped down the counters, and swept the floor. Then I put on a pot of decaf coffee and passed a cup to Peter when he came back into the kitchen. 'Gosh, this place is sparkling,' he said. 'And coffee, heaven.'

'Your dad's going downhill,' I said.

Peter nodded, and I saw tears at the corner of his eyes. 'So quickly. And his memory. I can't believe it. He was fine, well, okay, in the spring. Yesterday when I was mowing the lawn he wandered off. He's never wandered before. I found him soon enough, but—' He took another sip of coffee. 'This is too much information, but he can't control his bladder or bowels anymore.'

'If you hadn't been standing there to catch him,' I said. I didn't need to finish that sentence. He could have broken a leg, a hip, or worse.

'He's never been bad-tempered a day in his life until now,' said Peter. 'Never. Mom was the disciplinarian. Dad was always cheerful and good natured.'

Like father, like son, I thought.

'And he's started asking when Mom's due home several times a day.'

'Oh, Peter.' I reached my hand across the table for his. 'You've done so much. You've done so well.' I took a deep breath. 'Maybe now the time has come to think about long-term care.'

The tears that had threatened to fall, fell from Peter's eyes. 'Dammit,' he said. He stood in front of the sink to blow his nose. 'Sorry.'

'No need to say sorry, ever,' I said. 'I know you want the best for your dad. Maybe the best is professional care.'

'It breaks my heart to watch him,' Peter said, not turning around from the kitchen sink. 'He's confused, and he's afraid, and I understand why that makes him angry. He knows he's losing skills. He's worried that Mom has left him.' He blew his nose again and tossed the tissue. 'You're right. I have to see where his name is on the waitlist, figure out which home is the best fit. But...' He came and sat at the table again and drank the last of his coffee. 'It's my greatest fear, to die in an old age home. Lonely and scared and abandoned. I don't want my dad to end his days that way.'

I started shaking my head before he finished. 'He won't be alone. He won't be abandoned. You and I will visit him. We can go every day if that's what you need. We can go and have dinner with him every night.'

'You'd do that? You'd make that sort of commitment?'

Would I, really, commit to visiting on a daily basis an elderly man who would possibly soon not know who I was? Yes, I told myself. His son knew who I was. 'If that will help,' I said. 'If that's what you need. If it was my mother, instead of your dad, I'd go and see her every day.'

'Lily, I don't know what to say.'

'Say that you'll make some appointments to visit care homes this week,' I said. 'Say that you know what a tremendous job you've done and say that you won't see it as a failure on your part to admit that looking after him has become too difficult to do on your own.'

'I'll make some appointments for this week.' He tried to smile. 'I think we'd better forgo our walk this evening, but neither of us got pie. Would you like some blueberry pie? And a game of Scrabble, although I've not played for years, so I can't promise you a real match.'

'Pie and a game of Scrabble sounds lovely,' I said.

One of the perks of my position was that I had an office to myself in the back of the library and was pretty much left on my own to get on with the job. The following morning I went in early and made a list of all the care homes in the city. Over lunch I phoned each one of them. On the way home from work I stopped at Peter's to give him my notes. 'These three would love to meet with you,' I said. 'These two don't have the facilities you require.' I was trying to speak in code; on the sheet I'd written "*no dementia patients.*" 'I asked Kathleen's advice and she said start here, and here.' I'd starred those two.

'You two must be plotting something,' said Peter's dad from the living room. 'I can't hear a word you're saying. Up to mischief, no doubt.'

'I'm always up to mischief, Mr. Reynolds,' I said, raising my voice and walking into the living room. 'And I'm learning more tricks from my four-year-old niece that you can imagine.' I sat next to him on the sofa and chatted about Aidan and Madison, the sleepover we'd had last weekend in a tent in the yard. How we'd gone for a "midnight" swim at nine o'clock. 'Aidan loves being naughty,' I said. 'She adored breaking the rules and staying up past her bedtime.'

'I never had grandchildren,' he said when I finished the story. 'Great shame my son never married. He never met the right girl, you know.'

'Well, maybe it's not too late,' I said breezily.

'Huh. He's an old man now. Needed a wife to keep him young. My wife kept me young. Felicia. Felicia was my wife. Cancer took her and I got old.'

'I'm so sorry,' I said.

'Cancer,' he said again. 'Damn disease.'

Peter arrived with a jug of lemonade and three plastic cups. 'It's a scorcher out there today,' he said, pouring us each a half glass.

'It sure is,' I agreed. 'Hard to imagine in six months it will be minus forty.'

'Better get my truck fixed, Peter, if you want me to plow the driveway all winter.'

'I'll do that, Dad.'

Mr. Reynolds looked at me. 'Did you see my truck out front when you came in? Fifty-six Ford. Doesn't get better than that.' He looked at his son. 'Better set another place at the table. Better ask this young lady to stay for dinner, son.'

'It's Lily, Dad. You remember Lily.'

'Course I do. You think I've lost my mind. And why would she want to stay for dinner with two old men anyhow?'

'I'd love to stay for dinner, Mr. Reynolds,' I said. 'Thank you.' I volunteered to set the table and went into the kitchen.

'See that, son? Your old man can still pull 'em. I'll be your wing man.'

There was no sign of dinner underway, so I poked about in the fridge and made scrambled eggs and sliced tomatoes. I cut everyone's portion into small bites and put a spoon by each place, and made small talk through the meal.

'Thank you, Lily,' Peter said, when he came back into the kitchen after helping his father into bed. 'For making supper. And once again the kitchen is spotless, and once again you've made me a coffee.' He grinned, wryly. 'Lucky for me I've got such an able wing man.'

'Did he own a fifty-six Ford? I'm trying to remember, but I'm picturing a blue station wagon in your driveway when we were kids.'

Peter shook his head. 'He always wanted one, but every time he saved up the money there was something else. A diamond ring when he met Mom. Down payment on a house for his new bride.' He grinned. 'Then the baby. Later a new roof.' He looked at me. 'Life.'

'Life,' I echoed. I wondered if there was anything that Mum had coveted and never treated herself to. 'Is there anything you've wanted that you've never bought yourself? Do you have a hankering for a fifty-six Ford?'

'A thing? No, no *thing* that I can think of. I never was a car guy. Poor Dad. He would have loved me to be car crazy, to have helped him spend weekends fixing up an old vehicle.'

I had heard the emphasis. 'So not a thing—'

'My dad was right. It's a shame I never married.'

'He said you never met the right girl.'

'Well I did, in fact. But I was too scared of losing her. Instead of chasing after her, as I ought to have done, I stayed home and nursed my broken heart.' He looked directly into my eyes.

'You're not talking about your fiancée.'

'No. No, I'm not.'

'Oh, Peter. That was so long ago.'

'And yet I look at you and it feels like yesterday.'

I groaned. 'I'm forty, Peter.'

'I see you. When you smile, when I look up and see you talking to my dad, when you play with your nieces, when you laugh with Rose... you're the same woman I've always known and loved. Wiser now, and more beautiful, but she's there, she's you. I witness you.'

I witness you. I closed my eyes for a moment, to savour the beauty of that statement.

'The thing I most regret is that I didn't ask you out, ever. Until it was too late.'

'Why didn't you, I wonder?'

'The eleven years between us. Nothing now, but back then they made such a difference. And I thought- I thought you should date a few boys at university. Your own age, you know. I didn't want you ever to regret not having had chances.'

He could not have known that in my third year I slept with a man significantly older than him.

'And then you met Quentin, and you got so serious, so quickly. By the time I realized... I'd missed my opportunity. And he was younger, of course, and he offered you travel, which you were desperate for, and which was something I couldn't at that time. He was debonair, exciting, American... I was the boy next door.'

Peter knew me well. He had known me well then. 'I thought I needed excitement.' I tried to imagine a life where I'd stayed in Big Rock Lake after university. A life without having lived in England or Kansas or North Carolina or Hawaii. A life lived with Peter instead of Quentin. I guessed that Peter would not have been averse to the idea of adoption. 'I was a fool,' I said.

'I was the bigger fool,' Peter said. 'Too scared to chase after you. Too scared to... You gave me an opening and I made what I thought was the morally correct decision for both of us.'

'It was,' I said.

'I should have told you about my ex-fiancée, warned you how damaged I was.'

'And I should have told you that Quentin had been unfaithful.'

We both lapsed into silence. 'Coulda, woulda, shoulda,' I said.

'After that brief, glorious month,' he said. 'You went back to Quentin. I have often wondered what might have happened if I hadn't have pushed you away.'

It wasn't phrased as a question, but I wanted to explain. 'I was married,' I said. 'And I was pregnant. 9/11 terrified me. And—' I'd never said this aloud before. 'We had nine years of shared memories. It felt like such a large part of my life. I was worried what might happen if I lost that mirror, the ability to speak of those experiences with the one other person who had been there.' I wasn't sure I was expressing how I really felt.

But Peter understood. 'And now? With all the extra years' worth of memories? It must have been even more difficult to leave this time.'

I told him that the period of time after we had agreed to divorce, before I physically left, was one of the least stressful times of my marriage. 'But you move on, don't you? You have to move on.'

'You're only forty, Lily. You'll make new memories, you know that right?'

I nodded. 'Yes. And I already am. A new house, a new garden, a new job with a new friend, the twins. Lots of old and new people, to help me make new memories.'

'And maybe. . . us?' He looked at me. 'Please don't misunderstand me. I know I've got less to offer you than any time in the past. I'm not currently gainfully employed. I'm tied to my dad. I'm fifty-one and balding—'

'Don't sell yourself short.'

We said nothing for some time, but our silence was companionable. 'Last night I offered you pie and Scrabble,' he said. 'There's still some pie left. And I'd love a rematch.' And when he saw me to my car several hours later, he opened my door, and waited until I'd done up my seatbelt before he closed it and asked me to text him when I got home so he'd know I was safe, and then he leaned through my open window and held my chin in his hands, and kissed me. It was a gentle kiss, and brief, and full of promise.

I sent him a text as soon as I walked in my door. *I like us.*

He replied at once. *I like us too. Very much. I look forward to all the memories we'll make as us.*

Yes. I texted back. *Yes.*

Chapter Fourteen

BIG ROCK LAKE, FEBRUARY 2014

Waiting. Waiting. Finally an update: but only that there was no news. Then we waited some more.

A police officer brought the union representative to meet Rose. 'We don't have to discuss anything immediately,' he said. 'Just know that we're on your team.'

'What does that mean?' I asked Mum in a whisper. 'Why does Kent need the union rep?'

She shook her head. 'I don't know. I'm sure it's routine.'

A different police officer introduced himself to Rose and told her that he was in charge of the investigation.

'Investigation?'

'Regular procedure,' he assured her. 'Same as for any accident. Insurance company will need the paperwork.'

'Was he speeding? Was there something else? What—?'

'We'll keep you posted,' he said. 'First thing is to make sure your husband pulls through.'

'What's going on?' Rose asked Mum and I. 'What are they blaming Kent for? I thought it was a moose?'

'No one is suggesting Kent did anything wrong,' I said. 'You heard them, it's procedure. Paperwork.'

'He never never drinks and drives,' Rose said.

'And no one has mentioned that,' Mum pointed out.

'Never. Never,' Rose said again.

I briefly wondered if she was over-protesting the point. I scolded myself for so quickly assuming the worst of my brother-in-law.

She turned on me. 'You always think he's a big drinker, but that's because Quint never drinks.'

I was thrown. By the accusation, the bitterness in her voice, the way she spoke of my ex-husband as if he were still part of our lives. And I was instantly defensive. 'I've never said anything to—'

'You don't have to say anything. It's the looks you make. The way you watch him drink. It's uncomfortable, accusatory.'

'I'm—I'm truly sorry, Rose. I didn't—It was never intentional. I—I'm sorry.'

She sighed, the burst of anger gone. 'Oh, you get it from Mum, I know.'

'You're right,' Mum said. 'I taught you that, Lily. I watched every drink Bobby took. It's probably why he started drinking outside the home.'

'Mum!' I shook my head. 'You can't blame yourself for his alcoholism.' I shook my head. 'Every drink he had was his choice.'

'Choice?' Rose looked at me, then Mum. 'What choice? Alcoholism is an addiction. It's no more a choice than any other mental health challenge. And please, please. You're talking about him as if he was a drunk. Dad's not here to defend himself, it's not fair.'

'It's not fair,' Mum agreed. She looked above Rose's head and shook her head at me.

I understood, or thought I understood, that she wanted me to change the subject. And rightly so. Together we had helped Rose believe the fairytale we'd spun about Bobby. It wasn't fair to expect her to accept the different version we were giving her now.

'I'm sorry, Rose. I'm sorry I made you and Kent feel uncomfortable. I'm sorry I came across as judgmental.'

'I'm sorry I lost my temper. I think I get angry when I'm scared.'

I wasn't sure if she was talking about her outburst now, or nine months ago. It didn't matter. We reached for each other's hands, and she rested her head against my shoulder.

A nurse rushed by, paused, nodded at me. I smiled back. I couldn't remember her name, but I knew her face, the sound of her voice. She'd been working that New Year's Eve.

Big Rock Lake, 2008

Kathleen had guessed as soon as she saw me the morning after that Peter and I had kissed. 'You look happy,' she said. 'And I know my hubby is a kick-ass landscape artist, but it's gotta be more than a new herbaceous border that's making you smile. I think we need to take our coffee break now and sit outside so you can tell me everything.'

'Is it too soon for me to think about dating Peter?' I asked her.

'Too soon? You goof. You've known this guy since you were, what did you say, eight years old?' She held out both hands. 'I don't have enough fingers to count how long ago that was. Too soon!? What the heck are you waiting for? Any good that comes along your way in life, you've got to grab it with both hands and hang on. Don't hesitate. Go for it. Just do it. And if you don't interrupt me I'm gonna keep spouting clichés!'

We both laughed, and then I admitted that the 'everything' I could tell her involved nothing more risqué than two games of Scrabble, store-boughten blueberry pie, and a sweet goodnight kiss.

She laughed, then looked serious. 'One. August is too dang hot to fuss about in the kitchen baking pies, that is exactly what No Frills is for. Two. The whole time the kids were growing up I insisted on two things: church every Sunday, and Family Games Night every Friday. Frank, bless him, played board games once a week for twenty-six years to keep me happy. When Ben left home last year I said, okay, you have more than fulfilled your duty, now you can watch the football and hockey and baseball games on Friday evenings, or hang out with the guys, or do whatever the heck it is that men less henpecked than yourself do on Friday evenings. And he said to me, Hon, he said, "those board games are the backbone of my week. They have helped me with major decisions, they have averted arguments, they have bonded me to my children, they have bound me to my family. I will, however, give away our copy of Risk, if that won't break your heart".' She looked at me. 'Never underestimate the power of a game of Scrabble.'

The days Peter and I didn't see each other we spoke on the phone, and every day we sent countless texts back and forth. 'What did we do before cellphones?' I asked Rose because she and I sent almost as many texts back and forth.

'I guess we found other ways to communicate?' she laughed.

Or maybe we didn't. I wondered if Quentin and I had spoken this often about such mundane things as seeing a rainbow or hearing a loon call. I wondered if maybe that would that have made a difference. I thought that and then took a photo of a red maple leaf and sent it to Peter. It was still summer, but some mornings there was the suggestion of fall in the air.

'I downloaded my photos from my phone last night,' said Rose. 'I have to start learning how to cull. Three hundred from the past two weeks. I mean, I know my babies are the cutest ever, but they're four months old! Even they won't want a billion photos of their childhood.'

She was exhausted all the time but refused to complain. 'Sydney rolled from her front to her back yesterday,' she said. Mackenzie had performed that trick the previous week. 'That's the last time I'll watch my child's first roll. I keep thinking, all these firsts, I have to savour them all.'

I poked her. 'Never say never. I thought you'd stopped after Aidan.'

'Yeah, well we had. But you know, Kent never quite got around to getting the big snip and then. . .' She blushed.

'You're only thirty-one,' I said. 'You could have another two sets of twins.'

'Oh, don't! Don't even! Change the subject. Tell me what's new with Peter.'

'He's chosen the care home he wants for his dad, and he's on the waitlist.' I grimaced. 'It's a little icky, because someone has to die for his dad to get in.'

'Or move away?' offered Rose. Ever optimistic. Exactly like Tansy.

'Sure, or move away,' I said.

'Peter got him a GPS bracelet.' Mr. Reynolds' wandering was now a frequent occurrence. 'He still refuses to use a wheelchair.' That had been my suggestion, so that we could take him with us on our evening walks. I patted my stomach. 'We have to stop eating pie every evening.'

Rose groaned. 'Don't talk to me about losing weight,' she said. 'I think I'll keep wearing my maternity yoga pants forever.'

'Yeah, best to save them anyhow. In case you change your mind and have another baby or two.'

'No! No more babies,' she said. But she laughed. 'We are going to look at a cottage this weekend though. A fantasy really, but you know, it doesn't hurt to dream.'

But apparently not such an unrealistic fantasy that they couldn't negotiate a mortgage for it. A few weeks after that conversation Rose told me that they were going to buy it and would be celebrating Thanksgiving there. 'You'll come, won't you?' she asked. 'You and Peter.'

'It will be less stressful than that Thanksgiving Dinner after 9/11,' I said. She looked confused.

'With Quentin.'

'Was that stressful? I don't remember any stress. Was it the turkey? My first. Was it overcooked? Raw?'

'Your turkey was delicious. I hadn't expected Quentin to be there, that's all. And Peter had already been invited. I was in an awkward position.'

Understanding dawned on her face. 'Oh. Now that you mention it...'

'Did you tell Quentin?' I asked. 'When you phoned to invite him?'

Rose looked confused. 'Tell him what?'

'That I had been spending a lot of time with Peter?'

'I don't think so. I mean, I don't even remember making a phone call. That was so long ago.' She sounded hurt. 'You thought I was interfering in your personal life? And you're still upset?'

I was sorry I'd asked, and I wasn't sure I believed her answer, but my memory of that time had faded somewhat. The day Quentin had arrived I'd been hung over, and I'd discovered I was pregnant, and I must have been feeling guilty about my attraction to Peter.

'No, no, not upset at all,' I said. It was easy to change the subject: I asked her to tell me all about their new cottage.

In the end I had to send regrets for Thanksgiving. Three residents of the care home passed away and we were able to move Peter's dad into his new room on the Sunday afternoon.

The move itself went smoothly, and the three of us then went down to the dining room for lunch. Mr. Reynolds even consented to being pushed along the waterfront in a wheelchair. But when the clouds broke and it started raining, and we took him back to the home, and he realized we were leaving and he was not, his face crumpled. I'd seen that look on Aidan's face when she understood that there were different rules for herself and her older sister. It broke my heart to see it on the face of a five-year old, but it was all the more heart breaking to see on the face of a seventy-five-year old. He clung to his son's hand, and I could tell from the stoop of Peter's shoulders that he was taking full blame for his father's sorrow.

Saying nothing, I left the room and went in search of one of the staff members. 'My father-in-law,' this seemed the easiest term to use. 'He moved in today and—'

The woman nodded. 'Sure thing, Angel. It's always difficult the first few times. Let's go and get Mr. Reynolds off to an activity. That will help.' She was no-nonsense, and, of course, a professional. I noticed she addressed both Peter and I as 'Angel' but called Mr. Reynolds 'Warren.'

'Right then, Warren,' she said. 'Bingo is starting in the lounge in five minutes, and I need a lucky charm. Let's go and share a couple of cards shall we? I promise we'll split the winnings. These two will have to manage on their own for the evening, but I daresay they'll come back tomorrow for the Chef's turkey dinner. I've booked a table for three for the twelve noon seating. The wheelchair, that's a good idea, save you the long walk to the lounge.' And they were off down the hall.

Peter sat on the narrow bed and looked at me. 'Lily. I couldn't have done this without you. Thank you.'

'Sure you could,' I said. 'But you're welcome.'

'It feels like we have the evening off,' he said. 'We could do anything.'

'What would you most like to do?'

He looked shattered, and as if he really wanted to sleep, but he rallied. 'It's lousy weather,' he said. 'Shall we see what's playing at the movies? I can't remember the last movie I saw. Or I could take you out to dinner?'

'D'you know. We had lunch out today and we're having lunch out again tomorrow. How about we make a bowl of pasta at home?'

'That sounds even better.'

So together we cobbled together a pasta sauce from ingredients I had on hand, all the while watching the patterns the rain was making on the lake. 'You've done well, Lily,' said Peter. 'This is a gorgeous location.' He gestured at the muddy yard. 'And that is going to be a gorgeous garden.'

After dinner the rain stopped, so we braved the wind and went for a walk along my street. It was nine when we got back home. Peter hesitated at the front step.

'Would you like to come back in?' I asked, suddenly shy.

'I would,' he answered. 'I would like that very much.'

'Good,' I said. We moved towards each other at the same time, our lips meeting in a kiss. A kiss, and more, a promise, an agreement, a confirmation. He held my hand, walked me to my bedroom, and we undressed each other between kisses.

When I was naked, he stood back. 'You are so beautiful, Lily.'

I reached for him. 'Please. I need—'

'My dearest Lily. What do you need?'

'I need you. Now.'

'Slow down... let me worship your body a little.'

When, finally, he was inside me, I let myself go almost at once, calling out his name in some language known only to lovers. He joined me soon after, my name a passionate run-on chant. And then he gathered me into his arms and held me as both our hearts slowed back to normal.

'You're so beautiful. That was so beautiful.'

I struggled to find words to express my joy. How right it felt. How right we felt. If, like me, Peter thought at any point during that evening that it was almost exactly seven years to the day since we hadn't made love the first time, he didn't mention it.

I didn't tell Rose that we had consummated our relationship that weekend, but she must have worked out soon enough that Peter was spending several nights a week at my house.

As I had promised I would, I went to see his dad as often as he asked me to and sometimes stopped in on my own on the way to or from work. After his initial contentment at the end of the day-to-day stress of caring for his father, Peter began to grasp how empty his days had become. He went into his school to organize a return to work in January but was told that wouldn't be possible. Plans were in place for the winter semester; he could start again the following September.

I wondered if this was something he should take to his union, but he didn't have the energy to argue. 'Maybe it's better,' he said. 'I'll spend more of the daytime visiting Dad, and that will free up my evenings for you.' We had an understanding that we didn't need to spend every evening together. I still went to my book club, and still had the two older girls for sleepovers on a regular basis.

'You used to be very involved with Big Brothers and the Boy Scouts,' I said. 'Maybe you should do some more volunteering this winter.'

'Maybe,' he said. 'Maybe.' But he didn't contact either organization and I didn't push him.

I didn't always invite Peter to join Mum and me on Thursday evenings, but they got along well, and Mum admitted that she was pleased with the match. 'And Felicia would have been happy too,' she said.

I gathered the inaugural weekend at the cottage had not been a roaring success because the wet weather kept everyone inside. 'You can only play so many board games,' Rose had said. 'And the drinkers started sniffing around for the first drink of the day far too early.' She was sitting in our living room, each of us with a twin on our lap, while Peter entertained Aidan making pizza dough for individual pizzas.

'But it will be fabulous next summer,' I reminded her.

'It will. You and Peter will have to come often,' she said, lifting Mackenzie and sniffing her bottom. 'Ugh. Will you hold Sydney? This one needs a new bottom.'

Rose looked exhausted. Kent was on nights and, gauging from the bags under her eyes, Rose wasn't getting much sleep. 'Let me go change her,' I said. When I returned five minutes later, both Rose and Sydney were fast asleep on the sofa, and Mackenzie dropped off moments later. The three of them slept for an hour and a half, and when Rose woke up, she was a new woman.

'Can I do this every day?' she asked. 'Peter? Can I come and leave Aidan with you every afternoon for an hour or two so the twins and I can nap together?' She probably wasn't serious, but Peter said of course she could.

'So we can make pizza every day?' Aidan's eyes were wide. 'For real?' The pizzas had been baked and eaten after I'd taken a photo of Aidan's to show her mother.

'Not every day,' I said. 'One day this week you might go 'round to Granny's house and help Uncle Peter rake the leaves. Do you know he used to rake Granny's leaves when your Mumma was your age?'

Aidan always thought it was hilarious to hear stories about her mother as a young girl. 'That was a loooooooooong time ago,' she said.

'Sure was,' said Peter. 'I think there were still some dinosaurs hiding out in the bushes back then.

'For real?'

'No. Uncle Peter is making a joke.' This from Rose. 'Your Mumma is old, but she's not that old.'

Your beau is spoiling Aidan! Rose texted me a few weeks later. *And she loves it. Mads is ticked that she has to go to school and miss out on the playdates.*

He adores her, I texted back.

Ha! Well Kent has his wife back, so he sends his thanks as well.

November flew by, and soon there was snow on the ground and Christmas in the shops. I thought carefully about the ornaments I'd shipped back from Hawaii, still wrapped and boxed. I decided that perhaps this year I'd forgo a tree, but I didn't tell Peter, or tell him why. So I was truly surprised when I came home from work and saw a few tell-tale pine needles on the snow.

'Surprise!' yelled Aidan when I opened the door.

'Look what we got you!' said Madison. 'We chose it and Uncle Peter helped us to cut it down.'

'And now we're making decorations for you,' said Aidan. The dining room table was covered with construction paper and glitter glue and pipe cleaners.

'I'm better at cutting down a tree than making decorations,' said Peter. 'But we have planned a popcorn-and-cranberry garland too, and I have high hopes for that.'

The four of us strung yards of popcorn and berries on to bright red cotton, and when the tree was finished I declared it the best ever.

We had agreed to have Christmas morning at Rose's with brunch and presents, and then Christmas Dinner at my house. On Christmas Eve, Peter and I visited his dad, and then all three of us went to their church for Midnight Mass. Kathleen was at the door on welcome duty.

'Oh for pity's sake, Lily,' she said. 'Could you not have told me it's Peter Reynolds you're dating?' She shook a finger at Peter. 'And you're no better. All this time I've been bugging you to bring your girlfriend to church and she's my bestie!' She laughed.

I suspected when I went back to the office after the holiday break she might renew her efforts to encourage me to join the church, and I thought I might well agree.

In the middle of the children's present opening frenzy, I thought back to a year when Quentin and I had agreed not to exchange gifts and instead go out to lunch at an upmarket restaurant. I hadn't thought of him in a long time; I hoped he and Sonia were starting some new traditions which would become theirs. As if he could read my mind across the miles, my phone pinged with a text. *Merry Christmas HB*. I smiled.

'But we're all here,' said Rose. 'Who on earth can be texting you?'

'An old friend,' I said. And realized as I spoke that it was true.

Peter and I saw in the New Year at home with a bottle of sparkling wine, dressed in pyjamas and sitting in front of the popcorn and cranberry decked tree. A blizzard that day had covered the city, and it seemed an appropriate symbol for a fresh slate, a new start. 'Next year we'll have a tree in the yard,' I said. 'Let's hang some outdoor lights.'

'Sounds good,' said Peter.

'And in the summer we should finally make an oven in the back yard,' I said. 'Have everyone over for pizza.'

'Sounds good,' said Peter.

I laughed. 'I wonder what I could suggest that wouldn't sound good.'

'Hmmm. Pineapple on that pizza? Although,' he looked at the glass in his hand. 'Another one of these and I might even agree to that.'

When the phone rang soon after midnight, I assumed it was Rose, calling to be first to wish me a happy new year. It was going to be a good one, I had decided. But it wasn't good wishes, and it wasn't good news. It was the care home suggesting Peter come in as soon as possible. His father had had another stroke. Serious.

'Dammit. Dammit,' said Peter. He sounded as angry as I'd ever heard him. Neither of us was safe to drive. 'You get dressed,' I said. 'I'll call a taxi.'

Of course, as it was moments after midnight on New Year's Eve, there was an hour long wait, and an exorbitant charge. I considered calling Mum and asking her to come and get us but decided to hope a cab might come free sooner than the dispatcher anticipated. In fact, it was almost two hours before the cab arrived, by which time Peter was as anxious as I'd ever seen him.

We arrived at the care home to discover his dad had been taken to the emergency department. Another long wait for a taxi. A mess of people in the waiting room, many of them drunk.

'Dammit,' Peter said. Clearly this had become his mantra.

When we finally reached his father's room, I was worried we had arrived too late. I'd never seen Mr. Reynolds looking so pale or so fragile. Peter half-fell, half-sat in a chair by the bed, and started to cry. I touched Peter on the shoulder, then went to look for help. I found a young woman who must have been in her mid-20s but looked barely old enough to have graduated high school. 'Please,' I asked. 'Can you tell me what the prognosis is?'

'Are you a family member? I'm sorry, but I do have to ask.'

'I am,' I lied.

She may or may not have believed me, but apparently my word was good enough. 'We'll keep him as comfortable as possible,' she said. 'He'll be able to hear you, so do keep speaking to him.'

I thanked her and went back to the room, where Peter was still crying.

'Your dad can hear you,' I said. I raised my voice. 'Mr. Reynolds—Warren—we're here. The doctor wants to make sure you're not in any pain. Will you squeeze my hand if you hurt?' I had seen this in a movie. In real life perhaps it didn't work that way, or maybe, I hoped, he was not in any physical pain. Certainly there was no pressure on my hand. I kept his hand in mine and carried on speaking. 'Peter and I both love you very much. We love you very much. But if you're ready to let go, we understand. Your wife, Peter's mom, Felicia, will be waiting for you.'

Finally Peter found his voice and was able to say a few sentences. 'I love you, Dad. I love you.'

'Do you remember the first day we all met?' I asked. 'Felicia had made us a pie for dessert.' I couldn't remember if that was actually true but knew it didn't matter. 'And then you sent Peter over to rake our leaves the next day. And he took me to the movies and McDonald's. The most recent time we went to the movies he slept the whole way through.' I chuckled and searched for some more memories to share. There were lots, and I spoke for the next hour, recounting every memory I had in which Warren Reynolds played a part, however minor. When he could, Peter joined in. Mostly he held his dad's hand.

As the day was beginning to break, there was a sense of change in the elderly man's breathing. 'Shall I go and get the doctor?' I whispered to Peter.

He shook his head. 'No. Don't leave. Please, keep talking.'

I nodded, and raised my voice again, filling it with as much cheer as I could manage, with tears running down my cheeks. 'And hasn't this past year been good to us all? I'm so glad I was able to spend so many evenings with you, Warren. I'm so glad you've seen how happy Peter and I are together. It took us a while, and we needed your help, but we finally figured it out. You were an awesome wingman for your son, and I will be forever grateful for that. When you see his mom, tell her how happy we are. Tell her—'

There was a hand on my shoulder. I hadn't even heard the young nurse enter the room. I stopped speaking and turned to look at her.

'That was lovely. That was a truly lovely send off,' she said.

I understood this to mean that Warren had now gone to join his wife in some other place, not this one.

So the new year which had started with a moment of such hope began with funeral arrangements, which I quickly realized would be my responsibility. I called on Kathleen, who knew the church and knew the minister and knew what was needed. With Mum and Kathleen's help, I organized the wake, and Rose posted the necessary announcements in the paper and online. The church was packed, the service was lovely. Peter said very little through it all.

A few days later he started talking about how few short months his father had lived in the care home, how he ought to have kept him at home for the autumn, dammit, how he'd promised him he wouldn't die alone.

'He didn't die alone,' I reminded Peter. 'You were there. You were holding his hand. He heard your voice, and he knew you loved him.'

But Peter was unable to function. I recognized depression from the months after David's birth, and I understood, finally, how difficult it must have been for Quentin to live with me in that state.

'It will take time,' said Mum. Kathleen said the same thing. I knew they were right. Still, I insisted on trying to find something to interest him. Outings on snowshoes and cross-country skis, afternoons when we had Madison and

Aidan over, any evening talks I thought might interest him. I accompanied him to church every Sunday morning, to Kathleen's quiet satisfaction. He could rally himself for a few hours when the girls came to visit, but then the despondency returned.

'I'm sorry,' he said, often. 'I'm not much use to you.'

'I'm not with you because I want useful,' I always replied. ' 'I'm with you because I wanted to spend the rest of my life with the man I love.' Then I'd kiss him, and sometimes, on a good day, that made him smile.

Chapter Fifteen

Big Rock Lake, February 2014

The main doors of the emergency room opened, letting in a rush of cool air. An older woman held her partner's hand and helped him navigate around the floor mat.

She spoke to the front desk, then to her husband. 'We have to wait, Darling. We're on the list now. They'll let us know.'

She sat, and patted the seat next to her, but he shook his head, half-pacing, half-shuffling. He was clearly distraught, and he started muttering to himself. His wife stood, held his hand in hers, and walked with him, making soothing noises. Eventually she convinced him to sit.

Dementia.

Of course I saw it everywhere. Peter's diagnosis had changed everything.

Big Rock Lake, 2013

That had been a difficult day.

When he was called into the doctor's office, I followed him. Neither Peter nor the man about my age said anything as I sat. The minutes ticked by as Peter spoke about anxiety, sluggishness.

'Peter, your memory,' I said. I looked at the doctor. 'His memory.' I pulled a list from my pocket, smoothed it out on my lap, and started reading. 'A couple of weeks ago he stood in the middle of the kitchen and asked where the garbage can was. It lives under the sink, as it always has, as it did in his house, and his parents' house before that. Even with a list, he forgets to buy things at the grocery store. He didn't put the recycle bins out last Thursday. He doesn't know how old our twin nieces will be next birthday; they thought he was joking, but he really couldn't guess their age.' As I read on, I could feel Peter stiffening beside me.

I turned over the page, which was also full with examples, but I stopped.

'You've been spying on me,' Peter said, his voice cold.

'Not spying. I love you, I live with you, and I'm very concerned. You're too young to be losing your memory.' I met no one's gaze but looked down at my steel grey nails. A statement colour for power. I noticed the second fingernail on my right hand was chipped.

I saw the doctor nod through my peripheral vision and looked up. 'I'd like you to have an MRI to rule out any possible physical cause, and I'm going to refer you to the Memory Clinic in Toronto for further tests.'

Something in my stomach untwisted. 'You believe me.' This man with a doctor's education and a medical degree believed me.

He nodded. 'It sounds like MCI. Mild cognitive impairment.'

I clenched my lips against an instant angry retort. It's not mild. He can't work. He'll most likely never work again. I was counting on a second salary. I can't be his full-time caregiver. I didn't sign up for this. Instead, I listened, asked questions, thanked him.

We were silent on the drive home.

I'd booked the whole afternoon off, and I was glad I did. If I'd gone to the office and Kathleen had asked me how it went, I would have burst into tears. At home, I thought I could hold it together. I filed my list in the study and plugged in the kettle. 'How does a cup of tea sound, hon?' I asked.

'Good,' he said. 'It sounds good.' He sighed. 'Are you sorry you married me?'

'Not for a second,' I said. 'Never, never think that.'

'I am going to get a job, Lily. I'm not so stupid that I can't work.'

'No one thinks you're stupid. Darling, no one thinks you're stupid.'

'You watch,' he said, shuffling out of the room. From behind, he could have been his father as an elderly man.

'I'm watching,' I whispered.

And? Mum texted that evening.

I looked at my phone, not ready to share the bad news.

More tests to come, I replied, avoiding any mention of the diagnosis.

BIG ROCK LAKE, 2009

There had been signs. I'd not seen them for what they were, but there had been signs.

Rose said they'd celebrate the twins' first birthday May long weekend at the cottage. 'You must come,' she said, even when I told her that Peter's grief might put a damper on the weekend, and so I packed up the car and followed her directions. For the duration of the drive I kept up a cheerful patter about the arrival of spring and the plans we were making for the summer. Madison elected herself tour guide and showed me around the property while Kent and Peter sat on the beach with a cooler of beer.

The next morning they all went on an expedition to tour a sugar bush and eat pancakes with fresh maple syrup. I made my excuses. Rose further explained to the children. 'Aunt Lily has a fear of open fires. Like Aidan and spiders.'

'I hate spiders!' Aidan echoed. 'I scream when I see them and Daddy makes them go away.' When she came back, she told me that she and Uncle Peter had my extras. 'Maybe the twins can eat pancakes next spring, do you think so Mumma?'

'Maybe not next year,' said Rose. 'But soon.'

'Can they eat their birthday cake tonight?' Aidan wanted to know. 'Or shall Maddie and I help them?'

When they returned to the cottage Peter asked Kent if he could borrow the canoe. It was the first time I'd heard him ask to do anything on his own since the night his dad had died.

'Absolutely,' said Kent. He helped Peter launch it, and made sure the lifejacket, whistle, bailing bucket, and extra paddle were all in order. 'Sure you don't want me to come with you?' Kent offered. In that moment, I loved my brother-in-law.

Peter shook his head. 'I won't be long.'

When the twins went for their nap after lunch, Rose and I started dinner while the big girls decorated the cottage with streamers and each iced a cake. 'In case you ever wondered why you had those tacky streamers at Maddie's baby shower,' I said. 'It was because I had to buy a pregnancy test.' I had never told

Rose this story before. I had not been able to see its humour for a long time.

'I did wonder,' she said. 'It was very unlike Mum. And the blue streamers must have been caught in the printer because every sixth Y was missing from the end of boy.'

'Congratulations! It's a Bo!' This struck us both as hilarious.

'You two on the sauce already?' Kent asked, coming in from chopping wood.

'We aren't,' said Rose. 'But we should be. Shall we open the bubbles, or wait for Peter?'

I looked at my watch. 'It's four o'clock—he'll be back any time. Let's open them.'

But the three of us finished off the bottle, and the twins woke up from their nap, and still there was no sign of Peter. Dusk was coming on and when I went down to the shore to look for any sign of the red canoe, I had to swat away freshly hatched mosquitoes. If he'd capsized in water this temperature, hypothermia would hit in minutes. It was late May, but that didn't mean there wasn't still some spring run off—if he'd gone to explore a side stream, he may have run in to some unexpected rapids. The lake which had looked idyllic earlier, bright blue in the sunshine, was now dark and ominous. Still I stayed on the beach for another ten minutes, until the bugs were unbearable.

I went back to the cottage for bug spray, a ball cap, and long clothes. 'I'm worried about Peter,' I said. 'He should have been back long before now, and the sun will set soon.'

'He'll be fine,' said Kent. 'He's been canoeing longer than Red's been alive.'

It was true, but I was still concerned.

'You wait for him on the beach,' Rose said. 'I'll finish making supper.'

I waited until twilight, sitting anxiously in a beach chair, then getting up to pace the length of the cove, peering downstream for the red canoe. I started chewing my nails, a habit so long ago kicked I'd forgotten I ever used to do it. Rose came down again for an update, and I told her she should go ahead with the Birthday supper, the kids would all be hungry, and it wasn't fair to keep them waiting. Less than quarter of an hour later Kent came down to the beach with a plate of food for me. He must have wolfed down his dinner. 'I'm sure Peter's okay,' he said. 'But if he's not back in another half hour or so we'll give the coast guard a call, just as a safety precaution.'

I nodded, too tense to speak, surprised to find how comforting Kent's presence was. He had a string of good explanations for Peter's absence. 'Probably met a mate of his down the lake, had a few brewskis and got to chatting. You know. Or maybe he waited until dusk to throw in his line and the fish are biting.'

He hadn't taken any fishing gear, and I didn't think I'd ever known him to express any interest in fishing but was happy to believe that might be possible. 'Or, we all know Peter. If he met a couple of tourists who were lost, he'd paddle the length of the lake to take 'em home. He's got a heart of gold, that guy.' He slapped away a swarm of mosquitoes. 'Man these guys are fuckers, eh?'

I nodded after every story, and every few minutes checked my watch. Thirty-five minutes after my brother-in-law had come down, I looked at him. 'It's been over half an hour.' It was now truly dark. 'Kent,' I said. 'He's been so depressed since his dad died. I hope… I hope he…' I couldn't voice my deepest fear, not even under cover of the dark.

'Nah. Not Peter. Even if—and I'm saying even—even if he wanted to hurt himself, he wouldn't do anything that would put anyone else out. He wouldn't be dramatic, he wouldn't ruin the girls' birthday weekend. Listen to me, Lily. I'm a cop, and I've taken more anti-suicide courses than you can count. I'd have seen the signs, I promise you, and I would not have let him go off by himself.'

His words were instantly calming. 'Thank you,' I said. 'Thank you, Kent.'

'I think—'

Whatever Kent thought was lost. As he started to speak the silhouette of a canoe came around the point. I jumped up. 'Peter? Peter!'

'Lily,' he shouted back. 'Lily?' He paddled the last few feet towards shore.

The hours I'd spent worrying, thinking of all the worst-case scenarios: capsizing, rapids, hypothermia, came out in a rush of white anger. 'What the hell? Where were you? I've been worried sick, you've been gone for hours!' When I got close could I see the distress on his face.

Kent had waded out to help pull in the canoe. 'Hiya, Peter,' he said. 'Glad you're back.'

'Hi, Kent,' said Peter. 'It was the oddest thing. I must have been almost back here about four hours ago, but one bay over.' He pointed, vaguely, behind him. 'So I went down along the other shore, and when I got back to the float plane dock again, I knew I was at the wrong end of the lake.'

'The shoreline can be confusing, especially this time of year,' said Kent. 'You must be bushed if you've paddled the lake four times.'

'I wouldn't say no to a glass of water and a bite to eat,' said Peter.

We put the canoe away and walked up the path to the cottage. 'Darling, I'm sorry. I was really worried,' I said. 'I shouldn't have shouted.'

'I'm sorry,' said Peter. 'I'm really sorry.'

We walked into the cottage, and then, in the light, I saw how badly he'd been bitten. His left eye was barely open. 'Peter!' said Rose. She sat him down at the table. 'You must have a hundred bites on your face alone. And your arms!' They were a mass of blood and swollen patches.

'Yeah, they were buggers out there at dusk,' he said, retelling the story of turning around a bay too soon. 'I feel like such an idiot,' he said. 'I used to be able to read lakes. I can't believe how I got mixed up in such a familiar landscape.'

Kent gave Peter a glass of water and a bottle of beer, and Rose put a plate of food in front of him, and said she was sure she had something for bug bites.

'I drank all your share of the bubbles,' I said.

'I'm glad you enjoyed them.' He raised his bottle and clinked Kent's. 'I'm sorry you were all worried. I was an idiot.' He looked over at the older girls who were staring at his face. 'I'm sorry I missed the party, girls.'

'We were very worried, Uncle Peter,' said Aidan. 'And you are very naughty. And your face looks very funny. And now you must eat up very quickly so that we can all have cake, and there are two kinds to choose from and I decorated one of them all by myself.'

In our bed that night I again apologized to Peter for my greeting him with a stream of angry words. 'I was so worried when you didn't come back.'

'I was worried too,' he admitted. 'I have never felt that discombobulated. I was going to give myself another half mile and then kip down in the canoe for the night. Re-orient myself in the morning's light.'

'With all those bugs? You'd have been eaten away by morning.' And he'd been wearing shorts and a t-shirt. It was May, and the temperatures dropped at night. 'Surely there must be some other cottages on the lake for the long weekend. Didn't you see any lights? Couldn't you have stopped to ask directions?'

He said he hadn't wanted to bother people, had kept thinking that he'd come 'round a point and see Rose and Kent's place. He had passed a big bonfire and heard the sounds of drunken teenagers, but thought they'd be no use at all.

When we woke on Sunday morning Peter was as stiff as a board, and his left eye was completely swollen shut. I took him coffee in bed and left him to stay tucked up. Kent showed me a map of the lake, as we drank our coffee, pointing out the float plane dock at the far end, calculating how many miles Peter must have paddled. 'Solo,' he reminded us. 'I couldn't do it, not in an afternoon.'

'Why did he go so far?' Madison asked.

'Grief does funny things,' Rose said. 'Uncle Peter's daddy died and he is very sad. When my daddy died I was so sad I didn't eat maple syrup for a year.'

I looked at my sister. 'I don't think I ever knew that.'

'Nuts, isn't it? I think I felt it would be disloyal, somehow.'

I wanted to ask her more. The Maple Boil had been part of my childhood, not hers. Why did she connect Bobby with maple syrup? But Aidan curled up on Kent's lap. 'You won't die, will you, Daddy?'

'Not for a long, long time,' he said, hugging her tight. 'Don't you worry. I'm going to dance at your wedding and hound your Mumma for years to come.'

'What's hounding?'

'Like this.' He slammed his coffee mug on the top of the table. 'More coffee, woman!'

We all laughed, and soon after Peter joined us, walking slowly.

'You look like a zombie,' said Madison.

'I've discovered shoulder muscles I haven't used in months,' he said. He reached his arms above his head. 'Or… or maybe I AM a zombie!' He pretended to chase after Madison, who squealed with delight. And for the rest of the weekend, my Peter was back. He built sandcastles for the big girls' Barbies, pushed Aidan on the swing, helped Kent plan out future renovations over icy cold beers, and jiggled both twins on his knee when they fussed. Kent had the Tuesday off as well, so they were staying on. We left after lunch on Monday to head back home.

'There's a fire tower on a hill somewhere around here,' said Peter.

He was driving, so I looked at the map. 'Yes, a mile ahead or so.'

'Fancy a walk? It's clear, there should be a great view.'

There was a place to park a few cars by the trail head, and we clambered up the path through deciduous forest and over granite erratics. I imagined the strength of the glaciers, to have moved rocks this size. At the top of the hill was the fire tower, and we climbed up fifteen flights of steep stairs to the viewing platform at the top.

'Oh!' The forest of poplar and birch and maple was the bright green of first buds, which opened on to the lake, spread at our feet like a Group of Seven painting, deep blue apart from a few tiny wakes made by tiny toy boats. I watched a sea plane take off, silent in the distance. 'It's beautiful! It's so beautiful!' I turned to Peter with joy. 'I'm so glad we came to—'

He was on one knee, holding out a battered black velvet box.

'Lily. I've been wanting to ask you this question for more than half my life. You will make me the happiest, the proudest, the most blessed man in the world if you'll agree to do me the honour of becoming my wife. Please Lily, will you marry me?'

My hand flew to my throat. My first thought was 'so soon?' but then I thought of what he'd said. More than half a lifetime. And I remembered how worried I'd been on Saturday when I'd imagined him drowned, or in danger, and I dropped to my own knees and said, 'Yes. Yes, I will.'

He opened the box to reveal a thin gold band with a small diamond flanked by sapphires. 'If you would like a bigger stone, or a modern ring, then that's what you shall have,' he said. 'But I would also like you to have my mother's ring. She and my father were the happiest couple I've ever known, and theirs is the kind of relationship I'd like us to have.'

With tears in my eyes, I told him that it would be an honour to wear his mother's ring to declare our betrothment. He pulled the ring from its box and tried to slip it on my finger. It stuck at the knuckle.

We both chuckled. 'Your mother had tiny hands.' I remembered now. 'We'd better put it away. If we dropped it from here—'

We both stood, and Peter put his arm around my shoulder, and we looked at the view before us. We guessed at Rose and Kent's bay and searched for their cottage and watched the boats on the lake and the cars on the highway below us.

'I'm tempted to go back to tell Rose and Kent our good news.' But I also wanted to savour it for a little longer. 'And the girls will be thrilled. Especially if we ask them to be flower girls. Let's tell Mum this evening, in person, first.' I paused. 'I'm so sorry your dad didn't—'

'He gave me the ring in August,' said Peter. 'He said he'd been waiting until he was sure I'd found the right girl. He knew. He knew.' He looked up at the sky and whispered, as much to himself as to me. 'He knows.'

We admired the view for another twenty minutes, until we felt the tower beginning to shake, and heard another group of sightseers coming up the tower. 'Let's wait,' I said, 'and ask them to take our picture,' so we did. I had forgotten that Peter's face was still swollen, and his arms and legs were red with bug bites. I was tempted to tell them he'd just proposed, and I'd said yes, but they were a group of young people and I knew we'd look old to them, and I wasn't wearing a sparkling new ring, so I hugged the secret to myself. When I had the photo printed out a few weeks later I had to laugh at what a ragamuffin couple we made. It was hardly an engagement photograph to display in a silver frame, though I did exactly that.

Over the next few weeks we discussed our future, immediate and longer term. 'It makes sense for me to sell my house,' he said. 'I think we'd both much rather live here, by the lake, wouldn't we? We could pay off your mortgage.' And hen he admitted that he didn't mind if we were married in the church or not, osed that we hold our wedding and reception in our garden. 'That means ve to be next summer,' I pointed out.

as I know you're going to marry me, I'm happy,' said Peter.

He went back to teach in the fall, though it wasn't ideal. He was guaranteed a job equivalent to his previous position but was given a place in a school on the far edge of the district, a ninety-minute drive away on a clear day with no traffic. When the snow came in November, he had to leave the house at six in the morning and didn't get back home until well after six in the evening. By the time he'd had dinner, done the day's marking, and prepared for the next day of teaching, he was ready to drop.

Our wedding was perfect. A sunny day, our closest friends. When I'd married Quentin I'd had no idea how I wanted to celebrate; this time I was not only marrying the right man but marking the event in a way that made sense to both of us. Our honeymoon was spent in a cottage on the grounds of a lodge on the French River. Our breakfast was delivered in a hamper each morning, along with a packed lunch to take on a hike or paddle. We had dinner in the lodge the nights we didn't order room service and eat on our screened porch, overlooking the river. One evening we sat outside with a glass of wine and our books; I lowered my book and raised my glass towards Peter. 'This is the happiest I've ever been,' I said. And I meant it.

My happiness continued long after our wedding and honeymoon, but Peter's steadily diminished from September. The combination of the commute and his lingering grief was taking a toll on his health. I hoped the Christmas break would give him a chance to rest, but he was struck with the flu. Sometimes he barely seemed aware of his surroundings, and more than once I caught him writing notes which made no sense to me.

One Friday in February he slumped down at the table and started shaking.

'What is it? What's happened?' I held his shoulder, which was trembling.

'I think I'm done, Lily,' he said. 'Teaching is a younger man's gig. I'm a dinosaur in a modern world.'

He often said this—that teaching was a younger man's gig. But I'd never before seen him look so defeated. Over dinner he told me what had happened. In November he'd caught a student cheating on a test. Then the same student had not handed in his final essay. He'd failed the student, notified the department head and principal and the student's parents. The department head had called a meeting and promised, 'promised!' said Peter with disbelief, the parents that their son would pass the course and earn a credit. The student, full of bravado, claimed that he absolutely had handed in the essay and that Peter must have lost it.

'You didn't tell me any of this,' I said.

'I didn't want you think I'm such a failure,' he said.

'You're not a failure! But is there nothing more you can do?'

'I know when I'm beaten.' He shrugged. He was trying to work with the student. 'But where's his motivation? He's been told he'll get the credit; he knows I have no power. He doesn't care about the course and has no intention of doing any work at all.'

'And today?'

'Another meeting with the department head, who 'suggested' the fifty I gave the student was a slap in the face. It was. It was a slap in the face for every student who actually made an effort. The head has raised that student's mark to sixty-five. Which means I now have to add fifteen percent to all the other students' marks in order to be fair. Or defraud everyone else, making me no better than the student.' The student in question, Peter felt sure, was cheating in all his classes, but his colleagues were choosing to turn a blind eye. 'The school system is broken,' he said. 'Kids who should be held back are being pushed through.'

I was sympathetic, and empathetic, and then tried to think of any possible solutions. 'Would it help to go above the department head and speak to the principal, or higher, someone in the school board offices? Can you not request a transfer to a different school, somewhere closer to home? What can I do to help?'

He was quiet for a long time. 'You married a teacher, Lily. With a teacher's salary.'

'Peter... I didn't marry you *because* you're a teacher.' It took a moment for me to comprehend that he was asking my permission to quit. 'Do you want to leave?'

'Will you think less of me? I'll stay on until the end of the year, of course. But then look for something else. I have no idea what.'

'Of course I won't think less of you.'

'I may be penalized in terms of my pension.'

'It's only money,' I found myself saying. 'We can always earn some more.'

'Oh, Lily. I don't know what I did to deserve you.'

I had one last suggestion. 'If you're leaving anyhow, can you not stick to your guns and insist on a mark of fifty for the cheater?'

He said he might, but I suspected he wasn't willing to fight that last fight. I didn't push him, and never asked him about the final outcome.

The summer was little different than the previous year, apart from the fact ᵔeter claimed he was looking for work. He was bone-weary, and I could tell ᵔmucking about the garden, so I didn't push. We didn't need a second ᵔediately. Between the money from the sale of his house and my income we were fine.

When he still hadn't started a serious job search by Christmas I grew a little antsy, but he had a good reason to gently refuse every suggestion I made. In January, he came down with another bad flu, which he couldn't shake. When I finally forced him to go to the doctor, it was diagnosed as Chronic Fatigue Syndrome. The flu had been some sort of viral infection, and the doctor warned me that he'd be tired and sore for six months or more.

'It's bad luck,' said Kathleen one evening when I arrived at her house and burst into tears. 'It really is.'

'I meant it when I vowed in sickness and in health,' I said. 'I didn't think the sickness might come so soon. And I know two are supposed to live as cheaply as one, but I'm struggling. Is that churlish of me? And I can't have this conversation with Rose, because I don't want her to think I'm, you know, making a comment about her choice not to work outside the home.'

'Oh, Lil,' said Kathleen.

The following week when I was doing laundry I found an unopened envelope—inside, an overdue gas bill. I made a mental note to transfer all our bills from paper to online, into my name alone, and quietly take over their payment. On the outside of the envelope was a to do list: wash dishes, shovel driveway, cook dinner. A simple list, heartbreaking in its earnestness. I tried to guess what day Peter might have written this list but knew that he hadn't accomplished any one of those three things. There hadn't been a day recently when I'd not come home to dirty dishes by the sink, and a sticky counter. I shovelled the driveway by myself every evening before making a simple supper of pasta, scrambled eggs, or beans on toast. This was a list which an average person wouldn't write, would complete as a matter of course during a day spent doing other chores, real tasks. I took the bill and tossed the envelope into the recycle bin.

That Saturday, I invited Rose and the family to lunch.

'Look, Aunt Lily.' Mackenzie held out a wad of paper which had been folded over and stapled together. 'I wrote a book.'

'May I read it?' I asked, immediately sitting down and pulling her onto my lap.

'Of course. It's about giant moles. Everyone thinks there are sinkholes in the city, but it's really a gang of moles.'

'Ooh, sounds scary.'

'But in the end they're good, because they can dig out new tunnels for subway trains. And everyone lives happily ever after.'

'I love happy endings,' I said, opening the booklet. On the right-hand page, there was a sentence in neat printing, on the left a picture of a car half way down a hole.

'Wow,' I said. I looked up at Rose. 'This is really good.'

'Isn't it? Proud Mumma moment.'

I tried not to compare it to an almost illegible shopping list I'd recently found abandoned on the dining room table, riddled with spelling mistakes, with more words crossed out than completed.

Chapter Sixteen

BIG ROCK LAKE, 2013

The twins would be five in May.

'I can't believe it. Impossible,' I said to Sydney, when I went to collect Rose for a road trip to Toronto complete with concert and spa. 'I think maybe... two years old. I think I will buy you some baby toys for your birthday.'

'Noooooo. Silly Aunt Lily.'

'Well, three maybe. But that's the oldest you can possibly be. Three.'

'We're in school already!' Mackenzie pointed out. 'Three-year-olds don't go to school!'

'Well I don't understand how you grew up quite so quickly,' I said. 'Next thing I know you'll be wearing make-up and going out on dates.'

'Silly Aunt Lily!' they both said together.

'Don't call your aunt *silly*, girls,' said Rose. She sounded tired.

'I don't mind,' I said to my sister.

'Well I do. We don't use that word in this house.'

I made a face at the girls, which made them giggle, but unfortunately that didn't improve Rose's mood. 'Please, Lily. Don't encourage bad behaviour.'

I chose not to reply. Instead I asked them what their birthday party plans were. 'Two girls means two parties,' Sydney reminded me. 'Family and two cakes at the cottage, and also a big party with all our friends, with games and loot bags and more cake.'

'Two cakes,' said Mackenzie. 'Chocolate for me and pink for Sydney.'

'Our favourite flavours,' said Sydney.

'And what flavour is pink?' I asked.

Sydney looked at me as if I had lost my mind. 'Pink, of course.'

'Ahh.'

'I know your favourite flavour is carrot cake, but what about Uncle Peter?'

'He likes all the flavours,' I said. 'But he really likes pie. Blueberry pie.'

'Our daddy likes raspberry pie,' said Mackenzie.

'Then let's make him a raspberry pie next time you come for a playdate at my house,' I said.

Rose apologized for snapping as soon as we set off. 'Kent was supposed to be home at noon sharp,' she said. 'He walked in at two thirty with no idea why I was upset.'

'Busy at work?' I asked.

'I guess so. I used to know all his cases—the ones he could tell me about—but these days I barely know what he's doing. Sometimes I can't even remember what an adult conversation sounds like, we spend so much time talking about school and homework and parent-teacher nights and skating lessons and whether or not Madison can have her ears pierced.' She sighed. 'I have no idea how single parents cope.'

'Okay,' I said. 'First we're going to buy a coffee for the road, then your job is to find some good music. And all the cares and stresses you have, toss them out the window. They'll still be waiting for you when you get back, but this is our weekend.'

'Deal,' said Rose. 'Done. But I am sorry we're so late leaving. Now we'll be caught in rush hour and there won't be time for dinner.'

'Don't worry,' I said. 'We left a big cushion, we'll make the concert in good time.'

There was in fact an accident which closed two lanes, and we had to rush to use the washroom and get to our seats before the lights dimmed. The opening act was abysmal. My stomach was growling, and I began to think the whole weekend was doomed. But when the main act came on she was as good as we'd hoped, and the improved atmosphere across the stadium reflected our new found cheerfulness.

'That was great. Thank you,' said Rose, when we'd been seated at a table in a Greek restaurant half a block from the concert venue. 'I really enjoyed it.'

'Have we ever been to a pop concert together before?'

'Yes! How can you forget that Beatles tribute band Mum dragged us to? You were in High School and nearly died of embarrassment at being seen out in public with your mother and your sister.'

'Ahhh. I had deleted that evening from my memory bank,' I said. 'But it's all coming back now.'

'I can't believe I have a memory over you,' laughed Rose. 'You never forget anything from our childhood. Or ever.'

'I'm very worried about Peter's memory,' I said.

'Do you want to talk about that now?' Rose asked. 'Or is that stress from home that you tossed out the window when we left Big Rock Lake?'

'True. True,' I said. Nothing was going to change in a weekend. I had made him a doctor's appointment for the following week, and nothing was going to happen before then. And I could find lots of other happier things to talk about. We glanced at the menu and agreed on the Mediterranean Platter to share, replacing the taramasalata with extra hummus and adding an extra side of pita.

'Twins?' the waiter guessed.

'Sisters,' Rose grinned. I suddenly wished Tansy was here as well. I tried to imagine what she might look like, if she'd have enjoyed the concert too, if she'd like taramasalata or not.

'Do you miss Bobby?' I asked Rose.

She was silent for a few minutes and I could tell she was seriously considering the question.

'Honestly. No. I know he lived at home when I was child, but I don't really remember it. I am sorry the girls don't have a maternal grandfather though.'

'I was thinking about Granny and Grampa the other day,' I said. 'Our summers in Niagara-on-the-Lake. His garden. That little bakery in town. The joke shop.'

She shook her head. 'I don't think I've ever been to Niagara Falls.'

I open my mouth to correct her, then closed it. She'd been a baby; there was no reason she'd remember that trip with Mum. I needed Tansy here to share those annual summer holiday memories.

'We should take the girls to the falls,' Rose said.

We. Did she mean the two of us, or her and Kent? 'They'd love it.' I hoped she meant us.

'I bet it's crazy busy now with tourists. Maybe I'm not brave enough. It's like herding cats sometimes, trying to sightsee with four kids.'

'You're brave enough,' I said. 'You have always been braver than me.'

'No way. You're one of the bravest women I know,' she said.

I looked at her. 'Me?'

She tore a piece of pita and scooped up some baba ghanoush, but paused before eating. 'You bet. Marrying a man you barely knew who was going to travel around the world. Walking the Appalachian Trail by yourself.'

I interrupted. 'I didn't get very far.'

'You always say that. You started. If it hadn't been for 9/11 you would have finished, you know you would. That stubborn gene would have kept you going.' We both laughed.

'And,' Rose said. 'Going back to school to get a master's degree. And a doctorate. Then leaving your life—marriage, Hawaii, all that—to start over again. I think that's the bravest thing you've ever done.' She cut the last piece of grilled halloumi into two equal pieces and speared one.

'I never thought of that as brave,' I said, taking the other piece of cheese.

'It was. Super brave. I could never leave Kent.'

'Oh, you could if you had to,' I said.

She shook her head. 'No. I read somewhere that the one who loves less is the one with all the power in the relationship. He loves me, I know he does, but not in the same way that I love him. If we were to divorce, he'd recover. I never would.'

'You would,' I insisted. 'It would be difficult, but you would. You'd find your way and discover things you didn't know you'd lost.'

'Do you think I've lost things by marrying Kent?'

I knew I had to choose my words carefully. 'I think we all lose something of ourselves when we marry. It's part of the contract, by definition. In order to be part of a couple, we have to make compromises.'

She ate the last olive, then picked up the bowl and wiped it clean with a piece of pita. 'I'm not leaving Kent. I'm not getting a divorce.'

'I know.'

'I know you know.' A long silence. 'But... if I was given one wish it would be that you and Kent saw each other the way I see you both. I really don't understand how two of the people I love most in the world can't love each other like I do.'

'We like each other,' I said quickly. It wasn't even a lie. Some days I liked him a lot more than other days, but I didn't hate him. I didn't trust him, but I didn't hate him. 'And we both love *you*, which is what really counts.'

She nodded. 'I still think you're brave.'

'Thank you,' I said. I cut the last dolma in half and gave her the larger piece.
'I like Peter. But I liked Quentin too.'
'I know,' I said. 'He and Mum never really got on, but you two did.'
'Mum was convinced you married him because you were pregnant.'
'Really?'
Rose nodded. 'Really.'
'We spent so many years *trying* to get pregnant!' I snorted.
Rose looked at me and smiled. 'I bet she has never once thought of that. And I can't believe you're laughing.'
'Me neither. It's the biggest regret of my life, no children. Every month when I wasn't pregnant was the shittiest day ever, and my heart broke over and over again. But, oh, that Mum thought we were getting married because I was pregnant! That's the furthest possible thing from the truth.' Although it wasn't, not really. What if I hadn't terminated our first baby? Pregnancy. What if—I shook my head. Kathleen had told me a groaner of a joke the other day, and I remembered the punchline, so shared it with Rose.
She had jokes too, which were even worse, having come from the twins.
Maybe we were both tired. Maybe giddy after the concert and the wine and the freedom from all life's real responsibilities. But once we'd started laughing we couldn't stop, and when we tried to stop we started up again.
'You sisters have a good weekend,' the waiter said, when he gave us our bill.
We kept giggling on the way to the hotel and up to our room and all through a movie on television. 'We should do this more often,' said Rose when she turned out the light. 'A sisters weekend, just us.'
'I'd like that,' I said.
'What time is the spa booked for?'
'Ten o'clock.'
'Ummm, dreamy. Don't wake me a minute before nine thirty please. I can't remember the last time I could even imagine sleeping in until nine thirty.'
In fact, we were both awake at eight and had a relaxed breakfast before our spa treatment. Changing out of our clothes into the thick white robes, I looked up to see a three-way mirror filled with infinite number of reflections, and reflections of reflections, of my sister. Her words of the previous evening were so clear, for a moment I thought she'd spoken them aloud. *The one who loves less is the one with all the power in the relationship.*
She loves me less.
If I'd said the words aloud, instead of just thinking them, the mirrors

might have shattered. If this was a movie. But if this was a movie we'd look more like sisters.

'What are you thinking?' one of her reflections asked one of mine.

'We don't look like twins,' I said. 'You're young and thin and chic; I'm middle-aged and dumpy and grey. Ugh.' I looked away from my own series of reflections, which is what I really wanted to shatter.

'What?' She stood next to me, and put her arm over my shoulder, pulling me close. 'Of course we look like twins. You need another coffee. I bet the coffee is here is organic, fair trade, made from beans that have passed through a baboon's intestines. One sip will take years off your face.' She crossed her eyes and stuck out her tongue.

It worked. I smiled, and the morning was salvaged.

But lying on the massage table with the scent of jasmine in the air, soft new-age music playing in the background, my eyes covered with cucumber slices, I returned to the thought of power and imbalance in my relationship with my sister. If something happened to me, Rose would still have Kent and their four children. There was more at stake for me.

More uncomfortable was the thought that I was fully to blame. I had kept so much of the deep sadness in my life from Rose that she couldn't know that I needed her support. I'd always thought my lies of omission were a generous act on my part, but maybe there was a cost I hadn't counted on.

We met in the nail salon. Rose was having her fingers and toes painted bright blue. I sat next to her. 'Sorry,' she said. 'That seat is reserved for my dumpy, middle-aged sister who. . . oh wait! Lily, is that you? I thought you were a teenager.' She grinned.

'Ha ha,' I said.

'And,' she said, reaching out her hand. 'I bet you've chosen a barely there pink for your nails. Pass it over.' She looked at the woman who was filling the foot bath at my feet. 'Will you please choose the trendiest colours for this young lady, so she doesn't look like my grandma?'

'Ha ha,' I said again, but let the two of them conspire to give me teal toenails and metallic grey fingers.

'So what do you think?' the manicurist asked, when she was finished.

I smiled and held out my hands. 'They don't even look like my hands. I feel like I should be a hedge fund banker, or some whizz on Bay Street.'

'There you go,' she said. 'Remember that next time you reach for a pale pink. Chose a statement colour for power.'

'A statement colour,' I repeated, as Rose and I left the Spa. 'And that blue is gorgeous on you,' I added. 'You should look for a sweater in that colour. Something in cashmere for the cool spring evenings.'

'Yeah, because I have so many opportunities to wear cashmere in my life,' she laughed. She looped her arm though mine, just as we used to do when we were children.

'So. Lunch, and then we have the whole afternoon,' I said. 'We can each choose at least one thing. 'I'd love to go to the Bata Shoe Museum.'

'Well that's perfect, because there's an exhibit at the ROM I want to see.'

'Fun!'

'And if we have time, I'd love to go shopping.'

'Sure,' I said. 'I think I'll buy a lottery ticket. First time in ages. But don't worry, I haven't forgotten our pact—you'll get half of my winnings.'

As if she hadn't heard me, she kept talking. 'Starting with a junky party shop to buy all the crap for the twins' birthday party. I know—I made all the decorations myself when Maddie and Aidan were little. And I'm proposing to buy stuff that will end up in a landfill. Quentin would *not* approve.'

It always threw me when Rose spoke of Quentin as if his opinion mattered, or as if he was still part of the family. 'Oh, that rant of his,' I said. I smiled at the memory.

'Don't worry. Kent and I still repeat it from time to time. Our girls know it by heart.'

'Weird.'

'Yeah, a little.' She squeezed my arm in hers. 'Don't worry. We all love Peter. We're so happy that you married each other.'

'Is there a theme?'

'A theme?'

'The twins' party. I'm hoping five is still young enough for a classic, rainbows or jungle animals, not a video game character I've never heard of.'

'Under the sea.'

'Well that'll be super easy and super fun. Let's make a mental list. How many children will there be in total? And tell me, what the heck flavour is *pink*, really?'

A statement colour for power, I had told myself again on that Wednesday morning, as Peter and I waited in the doctor's office for his name to be called, and I looked down at my nails.

Peter followed my gaze. 'That's a pretty colour,' he said. 'Your fingers look really lovely.'

I reached over and held his hand in mine. 'Thank you. Rose and I had a lot of fun at the Spa.' And then we were called in to receive the diagnosis for Peter's memory loss.

I told Kathleen the day after Peter had been diagnosed with MCI. 'Bad news, good news. It's not going to get better. Well, unless he's got a brain tumour. But the doctor didn't think so.'

'I hope that's the bad news—?'

I loved that she could make me smile when I was on the verge of tears. 'The good news is that it's real. I haven't been imagining everything. That's positive, right?'

'Oh, Lil. I'm so sorry. I'm not going to hug you because if I were you, I'd start crying if you hugged me.'

'Poor Peter. However much this sucks for me, it must be so much worse for him. He knows, I know he does. He's maybe still in denial on the surface, but some part of him knows.'

'Now, or any time, tell me exactly what I can do to help. I'm going to start by bringing you dinner once a week. You can eat it, or freeze it, or feed it to the ducks.' I nodded, then shook my head, unable to speak for fear of crying. Kathleen squeezed my hand. 'And don't ever forget that you and Peter are part of our community. One thing about our church, we help each other.'

We finished our walk around the campus. At the door of our building Kathleen stopped. 'What's next?'

'An appointment with the Memory Clinic. But first the annual long weekend at the cottage for the twins' fifth birthday celebration.'

I wasn't sure why I was reluctant to tell Rose the outcome of the doctor's appointment. I told myself I didn't want to spoil the long weekend, take the focus away from the birthday girls, but it went deeper than that. The power imbalance, perhaps, which I had been thinking about off and on since our weekend in Toronto. I had established such a strong relationship with all four of my nieces and I didn't want Peter's illness to put that into jeopardy. I didn't want Rose to be scared that he'd forget to turn off the stove and burn down the house, so nix any more sleepovers. But there was more, too: I had been the one who couldn't get pregnant, I had been the one whose first marriage ended in divorce, I didn't want to be the one with a sick husband.

Peter had been withdrawn since the doctor's appointment, but when I arrived home from work on the Friday he was chirpier. On the top of his bag were two boxes, wrapped in bright pink paper. 'Ooh, what are those?' I asked. I'd bought and wrapped the girls' presents from us - swimsuits and matching beach towels.

'Surprises,' he said.

'Exciting.' I hoped he had bought something age appropriate. Last time we'd spoken he'd thought the twins might be turning ten. Or two. I wondered if my joking with them about how fast they were growing up was confusing to Peter. I added that to my mental list of things to remember—stick to the facts.

In fact, his presents were perfect. 'Ooh goody,' said Sydney. 'If it's from Uncle Peter you know it will be a good one.' She had chosen to unwrap his first, and pulled out a bright pink child-sized baseball ball, with a pink baseball and a pink ball cap. 'Let's go play right now,' she said.

'Aren't you going to open the rest of your presents?' Aidan asked.

'She doesn't have to open them all at once,' said Kent. 'She can savour them the whole weekend if she wants to.'

Aidan's face fell. 'But I want her to open mine,' she said.

'I want to open yours,' said Mackenzie. 'I want to open yours right now.'

'Me too!' said Sydney, the baseball set momentarily forgotten as she and her twin opened the Barbies Aidan had bought 'with all my own allowance.'

For Mackenzie, Peter had bought the fried-egg water mattress that had been hanging in the window of the toy shop for months. 'How did you know exactly what I wanted?!' she shouted, jumping down from her chair and rushing over to give him a bear hug with no prompting at all. 'I wanted this for my whole life! Daddy, Daddy, blow it up for me right now.'

'You have to share,' said Aidan. 'You have to share with everyone.'

'But me first,' said Sydney. 'Because we are the special twins.'

'You're special all right,' their father said, engulfing them both in a hug. 'Now I thought there was a rumour about some cake for dessert. Two cakes, with candles that need blowing out.'

'Make a wish. But don't tell us,' Aidan reminded them.

'I never need to make another wish,' Peter whispered to me. 'All my wishes came true.'

I looked at him, at the love in his gaze, and smiled back. 'Mine too,' I said. 'Mine too.'

The next day was a perfect beach day, blue sky and sunshine, more summer than spring. In the morning we all swam—or splashed about—and those aged ten and under played with the new blow up fried egg. After lunch, Rose and I sat at the edge of the lake, half-facing the beach, half-facing the bay, watching as Kent, Peter, and Aidan played ball with the twins.

Over and over again, Kent gently threw the pink baseball to Sydney. Sydney swung the bat after the ball had passed by her. 'Lookit me, Daddy. Lookit,' she squealed, dropping the bat in the sand and clapping her hands.

'My turn,' said Mackenzie. 'My turn, Daddy.'

'Everybody gets a turn,' said Kent. 'Syd, you have to swing the bat as soon as I start to throw the ball, okay? You have to try to hit the ball with your bat.' Aidan and Peter were the catchers, throwing the ball back to Kent.

'Honestly,' Madison muttered. 'Doesn't Dad know the twins are too young?' She flounced off the chair. 'I'm going to go out to the end of the dock so no one can bother me,' she announced.

Rose looked at her watch when her eldest daughter was out of hearing. 'Because right about now the boys' camp boys will paddle by, and she's much more noticeable if she's lying nonchalantly on the end of the dock, instead of sitting next to her old mother and aunt who will cramp her style.'

We both laughed.

'I hit it!' Sydney said. 'I hit the ball!' We both turned to look; the ball was three feet behind her, and her bat was on the sand at her feet, but she was dancing with pleasure. 'Your turn now,' she said, passing the bat to her sister.

Mackenzie managed to tap the ball with the bat.

'Almost,' said Aidan, scooping up the ball. 'Good try, Kenzie.'

'Good try, Kenzie,' Sydney echoed.

'Okay Mackenzie, here comes another one,' said Kent. Start swinging... now.' Mackenzie missed by a country mile. 'Again, Daddy. Again!'

I sat up suddenly, spilling my beer down my t-shirt.

'What? What is it?' Rose asked. 'Are you okay?'

I shook my head. 'Nothing.'

'You've gone pale. Are you sure you're okay?'

I managed to nod.

Again, Daddy. Again. The same words. Kent must have heard the same ghostly echo. I turned to look at him.

Rose, having no way to know what I was thinking, misunderstood my glance.

'He's such a great dad, isn't he?' asked Rose. 'He would have loved a son. Not that he doesn't love being the father of four girls.'

I never had to bite my tongue. I was never worried I might inadvertently say something, not even times like now, when I was gently tipsy. But sometimes, like then, I did think to myself, *He does. He has one. He has a son.* When these moments arose, I always let them pass.

She laughed. 'I can't believe you thought for one second I'd ever leave him.'

'What?' Suddenly I was terrified I'd had one beer too many this time, and I'd spoken aloud.

'In Toronto,' she said. 'You said I'd survive if I divorced him.'

My heart slowed to a more regular beat. 'Yes. But that doesn't mean I thought you were going to leave him.'

'Maybe. What I heard was that you had considered the possibility.' She took a drink of her beer. 'But anyhow, I love that man. I love this cottage. I love these weekends.' She handed me another bottle of icy cold beer. 'This is the good life.'

The day was full of echoes of things I'd heard in the past.

'Do you remember the fall of 2001?' I asked.

She looked at me and laughed. 'You and your memories. Which one is this?'

'It was unseasonably warm. We had a barbecue and ate outside—in your back garden—the week before Thanksgiving. Peter was there, and his dad, but before they came you were imagining the future, with a toddler and a baby on a blanket in the garden. You were pregnant with Madison. You described your dream cottage. And this is it. It's remarkable, but this is exactly what you wanted.'

'It is. It's perfect.' She took a long swig of beer. 'I guess we'd been thinking about it for a while.'

'It's like you had a list, and you waited until you could tick off every detail.' I looked at her. 'What am I saying, of course you had a list!' It was supposed to be a tease, a gentle joke. 'You must have known about this one before it even came on the market.'

'We were watching a few cottages,' she said. I heard hesitation in her voice.

'You chose well,' I said. 'Worth the second mortgage.'

'Lily.' She was sitting up straight and looking directly at me.

'Hmmm?'

'I've—I've actually been meaning to tell you for a while.'

I stopped watching the girls. Peter was leaning over, holding the bat, with Sydney's hands on top of his. I turned to face my sister. 'Tell me?'

'No reason you'd remember,' she said. 'Saturday March 24th, 2007.'

I did. I did remember exactly where I was, as it happened. The General Hospital, Honolulu. The last cruel joke my defective womb had played on me, a baby conceived without a single IVF treatment who grew in the wrong place. I spent three days in the hospital. The first day confirmed an ectopic pregnancy. The foetus could not be moved to my uterus, and there was no chance of survival. The second day a doctor removed the pregnancy tissues and both my fallopian tubes. The third day I curled into a fetal position.

217

Another thing about my life I had never told Rose.

The following month I'd found the condom in Quentin's jeans pocket and noted the irony that we had almost been placed in the position for a second time of having to mend our marriage whilst bringing a baby into our broken relationship.

How would my sister respond, I wondered, if I told her where I was on the 24th of March, 2007. 'Having abdominal surgery,' I could have said. 'Losing my last possible hope at a biological child.'

'—we called you,' Rose was saying. 'You must have been away on holiday because you didn't answer. We tried three days in a row. And by the fourth day—I hope you understand—we reconsidered. I mean, it was such a long-standing joke between us, but it was always a joke, right? You'd have done the same thing. Kent pointed out that you hardly needed the money, that half of the total sum wouldn't change your life, but that the total sum could change ours.'

'What are you talking about, Rose?'

'The 6/49. Our numbers came up.'

It took me a few moments longer to understand she was talking about a lottery win that she had never before told me about. A significant one.

'—a list, of course, and did the math.' She kept talking, justifying their choice.

I remembered how the nurse held my hand, let me grip it through the pain. A young man, with a soft voice. I hadn't heard all the words he'd said but took comfort in his presence. I noticed my hand was on my stomach now.

Rose was still going on. This was clearly a story she had been telling herself for six years. She believed what she needed to believe. Now she told me what had been on the list that she and Kent had drawn up. The mortgage on their house had been paid off, university funds had been started for the two girls, and there were small upgrades like a new washer, nice towels, and name brand groceries mixed in with the low price No Name. 'That's when it really hit me,' said Rose. 'I opened the kitchen cupboard and it wasn't yellow and black. So when we saw this cottage on the market, well, we could afford a mortgage again.'

The one who loves less holds all the power.

'And that's why we don't buy lottery tickets anymore. We had our luck. We want someone else to have luck now. You don't mind, do you?'

I thought of all the times I hadn't been fully truthful with her. 'I don't mind about the money,' I said. 'I'm glad you started university funds for your daughters and paid off your mortgage. I love this cottage and I think it's a great investment.'

'But? I hear a *but* in your voice.'

'I need time to process this,' I said. 'You've known for six years. I found out seconds ago. But if you need an instant answer, right now, I'm not sure I'm pleased you've told me. Honestly, I think I might have preferred not to know.'

'Oh. But it's been killing me,' Rose said, clearly hurt. 'I hated lying to you.' Her voice grew defensive. 'And Quentin was always throwing money around, so we knew you were loaded. He used to say it was only money, you could always earn some more.'

'He did say that. Once. When Madison broke his brand-new television. When you came to visit us because he bought your plane tickets.' I could hear how cold my voice was. 'It's not about the money, Rose. I'm happy you won money. It's about—.' I wasn't sure what it was about. The breaking of our lifelong childhood pact, the secrecy? One of the twins hit the ball, but I didn't turn to see who it was. There was shouting, and applause, and I could hear high fives all round.

'The twins,' I said slowly, doing the math. 'They're your lottery babies. Not an attempt to save a failing marriage, as some people might have thought—'

'Who? Who thought that? Did you think that? Did Mum think that?'

I didn't answer. '—but an acknowledgement that another child was a financial possibility. And surprise—twins. That must have been the very last nail in the "share the winnings with my sister" coffin for you.' I wondered if any of the lottery winnings were spent on the other woman and her son. I sighed.

'You don't know everything.'

'No. No I don't. I can only know what you tell me.'

'What's that supposed to mean?'

'It's not supposed to mean anything. It means that you have chosen to share the truth when it is convenient for you to choose to share it. I don't know how that's honest. It means that I can't read your mind. It means that you're hurt that anyone would assume you don't have the perfect marriage, even though it sounds like you doth protest too much.'

Her voice was cold. 'The state of my marriage is actually none of your business.'

'You're right. It's not. And you have assured me many times that you are very happy and that you are not going to leave your husband.'

'I am not like you.'

'My turn to ask you what you mean by that.'

'I will do everything I can to make my marriage work.'

I shivered, even though I wasn't the least bit cold. 'You're suggesting that Quentin and I didn't do everything we could to make our marriage work?' I felt a white flash of anger. 'Did I tell you about the therapy sessions? The years of IVF treatments? The promotion he turned down because it would have meant another seven-month deployment?' I drew a sharp breath. 'And if you were to discover that your husband was falling in love with, was *fucking*, another woman, you wouldn't even consider leaving him? You'd carry on, stay married?' I was aware that I had to stop talking, that I was starting to say things I could never take back, never un-say. We can hurt the people we love so easily, so much more deeply than strangers. And I didn't want to hurt Rose.

'Kent is nothing like Quint. We have children. And he'd never cheat on me.'

'You sure about that?'

There was silence between us for a long time.

When the twins got tired of playing ball and started building a sandcastle with Aidan and Peter, Kent came and sat on the end of Rose's chair, took a beer from the cooler, and passed Rose and I one each. I set mine beside the other one, untouched, in the sand. 'This is nice,' he said. 'It's lovely to sit in silence sometimes, eh?'

It was a throwaway comment. Idle chitchat after two hours of non-stop talking from the twins. But I blamed him for putting me in this position, for the secret I knew about him that had now grown from a crack to a chasm between Rose and me.

'We're silent, your wife and I,' I said, 'because we've argued.'

'Why would you say that?' Rose hissed at me.

'You made a point of saying how you want there to be truth between us. So, there you go. Truth between all of us.' Though not the big truth. Not the real elephant in the room. A herd of elephants. They waved to me from the middle of the lake: *Again, Daddy. Again.*

'I told her,' Rose said to Kent. 'About our lottery win.'

'Ah.' Kent sounded distinctly uncomfortable, and I imagined he was wishing he'd offered to help with the sandcastle too, or gone to chop some more wood, or was anywhere but sitting on the end of that deckchair, between his wife and his sister-in-law. 'Red. We agreed we'd never tell.'

'You suggested. I never agreed.' Rose's voice was filled with anger bordering on frustration. 'And anyhow, last week we both said that we'd start telling the truth. No more white lies or half-truths. We did agree to that, with each other, in front of Dr. Corbett.'

There was a sudden frostiness in the air, and I guessed that Rose had not intended to mention Dr. Corbett, local marital therapist, in front of me—ever, but especially not right now. Suddenly, it made sense why she'd come clean about their lottery win. Telling me was some sort of ten-step thing. And now the secret Kent and I shared, even though she knew nothing about it, made us the bad guys. I wondered if Kent was as insistent about truth-telling as his wife said she was.

And marital therapy. So she truly was doing everything she could to make her marriage work. I wanted to reach over and hug my baby sister but knew if our roles were reversed that is not what I'd want. I'd want her to leave. I'd want to be alone. Saying nothing, I stood and went over to the sandcastle village. After admiring the castle and surrounding town, I said, 'Uncle Peter and I are going to go for a little walk now, girls. We'll see you later.'

'Later 'gater,' said Sydney.

'My fried egg is the best ever!' Mackenzie yelled. 'Thank you, Uncle Peter!'

'You aced their birthday presents,' I said as we walked up the path to the cottage.

'I love those girls,' said Peter.

'And they love you.' I hoped I hadn't put that relationship at risk.

I didn't speak again until we'd changed into long pants and running shoes and were in the car. 'Rose and I argued,' I said.

'Oh, that's a shame, Lily,' said Peter.

'They won the lottery. She and Kent won the lottery six years ago and never told me.'

'Well. That's nice for them. That they won.'

How could his cheerfulness grate on my nerves? That wasn't fair of me. 'Rose and I always had a deal,' I said. 'Since... since, forever. We promised that if either of us won the lottery, we'd share the prize.'

'Don't let a bit of money come between you. Are you worried about money? I am going to get a job. I mean that.'

'It's not about money. It's not about us.' I thought it safer to ignore his pledge to get a job. 'I'm hurt. Hurt that she didn't tell me. That she didn't tell me then. And that she told me now. Why couldn't she have kept it to herself? Like all the money.' I knew I wasn't making a lot of sense, but I didn't want to tell him that she thought I had somehow not done enough to save my marriage to Quentin. And I knew she was right. I was a quitter; I'd stopped trying and given up. 'I'm not entirely sure why I'm so hurt,' I said. 'But I am.'

'I dare say it'll blow over,' said Peter. 'Money can be a funny subject.'

I agreed. And then we reached the trailhead for the fire tower and I stopped the car. 'Our engagement walk,' I said.

'Ah yes. Lovely.' He stood at the entrance. 'Which way shall we go?'

There was only one way. A single path uphill. I understood that it was going to be up to me to lead from now on. I hoped the view from the top would be as pretty as I remembered.

Chapter Seventeen

I deliberately took my time climbing the hill and lingered at the top. When we reached the car I headed not for the cottage but for the nearest LCBO, where I blew a ridiculous sum on a bottle of Champagne. The real stuff. I walked into the cottage waving it and passed it to Rose and Kent. 'Belated congratulations,' I said. 'Really, I am so happy for you. Your big win. I mean it. It was a surprise when you told me, Rose, but I am truly happy for you. And I love that you're so generous and keep inviting us to your cottage.'

'Thanks,' said Kent. But it was clear from his voice that he was not in a good mood, and I wondered if words had been exchanged between them after Peter and I left.

'Shall we drink to your numbers coming up?'

'You go ahead,' Rose said to me. 'I drank beer all afternoon, I've had enough alcohol for the day.' She plonked the bottle on the back of the counter by the salt and pepper.

So as a peace offering, it was a bust. I instantly begrudged the money I'd spent.

Madison entered the room and looked at her mother. 'What's for supper?'

'I don't know! I don't know what's for supper! Why are you asking me? Why am I always the one who organizes supper? Ask your father or your aunt.'

Rose left the cottage, and the door slammed behind her.

'Honestly,' my eldest niece muttered. 'It was only a question.' She stomped out of the cottage, also slamming the door. It rebounded on itself and the top hinge popped off, leaving the door on an angle.

'Don't slam the door, goddammit!' Kent yelled. 'For fuck's sake,' he muttered under his breath. 'No one gets to complain when the cottage is full of mosquitoes.'

Sydney and Mackenzie had been watching with wide eyes, and when the third person yelled it must have been too much. They both burst into tears.

'Now look what you've done!' Aidan shouted. 'You made them cry on their birthday weekend.'

Kent dropped to his knees. 'Oh Babies, I'm sorry. Daddy and Mumma are tired. We didn't mean to shout.' He reached out his arms to engulf Aidan and the twins.

I thought about packing up and leaving. Clearly we were in the way—neither wanted nor particularly welcome. But our leaving might be taken as an affront rather than a kindness. 'Let's see what we can find for dinner,' I said to Peter, going into the kitchen. I spoke loudly enough that everyone could hear, in case Aidan wanted to help, or Kent knew of a local pizza parlour that delivered. But no one replied, so I opened the cupboards and fridge. I assumed the hamburger meat had been intended for tonight's dinner, but food on the table as fast as possible seemed more logical than taking the time to cook the beef. I put on a pot of water for pasta, and mixed eggs with cream and parmesan while I fried some bacon, and asked Peter to set the table then make a salad with whatever he could find.

'This isn't real pasta,' Mackenzie said when I served her a bowl. 'Real pasta has red sauce.' She picked at it.

Kent declined the offer of supper and worked away at fixing the screen door.

Sydney ate quietly. Of Rose and Madison there was no sign. I tried to keep a conversation of sorts going through the meal, despite the mood. As soon as the twins had finished, Kent took them off to bed. Peter and I cleared away and washed the dishes. 'Would you like to play a board game?' I asked Aidan, who was slouching on a chair in the screen porch, reading ancient copies of Mad magazines, but she shook her head no. So Peter and I sat with her, books open in our hands, until the light was too poor to see any words on the page.

I said good night to Aidan, deciding that she was old enough to see herself to bed, or not, and Peter and I went to our room. 'Let's leave as soon as we can tomorrow morning,' I whispered. 'Right after breakfast.'

'Righty-oh,' said Peter. 'That was lovely pasta, hon.'

I curled into him and lay my head on his shoulder.

I didn't hear Rose come back, but nor did I stay awake listening for her footsteps. She was in the kitchen when we emerged the next morning, making coffee. 'Did you use up all the bacon and eggs that I brought for breakfast?' she asked me.

'I made Carbonara for supper,' I said.

'Not helpful,' she said.

'I saw muffin mix and boxed cereals, so I knew we'd be okay for the morning.'

A big sigh, as if her day was now ruined. 'Girls, who wants to go out to the Inn for breakfast?'

'Peter and I will leave you to a family breakfast out then,' I said. I kissed Aidan and the twins and asked them to say goodbye from me to Madison when she woke up, then said goodbye in the general direction of the kitchen where both Rose and Kent were silently drinking coffee.

'Don't feel you have to leave,' said Kent.

'Stuff to do,' I said, unable to tell if he was trying to be polite or if he hoped there might be less hostility in the room with Peter and me there. I opened my mouth to thank them for a great weekend, but there was no way to phrase that. Instead I turned to the twins, who were playing with their new Barbies. 'We loved being part of your birthday celebration. Thank you, girls.' There was no response, so I lifted my hand in a casual wave and left.

'That was an awkward parting,' I said when we were in the car and heading home.

'Oh, I think everyone's tired,' said Peter.

'Let's get a coffee to go and have brunch when we get home,' I suggested. 'In case they change their minds and don't go to the Inn for breakfast.' I didn't want to be sitting at a table in the town's other restaurant if they all walked in.

'Sure,' said Peter.

I reached out my hand and patted his thigh. 'Thanks, darling, for always being so good-natured and cheerful.'

'It's the easiest thing in the world to be cheerful when I'm with you,' he said.

'Aww. Corny. But sweet.'

'And true, as it happens.'

'I wasn't expecting to be at home today. Is there anything you'd like to do? Is there anything we can do in the garden?'

'That's a great idea,' he said. 'There's always something to do in the garden.'

When Kathleen asked if we'd had a good long weekend I didn't answer but asked instead for details about hers. I didn't speak to Rose for the rest of the week, and every time I thought about texting her I hesitated and typed nothing, and then put my phone away.

On Friday she rang me at work soon after I arrived. 'I have "Sunday Lunch" written on the calendar. Is that at yours or Mum's?'

'Mum's,' I said, wondering if she would have cancelled if I'd said it was due to be held at my house. 'There'll be two more birthday cakes for the girls.'

'Oh god, more cake.' There was a long silence and I wondered if she'd hung up but the phone hadn't disconnected us. 'Okay. I'll see you there.'

'Yes,' I said. 'See you there.'

I hung up the phone and then lifted it again, making sure there was a dial tone. I propped it between my shoulder and my ear, so that if anyone came into my office I'd look as if I was on a call. I wasn't sure what I was going to do, but I couldn't face seeing any of my colleagues. There was the ping of a new email, from the university's health and wellness team. Usually I barely scanned them, but this one had 'dementia' in the subject line, so I opened it to read more closely. It was notice of a brown bag lunchtime seminar series for the sandwich generation, caring for a loved one with dementia, starting today.

Moments later my email pinged again. *Wanted to make sure you've seen this,* Kathleen wrote, forwarding me the same email.

I did, thanks, I wrote back.

Going?

Yes

Want me to come with? Extra pair of ears and all that.

I thanked her and said yes, if she wasn't busy. Then I put down the phone and got on with my day, and I might have forgotten the lunchtime meeting if Kathleen hadn't stopped by my office to collect me. I was amused to find I recognized the classroom where it was held from an art history course I'd taken all those years ago.

The facilitator started with a general outline of what we'd discuss, then asked us to introduce ourselves.

When she reached me, I gave my name and said I worked in the archives.

'Welcome, Lily. And do you have a parent who is living with dementia?'

'It's my husband who has memory issues.'

Next to introduce herself was Kathleen. 'I'm here with my best friend,' she said, patting my arm.

'So,' said the facilitator. 'First thing. You are not alone.' She gestured at all of us. 'It will feel like you are. Often. But you are not.'

She started with a PowerPoint, an overview of the various types of dementia, and some of the signs and symptoms of each. She gave us each leaflets and some homework.

'Well?' asked Kathleen as we walked back to the office. 'Helpful? Helpful enough that we'll go back next week?'

'For sure helpful enough to go back,' I said. 'But you don't have to come.'

'I know. But if it was me, you'd go.' She held out her baby finger. 'Pinkie promise.'

'I always wanted to pinkie promise,' I said. 'I didn't ever have a bestie in grade school because I was a bushie. And by the time we moved everyone else had outgrown that phase.'

'Not me.' She grinned, and I reached out my baby finger and we walked back to the office that way, like a couple of seven-year-olds.

At my desk I skimmed through the leaflets. So much sounded so familiar. There had been many early signs. Of course it was easy to see them with hindsight. I wondered how I'd missed them, or managed to ignore them, so successfully for so long. I allowed myself five minutes to wallow in self-pity. I had survived the pain of Quentin's infidelities, David's death, the loss of all our other unborn babies, and having to start over again in mid-life. After so much loss, everything that came after should have been easy, or at least easier.

I wanted to ring Rose, but hesitated. It was too soon after our argument. And it was clear she had enough to deal with. Peter's memory loss was a problem I could deal with by myself. And I remembered the facilitator's speech. I was not alone. Kathleen, for one. Mum, for another. I looked forward to seeing her on Sunday.

There was roast chicken for lunch with stuffing, gravy, roast potatoes, and baby spring vegetables. 'Oh that smells delicious, Mum,' I said, hugging her.

'Mumma said exactly the same thing!' Sydney said. 'Kenzie and I do that too. Because we're twins.'

'Hey, Lily,' said Rose.

'Hey, Rose,' I echoed, understanding that at least we could agree that Mum did not need to be dragged into our quarrel.

The three youngest girls chattered all the way through lunch; I noticed Madison said very little and hoped she'd not been damaged by the arguing she'd overheard at the cottage.

'We thought we'd do the White Bear Trails into the old growth forest next Saturday,' Kent said, when there had been a long pause in conversation.

'Oh, I love those walks,' said Peter. He turned to Madison, who was on his right. 'Some of those trees are over three hundred years old.'

'Really?' She sounded intrigued.

Peter nodded. 'Can you imagine the stories they tell?'

Sydney's eyes widened. 'Uncle Peter, can the trees really tell stories?'

'Well, not in words,' he said. 'Not like you and I tell stories. But the scientists who understand trees can decode their messages.'

'Like, if you count the rings in a tree, you know how old it is,' Madison explained. 'And if you measure how far apart they are, you can tell if there was a drought one summer, or lots of rain, or even a forest fire.'

'I'm impressed,' I said to Madison.

'Trees are cool,' she said. 'I think I might be an environmental arborist when I grow up. You guys should come on the hike with us,' she added.

'That would be fun,' said Peter.

I looked at Rose, but her face was unreadable. 'Lovely,' she said.

'Great,' I said. 'I'll bring the picnic. Will you come too, Mum?'

She shook her head. 'I remember those trails. I think they're too steep for an old dame like me.'

'You're not an old dame,' Rose and I both said at once. Without thinking we also both laughed. I felt a subtle shift in the ice between us, the hint of a thaw. Maybe Peter was right, it was an argument, but we were sisters. It would blow over.

Thursday and Friday night I stayed up late making perfect tiny picnic treats *à la* Martha Stewart. I could understand why Rose got fed up being the one who was always expected to provide every meal, every day. In as much as a single picnic could say sorry and hold within it the promise of pulling my own weight with regards meals at the cottage in the future, this one would.

On Saturday morning I set the alarm for five so that I could do the finishing touches. At seven I went to wake Peter.

'What's up?' he said. He looked confused, and pale. 'What day is it?'

'It's Saturday. We're going to Temagami to hike the White Bear Trails with Rose and Kent and the kids.'

'Bears?'

'The White Bear Trails.'

'Oh.' He gave no indication he had any recollection of our plans. 'What day is it?'

'Saturday. It's Saturday. We're going for a picnic.'

'I don't think I want to go on a picnic.'

That threw me. I couldn't remember the last time—if ever—he'd objected to plans we'd made. 'Come downstairs and have a cup of coffee and see how you feel,' I suggested. He pulled on his green dressing gown, shuffled downstairs, and sat on the sofa. I gave him a cup of coffee and he said thank you, then put it on the table in front of him.

'What day it is, Lily?'

'It's Saturday,' I said. 'Saturday.'

'Please don't snap, I only asked you what day it is.'

'I'm sorry if I snapped. You've asked me what day it is twice already in the past ten minutes.'

'I didn't remember.'

'I know, hon. I'm sorry.' I remembered the booklet from the lunchtime seminar. Mornings and evenings are often times of increased confusion. 'Why don't you go get dressed for the picnic?'

'Do I have to go?'

'Oh, Peter, my love. No. Of course you don't have to go. It's supposed to be fun.'

'I don't think I'll have much fun today.'

I had handled the whole conversation all wrong. But Kent had said we'd leave at eight on the dot and I didn't want to be late. There wasn't time to start over with Peter and cajole him into joining the expedition. 'Are you sure you'll be okay by yourself here alone?'

'Of course. I'm here all alone every day when you go out to work.'

His voice broke my heart, and I closed my eyes, wondering if I should call Rose and send regrets for both of us. But I'd promised to provide the picnic, and to leave her with only half an hour to assemble a lunch wasn't fair. It would look odd if I dropped off food but didn't go with them—as if I was prolonging our argument. Plus, I wanted to go. I wanted the walk, the exercise, the fresh air, the time with my nieces, the chance to mend fences with Rose.

'Okay, Peter,' I said, kissing his forehead. 'I'll be back this afternoon.' He said nothing as I packed up the picnic and got ready to go, other than muttering *Saturday* to himself a few times. 'I love you,' I said from the hallway, waiting, expecting him to come and say goodbye.

'It's Saturday,' he said. 'I know it's Saturday today.'

'I love you, Peter,' I said again.

The moment I walked down their driveway I began to wish I'd cancelled. All four girls were in the backyard. 'Mumma and Dad are tired,' Aidan told me.

'Yeah, and grumpy,' said Madison. She looked behind me. 'Where's Uncle Peter?'

'He's tired too,' I said. 'And sick.'

'Oh.' She sounded genuinely disappointed that he wasn't coming on the expedition, and I made a mental note to tell him when I got back that his eldest niece had missed him.

In the kitchen, Rose was barking orders up the stairs. 'Get showered and get dressed.'

'Goddammit, I'm not a child,' Kent yelled back.

'Then get showered and get dressed,' she said to him. She looked at me. 'We both stayed up too late last night. We won't be ready to leave at eight.' She passed me a block of cheese. 'Can you please cut this into cubes?'

'I've brought two kinds of cheesy snacks,' I said. 'Cranberry Brie Bites and Cheddar Shortbread.'

'Aidan won't like those,' she said.

She opened a plastic bag of new potatoes, dumped them into a pot, and put a jar of Hellmann's on the counter.

'I've brought potato salad too,' I said.

'Normal, regular, potato salad? Potatoes with mayonnaise and chives? Nothing fancy or weird?'

'Are chilies, cilantro, and cumin *fancy and weird*?'

'For the love of—Lily. My children are five, ten, and eleven. They eat spaghetti with red sauce from a jar and peanut butter sandwiches on white bread. You know that.'

Her bad mood was infectious. 'Well I hope everyone's hungry,' I said. I started cutting the cheese into cubes. 'I said I'd bring the picnic and I have. More than enough food for everyone.' And you're not the only one who's tired, I thought.

'What else?'

I took that to mean the menu and started to recite it. She stopped me after the smoked chicken and sun-dried tomato sandwiches with pesto, and tuna and avocado puff pastry fish.

'Smoked chicken? And no one likes fish. You may as well leave those here.'

'You love fish,' I said. 'We ate fish all the time in Hawaii. Mahi-Mahi and grouper and tuna. Even Madison loved fish, and she was a fussy eater back then.'

'Lily, no one in this household eats fish. I never cook fish.'

I wasn't sure if she was having me on or really had no recollection of all the fish we'd eaten in Hawaii. I wasn't going to unpack the entire picnic to leave behind one item. Although I was tempted to show her what they looked like: tiny fish-shaped bites, so cute they'd melt her heart. They had taken a lot of work to make and decorate, and I knew they were delicious because I'd eaten three of them. I carried on cutting the orange cheese into cubes.

Desperate to break the silence, I asked if she'd been following the Instagram account of a quilter whose blog we both read. 'No recent shots of her belly,' I said. 'I wonder if she's had her baby.' This was a safe topic to discuss because we agreed. We were thankful not to have had our lives documented and shared with the world on a daily basis from birth. Although a few more photos from our childhood would have been nice to have.

'I'm too busy to look at other peoples' photos,' she said. 'It's just a waste of time, Instagram.' She passed me a bag of carrots.

It felt like she was judging me. I peeled carrots and cut them into sticks and said nothing more. It was almost ten before we'd loaded the car and were ready to leave. I could have slept in for an extra hour. I could have coaxed Peter into coming. I hoped he was okay.

'Seat belts on,' said Rose after there had been a minor squabble over who would sit next to me. It was her forced cheerful voice. There were clicks all round, as we did up our seat belts. Though not, I noticed, from the driver's seat.

Kent turned the key in the ignition.

'Kent?'

'What?'

'Your seat belt?'

No answer. He drove along the road and turned towards the highway.

Let it go, I told myself. *Not your business. Not your problem.* But all the times I'd said nothing came rushing back. Most of all, the secret I'd held for twelve years, about his secret son. 'We've all done up our seat belts, we're waiting for you.'

'It's fine,' said Rose.

'It's not fine,' I said. 'He's driving the car. If we're in accident and he flies through the windshield, where does that leave us?'

'Kent is the safest driver on the road,' said Rose. 'We won't be in an accident.' She sounded drained.

We were on the highway now, driving north. 'Yes, it's the other drivers over whom we have no control. Those are the ones I'm worried about,' I said. 'And what kind of message is he sending to your children? You demand they do up their seat belts, but you don't care that he doesn't bother? Do as I say, not as I do? Surely your brains are more useful in your head, Kent, than mashed to pulp at the side of the road. And what good are you to anyone if you're hooked up to life support in a hospital?'

'Lily! Stop yelling at my husband.' Rose turned and glared at me.

'No.'

I didn't know I was going to say 'no' until the word came from my mouth.

'No, Rose. You don't get to tell me who I can and cannot speak to. He is my brother-in-law, he is married to my sister, he is the father of my four nieces. I have every right to state my opinion.'

'Your opinion. *Your* opinion? You know nothing about his job. Policemen never wear seat belts.'

'In cop cars, maybe. On the job. This is not a cop car. He is not on the job. Right now he is off duty, being a father, and setting a shitty example to his daughters.'

'Do not swear in front of my children.' Rose's voice was ice.

'Stop the car.' I couldn't breathe. I couldn't see. I couldn't stay in that car one moment longer. 'Stop this shitty fucking car, for fuck's sake!' I yelled.

Kent slammed on the brakes and swerved on to the side of the highway. 'It's not safe to walk along the edge of a highway.'

I didn't reply. I didn't give Sydney time to get out, but climbed over her, then grabbed my backpack which knocked against her face. 'Sorry,' I whispered. 'Have a fun time.'

'I won't,' she said, tears already welling in her eyes. 'Not now.'

I shut the door and Kent took off, sending a spray of gravel against me. I watched him speed away, him and his family unit, and knew I was no longer considered a member.

It took me three and a half hours to walk home. When I reached the lakeside park quarter of a mile away from my house I sat on a bench. The wind had come up, and I closed my eyes, hoping the sound of the waves would bring me a modicum of peace, but all I could hear were the angry words Rose and I exchanged.

When I turned to leave, I noticed the 'No Exit' sign across the street. A metaphor for my life? For the first time I felt truly trapped. I didn't know if I could repair the damage between Rose and me. I owned a house. My husband was losing his memory. The health benefits at work were more necessary than I'd ever imagined they'd be. My home wasn't really the refuge I sought right now. But there was nowhere else for me to go.

There was no indication that Peter had even moved since I'd left. He was still sitting on the sofa in his dressing gown, an untouched cup of coffee in front of him.

'Hello, Lily,' he said, when I walked in. As if I'd been out of the room for a moment or two.

'Hey.' I sat next to him. 'You remind me of my grampa. Every morning in the summer he'd go and tour the garden in his dressing gown. Tansy and I followed him, listened to him talk to the plants, helped him pick off deadheads. He'd always find us a treat—fresh peas, a green bean, a carrot pulled from the earth and washed under the tap by the shed, a Cox's orange pippin. That's still my favourite apple.' I painted my past as well as I could.

'Was that your mum's father or your dad's father?'

He was following the conversation, even if he had forgotten that I'd never met my paternal grandparents. 'My mum's,' I said. 'Tansy and I spent two weeks with them every August at their house in Niagara-on-the-Lake.'

I thought of those holidays with my older sister and my stomach cramped. A physical pain of longing.

'I forget. What day is it today?'

'It's Saturday. We have the whole day to do anything we'd like to do.'

'You don't have to go to work?'

'No, I don't have to go to work.'

'We could go on a picnic.'

Chapter Eighteen

When the phone rang in the early evening, I knew I wasn't yet ready to make peace with Rose. I wasn't sure I'd ever felt more alone, even at the lowest point of my marriage to Quentin. 'I don't want to talk to anyone,' I said to Peter. 'Let's let it go to message.'

But he wasn't able to ignore a ringing telephone. 'Hello.' And moments later my mother's name. He listened for several minutes, chatted a bit, then passed me the phone.

I drew a deep breath to steady my voice. 'Hi, Mum.'

'Hi Lily.' She told me her news and I was able to comment. But then, 'and how was the picnic?'

'Ah. Plans changed. Peter and I didn't go,' I said. 'We spent a very productive afternoon in the garden instead.' I listed all that had been accomplished, making sure I didn't specify who had done what.

'You always were the one with the green thumb,' she said.

'Really?' This was not how I thought of myself.

'Oh yes. Remember the year you were six? That winter we ate your zucchini almost every meal. Bobby and I joked that if you'd not grown so many zucchini we might not have survived the winter.' She laughed.

'I love that a memory of Bobby can make you laugh.'

I could feel her smile down the phone. 'It wasn't all bad. And even I can't hold a grudge forever,' she said, and laughed again.

She ended the phone call as she always did. 'I love you.'

'I love you too, Mum.' I hung up, lifted the receiver to make sure the connection had been broken, then hung up again and turned to Peter. 'I said I didn't want to speak to anyone.'

'You can't not speak to your mother.' In his voice, the same calm reason of the day he'd told me that he cared for his father, because there was no one else. 'What if she had a heart attack this evening and you'd not spoken to her?'

He was right of course. I'd feel guilty for years if I'd not spoken to her and then she died. But more than that, the alert look on his face: standing before me was the man I'd fallen in love with, and not seen for so long. 'I love you,' I said, reaching for him and holding him close.

'I love you too,' he said, returning my hug.

We should hug more often, I thought. More physical contact. It's good for both of us.

'A memory of Bobby made Mum laugh,' I said. 'She said she can't hold a grudge forever. Maybe Rose and I will get through this patch.'

'You will,' Peter said. His voice was confident.

I lay in bed that night wishing for some of his confidence. I turned on my bedside light and picked up a book, put it down without reading a word on a page. I picked up my phone imagining what I could possibly say to Rose in a text, then wondered if they'd gone on the hike, or decided to abort the mission, turned around and gone home. I tried to remember my six-year-old self, a few months older than the twins, growing enough zucchini to feed the family through the winter. I wondered how both Rose and I had escaped the alcoholic gene. If the gene I had inherited was worse-the belief that truth was optional. And then I wondered what Tansy would be doing if she were still alive, where we'd all be now if Tansy had lived.

The ping of an incoming text startled me. *All good,* read the text from Rose and I nearly smiled as I opened the attachment. Maybe a photo from the picnic? I glanced at the top of my phone. Two a.m. She couldn't sleep either.

It was an Instagram screenshot, from the quilter's account. A shot of her belly and two almost identical baby quilts. 'Keeping our baby's name a surprise from everyone, ourselves included! But ready either way!'

I blinked. 'All good' referred to the pregnancy of a stranger, not to the relationship between Rose and me. I enlarged the photo, studied the quilts as if they held the answer. They were almost identical, pale yellow with grey elephants, one had an R in the middle and the other an S.

Wow, I started to compose a text. *So much work. She couldn't have added the first initial after her baby's birth?* I hesitated, imagined a possible comeback. *You have no idea how busy and exhausted she'll be.* I didn't. I couldn't know that, as I'd never joined that club of new mothers. I deleted the text.

Good to know. Smiley face.

But was it good to know? I didn't actually care at all about a stranger's baby right now. And could a simple 'good to know' sound unintentionally sarcastic? I deleted that one too and put down my phone. Was there an underlying message? Rose had made the time to check the Instagram account and update us both. Was it, in some way, an apology?

Should I send a cheerful 'hope the picnic was fun?' No, because I had chosen to leave the day. But if I didn't mention the picnic at all, what might that indicate?

I had no idea what to say to my sister.

The next morning, I opened her text and the attachment again, and again I studied the two quilts. 'Sorry we argued,' I texted her. But she never replied.

It was extraordinary how easy it was to live in the same small city, so close to each other, yet never cross paths. Sometimes during the summer I crept onto Peter's Facebook page to see if Rose had posted any photos, but she rarely did. If Mum was aware that her two daughters weren't speaking to each other, she said nothing. I remembered how she'd waited for me to tell her about Quentin's infidelity and knew she wouldn't push. When she came to dinner, she mentioned what Rose and the girls were up to, but never asked me for more details of their lives.

Our garden bloomed, our sunflowers grew above the garage until we could see them from the upstairs hall window, and our tomato plants were heavy with fruit. Peter and I spent the weekday evenings picking blueberries, then making them into jam and pies for the winter. When the tomatoes ripened, we canned sauce and cooked great batches of Ratatouille for the freezer. After our evening's work we'd cool off with a swim, then sit on the deck with books, one of us pretending to read. He struggled to play Scrabble, so I put the game away. There was no more talk of his finding a job.

In August we went back to the Memory Clinic in Toronto for a second appointment. He was given a test he'd been given before; this time he couldn't draw anything that resembled a clock face. I thought of his dad not being able to read the time. There was also a dot-to-dot puzzle he wasn't able to complete. The first time he'd managed to do it, he joked that the twins would have been faster. This time he grumbled that it was stupid, impossible. I bit my lips to stop from crying and turned my face away.

I asked many questions but was given few satisfactory answers. The specialist admitted surprise at how quickly Peter's memory was declining. His diagnosis was changed from Mild Cognitive Impairment to Younger Onset Dementia, and he was given a new prescription. He could reach a plateau and stay at that level of functioning for some time, the specialist reassured me. What does 'some time' mean I asked, ten years, fifteen? There was a moment of hesitation. Three, said the specialist. Maybe three.

As soon as we got home I tucked Peter into bed and went to the pharmacy. As if having his prescription filled and starting him on the new medication the very next day might make all the difference.

Big Rock Lake, February 2014

Kathleen texted me.

'They're organizing a donor drive at the university,' I read. 'The students are posting and reposting all over the socials.'

'Oh...'

'Is there anywhere you don't want it advertised, Rose? Kathleen's thinking about Madison and Aidan seeing it.'

'All these decisions. I don't know.' Rose sounded worn out.

'I know,' I said. 'I know.'

Mum wrapped Kathleen's prayer shawl around Rose's shoulders, then kept holding her.

'What am I going to do? How am I going to do this?'

'One decision at a time. One moment at a time,' Mum said.

'I don't know if I'm strong enough.'

'You are,' I said. 'You're so strong. You were terrified of flying after 9/11 but you got on a plane to come and visit me when I needed you.'

Rose shook her head. 'I don't think I am. I'm not like you. I couldn't have. . . David.' She started to cry. 'Oh god, Lily. I'm so sorry I took his photo down from your wall. I really didn't—'

'I know. I know. I wish I'd said something then. I wish I'd said a lot of things.' Maybe it wasn't too late. Maybe I could share the ugliest secrets of my life and... would it be too much to hope that the act of divulging them might help me finally let them go?

'I raised two strong daughters,' said Mum. 'Kind, intelligent, generous, beautiful and tough.'

'Three,' I corrected her. 'You raised three daughters.'

'Tansy,' Rose whispered. 'Tell me about her? She was my sister too. I know I... I never knew her, but... I am one of three.'

One of three. Did she really feel that way? I never had. I'd been a younger sister for a long time, and then I'd become an older sister. I'd been the middle girl of three for so few days, I couldn't remember what it had felt like. But there were photographs. Half a roll taken on one of the sunny April days. They were slides, later made into prints, and three of them are out of focus. But in the best, Tansy is sitting on the porch, holding newborn Rose in her arms. I am snuggled up to both of them. All three of us are smiling.

'She taught me to read,' I said. 'She held my hand when I was scared. She always let me be the princess and she was the dragon. Once, we—' I shared every single happy memory I had of our wonderful, perfect, older sister. I smiled at the memories; I smiled too because for months my therapist had been recommending I do exactly this. Tansy's death, David's death, my termination, my lost babies—all the trauma that I hadn't fully dealt with: she'd suggested I start by talking, sharing memories, and now I was doing just that.

When I'd finished recounting every memory I had of her, real and imagined, Mum took over. The years of Tansy's life I hadn't known and couldn't remember. The firstborn, eldest daughter, as loved by her mother.

Part of me was watching from a distance, listening to Mum talk, while another part of me tried to change that last day. Reorder the events, my reaction, so that when Tansy grabs the crumpled blue form from my hand I laugh. Mum is closer, and has already set baby Rose on the ground, far away from the fire, safe, so she has two free hands. And then Tansy throws the form into the fire and it's the only thing lost.

But that isn't how it happened.

Big Rock Lake, 1976

This is what I remember and how I remember it, though I am aware that it is the memory of a memory of a memory, and that over the years I have added details and embellished in some places, let other facts fall away. The piece of paper was wrinkled from having been shoved deep down by Bobby's hand. When I pulled it from the pocket, I noticed the colour, same as a robin's egg, and my mother's signature, which had never changed. The slanted J, then a scrawl of illegible letters, a capital M followed by another illegible scrawl. I pulled that robin's egg blue piece of paper from the pocket of his jacket—I can see it clearly... and...

1976. There was excitement about the Olympic Games which would be held in Montreal; some of the kids in Tansy's class were even being taken there by their parents. But we had an even bigger excitement than that to look forward to. At Easter we were told that we were going to have a new baby brother or sister, and a telephone. The talk of a new sibling made Tansy giggle; I didn't understand why. I wanted to know if it would be a boy or a girl, and where would it sleep? I had just been given a bedroom of my own and had a suspicion this might not last. 'In the top drawer of our dresser, as you both did,' said Mum. She pulled out the drawer to show me how it became a bed big enough for a baby. And a telephone? We had never needed a telephone before.

'And we still don't,' said Bobby, in a foul mood every time the topic was raised. 'Next thing your mother will be demanding city water. And a road right to our property.'

'It's time,' my mother said, every time that Bobby argued there was no need to disrupt the peace and quiet with a telephone. 'You didn't want plumbing or electricity installed when we first moved here,' she reminded him. 'But now you love it.' And she didn't want city water, she was more than happy with our well water, soft and free of any additives. And yes, she'd be happy to be able to drive the old jalopy all the way to our house, instead of having to park half a mile away at the end of the lane, especially in the winter, but they would tackle one modernization at a time.

I had not understood that the arrival of the baby would necessitate my mother's departure to the city hospital. 'But I was born here,' I said, pointing at the floor in the living room. 'You told me. Right here.'

'Yes, Lily Love,' said Mum. 'That was a crazy thing I did. I'm thankful there were no complications. But I'm not going to take any risks with this baby.'

Years later, I would do the math and guess that the time between my birth and my younger sister's represented eight years of miscarriages. Of course my mother was not willing to take any risks with this delivery.

It had never been the three of us—Bobby, Tansy, and me—without Mum. It worried me, and perhaps it worried Bobby as well. Not Tansy, who was more than capable and happy to tie on Mum's apron and cook dinner, and generally keep the household running. Mum was due home in three days, but when she didn't appear as we expected, Bobby fussed and fretted, wondered why she hadn't had the baby at home.

'Or we could drive into the city and actually visit her in the hospital,' Tansy pointed out.

Bobby shook his head at the suggestion. 'Can't make me go into one of those death factories,' he muttered, taking a drink and settling in his armchair for a few minutes before he started pacing again.

On the fifth morning, Tansy dragged a stack of buckets from the shed and shook Bobby awake from where he'd fallen asleep in the armchair with an empty jar beside him. 'The trees are ready,' she said. 'I can smell the sap rising. We have to start tapping them, it's spring and it's tradition. The Maple Boil.'

It was my favourite childhood tradition, the Maple Boil. We had been doing it since forever, Tansy told me, and because she was three years older than me, and my idol, I didn't question anything she said. Mum, when pressed, once admitted it had been a more recent whim, maybe even starting the year I was four.

Bobby might have shaken his head. Said something like, not without your mother. She has to be here—that's the tradition. But my sister must have insisted, and promised Mum would be back, and that Mum would be angry if we weren't making syrup like we always did.

'I can't do it without your mother,' he said then. 'I'm a goddamn wreck without her.'

I don't know where my words came from. Which adult, of the few in my life, I was imitating. They were as much a shock to me as they must have been to my father and sister when I opened my mouth and started speaking.

'If you'd done what you promised then the telephone would have been installed and you could telephone the hospital and then maybe you wouldn't be so worried.' My voice was cold. 'It's a piece of blue paper. Mum filled in a form on a piece of blue paper and asked you to mail it. One lousy thing she asked you to do. She didn't expect you to install the telephone yourself. All you had to do was sign it then walk down the lane to the highway and put the form in the mailbox, and you couldn't do it. So stop feeling sorry for yourself, it's your own damn fault. And that's the goddamn truth.'

Bobby raised his hand as if to bring it down across my face—something he had never done before—then backed away, looking at me in horror. Down at his hand. Back at me. 'I don't have a piece of paper,' he said. 'I don't know what you're talking about.'

'I'm talking about how lazy and useless you are!' I yelled. 'You want the truth, that's the truth for you!' My face stinging as if he had actually hit me,

I turned and ran out of the house, up the hill and down the other side to the river, where finally I allowed myself to cry. But in my defiance, I'd left without a coat, and as soon as the sun started to set I had to go home. As I approached the house, I heard the tap tap tapping of spouts being hammered into the maples. Bobby and Tansy were outside, getting everything ready. He had hung my coat over a bush and he put it around my shoulders, and I took this as an apology, and, of course, I forgave him.

Not half an hour later, we heard the sound of a vehicle as our neighbour's tractor came up the lane. Our mother got out, and Bobby ran to her, and I watched as his shoulders relaxed and his proper smile returned.

'I was worried,' he admitted later, when we were all cooing at the sleeping baby girl in Mum's arms. 'It seemed to take longer than I'd imagined it should.'

'She's going to be an obstinate one,' Mum said, smiling down at my new sister. 'She was in no rush, no rush at all. She waited until she was ready. Now where do you suppose she gets that stubborn gene from?'

'Huh,' Bobby said. But he didn't take his gaze away from the perfect little girl. 'We sure make beautiful babies, J.'

'We sure do,' Mum agreed.

'What're we going to call her?'

'I was thinking Rose,' said Mum.

'I was thinking Maple-baby,' said Tansy, and fell to the ground with the giggles.

For several days after baby Rose came home, life was perfect: Mum and Rose, and brilliant blue spring weather with cool nights and warm days. Bobby, Tansy, and I collected the sap, and started boiling it down. We made taffy on the snow, Mum made pancakes, and we drenched them with fresh syrup. On about the sixth afternoon—I'm guessing Rose must have been about a week old—Mum brought her out to watch us work. Remembering it now, I can smell woodsmoke from the fire, and maple sap, already with a hint of the thick, sweet syrup it was about to become.

The whole thing couldn't have taken more than a minute, though it always plays out in slow motion for me. Mum walking towards our boiling station, baby in her arms. Bobby, pausing to take off his jacket after building up the fire, about to crack open another jar of shine. I was standing back from the open flames, as instructed, so I was a little chilly. I shrugged into his jacket, putting my hands in his pockets and, without thinking, I withdrew a piece of paper I found in one of them. It was robin's egg blue, and I knew immediately what it was. The request form for the installation of a telephone system.

'Hey, Bobby,' I said. I waved the paper at him. 'I told you that you had a piece of blue paper. This is the form you were supposed to sign and mail. You said I was a liar. You called me a liar and you tried to hit me, but I wasn't lying. And that's the goddamn truth.'

Why did I insist on using those words again? What could I possibly have wanted, expected, his reaction to be? Was I trying to punish him for almost slapping me? Or had I never before realized that my father was so adept at lying, and was I wondering now what else he'd lied about that I had accepted as truth?

'Hey! Hey, Lily!' Tansy reached for the piece of paper, taking it from my hand.

I'm sure Tansy was trying to divert attention to stop a potential argument. But I didn't laugh. Instead I started to yell, angry at my helplessness, angry at having been accused unjustly, and I grabbed at the paper, determined not to let my sister burn it. It was proof that I'd been right and Bobby had been wrong.

Bobby grabbed for it as well. Perhaps he was embarrassed, or maybe he planned to mail it, thus fulfilling his promise to his wife.

Somehow, between the two of us, we pushed against Tansy. There was a patch of slush in the shade which had frozen to ice—it ought to have melted with the heat of the fire, but it hadn't. Tansy slipped, slid. Her arms windmilled back, but she couldn't stop herself.

No one reacted quickly enough. Mum had to put Rose down, Bobby had to take the moment to realize what was happening, and I. . . I was immobile, paralyzed by the inhuman noises, from the bright red jacket engulfed in flames, which I knew was my big sister Tansy.

There was no telephone. There was no goddamn telephone and so no way to call for an ambulance. Not that it would have made a difference. It was Mum who pulled Tansy out of the fire, rolled her in the snow, carried her in her arms, yelling at me to bring Rose, and ran, we ran, we ran to the neighbours' a half mile down the lane.

That's impossible. I was eight. I could not have kept up with Mum with Rose in my arms. And where was Bobby? But this is what I remember, possible or no.

Rose started screaming too, of course, and Tansy's screams changed to a low moan, an occasional whimper. Still, I knew it would all be okay. There would be a nurse in a white uniform at the hospital and she would make Tansy better. Our neighbour drove Mum to the hospital in his pickup with one hand on his horn the whole way. (How do I know this detail? I can't. I must have made it up.) His wife gathered Rose and me into her arms, suggested we kneel and pray. I was still wearing Bobby's jacket and I shook it from my body.

There was a police investigation. I was asked what my father smelled like but didn't understand the question. Like he always did during the maple boil, I would have replied. Of woodsmoke and sap and syrup. That his breath smelled of shine was normal and would not have been worthy of mention. I was asked about abuse but didn't understand the question. 'Abusive'? That was not a word I'd have used to describe my father.

Until that day six years later.

The second time I heard Mum call my father Robert.

Bobby had grown increasingly more distant and absent from the house. Rose was six, and in Grade One, full time school. I was fourteen and more than capable of organizing our packed lunches, getting Rose to the school bus stop on time, starting dinner before Mum got home from her job with the university press. Occasionally Bobby joined us for dinner, more often than not he didn't. We left the back door unlatched for his comings and goings; he had lost so many house keys over the years that he no longer bothered to carry one.

That Friday was the last day of college, and Felicia Reynolds dropped by to warn us that the student house down the street was hosting a big party that evening. She suggested we lock our doors. The previous year a drunken student had gone into their house by mistake and vomited all over the living room floor before curling up on the sofa and falling asleep. Of course, Mum told Bobby to ring the bell when he came home; of course he forgot. I woke in the darkness to the sound of glass shattering and a string of cuss words. I tore downstairs, steps behind Mum.

The light came on, and I had a brief impression of my father lying in a pool of blood, before Mum turned to block my view. 'Go back upstairs, now, Lily,' she said. 'Stay upstairs and make sure Rose is okay.' Her voice was shaking, but firm, and I didn't argue. I spent the next hour cuddling Rose on her bed, telling her it was all okay, reading to her to cover the noises from below. First some shouting, then the unmistakable siren of an ambulance, its lights making vibrant patterns on the bedroom walls, and then an eerie silence.

We must have fallen asleep eventually. When we woke, I played with her in her room for as long as possible, dreading to imagine what we might see if we went downstairs. When she was cranky with hunger, I told her I'd serve her breakfast in bed, and crept down to the kitchen. My mother was on her hands and knees, scrubbing at the floor, a bucket of pink water beside her. There was a breeze and I looked at the door, noticing for the first time that both glass and screen were missing.

'Is Bobby okay?' I asked in a whisper.

Mum nodded. 'He will be.'

'Rose is hungry,' I said, still whispering. 'I told her I'd take her breakfast in bed.'

Mum smiled. 'Thank you, Lily. That was clever of you.' Together we assembled a tray with all Rose's favourites: a bowl of store-boughten cereal, chocolate milk, and white toast with butter and melted brown sugar. 'You can go into my room and watch TV if you like,' she said as I left the kitchen, carrying the tray.

When I next went down to the kitchen, Mum was dressed, and the floor was spotless. Peter arrived at the kitchen door minutes later. 'We heard the ambulance last night,' he said. 'I—we, that is, my mother and father and I wanted to make sure you're all okay.'

'Thank you, Peter,' said my mother. Had any other neighbour asked, she might have bristled at the intrusion, but her smile towards Peter was genuine. 'Bobby had an accident and needed a few stitches, but he'll be fine.'

Peter nodded and turned to go. 'It looks like this door could use a little TLC.'

'It's a big job,' said my mother. 'I'll call a repairman.'

'I can't do the glass,' Peter admitted, 'but I fit new screen on all our doors last year. I'm sure I have a piece of mesh, so at least you can keep the bugs out.'

'Well, if you're sure.'

He smiled, that easy good-natured smile we all loved so much, and said he'd be back with his tools in 'just a mo.' Then he paused. 'Unless now's not a good time?'

'Now's a fine time,' said my mother. To clarify she added, 'Bobby will be kept in hospital over the weekend.'

Peter had finished trimming the new, taut screen and was starting to rehang the door when we heard a car pull into our driveway. It was a grey cab, and Bobby, in a dirty t-shirt and filthy jeans, a big bandage on his arm, got out and yelled to Mum for some money to pay the fare. With a tight smile she went outside, Rose dancing after her, and paid the taxi driver. 'You should rest,' I heard her say as they came through the front door. 'You were supposed to stay in hospital to rest.'

'Stay there? In that place that killed our Tansy? I couldn't leave fast enough.'

Rose had been trying to hold his hand. Now she looked up at him. 'The hospital killed my big sister?' she asked.

'No, Rose,' said Mum. 'She had a bad accident and the hospital wasn't able to save her. It was very sad.'

'What your mother is trying to say,' said my father. 'Is that it was my fucking fault. I'm a good for nothing drunk and I killed her. And I *am* a drunk, and I have a raging hangover, and what I need more than anything right now is a beer.'

I stood in the kitchen trying not to listen, trying not to look at Peter, willing Mum to divert Bobby upstairs. But into the kitchen Bobby came, where I was frozen next to the fridge. 'Pass me a beer, will you?'

I stared at his t-shirt, which was covered with blood, and his jeans which were shredded at the knees. 'Bobby?' I was going to ask if he was okay, but that's not what I said. 'All you had to do was ring the bell,' I said. 'If you had rung the bell, someone would have opened the door for you.' There had been enough bull already to last the entire summer, and I wasn't going to put up with it anymore.

'Make yourself useful. Get me a fucking beer!' he yelled at me. He must have known I was right. I was right that all he'd had to do was ring the doorbell to be let in. I had been right back in the spring of '76 that there was a blue form he had to post.

Rose burst into tears.

'I'll put on a pot of coffee,' said Mum, gathering Rose to her with one arm and reaching for the kettle with the other.

'I don't want a fucking coffee, J. I want a fucking beer. If that's not too much to—' He stopped mid-sentence, noticing the new screen door. 'What the hell?' He looked at the door, then at Peter, who was hurriedly trying to pack the last of his tools, no doubt hoping to slip away from the house before the shouting escalated. 'You did that I suppose? Fixed the mess I made when I came home too stoned to open the fucking door?'

I had never heard Bobby thank Peter, not once, for everything he'd done, and I relaxed in anticipation of what I knew was going to be a thank you big enough to make up for all the times he'd not thanked him.

But that wasn't my father's intention. 'Always fucking meddling, aren't you? Sticking your nose in our business. Hanging around here.'

Peter looked as shocked as I felt, and Mum's face fell. 'Bobby. Language. Peter offered to fix the screen and I said yes please.'

'I'm sorry, Sir. I was trying to help,' said Peter.

'We don't need your fucking help,' Bobby said.

'Bobby. Enough swearing in front of Rose.'

I knew I should have taken Rose out of the room, but shame rendered me immobile. I knew my father was an alcoholic. But I had been pretending it was a family secret.

If Bobby had heard Mum, he ignored her. 'You think I can't fix a fucking door? You think I'm too goddamn useless to fix a fucking door? What the fuck? Or is there another reason you spend all your free time here? You got the hots for Lily here? You know she's fourteen, right? Still a flat-chested kid.'

Peter had thrown the last of his tools into his red box, and was already halfway down the steps, when my father roared. 'Don't you turn your back on me when I'm talking to you! I asked you a question!' When Peter said nothing in reply and kept going, my father lunged after him. 'You touch my fucking daughter, I'll kill you. You understand?' The lack of response must have further frustrated him. He punched the newly patched screen door, and when it didn't come away in his hands, he smashed it off its hinges. 'And don't forget to take your fucking door! And don't ever fucking come back here! You are not fucking welcome.'

'Bobby! Stop!' I could finally move. Finally speak.

He turned, looked at me, raised his hand, and brought it crashing down, knocking me sideways, off the steps and on to the ground.

He turned back to enter the kitchen, to be met by my mother, with the telephone receiver in her hand. Her voice was quiet. 'Robert. Leave.'

'What?'

'You are no longer welcome to live here. I'm serious. If you come one step farther into this house, I'll call the police.'

'What the fuck?'

'If you come one step farther into this house, I will call the police. You may not come back here, ever.'

His eyes narrowed. 'Peter's not sniffing after Lily at all is he? He's hanging around you for some afternoon delight.'

I stood, slowly. I was going to be bruised, but I was okay. But that Bobby had made such a scene, that he'd called me flat-chested, that he'd suggested Peter might have the hots for me, it was all too much. 'Come on, Rose,' I said, taking my still-howling sister's hand. 'Come on.' I wasn't sure where we were going, but we had to get away from this house, away from this noise.

'Take money from my handbag in the hall, Lily,' my mother said. She was still speaking in that dangerously quiet voice. 'Treat yourself and your sister to a movie and popcorn, but please be home by five o'clock.'

I did what she said, and as we left, I heard her say to Bobby, 'I'm done. It's over.'

I knew families could change shape, and I knew it could happen in an instant. I hadn't known it could happen more than once. But there it was. When I came home there would be Mum, Rose, and I living in our house. No Bobby, ever again.

Here's where I wish I could say that, too late to save his marriage or his health, my father stopped drinking—but he didn't. Without Mum, he gave up. He rented an apartment downtown and invited Rose and me for lunch occasionally. I went with my baby sister but barely spoke to him when we were there, not out of any sort of loyalty to my mother, but because I had no idea what to say to him. We couldn't even reminisce about the old days, because then we'd have to acknowledge Tansy's death.

Peter spent that summer of the door working as a tour guide in Algonquin Park. When he came back in the fall, his mother's cancer had returned. My mother visited often with meals for Peter and his father and books to read his mother, but whenever she invited me I found a way to decline. When I saw Peter at his mother's funeral in January, I wasn't sure what to say. Some months later my mother reported that he'd landed a teaching job in a school on the other side of the city, and by this time she'd developed a routine of inviting his father to dinner every Thursday evening. I was fifteen, still flat-chested, and my skin was a mess of acne. I hadn't told any of my friends about my parents' separation. And no one ever asked.

Bobby's liver couldn't cope, and he died of cirrhosis four years later—a decade after Tansy, almost to the month. What he did save, though he may never have been aware of this, was his relationship with Rose. She was six when he left, ten when he died. Young enough that her memories of him as a father were not automatically coloured by his alcoholism. Innocent enough that none of us disabused her of the notion that any early memories she had of him drunk and out of control were anything other than a funny man who sometimes made her laugh doing funny things.

Something else my therapist had recently pointed out: We enabled her, Mum and I. We helped Rose remember Bobby in the very best light possible, recalling and recounting all the good memories. When Rose spoke of him with love and respect, that was due in part to the elaborate ruse Mum and I had engineered. No wonder Rose was shocked by the venom in my tone when my act failed. And, my therapist had gently asked, was it any surprise that I rarely spoke about the things that mattered most to my loved ones? I had spoken up to Bobby and Tansy had died—what had that taught me? That it was dangerous to speak out? That calling out people could have disastrous consequences? She always spoke in questions, leaving me to think about the answers.

Big Rock Lake, February 2014

'Why is it taking so long?' Rose muttered. She stood and started to pace. 'Why won't anyone tell me what's going on?' She looked at her watch. 'The first twelve hours are the most crucial. Should I demand information?'

I was watching the station for any signs that there was news, so I saw the tall blonde woman approach them. A tall woman who looked familiar. Her hair was blonde, pulled back in a ponytail. '—Dr. George,' I heard her say. The double doors buzzed and she was let through. As she walked away, she looked over her shoulder. I felt she was seeking out Rose, but her gaze caught mine and then she was gone.

'Who was that?' Rose asked. She'd noticed the other woman too.

I shrugged. 'I think I bumped into her in the coffee line.' Had I spilled coffee on her? No, I couldn't have.

Rose sat again. 'I'm so tired. So tired.'

I nodded. I knew tired.

'When Sydney starts gymnastics next week; she'll need a ride to and from.'

'I'll sort it out,' I said.

'And Kenzie's got a sleepover birthday party. She hasn't bought a present yet.'

'I'll take her shopping.'

'Oh darn. And I'm supposed to be hosting quilt guild next week.'

'Don't worry about that,' I said. 'Don't worry about any of that.' But I knew those were the easy worries to fuss about. 'Quilt guild?' I asked, belatedly processing what she'd said.

'I know, right? Would you ever have pegged me as a quilter? I started on a whim during the summer and I've become obsessed.'

Kathleen rang, checking in, letting me know that Peter was at his day programme and not to worry.

And then a woman in a white lab coat came towards us. 'Mrs. Hayton? Mrs. Rose Hayton? You may come and see your husband now.'

Rose reached out both her hands, and Mum and I each took one. She gripped tight as we walked through the double doors and down the hallway to the intensive care unit. The doctor pushed open a door.

And there he was. Kent, but not Kent. *Lifeless* was the first word that came to mind, and I clamped my lips together tightly, to make sure I'd not spoken it out loud. He was drained of all colour, his bruised face almost unrecognizable, the rest of him lost in a neck brace, wires hooked to monitors, casts, bandages. . . . The man connected to tubes and machines didn't look like Kent at all.

'Five minutes,' said the doctor and turned to leave.

I followed her into the hallway. 'Please,' I whispered. 'Is he going to recover?'

'He lost a lot of blood. He's lost both his kidneys. He needs a transplant, urgently. We're concerned about his skull and his spine. He's broken an arm, both legs, at least three ribs.' There was more, but I couldn't keep track.

'But will he get better?'

'He's lucky he was found when he was. Another ten minutes and he'd have died.' The doctor patted my hand; I'd grabbed her sleeve and she was trying to extract herself from my grasp. I let go and watched her walk away. I didn't know if that had been a *yes*, or a *no*, or a *we can't be sure*.

When I turned, Mum was standing in the doorway to Kent's room. In a loud voice she said, 'A full recovery. Wonderful.'

I remembered again how the nurse had encouraged Peter and I to talk, saying that his father's hearing would be the last thing to go.

'Syd must be excited about gymnastics,' I said clearly. 'This is the first activity she's done without Kenzie, isn't it?' As if we were sitting at the kitchen table having tea. As if we'd seen each other earlier in the week. As if the wall we'd erected after the fight in the car on the way to the picnic had never existed. 'What will Kenzie choose to do, do you think?'

Rose said nothing, but Mum spoke: 'She told me she's excited for her birthday this year because she's going to ask for a horse.'

Rose found her voice. 'That girl is horse crazy.'

I didn't know that about my niece. What else had changed in the past nine months? Nine months of her life—I tried to do the math—was a full fifteen percent? A long time. 'Are there any riding stables near your cottage?' I asked. 'Could she take lessons this summer?'

'That's a good idea,' Mum said. 'I think you're planning to put in a new deck this summer, aren't you? You'll be spending a lot of time there.'

Rose nodded. 'A new deck. Yes, that's the plan.'

'You'd better recovery quickly, Kent,' I said. 'Or your daughters will paint the deck pink. You know they will. You know that's Sydney's favourite flavour, colour, everything.' I tried to laugh.

'Yeah, and I have a feeling their Uncle Peter would let them.' Rose was trying to make a joke too.

'He loves those girls so much,' Mum said.

That was true. He didn't necessarily remember their names, but he smiled at their photographs.

'He spoiled them rotten at Christmas.'

It had, of course, been me who bought, wrapped, and labelled the gifts for our nieces.

'They wrote thank you letters, didn't they?'

I nodded. 'Yes, lovely letters.'

'They all missed you. The twins have never had a Christmas without you. But I've never asked: how was Vancouver?'

I hadn't wanted to face Christmas without Rose and the girls, or be forced into faking false joviality with Mum, so I'd booked a holiday in Vancouver which was not entirely successful but did get Peter and me through the holiday. I had told Mum about the day Peter left the hotel room and got lost, about his inability to use a toilet by himself, my realization that he'd become an exit-seeker and would now need round-the-clock care. I searched for something positive to say. 'Warm. Pretty. Kent, I guess you're lucky Kenzie didn't think to ask Santa Claus for a horse.'

It was a surreal conversation, the three of us, all speaking to the man lying in the bed between us, but I saw that I could talk to Rose this way, could tell her anything I'd not been able to say since our argument.

We were allowed to stay with him for twelve minutes, and then we were asked to leave. Mid-afternoon, Mum took charge. 'I'll go and collect the girls from school with Carla,' she said. 'Rose, I'll have supper on the table at five thirty. You leave Lily here at five fifteen so you're at my house in time for dinner.'

Rose looked dazed. 'I can't leave.'

'You can leave. Lily will look after Kent and she'll call you the moment he wakes up.' All three of us knew that wasn't going to happen. 'Your girls need to see that their mother is okay. They need to watch you eat dinner and hear you tell them that their father is being taken care of in the hospital and will be home as soon as possible. Then they need you to help them with their homework and get them ready for bed.' There was no space between her sentences for Rose to disagree.

'Will you collect Peter from Kathleen's on your way home?' I asked Mum.

'Of course.'

'And are you okay to watch him for the evening?'

'Of course.'

Rose waited until Mum had left before asking why couldn't Peter drive.

'He's had his licence pulled,' I said.

'His licence pulled? Whatever for?'

'He's not safe to drive.'

'Not safe?'

We'd both lost nine months of each other's lives.

Chapter Nineteen

BIG ROCK LAKE, NOVEMBER 2013

One weekday night in mid-November I'd woken to an unfamiliar noise. Peter wasn't next to me in bed. The clock read 4:12 and I tried not to give in to the instant irritation that my night's rest was over.

Any hint of that annoyance left me when I reached the living room. Peter was sitting on the sofa in his green dressing gown, my old wedding album open on his lap. The sound I'd heard was crying. Not his usual silent tears, but body-wracking sobs.

'Darling.' I passed him tissues and sat next to him on the sofa. 'Peter. What's wrong?'

He blew his nose, then pointed at an eight-by-ten photograph of Quentin and me. 'This is you.'

I nodded. 'Yes. It's me.' A long time ago.

'This must be our wedding album. But I have looked at every photograph and I don't remember a dang thing.'

Maybe it would be funny later. He had been invited but hadn't come. He hadn't been there, so of course he didn't remember a thing. It wasn't his memory because he couldn't forget an event he hadn't even attended. I'd tell Rose later, and then I'd be able to laugh about it. With a sinking feeling, I remembered that Rose and I no longer spoke. Had not spoken to each other at all since that day in June.

I pushed her from my mind. Right now Peter's pain and sorrow were real. Heartbreakingly real. I pulled him into a hug.

'You are so beautiful, Lily.' He pointed down at the photograph in the heavy blue leather book.

'Thank you.' So young then, so full of hope. And no wonder Peter had been confused. The ivory silk dress had been an extravagance. I'd saved it and re-worn it for my second wedding. I had joked with Mum and Rose: reduce, reuse, recycle. The ivory had yellowed into the colour of fresh clotted cream, and I'd had it shortened, using the leftover fabric for an extra panel. It ought to have been over the top for our back garden wedding, but it had been perfect. Not the white dress of a young virgin bride, but a gorgeous statement of belief in second chances.

I had believed in second chances on that day. And I had vowed, I knew I had, for better or for worse, in sickness and in health.

'We have some better photos,' I said. I went to the bookshelf for our much slimmer, much less expensive album, the one we'd made ourselves with pictures taken mostly by our guests. 'Look,' I said. 'There we are. Look how happy we are.' We stood on the fresh lawn, where the tomatoes were now planted. In the background, slightly out of focus, the lake, sun catching the tops of the waves. My dress did look stunning. And Peter was looking at me with a mixture of awe, disbelief, and love.

'I was so happy,' said Peter. 'I was so happy to be marrying you.'

'Me too,' I said. 'Look how happy I am. Look how happy we both were. And isn't it lovely that we're still so happy now?'

'Are you?' He turned to me. 'Are you happy? I'm not much of a husband.'

'You're my husband,' I said. 'I chose you, and I'd choose you all over again if you proposed to me right now.' I didn't care what anyone might think about the importance of truth telling. I was not going to tell this man that I wished I'd never married him. I moved as close to him as I could, so that we were cleaved together as one, and started at the beginning of our book. Page by page, photograph by photograph, I pointed at the guests and named them, and the food that we'd eaten, and reminded him—reminded both of us—what a happy day it had been.

Later, when I'd tucked him back in bed, I opened the big blue album again. There I was, young, pretty, ready to take on the world with Quentin at my side.

What advice did I have for that young woman? 'Don't do it!' But I wasn't sure, even now, that I'd tell the young me not to marry Quentin. 'Do it differently.' That would be better advice. Certainly I could have made more of an effort to integrate myself into the military communities where we lived, befriended the other wives. I could have tried harder. And together Quentin and I should have explored the things we had in common, made time for each other's interests long before we finally did. Had he ever asked me to workout with him? I assumed he must have done, and I must have said no, until he stopped asking. I couldn't picture him on the Appalachian Trail, but nor could I picture myself there any longer. I thought of the woman at the bar, who had called me Sweetie, lent me her phone on 9/11. Tried to envision her face but couldn't. How old was she then? As old as I was now? Probably younger.

The last page of the album was a shot of the two of us, hand in hand, looking over our shoulders as we strode off into our new life. Did I miss that life? No, but I missed the parallel life that we failed to find. The one we didn't lead. I missed David. I missed the other children we'd never had, the family holidays we hadn't taken. I wondered if Quentin and Sonia had been successful in having children. Wondered if he ever sat in the pre-dawn light like this and thought of me. I sat for a long time, until the sun rose and it was time to make coffee, pack a lunch, have a shower, head to work. I lifted the heavy blue album to the top of the bookshelf and pushed it back where Peter would be less likely to stumble across it. Our own album I left in the centre of the coffee table.

In the support group session at the Alzheimer's Society that evening there was a discussion of doll therapy as meaningful work for some dementia patients. I disagreed through my tears. 'In my opinion, that is not meaningful work.'

'Well, not work, exactly,' conceded the facilitator.

'Nor meaningful,' I said. I closed my eyes, not embarrassed by my tears, but to shut out an all too clear image of Peter holding a doll in his arms, cooing to it, singing, comforting a lifeless piece of plastic.

'You may change your mind, if you see that it makes him feel better, useful, less lonely.' The facilitator's voice was full of compassion, as if she'd had this conversation before.

I didn't reply. There had to be more value to a life—his life—than that.

As this was the last in this series of sessions, there was a survey for us to fill out. Was it helpful? What had been most practical in our day to day lives? What suggestions did we have for future sessions? I held my pencil above the boxes, then put it down, and put the blank survey back in the pile. I would come back to the next series of sessions, but I was glad to have a break. I found it heartbreaking to speak to people whose loved ones were worse off than Peter, to be given a hint of what was ahead for us.

Had that really only been November?

Big Rock Lake, February 2014

'Lily. I didn't know,' said Rose. 'I had no idea. I'm so sorry.'

I shook my head. 'It is what it is. I have a respite worker twice a week so I'm free to do the grocery shopping, pay bills, spend a few hours not being a full-time caregiver.'

'But what will you do?'

I shook my head again. 'Keep him at home for as long as possible.'

Rose reached for my hand. 'But—Are you saying- A long-term care home? He's... he's only sixty.'

I nodded. I knew.

'What am I going to do?' She sounded terrified. 'If Kent's brain damaged? If he's a paraplegic. If we need round-the-clock care and I need to get a job to pay all the bills. Who'll care for the girls if I have to go back to work? And what job can I possibly apply for?'

'You'll manage. We'll manage.'

'I wonder if I could have graduated med school,' said Rose.

'Of course you could have, if you'd wanted to. But you fell in love, and got married, and you have a good life,' I said. 'You have a great life.'

We were interrupted by a technician and a nurse, who asked us to follow them into a cubicle off the main hallway, where they asked us if Rose would like to have her blood work done now.

'Blood work?' asked Rose.

'To see if you can give your husband one of your kidneys.'

There were questions first, and it quickly became clear Rose wouldn't be a match. Not even a bad match; she'd had kidney stones when she was nineteen. 'The wrong kind of kidney stones?' Rose sounded defeated but she rallied. 'Our daughters? My mother?'

The girls were all too young, and Mum too old. Rose scanned the information she'd been given. I knew what she was going to ask me before she spoke.

'Will you get checked, Lily? Even if you can't give him a kidney, if you donate to a stranger it moves Kent up the list by one. It will make a difference.'

I was supposed to say *of course*. I was supposed to open my mouth and say those two simple words. Immediately. Of course I would donate a kidney to Kent if I happened to be a match, or I would donate to a stranger if Kent and I didn't share the right blood type. Never mind that I didn't love Kent. My kidney wouldn't be for Kent. It would be for my sister, who loved her husband, and for my nieces who loved their father. Perhaps for a stranger, whose life it could help.

For the split second before I was able to make my throat work, push those two simple words up from my diaphragm and out into the room, I suddenly held all the cards. The imbalance of power between us—me, with this simple thing my sister needed—was palpable. It was exhausting. Was this what Rose had carried all her life?

'Of course I will,' I said. 'Yes, of course. Of course. Of course.'

Rose whispered. 'Thank you.'

'What are the chances?' I asked the technician. 'We're sister and brother-in-law. Is there any hope that my kidney might be a good match?'

'There's always a possibility.' It didn't feel like a line he'd been taught to say, it felt like he believed there was always a hope that sometimes things would work out for the best. 'Is there not a blood relation?'

Rose shook her head. 'His eldest daughter is three months too young. Unless you can make an exception—?'

'No other family members?' the nurse asked. 'A brother? A sister?'

Rose shook her head. 'Three sisters, but they're all adopted.'

'No other children by a previous relationship?'

Again, Daddy. Again.

I held my breath.

Rose shook her head. 'No. No other children.'

So. All this time I had wondered if she knew. Now, in this room, would be the time that Rose would have to admit Kent had fathered another child, and do what needed to be done to save his life.

But she didn't know.

She had no idea.

I walked to the window and looked out at a deep orange sunset. I heard the nurse and technician leave, and said, without turning around I said, 'I lost my big sister, Rose. I lost my first husband. I'm losing Peter. It terrifies me that I could lose you.'

'Lily?'

'It's my biggest fear. The past nine months, without you, have been the worst.'

'I'm so sorry. Really. If I could change one thing in my life, I'd have told you about the lottery.'

'It doesn't matter, Rose. Really, it doesn't.'

'Everything got crazy.'

'I know. I understand. Life.' I tried to express what I was finally starting to understand. 'I regret the big lies, of course. But it's the lies of omission that eroded us. I think I told myself I was being kind, saving you from unnecessary pain or worry. Shielding you, as if you were still a child. I'm sorry. I'm so sorry.'

My sister reached for my hand. 'I accept your apology.'

'I guess I have to stop calling you my Baby Sister?'

'Yeah. I asked you to retire that nickname when I introduced you to Kent.'

'Oh—' I could feel myself tensing. Reminded myself to take a deep breath. 'I'm sorry,' I said again. 'I'll try to do better.'

'I'm sorry too,' said Rose. 'There are things I could have—should have—told you. Soon after we met, Kent was first officer at the scene of a car accident. It was an old car, just lap belts in the back. One of the children was killed.' She swallowed. 'Severed, Kent said. The belt sliced the little boy in half.'

I gasped. 'And that's why he doesn't wear a seat belt.'

'We argued for years about the girls wearing seat belts. It's why I kept Maddie in a car seat long after she should have graduated to a booster.'

'I had no idea.'

'No. How could you? But you struck a nerve that day, for sure.' The tiniest smile flashed across her face.

'I've missed you.'

'I've missed you too.'

My phone alarm startled us both.

'Damn,' I said. 'OK. I'm going to call you a cab.' When she protested, I overruled her, reminding her what Mum had said about the girls needing to see that their mother was okay.

'But I am not okay,' Rose muttered. 'And they will see that.' But she let me call her a taxi and wait with her at the door until it came.

Without asking for permission, I went back to Kent's room. The tall blonde I'd seen earlier was standing beside his bed, reading Kent's chart.

'Dr. Hannah George,' she introduced herself.

I hadn't been imagining the familiarity. 'We met once before,' I said slowly.

'We did?'

'Not formally. I'm Lily Reynolds. That will mean nothing to you. I'm Kent Hayton's sister-in-law.'

She nodded. Yes. She knew. 'I asked my colleagues. I didn't know which one of you was Rose.'

'I saw you once,' I said. 'With your son... and Kent. In front of a lakeside condo by a coffee shop. Playing ball.'

'Oh. So you know who I am? You know about Dominic?'

'Dominic?'

'My son.'

'Your... and Kent's son.'

The other woman nodded. Closed her eyes briefly. 'I've been wondering all day how to open this conversation... and you already knew.'

'I was never completely sure. I suspected, but—'

'And Rose?'

I shook my head. 'I don't think she has any idea. I don't even know what the truth is.'

The doctor put down the chart, gestured towards the hallway, and I followed her out of the room.

'The truth. Yes, I owe Kent's family the truth.' She sighed. 'It's all so long ago now. I was in Grade Thirteen and Kent was in Grade Eleven. It was one school dance, a bottle of vodka, and a couple of kids fooling around at the end of the night. But as we all know, it only takes a moment of fooling around to make a baby.'

For some, I thought. For the lucky ones.

'I contacted him. It was agreed that the pregnancy would be terminated, and I would go on to university as planned. I had a very good scholarship. And that would be that, the problem solved, all hands washed clean of any responsibility.' She tilted her head. 'But... when it came time for the abortion, I refused. Headstrong, young. Determined to have it all, a baby and a medical degree, and prove I could do it myself.'

'And you did,' I said.

'Not by myself,' she said. 'My mother raised Dom. My father bought us a home; that condo in Blueberry Bay. It wasn't only student debt I had to repay when I earned my degree. And Kent. He had no say in the changes to his life. Emotional or financial. He spent eighteen years paying me for the decision I'd made when he was barely seventeen.'

I gave myself permission to ask difficult questions. 'Is Kent still in contact with... with Dominic?'

Hannah shook her head. 'I don't think so. But I couldn't be sure. I married when Dom was seven. A man with a son almost his age. When our marriage ended and we separated, Dom said he'd like to live with his stepfather and stepbrother. My ex remarried, and so my son lived with two step-parents, neither of whom was biologically related to him.' She looked at me and raised her eyebrows. 'The modern world, eh?'

'Lived—?'

'He has his own place now.'

I let out the breath I'd held. 'But it sounds as if you're still on good terms with him?'

'As much as one can be, I suppose. I am my father's daughter, and haven't shaken all his outdated beliefs. I'd assumed Dom would go to university, but he's chosen an apprenticeship in the trades.' She stared into the distance for moment, then snapped back. 'And Rose knows nothing about Kent's past, with me?'

'I'm sure she doesn't know about Dom. But I think—I think Kent stood you up the night he met my sister. His staff party.'

She rolled her eyes. 'That holiday party. Yeah. I was glad to get out of it. Then he phoned me a few days later and told me he'd met the woman he was going to marry, and he hadn't told her about Dom, and would I mind very much if he didn't. I didn't mind at all. Rose was nothing to do with me.'

It occurred to me that Hannah, with all her career success, might be lonely. That perhaps she didn't have many female friends. I thought of how lucky I was to have Kathleen in my life.

'But you didn't remain in touch, you and Kent?'

'Goodness no.' A half laugh. 'Ancient history. I mean, it's a small city, right? We must pass each other on the street sometimes. I don't know that we'd recognize each other.'

I had spent the best part of a year not seeing my sister in this city; I understood how easily Hannah and Kent could have lived completely separate lives.

'I wouldn't have known him,' she said, nodding towards the room where he lay hooked up to life support. 'His condition is serious.'

This was my opening. My best hope for helping my sister. 'So will you... would you... Please, would you be willing to ask Dominic if he might consider having tests done to see if he'd be a match for Kent's kidney? If—do you think there's any chance he'd consider being a donor?'

That half laugh again. 'Whatever I think will be of no consequence. But yes, of course. That was my thought too. And don't worry, he'll say yes.' She glanced at her watch. 'I have to run.'

I gave her all my numbers—cell, landline, and work—and thanked her several times for even considering my request. 'Thank you. Thank you so much.'

'It was... interesting to meet you, Rose's sister,' she said. 'I'm trying to picture the life Kent has made.'

'He loves his life. He adores Rose. They have four intelligent, wonderful daughters.'

The other woman nodded, and I watched her stride off and wondered when—if—I'd hear from her. I thought to Google 'Dominic George Big Rock Lake' and dozens of images popped up on my phone. The young man was the spitting image of Kent. No doubt at all they were father and son. I was briefly angry at Kent again. He could have told Rose. Surely at some point he could have told her. *Years ago, before I met you, I had one night of sex which resulted in a son.* How difficult was that?

But I knew.

I knew how it happened.

I knew how shame and fear silenced even the best intentions.

The lies of omission that I had told my sister were countless. About Bobby, about our childhood. That I was happily married to Quentin. By the time I admitted how bad things were, I'd been telling myself—and her—that it was great for too long. At some moment it became too late to backtrack, to explain. I couldn't pick up the phone—I couldn't even imagine having that conversation when we were alone together. Rose was the person I loved most in the world, for so many years, but I couldn't tell her about my life, and so my life became a secret, a lie.

In place of the angry grudge I'd harboured against Kent for over a decade, suddenly I felt a surge of acute pity. He loved Rose. He loved her so much he was terrified of losing her. And the longer he said nothing, the harder it would have been to explain why he'd never mentioned it before. *Oh by the way, did I never tell you that I have a son? Dang, that was remiss of me.* By the time Madison was born it must have been almost impossible. *Our daughter has a step-brother. Maybe we should invite him over for a playdate.*

He'd paid child support. How had he justified or hidden those payments from Rose? That lottery win must have lifted a financial weight from his shoulders. I closed my eyes. Seeing Kent in this new light was throwing into sharp relief, my prejudices and failings.

I stood by his bed, and reached for his hand. 'Forgive me, Kent? Please, forgive me.'

I should have given Hannah George more credit. She was a doctor, accustomed to making difficult decisions without delay. She called me three quarters of an hour later. I tried not to sound too desperate when I answered.

Despite her assurances, it was possible Dominic might not be interested in giving away one of his kidneys. He might not be a match. He might have a medical reason why he couldn't donate.

'Dom would like to see Kent and meet Rose.'

'I—I see.'

'He's had the blood work done, and started the other tests, and it appears he's a solid match. He'll give Kent a kidney. But he wants to see him first. He wants to see his biological father, and his biological father's wife. Maybe in the future, his half-sisters too, depending on how things go.'

'That sounds more than fair.' I took a deep breath. 'Thank you. And that was quick. I didn't know test results could come back so fast.'

A short laugh. 'I'm not above pulling favours when I need to.'

'I—Thank you,' I said. 'Do you think he would be willing to come to the hospital to meet Rose when she comes back this evening? After she's put her girls to bed. Say nine, to be safe?'

'Sure,' said Hannah. 'Nine this evening will work well.'

How much would Rose want to know about Hannah and Dominic? There wasn't much I could tell her. I wondered, briefly, if I could avoid admitting that I'd known about Dominic since 2001, decided that I going to be truthful, I wasn't going to hide anything. I was going to create a more honest relationship with my sister, regardless how difficult and uncomfortable it made me. It was ironic that it was Kent's accident that had brought us back together and was now the very thing that might split us apart forever.

Rose came back to the hospital at ten to nine. That didn't leave me much time to prepare her. I took her hand in mine and started speaking in a soft voice.

'Do you remember when you told me about your lottery win? My first reaction was that I wished you hadn't told me. That I would have preferred not to know. But you said that the truth was always better, even if it hurt.'

'What truth?' Her eyes grew wide. 'What have the doctors told you? What's happened?'

'No. No bad news,' I hastened to assure her. 'This *is* about Kent. But it's good news. It's about a new kidney for him. There's a very good chance that it's a very good match. But before the donor gives Kent his kidney, he wants to meet him, and you.'

Rose gripped my hand. 'A kidney? Really?'

'Yes.'

'A match?'

'We believe so, yes.'

'And the donor wants to meet me? Why?'

'Rose, I need to tell you about this person, and I'm worried that will make you angry.'

'I won't be angry,' said Rose. 'I've used up all my anger.'

'I'm scared I'll lose your friendship,' I said, tears welling, and a lump growing in my throat. 'If I do lose you, I'll understand. But I need you to know, right now, how much I love you.'

'I love you too, Lily,' she said, her voice rising with panic. 'Really. Please. Let's never argue again. Not like that. I couldn't bear it. I'm sorry I wasn't there for you, not there for you properly, when you were so unhappy. The babies. . . David. . . and Quentin. . . And now, Peter's memory. At supper. . . he's going downhill so quickly.'

I blinked away tears, nodded.

She finished in a rush. 'I love you. I know I can never replace Tansy—I'm sorry I can't share those childhood memories with you—I—'

I pulled my sister close to me, cutting her off mid-sentence. 'One of your daughters changed my ring tone for your number,' I said. I started singing the Taylor Swift song: "And I don't try to hide my tears, my secrets or my deepest fears. Through it all nobody gets me like you do. . ."

-the end-

Gratitude

I am so incredibly lucky.

One

When I was living in Cambridge I made two best friends, Amy Crawford and Tiffani Angus, and at least once a week we went for drinks and dinner and put aside all dissertation and teaching discussions in favour of writing and reading conversations. One evening Tiffani asked me, 'What scares you the most?' After I answered she shook her head. 'Nope. I'm calling BS on that answer. What truly scares you the most?' And then, 'Well, when are you going to write about that?'

Two

In January 2017 I was given the opportunity to focus on writing for a month at Hawthornden Castle. I arrived with a firm idea of the short stories I was going to write—but the first day I instead rose to the challenge Tiffani had set me … and this novel was born. Never before have I written so much, so well. Never before have I so completely inhabited my characters' fictional world; I walked with my characters around the Castle, across fields, through the woods. They woke me in the night, they sat with me at lunch, we had long conversations together. Thank you to the late Drue Heinz and selection committee for giving me this incredible gift, and Hamish Robinson and Ruth Shannon for making it so magical.

Thank you my fellow Fellows, Gaia Holmes, Lindsay Macgregor, Keith Mansfield, Sue Reid Sexton, and Jakob Ziguras for that marvellous month, filled with daily inspiration at breakfast (well, from the four other early risers), and readings every evening. I can't imagine when I'll next attend 28 dinner parties in a row, but when I'm asked for my "ideal guest list" for *Vanity Fair's* Proust questionnaire, you will be it!

Three

That was a rough first draft. Thank you to everyone who helped me find the novel within, especially my very first readers, the Book Club's Cat Murton Stoehr and John Picard—your thoughtful and honest feedback helped me focus, and editor Adrienne Kerr—you asked difficult questions and interrogated my answers. Marion Agnew, your super close reading greatly improved my novel, and your friendship is such a bonus.

Four

After six years in the UK, I moved back to Canada on a Sunday afternoon. I started working at Nipissing University the following morning. Cindy Brownlee and Gemma Victor welcomed discombobulated, jet-lagged me with a lunchtime walk and afternoon coffee break. These daily rituals, along with your unconditional friendship were an anchor during the years my husband and I lived with his early onset dementia. I love you, my friends.

Five

Funding from Canada Council for the Arts, the Ontario Arts Council, and The Writers' Union of Canada enabled me to support myself whilst writing.

Six

Heather Campbell, Mitchel Gauvin, and Matthew Foti of Latitude 46 Publishing: thank you for your belief in my work and this novel, and thank you for making it into the beautiful book it has become.

Seven

Community is such a precious gift. I am honoured to be a member of the Conspiracy of 3 and the Writer's Union of Canada. Jennifer Rouse Barbeau, Rod Carley, Kim Fahner, Barry Grills, Laurie Kruk, Margaret Macpherson, Zoriça Markovich, Meg Parker, Steve Pitt, Donna Sinclair, Heather Stemp, and Denis Stokes—you are amazing human beings and you've set the bar high! You are deeply talented writers, wonderful literary citizens, and I am so proud to call you my friends.

Kerry Clare, you welcomed me into the literary world of Instagram, taught me how to blog, and gave me much needed hope, especially during the long, dark days of the Covid pandemic. Thank you for lighting my way and reminding me that "all will be well."

Thank you Pamela Mulloy, Margaret Watson, Nicole Smith, and Kitty Lorriman. When we gathered at the New Quarterly's Write on the French River Retreat, you helped me understand that my "dementia novel" was, in fact, my "sisters novel."

Amy Long, thank you for introducing me to the songs of Taylor Swift as well as a host of fantastic books through your super fun Insta account, @taylorswift_as_books.

Debra Martens, thank you for patiently instructing me how to read and write about a novel with a book reviewer's lens.

Alison Gadsby, you welcomed me to your reading series, Junction Reads, weeks before Covid shuttered in-person events, then guided me through the new normal of online events. Thank you.

Thank you Rebecca Hunter and Debra Lamb, Rachel Holden, and Joan Morrison for convincing your book clubs to read my short story collection and then inviting me to join your meetings.

My students—every semester you inspire me with your wisdom, generosity, and enthusiasm, and teach me how to be a better version of myself.

It breaks my heart that I will not be able to give my therapist, Sharon Chayka, a copy of this novel. She died on April 9, 2024.

Eight
Donna Landry and Lorie Fairburn—you champion my writing and my life. Yoga classes, hikes, pizza nights, road trips, wine, deep dive conversations, all the food, and faith. I am truly blessed to call you my friends.

My Gang of Four, always. Karen Dunn Skinner, Laura Kollenberg, and Maureen Patterson - my besties, you have played the long game, loving me through all my choices, mistakes, and triumphs, and I am thankful every single day that I don't have to live in a world without you in it.

Nine
David, I love all the memories we've made, and I love the life we're making.

Ten
My family, for everything. My sister, Caroline. My mum, Elizabeth. My brother-in-law, Timothy, and my nephew and nieces, John, Sarah, and Jody. My extended families—the Selanders and the Holdens. You don't have to love me-or even like me-just because we're related; I am beyond lucky that you choose to.

This novel is a love letter to you.

Discussion Questions

1. Judith says, "I didn't teach you, as children, how to have difficult conversations." What did their mother try to teach Lily and Rose? What lessons did they each learn from her?
2. The title of this novel is *Lies I Told My Sister*. How do each of: Lily, Rose, and Judith define 'lies'? What about Quentin, Peter, and Kent?
3. Of all the lies the sisters tell each other, which are the most egregious? Why?
4. Lily appears to learn that she can only be honest with others if she's willing to be honest with herself. Why do you think she became so good at telling herself stories that weren't true? What role does truth play in Lily's life?
5. Lily finds it difficult to speak up: she doesn't talk to her mother or her sister about the painful things in her life—Tansy's death, her abortion, her IVF treatments, her marriage. She does, however, confront Quentin about his infidelity. Why do you think this is?
6. It takes Lily a long time to make a friend; Kathleen seems to be the first real friend she has, apart from her younger sister, Rose. Why is this?
7. Lily often notices the kindness of strangers (the volunteer driver, the woman in the bar on 9/11); in what ways is she kind? In what ways is she cruel?
8. Lily appears to view life through a perspective of loss and "the dark, the danger, the possibility of menace." How does Rose view life? How do these perspectives serve them? Work against them?
9. Lily is quick to note what she considers her faults and weaknesses, but what are her strengths?
10. Kent's accident allows Rose the chance to reach out to Lily. If Kent hadn't been in an accident what do you think would have happened to her relationship with her sister?
11. Lily's greatest fears include the loss of her younger sister, Rose, and the loss of shared memories. Peter fears dying alone in a care home. What is your greatest fear?
12. The novel opens and closes with lyrics from the Taylor Swift song "I'm Only Me When I'm With You." Its lyrics include: "And I don't try to hide my tears/My secrets or my deepest fears/Through it all nobody gets me like you do." Who do you feel "gets" Lily the best? Would Lily agree or disagree with you? Who gets you the best?